SOMETHING

WICKED

T.R. Kester

Contents:

SOMETHING WICKED

Copyright © 2017 by TR Kester

This is a work of fiction. Similarities to real people, places, or events are entirely coincidental.

DEDICATION

In Memory Of
Jason Kester (1979-2005),
Una Fay Eastham (1929 - 2012), **Amy Delamere** (1990 - 2014)

Thank you to
Maria Merlino- Chiarolli, my high school counsellor and best friend, who helped me through enduring the loss of my older brother Jason and encouraged me to write. Just like the powerful force of good she is in the community, Maria is a powerful force of good within the book.

Neil Moreton, who gave me love and being in love, Melissa Kester, my sister, my confidant, Aunty Christine, without whose encouragement I would not feel as confident as I do about Something Wicked, and also Kerry Carlson who assisted in the proofing process. Tiffany Dean, for your integrity, wisdom and Cosplay, Aunty Evette and Judy Green, who never gave up on me, Di Atherton and Jill Webb, thank you for your friendship and allowing me to experience Canada. Kimberley Gordge, you are my idol. You are stronger than you realize. Thank you to my parents for always believing in me.

And thank you to you, the reader, for giving this book a chance.

DISCLAIMER

This book is a work of fiction. Any resemblance to persons, living or dead, is purely coincidental. The characters are productions of the author's imagination and are used fictitiously.

Edited by Word Writer Professional and Susan Horsnell.
Note about Editing -
Editors, correct and suggest
Authors, accept or reject.

CHARACTERS

<u>POGUE WITCHES</u>
Aaron
Noah
Perry
Bermuda
Isadora
Shane

<u>ROMANI COVEN</u>
Pilar
Madelyn
Addison
Dantalian
Persia
Brady

<u>EXTENDED FAMILY</u>

Ravenna - *Wife of Aaron Pogue*

Connemara Penthal - *Wife of Noah Pogue*

Kathryn Penthal - *Sister of Connemara*

Andromeda Pogue (New) - *The twin sister of Bermuda, resides in Vancouver, Canada*

Mars Romani (New) - *Twin brother of Persia and Dantalian*

Serene Rein - *Step-daughter of Pilar and elf Queen of the Autumn Forest.*

<u>GOOD WITCHES, ROMANI AND GOOD MAGICAL BEINGS</u>

Julyanne (New) - *A powerful witch, and High Priestess of British Columbia, Canada*

The Morrígan - *An Old One who resides in The Dream/Spirit Realms*

Diana - *Goddess and lover of Julyanne*

Gaia, Rhea, Pan & Dionysus - *Deities of Earth located in Butchart Gardens*

First Nations - *Canadian aboriginals who inhabitants of the Dream Realm*

_Chief Alo - *Leader of the Omega clan*

_Proud Buck - *Chief of the Forest Clan*

_Grey-Wing - *High Chief of the Bold Clan*

Carmen Penthal - *The deceased sister witch of Connemara & Kathryn Penthal*

Aryan - *A Mongkukulam (Filipino witch) who came to be possessed by the Old One, Vesta*

Daemon - *Dream gods who preside of the Dream Realm*

_Phantasos, Morpheus & Phobetor

Tempest Pogue - *Ancestor. Grandmother of Aaron, Noah and Perry Pogue*

Philomena Beaumont - *Ancestor. Sister of Tempest, Great Aunt of Aaron, Noah and Perry Pogue*

Amethyst - *Pogue Ancestor, begins to haunt Bermuda*

Andros - *A male witch. Possesses the power of Matter Alteration, using mirrors as portals for transportation*

Atropos, Lachesis and Clotho - *Three Sisters of Fate*

Genvera - *Leader of a group of mystical Griffins*

Pridham - *A female Custodian appointed to the Pogue Family*

Renae & Basset - *Custodians appointed to the Romani Family*

Oracles of Phaedra - *A powerful trio who can foresee all*

<u>DEMONS AND EVIL BEINGS</u>

Paimon - *An ancient demon king, gay lover of Asmodeus and servant of Twelve Disciples of Malignant*

Dark Promise Coven - *A congregation of evil witches that follows Alera.*

_The Judges - *Evil witches turned into demons as a reward for their worship to Asmodeus*

_King Solomon - *In ancient times was a devout follower of Alera*

Asmodeus - *An ancient demon king. Entombed in ice by the goddess, Rhea*

Kamenwati/Kamen - *Powerful Nightmare Soldier & Rafaela's right-hand demon*

_Mangiare Demons - *Specie of Nightmare Soldiers, sub-specie of Incubo*

_Kati - *One of three Mangiare Demons in the Dream Realm*

_Laedo - *Sub-specie of Nightmare Soldiers, the name means incapacitate in Latin*

Haarlem Blackheart - *An evil pirate, whose ship is the Nautica*

Abiteth, the Devourer - *A devourer of the beautiful and light*

Slither/Sheppard Romani - *An evil Romani and brother of Pilar*

_Snake Demons - *minions of Slither*

Melpomene - *The Muse of Tragedy and seized control over Limbo*

Rasima/Ima

Morgana

Modesto Coven

BEGINNING

Weeks go by slowly and agonizingly. The pain of loss and the grief it brings is inevitable to say the least, but noteworthy; it's insufferable.

The impressive, towering gothic headstone of Lindsay Pogue reads: *Loving Mother, Devoted Wife. Innately powerful and strong willed. Born January 5th 1940 – Died July 10th 1986.* Emotional agony becomes a bodily function, like breathing. Over time, weeks became months, months turned into years and, years turned into the future… and now, it is the present day.

Aaron Pogue, born on January 10th, once possessed the power of Deflection. As the eldest, he was perceived to be the strongest and most powerful…but was just the opposite. He came into his power quickly, at the age of three…early even for a witch, so he was perceived to be powerful. At the age of twenty, he was attacked and bitten by a Wraith, and as a bitter person, he quickly turned into a Wraith.

As written by Patrella Pogue, the *Book of Shadows* states, *Wraith Venom, when entering the body with negative outlook, will consume its host and turn them into a Wraith.* Lasting almost forty-eight hours, Aaron was finally cured when the Wraith that attacked him was vanquished by his brother, Noah. He hid his fragile, traumatized psyche flawlessly…and it led to his eventual withdrawal from the craft.

Now, having entirely renounced his magical heritage, Aaron Pogue is now a mortal – for what he believed was for his own safety. He is best described as being unjust, cold and judgemental.

Noah Pogue – born on May 13th, possesses the power of Probability Manipulation. As the middle brother, and reputedly the most handsome – as credited by WC (WitchCraft Magazine – the magical world's equivalent to GQ). That publication described him as the most desired bachelor; not because of his sex appeal, but because of his humble persona and paternal nature. If you wanted to marry into the Pogue Line of witches, Noah was your guy.

Noah studied law at Harvard to become a District Attorney, and he is the only one of the three Pogue brothers to neither turn nor become evil. At twenty, he married his highschool sweetheart Connemara Penthal – an enchanting beauty with whom he sired a son; Shane Penthal.

Bitter toward his older brother, as a result of feeling betrayed, Noah took over as Head Witch and assumed the title as the most powerful of the three...even though his power came by a twist of fate. He accepted his duties as a Custodian, a healer with a direct line of communication to a higher power, and succeeded greatly while maintaining his mortal world occupation.

Noah fights the good fight, never backing down, and vanquishing demons to protect the world for future generations of witches. Noah is heavily spiritual, he doesn't believe in God as such, but believes there is a higher power.

The third and youngest brother, Prometheus Pogue – born on September 9th, possesses the power of Sensazione – a superior mental ability made up of intuition, empathy, telepathy, sensing, mediumship and foresight. As early as the age of ten, Perry was a heartbreaker...he had girlfriend, after girlfriend, after girlfriend...one was never enough. At the age of seventeen, he unknowingly rendered a girl pregnant...and he still doesn't know to this day. Juggling university with his witch duties, he somehow made them both work, and he graduated with honors in Publishing.

The most susceptible to his mother's death and unable to control his grief, Perry fell into sex addiction. Directionless, he headed for Los Angeles, where he underwent rehab and chanced upon a modeling agent. His prestigious career of underwear modeling began when he was twenty-six, and it lasted for ten years.

Now thirty-six, Perry is an executive editor of WC Magazine in its Los Angeles office, and he maintains his aversion to being tied to one woman...they say old habits die hard.

Perry is the only Pogue to have been turned evil more than once. First, he was turned into a male Banshee when his grief was inconsolable, and he was subsequently cured. Next, he became a Seeker – a hideous looking, cloaked, harbinger demon that feeds upon the life-force of a mortal. As if that wasn't enough, he was attacked by an Undine – a Demonic Mermaid, before he was turned into a vampire and it stuck...with no possible chance of reversal.

INNOCENT

Above the North Pacific Ocean flew an unlikely creature; a winged cougar. Its feather and fur, normally ash grey, gleamed silver under a pale moon.

The down-draft from its massive wings caused the luxury yachts below to rock on their moorings, yet if anyone glanced up at the disturbance, they would have seen nothing.

As the beast flew toward the rapidly approaching shore, the city lights caught the glow of its surprisingly kind, sapphire blue eyes. Within seconds, it crossed the four-mile distance, and upon reaching the beach, shot upward into the sky before disappearing in a burst of white smoke.

The *Hollywood* sign's light burned brightly in the night. Lush and hypnotic bass notes pumped out of the inner-city nightclubs and pounded through bodies like a second heartbeat.

Vertigo, the place to be in LA, was the most lucrative hotspot if you wanted to see a celebrity. The dry-ice fog smothered the full dance floor. The lights flickered and shone in a myriad of colours. On stage, the iconic Lady Labyrinth prepared to perform in the club.

"Clubbers!" a female voice called. "In proper Vertigo tradition, give it up for the sensational...Lady Labyrinth!" The patrons in the club cheered, their hands in the air they applauded.

"Are you ready, Vertigo?!" Lady Labyrinth encouraged in a loud cheer, "for all my little monsters who are BORN THIS WAY!!"

Like a clap of thunder, the classic pop track brought an explosion of life to the already buzzing club.

On the dance floor, surrounded by other energized people, a male danced with a young woman.

He traced his hands up and down her sides, pulling her up against him, her blue eyes hypnotizing his as she ran her fingers through his short dark hair. The club had a set dress code; his attire was designer jeans, a charcoal short-sleeve shirt and slick shoes. She was dressed as a typical street walker, but with more expensive taste. Her attire left little to the imagination.

Bum in, boobs out, a wicked smile, long blonde hair and a nice tan you just wanted to taste...she knew how to tease. The song reached the chorus and the atmosphere in the club rose to a climax.

Slowly bringing her arms down, she rested her hands on his chest.

Leaning in, he began to kiss her neck making her throw her head back in a sensual abandon as she swayed her hips.

Blocking out the pumping bass and music, until all he could hear was silence, he felt her pulse race, and it was like nothing he'd ever felt before. Moving her neck away more, she turned around and rubbed her back up against the front of his body as he placed his hands on her hips.

His arousal became obvious as his body shuddered slightly and his eyes rolled back. Opening his eyes, they changed from green to yellow, revealing the creature within. Quickly, they reverted back to their green state as he engaged his prize beauty.

At the bar, another female with long ruby red hair sipped a cocktail. Rotating around on her stool, the male appeared in her direct line of sight.

A passage began to form as people subconsciously parted for a better view.

Her beauty was remarkable; a goddess...so enthralling and attractive that the air around her swayed as she radiated heat.

"Hey, Red!" A young man with a cocky grin tried to flirt with her. "What's a woman..."

She turned her head and gave him a glare, "I'm gonna stop you right there." Her beautiful, maroon-coloured eyes shone like a complex ruby under the down-lights, and he immediately fell silent. "Save me the agony of hearing your yawn story."

With a look of chagrin and an unattractive red flushing his features he stiffened his posture.

"Oh, don't look so hard done by. You knew I was out of your league the moment you saw me." she continued, "Now, shoo! I'm here on business!"

With that he turned and stalked away, shoulders hunched with embarrassment.

"What am I? A cougar?" she asked herself in a whisper, almost insulted.

To the side, a croaky, heavily lined and even more heavily made-up woman spoke to her. "Honey, trust me. These young things have a lot of stamina."

Glancing at the woman, the red-head growled, "Go back to the nursing home, and pray that the kind doctor will give you something to put you out of your misery!"

Displaying her power of Pyrokinesis, she opened her hand, and her mobile phone appeared in a spontaneous shimmer of small flames.

Moving the phone to her ear she uttered, "I really don't know why I had to do the Cougar Town, nightclub watch!" She glanced about bitterly as she listened to the person on the other end, "Yes, yes! I have located him. Hostile is dancing with the girl..."

The woman beside her, shocked by what she had just witnessed, remarked.

"What are you?!"

The red-haired female glanced back, "A witch!" the startled woman's eyes widened, "It's more than I can say about you, you cradle snatcher! Go home to your husband!" she remarked, before disappearing from her seat in a delicate shimmer of flames.

Back on the dance floor, the male's date pressed her bottom lip with her teeth as she raised her arms up into the air.

"I want to taste you..." she purred, placing her hands on each side of his square, chiseled face as she pulled his lips to hers and they locked in a frenzied kiss.

Atop the stage, Lady Labyrinth continued to perform.

Pulling his lips away with a gasp the male spoke. "Want to go back to my place?" Facing him again, his partner gave an obvious smile and a coy wink. Her silent consent was enough for him.

"Let's go." He said, and they began to move off through the crowd.

Along a dark street, lit by the occasional street lamp, the music of the nightclub was long behind them, and the male escorted his prized, innocent date back to his house. The apartment buildings cowered in the shadows as they felt his presence.

"Isn't the night incredible..." she whispered, hugging his arm as they walked along.

He dismissed her comment as he watched the path ahead.

Turning her head, the woman glanced across the street at a small park adorned with tall pine trees. Among the dark trees, faintly distinguishable glows of silver captured her attention for a second, and a smile curled her lips at one end.

"Let's go through the park." She suggested.

He glanced out the corner of his eye, saw the darkness and found himself silently agreeing with her.

"I'm feeling courageous; what about you?" her eyes sparkled innocently, and then she spoke his name, "Peter; do you feel like being spontaneous?" Her smile broadened.

He smiled at her convincingly. "The night is young." He said, before they began to cross the street in the direction of the adjacent park.

Another female, tall and beautiful, exited a parked car as the two disappeared into the park.

Raising her phone to her ear, she uttered the words, "I have located him."

Stepping away from the classic red Chevy, even the poor lighting captured her other-worldly beauty.

On her right wrist she sported a tattooed symbol of the triple goddess; a sign that she was a member of the Triad.

With her back to the vehicle, she waved her hand, and the car door slammed shut.

A sudden blur of luminescent green came hurtling out of the darkness toward her. Halting abruptly, the green, astral energy coalesced into a male with apple green hair and green eyebrows that sat above azure eyes.

"Zane; about bloody time!" the female complained.

Zane, the only male member of the Triad, stood six feet tall and was built like a weight-lifter.

Without even puffing from the exertion of using Astral Speed, he replied with a grin.

"Pilar, do you have any idea how many fricken hills there are in Los Angeles?"

"No." She replied, "but I get the feeling you're going to tell me anyways."

Sucking in air, he puffed out his chest and boasted, "Not enough to tire me out! Where are Siobhan and Juliann?"

She narrowed her eyes and twisted her lips as she responded with a look of displeasure, "Wow, I'm proud." The sarcasm was evident as they both exchanged glances with one another. "Siobhan was on nightclub duty."

"And Juliann?" he queried cautiously,

Pilar responded sarcastically. "Bush walking."

In the clear, night sky, a noticeable cloud of white quickly began to manifest itself. Its choppy texture rolled and curled as it pulled away from the dark and poured down in a cascading stream.

Reaching the ground, it spun like a tornado…minus the deadly wind. The night air of Los Angeles changed as the surface of the street flooded with fog before dispersing and leaving a man in its stead. Noah Pogue stood in the middle of the suburban street.

Noah was one of those people who just had natural good looks. The more he aged as a man, the more his features became stated. His sapphire blue eyes captured the glow of the street lamps and revealed a caring disposition. Though it was dark, the light improved his already perfect olive tan.

On the inside of his right arm, close to his wrist, sat the birthmark of a Celtic sun; a recognizable symbol that revealed him to be a Custodian. But he was also a witch. The Therianthrope mark defined the blood that flowed through his veins and his ability to shapeshift into a winged beast.

Using his limited Custodian ability to sense, Noah turned his head away from the impressive apartment complex in front of him. He glanced out the corner of his eye, with his attention directed to the blackened park that separated two neighborhoods.

Beyond the darkness, some distance away, was another street. An ill-omened feeling began to permeate within him.

Levitating across the bitumen, he disappeared in another rush of smoke.

~*~

"**Y**ou have an odd fascination with parks at night." Peter commented, as he walked beside his date.

He looked up into the towering trees as they walked the gravel track.

She shyly lowered her head and curled some hair behind her ear, before smiling and turning her gaze back to him as she spoke jovially. "I hope you're not scared of the dark."

"Not at all." He bumped her playfully and then looked ahead into the thick black of night.

The textures of the rough barked pine trees were becoming more indistinguishable as they ventured further.

He said rather coyly, "I've got a hot woman to protect me."

A distance away, enough not to be noticed, another female was captured by the poor light that shone through foliage above as she peered out from behind a tree.

She was a Triad member with long, golden-blonde hair and an oval-shaped face and green eyes.

Using her power of Advanced Telepathy, she projected her thoughts, "I see him."

The young woman holding Peter's arm gave him a suspicious, *you so don't know what you've gotten yourself into* look.

Raising his head, he murmured at her, "Is it me..." caution now obvious in his manly voice, "or is it getting darker?"

The darkness blanketing him had a disorientating effect, and the deafening silence sent shivers up his spine...he had not counted on this happening.

Halting, he turned to his date, "W-why?" She had vanished from his side.

Staggering about with a lost look and hesitant dread in his eyes, he began to fear the grizzly fate that awaited him. Behind him, a stick snapped, and a tall, black figure slipped out into the poor light.

"You lost, mate?" The thick, British accent surprised him, and Peter turned quickly, acknowledging the man, who apologized. "Sorry. I didn't mean to startle you. You look lost."

At first sight, Peter mistook him for a harmless council man working late to keep the park clean. But then, he began to sense something more atrocious.

The British man began again, his face this time morphing as he spoke.

"You know, all sorts of things lurk in the dark." His brow protruded, and each iris turned a demon yellow. His cheek bones rose, his eyes sunk into subtle shadow and his sharp canines rose to the occasion.

~*~

Some years earlier, on a stormy winter's night, Caydit Packrem, Vampire Sovereign of the Los Angeles Nocturne League was out hunting in Treadwell when she crossed paths with a Pogue Witch. Local Vampire Empress, Anessa, had already banished Caydit some one-hundred years prior for murdering a gypsy coven in the area, and also for bedding the Vampire King.

"A Pogue Witch." Caydit spoke with caution and a hint of suspicion in her voice, "requesting to meet with me?"

A flash of lightning revealed a tall male with short blonde hair and amber eyes.

"I have a proposition for you, Sovereign!" the male replied in his deep voice.

"Witches cannot be trusted! Just like Slayers!" Caydit retorted, her eyes hungry, "but go on; I am listening!" Extending her arm, she moved her fingers individually, showing off her sharp fingernails. "Speak, before I tear out your jugular!"

"I want you." He began with conviction. Making no secret of the vindictiveness in his voice, "to teach my brother a lesson about being irresponsible!"

Caydit remarked sarcastically, "You're kidding, right?"

"I want you to turn Perry into a Vampire!" he said coldly.

OFF THE BEATEN TRACK

Although the darkness limited his senses, Peter sniffed and then hissed through crumpled lips, "Vampire!"

The intruder gave off a demonic growl and then lunged forward.

Widening his eyes in disbelief, Peter, out of reflex, suddenly engaged in hand-to-kick combat. Immediately, he blocked the vampire's punch with his arm, and then swung a punch of his own back, only to have the vampire evade it.

He swung another punch.

Blocking the attack, the vampire pushed Peter's arm and struck him across the face, causing him to stagger back.

Turning around to gain better ground, the vampire came at him again. Peter propelled himself into a roundhouse kick, striking his foe in the face. Landing back onto his feet, he stared down his opponent.

The vampire growled. "Skilled...mortal." As he reapproached. His yellow eyes gleamed with an intense hunger. "But it won't be enough to save you!"

Leaping into an upper-cut kick, he forcefully struck Peter in the chest.

Crying out as the force of the vampire's attack launched him back into the darkness, Peter crashed into nearby bushes. Above him, in another concentrated rush of white smoke, Noah Pogue appeared. A large, solid branch managed to support his weight.

Deeper into the park among the thick shrubs, Peter's date knelt down to a heavy, circular, iron manhole-cover. With a single heft, she ripped it free and tossed it away without a second thought. Nearby, a blonde-haired, female Triad member watched the proceedings from behind a tree, her green eyes gleaming subtly in the shadows.

Peering into the disused cave – a nest – Peter's date growled, "Get out!" as her face morphed into that of a vampire's. "I have brought us a snack!" Stepping to the side of the manhole, she let four vampires out – three female and one male.

Peter's innocent date was as far from innocent as possible, and she raised her dainty hand to the poor light and stared lovingly at her fingernails. All five nails suddenly extended and became razor sharp.

"I'm going to rip out his jugular!" she purred sadistically.

~*~

*O*ver the past years, the bodies of thirty-five missing people had been found...drained of blood, with either a neck wound or a wound to the thigh at the femoral artery point. The popular and idiotic theory was...dog attacks. It was later revealed by the media that a total of seventy people were actually missing, but being Hollywood, nobody had the sense to be remotely fearful or reluctant to venture out of doors after dark, regardless of the attacks.

The thirty-five undiscovered bodies re-populated the Nocturne League, a group of Vampires under the jurisdiction of Caydit, the sadistic, and very bitchy, Sovereign Vampress of California.

Caydit was nowhere near as old and powerful as her creator and Southern Hemisphere counterpart – Anessa, The Vampire Empress.

Back on the gravel path, the male vampire looked into the darkness, waiting for Peter to reappear. Between him and his next victim, shimmering orbs began to spiral around as they manifested. Gathering into a single shimmer, they blazed for a moment before a young woman emerged.

"Nice parlor trick, Witch!" The vamp greeted her with a scolding glare, coupled with a deep and chesty growl. "I am immune to your powers!!"

Isadora merely sighed, caring little that he had the upper hand.

In the breeze, her long, honey-blonde hair floated from her face and danced to the side. Her indigo colored eyes revealed her fierce power as they challenged his demonic ones. The witch's confident stare wiped the gloat from his face.

Her glossy lips smirked, "I might be blonde, but I'm not totally stupid!"

In the dark, she stood tall and poised. Watching him sway with anticipation as he feverishly licked his lips, she raised her hand, prompting him to approach.

"Bring it on, ugly!"

Isadora stepped forward.

"Ready to die!" the vamp growled, swinging his fist at her.

The true beauty of a vampire's fingernails was not aesthetic – it was more practical than that. They could slice through solid metals...slashing a human was as easy as sliding a hot knife through butter.

Glancing out from behind another tree, the blonde Triad member used her telepathy to inform her comrades, "Isadora has engaged a vampire!"

Ducking down, Isadora evaded the vampire's attack. As she rose again, she pushed his arm away in the opposite direction and grunted as she struck him across the face. She used her left fist, and then she swung her right, each time effortlessly evading his attacks.

The force of each punch made him stagger.

She approached him again in a smug manner, her heels crunching in the gravel. She halted, raised her foot and kicked him in the gut, quickly raising her leg higher and kicking him in the chest.

Stepping back, she regained her composure.

She stood with her arms braced and fists locked...all in preparation for his next move.

"Beaten by a girl!" she taunted him.

Breathing in deeply, the bones in his body cracked as his chest expanded.

"You all break the same!" he growled, before charging at her. "One should always appreciate the taste of a fine witch."

Sarcastically, Isadora remarked, "I'll bet!" and as he came within reach, she extended her arm and struck him in the face.

As he slowly floated to the ground, she whipped a wooden stake from her back pocket and drove it into his heart. Screaming out in pain, the man's flesh and clothes disintegrated to dust. As his skeletal figure finally settled onto the ground, it broke apart, collapsing into fine white dirt.

"You all break the same..." she mocked, looking down at his white outline in the gravel.

A cold shiver shot up Isadora's back, causing her to gasp softly as she saw a tall, dark figure out of the corner of her eye. As it approached her, a deep, chesty animal growl emanated. It opened its arms to bind its prey.

"I smelt you!" it growled, in a deep, masculine voice.

Isadora screamed. Spinning around, she grabbed the figure by his shirt, turned again and launched him at the monstrous trunk of the pine tree to her immediate left.

As he slammed against the tree, the sounds of cracking pine filled the silence of the park.

The male groaned and then fell to the ground.

With another growl he questioned her, "Where is your nest?"

Isadora abruptly stiffened, and her goddess-like beauty contorted with outrage, "I am not a vampire, you half-wit!"

His piercing yellow eyes flicked up from the dark, connecting magnetically with her glimmering, indigo eyes.

"I can smell the stench on your clothes and skin!"

Narrowing her eyes with the insult, she growled, "That stench is Burberry!" Isadora has exquisite taste in fragrances. Arching her arm and gripping her wooden stake tightly, she threatened him, "I will stake you like I did your bigot, British friend!"

Standing her ground, she watched his eyes move through the dark as he got to his feet and then approached her. As he neared her, she drew on her power of Energy Manipulation and the air surrounding her suddenly rippled like water. With a brisk, single-handed gesture, she forcefully propelled him back into the tree again.

She murmured, "...odd, vampires are immune to a witch's powers!"

Satisfied the effect that her power had wrought, she lowered her hand back to her side and watched the dark as she called out a name.

"Perry...?" briskly raising her hand again, Isadora commanded the foliage in Italian, "Luce! (Light)"

Glittering magic danced across the branches of the pine trees, and they easily parted, flooding the dark with moonlight. Brushing himself off, with his face now morphed back to normal, Peter, or Perry, stared at the beautiful young witch before him.

He spoke her name, "Isadora?"

Isadora only managed to utter, "P–" as a blackened figure charged out from the dark and snatched her into the velvet black. Her scream echoed in the distance.

Turning his head, a large fist struck Perry in the face, throwing him into a spin and onto the gravel.

Slithering out into the moonlight, his date reappeared...all vamped out.

"Hello, Peter!" she greeted him sarcastically, now fully aware that it wasn't his real name. "I've been looking for you. Are you ready to die?" Her stunning, immortal smile was utterly captivating.

In the glow of the moon, a rush of smoke plummeted down from the foliage and onto the ground. Noah emerged as the inky blackness masked his facial features.

Growling, the vampire became hostile and territorial, "a Custodian!"

Painfully, Perry murmured, "Noah?" as he raised his bloodied face from the ground.

~*~

Crashing through the shrubs in darkness, Isadora hit the ground hard and rolled across the painful pine needles that blanketed it.

"Ugh! Son of a bitch!"

Pouncing onto her body, the black figure, another female vampire, pinned her down. Screaming, she felt the vampire's open mouth against the bare skin of her exposed neck.

The icy breath of its voice numbed her skin, "I've always wanted to taste a witch!"

"Get off me, you bloody leech!" Tucking her legs in, she shoved against it with all of her might, launching the vampire off, and consigning it back into dark.

Quickly, she scrambled to her feet.

Isadora commanded the foliage again in Italian, "Luce! (Light)." Almost immediately the branches that were laced together in glittering magic parted, letting in the moon's full gaze. "Come out scumbag!"

She scanned her surroundings slowly. and as she turned, a fist, out of nowhere, knocked her to the ground again.

Stepping into view, the beautiful female vampire revealed more of herself – short, red, pixie-styled hair and stunning orange coloured eyes. Licking her lips, she looked hungrily at her prey in the dirt.

Folding her arms, she growled menacingly "Lights out, witch!"

Turning over in the dirt, Isadora swung her leg out. "Kiss the ground, bitch!" she spat, as she knocked the vampire's legs out from underneath her.

Rolling back over onto her stomach, she began to crawl away. Pressing her hand against the pine needles, she hissed with unexpected pain as one penetrated her hand. As she quickly pulled it free, a droplet of blood fell in the dirt.

A deep growl sounded, and the vampire's iridescent orange vampire eyes shone with thirst. The smell of Isadora's blood permeated the tasteless air around it.

Isadora's beautiful, indigo eyes stared up at the vampire. "Oh, you have got to be kidding me!" Rising to one knee, she turned, crying out as she avoided a punch. Rolling away to the side, she evaded another.

Getting to her feet, Isadora then caught the third punch and struck the vampire back in the face.

"You never give up, do you?!"

Energy rippled beneath her feet, and she used her power to levitate from the ground. With a hearty grunt, she turned herself in the air, striking again; this time with a kick.

Retaliating, the vampire grabbed her foot and swung the teen, catapulting her into a tree.

"Give it up, gorgeous!" the vampire laughed maliciously.

"I'll take that as a compliment!" Isadora retorted, "at least," she continued, maneuvering herself into a cartwheel and hitting the vampire twice, "I'm attractive. What's there to like about you?" she caught the vampire's flying fist with one hand. With her free hand, she punched her foe in the gut. "Bloody ugly is what you are, Cupcake!" She punched her again, this time in the face, and turning side on, she then elbowed her in the nose.

"You insolent witch!" the vampire hissed back. With incredible strength and stamina, she struggled against Isadora's martial arts skills, "I will rip your throat out!"

Isadora retorted sarcastically, "I'd like to see you try!" completely unaware that a second vampire stood directly behind her. Grabbing her by the arm, the male flung her away to the side like a ragdoll.

Screaming, she soared in between the trees and then hit another tree that appeared to jump out from the shadows in front of her.

"Kill her!" the female vampire ordered imperiously.

With a nod of his head, the male understood, but as he turned to do her bidding, a blur of green astral energy shot past him, and the hulkish vampire roared in agony.

His flesh and clothes spontaneously disintegrated, and his skeletal figure dropped to the ground and then collapsed into a pile of fine white dirt.

Apprehensive, the female vampire screeched, "What the…?" moving her gaze from the pile of white dirt to her surroundings.

Behind her, the blonde telepathic witch stepped out from behind a tree.

Some distance away from her, another female stood poised in the moonlight, accompanied by the fiery, red head – the female from the night club.

Sensing the unseen – the male Zane, with the power of Astral Speed – the vampire raised her arm and then abruptly slammed her elbow into Zane's gut.

"Take a hike, Quicksilver!"

He halted abruptly and groaned.

Moving so quickly that every movement was a blur, the vampire grabbed him by the scruff of his green shirt and propelled him back with brute force.

"I hate witches!! You are nothing but a filthy, bubonic plague!" Bringing her arms back down to her side, the vampire smirked confidently.

"Good night." A stern, feminine voice came from behind her. Turning, the vampire was greeted by the red-haired female. "…bitch!" she spat.

Using her own power of Pyrokinesis, the red-headed witch blasted the vampire with a ferocious torrent of flames from her mouth – Conflagration Breathing. Consumed by an evil, fiery fate, the vampire screamed.

BROTHERS GRIMM

Many years earlier, following a failed interaction with one of the Pogue Brothers, Caydit Packrem had hunted down and lured Perry Pogue out into the open. It had happened one night as he had visited his mother's grave in the cemetery on the Old North Road.

"Hello, Mum." he greeted the angel-adorned concrete block. "How are you? I miss you." He knelt down and placed the bouquet of flowers for his mother beside her photo. "We've drifted apart, Mum. Without you, our family is broken…"

"Oh." An uncaring and acidic voice said from somewhere out in the darkness. "I wish I could give a shit!" The Sovereign Vampire was about to attack.

Startled, Perry jumped to his feet and spun around, looking in every direction for the person who had interrupted the conversation he was having with his mother's grave.

"Hello?" he queried.

Staggering around in a circle, he balanced himself, but trod on a stick, snapping it as the silence was broken. The dark was a bit disorientating, but a short distance away, there were street lights. He narrowed his eyes and made out the delicate silhouettes of houses along the street.

He turned around again to face his mother's grave. "What's wrong?" Caydit remarked menacingly, as she grabbed him by the throat. Perry choked as he struggled to pull her hand away. "Were you expecting your mother dearest?" she continued spitefully, her human-looking face morphing into a vampire's, "was she about to make a ghostly appearance?" With a demonic growl, she pulled Perry in close and sank her teeth into his neck. He struggled to cry out, but she muffled his mouth with her other hand as she drank his blood.

Aaron, Perry's eldest brother, and the man who had orchestrated the attack, then stepped out from behind a tree.

~*~

Everything was still, quiet and ominous.

The moon's full gaze permeated the shadows, driving them back to reveal a small portion of park and the gravel path where Perry lay.

"Noah, you have to go!"

Raising his bloodied face from the ground, he tried to warn his older brother about the grizzly beings that lurked close by.

"No. Stay. I'm going to enjoy this!" his date remarked modestly.

Although dressed as a heavily made-up street walker, she was actually quite breathtaking in the moonlight as it shone through the foliage.

Noah stood cautious and watchful.

Intrigued by his presence, she eyed him up and down as though he would be her next victim. He was able to sense her slyness as she placed her hands on her hips.

"I might be immune to the powers of a witch, but I have no issue beating you down, Custodian!"

Noah disregarded her portentous small talk as hollow words. He chose instead to remain silent and standoffish.

Raising her hand to eye level she stared lovingly at her razor sharp, blood-red fingernails and blew gently against them. Hearing Perry stir in the gravel, she shot him a mocking glare.

"Perry Pogue, the womanizer. I would say it's an honor, but you're so below respect on my radar that it's not funny. Cayden wants you dead!"

Nearby, Noah tightened his fists until his knuckles cracked.

The vampire turned to Noah with a territorial growl.

"Easy, fool. Only a Slayer can vanquish me!"

In reply, Noah made an odd sound before he grinned and extended his arm at her. Flexing his biceps, something happened, and Perry's date screamed out in agony. Her entire body suddenly exploded into molecules, and then fell to the ground in a fine veil of white dust.

"I proved you wrong!" Noah laughed at the dust. "Some of us can manipulate probability by amplifying the moonlight and turning it into kinetic energy. As it turned out, you weren't immune to the probability of disintegrating into a million pieces!" The gravel path crunched beneath the soles of his shoes as he moved over to Perry. "Are you okay?" he queried, halting at his brother's side and kneeling. "Let me see your face."

"No..." Perry turned away from his Custodian,

Placing his hand on his innocent's jaw line and chin, Noah turned the young male's face and their eyes connected like magnets. "I am your brother." His warm and caring sapphire eyes looked over his younger brother's complexion. "Vampire or

Witch...Brother..."

Perry's eyes glimmered as he appreciated this affection.

"I love you just the same, *Rufus*," he said, using his pet name for his brother. "Now, let me heal you!" Gently, Noah placed his hand on his brother's face, and the bloodied cuts healed instantly, disappearing as though they had never been there. Taking his hand away, he took his brother by the arm and began to help him back to his feet.

He queried again, "Are you okay?"

Brushing his clothes, Perry's face morphed from vampire back to human, and Noah smiled. "I see you've still got your powers."

Shyly, Perry stood with his face tilted toward the ground as he spoke to his older brother. He envied and admired the control Noah had over his powers of Probability Manipulation.

Perry reminded him, "Vampires are immune to the powers of a witch." As he was only half Custodian, Noah had limited access to the powers of that role – because he was also half witch. To wield either beings' power fully, witch or Custodian, he would have to renounce one or the other.

"They're cloaked by an ethereal shield that acts as a second layer of skin. It reacts to sunlight and grants immunity." Perry continued.

Noah replied, "You're welcome, know-it-all, but I'm not entirely a witch, and neither are you." As he spoke, calm settled into his eyes.

Shifting his gaze, Perry's memory took over, and he recalled the attack over a decade earlier. He remembered Cayden, the 15th century vampire who had kidnapped and tortured him for slaying her lesbian lover. As the images in his head flickered like an old TV, he recalled her feeding on his femoral artery until he was only seconds away from death.

Forcing him to feed on her own blood, she then sired him...but not to completion. He had been turned, becoming half vampire, half witch. Somehow, the witch side of him camouflaged him from other vampires, so he gained their strengths but none of their weaknesses, enabling him to walk in daylight, control his hunger and have immunity from wooden instruments, crosses and silver.

Noah waved his hand across his brother's eyes, "Hello?"

A vague look crossed Perry's face before he returned to the present. He looked at his brother again.

"Where did you go?" Noah asked, clearly confused.

Before Perry could reply, yet another female vampire appeared, iridescent with self assurance as she glided across the ground and crossed Perry's line of sight. A veil of moonlight swirled around her like a light fog, and she uttered a chesty growl.

Protecting his brother, Perry snarled, "my turn!"

Catlike, he leapt through the air and threw himself at her as she readied herself to pounce on Noah. She looked Chinese-American, about nineteen years old, and she growled throatily as Perry crashed into her; knocking both of them to the ground. Tucking her legs underneath her as she fell, the vamp gave a grunt and propelled him away. Through the air, Perry rolled into a somersault and skidded across the gravel, dog-like on his hands and feet.

Flipping back up onto her feet, the vamp turned, her long, layered, baby blue hair fell delicately as it framed her face, and the effect gave her a strange beauty as she raised her fists and prepared to fight.

The vampire growled, "Cayden is not happy with you!" clearly trying to intimidate him with her yellow, demon-eyes as she addressed him. "Half breed!"

Rising, Perry swung his leg, hoping to strike her with a kick. Using only her forearm, she blocked his kick and punched him in the face. Then, she pulled him close and kneed him in the gut…hearing him groan put a smile on her face.

She toyed with him, "I promise I'll make your death quick!"

Abruptly, Perry jerked his neck forward, "Kiss my arse!" he snarled, head-butting her in the face before he leapt up and struck her in the gut. He rose a little higher and kicked her in the face…the force of his attack flipped her backwards. She crashed onto her stomach in the gravel, while he landed back on his feet.

Perry growled, "There's no such thing as an easy death!"

Recovering, the vampire levitated, her face now fully vamped. She gave off another chesty, pissed-off demon growl.

Standing back, Noah watched, intrigued. Again, Perry and the vamp engaged in combat. She blocked Perry's fist with her left hand and punched him back with her right.

Anticipating her next attack, Perry returned the compliment. Grabbing her by the arm, he then twisted it.

Clenching her other arm, he twisted that too, then raised his leg and kicked her in the gut, launching her back into a tree with rocket-speed. The giant, solid pine groaned and cracked under the force of the impact. Impaled on a broken branch, she screamed out in agony. Her clothes and flesh disintegrated and her bones fell to the ground, floating to the ground to form a small pile of white dust.

~*~

Elsewhere in the park, bathed in moonlight, the Vampress screamed as the red-headed witch blasted her with flames. Looking on from the side, the brunette's eyes widened in shock, and her breath fled from her lips.

The magical atmosphere made visible by the rich and intense flames, acted as a barrier of glittering energy that kept the fire at a nose distance away from the vampire's face.   "Such passion!" The Vampress stopped screaming, her voice now thick with seduction. "I can feel your heart race!" Striking out, she punched the fire-breathing witch in the gut. Briskly spinning on the spot, she extended her leg, kicked the witch and sent her soaring back onto the ground.

A loud groan came from the shadows. Turning, the vampire was struck by a powerful and visible seismic wave. She grunted – making it obvious that she was unaffected. The power gave off a pulse, and it reacted to the magical atmosphere, surrounding and deflecting from her, blasting pine needles off of the nearby trees.

"Cool parlor trick, witch!" She laughed maniacally.

The blonde witch squinted her eyes, screwed up her lips and discharged low-level pulses of energy from her outstretched hands.

"I can create earthquakes. Want me to make the ground swallow you whole?" she threatened.

"Impressive," the Vampress replied, looking almost flattered as she turned to face the small group of witches who had joined their brunette companion. "My, my…" she mocked them, "what an honor it is to be in the presence of true and great power here in Los Angeles." She pointed to the brunette first.

"Pilar," she announced, a smile curling her red lips as a look of intimidation moved in Pilar's face, "the gypsy-witch who can inflict paralysis and manipulate the human body."

She then moved her pointed finger to the blonde. "Juliann Quake, as you're known in demonic circles; the one with the power of Pulse Manipulation."

Turning her head, the Vampress looked down at the red-head and lowered herself onto one knee…but not out of respect. The vampire clearly despised her. "Siobhan…the Firestarter and the eldest sister…" Glancing to the other side, she frowned upon the male as he sat against the tree. "Zane…Quicksilver. You four are revered and feared as gods amongst legends. Four siblings…the wielders of The Triple Goddess!"

Raising her chin slightly, whilst displaying a stern and repulsed glare, Pilar used her power of Paralysis. With a seductive echo to her arrogant huff, the vampire smirked as the gypsy-witch's power reacted with the magical atmosphere giving off a loud, whip-cracking bang.

The Vampress chuckled modestly, "nice try, but you are all the same." The pine needles that blanketed the ground crunched beneath her shoes. "Power, power, power," stepping into the moon's gaze as it peered in through the branches, her magnificent, orange vampire eyes ignited with a glow. Behind her, a black figure emerged. Unaware, she continued to speak, "don't you ever get sick and tired of your own ego?"

Noticing the figure, Juliann's facial expression became uneasy.

Gesturing her hand and briskly flicking it in an attempt to afflict the Vampress with paralysis, Pilar drew her attention. With a mocking face and jovial tone, the Vampress stopped with her hand firmly placed on her hips. "Please."

With a brisk swing, the dark figure attempted to strike. Turning abruptly, the Vampress tore the stick from Isadora's hands, threw it away to the side and then pulled her by her blonde hair.

"I really hate you!" Isadora screamed.

"Indy!!!" Pilar cried out, as she ran at the vampire.

Turning slightly, the Vampress forcefully shoved the brunette in the chest and catapulted her backwards. "Back off! You're in my territory now!"

Screaming as she moved through the air, Pilar crashed into Juliann, knocking them both to the ground. Pulling the young witch around in front of her, the vampire glared down her enemies and then arched her jaw. Opening her mouth, she moved her fangs to the innocent teen's, tasty neck.

"Mm, you smell like peaches!" the Vampress announced, giving off a deep growl. "Welcome," a seductive chuckle slipped from her parted lips, "to the dark side!" With another growl, she plunged her teeth into the witch's neck.

Isadora screamed out in agony.

Raising their heads from the ground, both the blonde and the brunette watched with terror. The young witch's head hung to one side as the Vampress fed on her...blood dripped down the side of her neck.

In between two towering pine trees, a cascade of smoke appeared as Noah transported himself and Perry to the location of the scream. The smoke floated across the ground giving the darkened park eerie, un-dead appeal.

Stepping forward, realization immediately swept across Perry's face.

Cautiously he uttered, "Cayden!" loud enough for his brother to hear, "She's resurfaced!"

The tone of his voice acknowledged a personal terror.

Terrified, Noah yelled out in anguish, "Indy!!!"

Pulling her mouth from the young witch's neck, Cayden — the now identified Vampress – gasped as she quenched her thirst.

"Her blood is incredible; so much power!" she said, licking the remaining blood that wept from the neck wound. "She is such a saint!" Slipping her arm away, she licked her fingers as Isadora's unconscious body fell toward the ground, "for a Pogue..."

A sudden gust of wind blew up from the ground, causing Cayden to shield her face from the projectile pine needles that shot up with the dirt. Green astral energy – captured in slow motion – rushed past. Zane caught Isadora as she fell into his arms, and he then abruptly shot off in another blur of green.

As he watched, bound in confusion, Perry murmured, "What the...hell?"

Shifting his gaze away to the right, he watched the brunette, blonde and red haired women, and then noticed a fast moving, green blur. Reappearing, the green blur...Zane, cradled Isadora in his arms as he stood by his sisters.

Perry murmured in his brother's ear, "You involved the Triad?"

"They are powerful," Noah growled underneath his breath as he watched the Vampress ahead of him without moving his eyes. "They—"

Perry finished his brother's sentence, "they helped you locate me…" Looking back over to them, one by one, he appeared curious. "…the Stepford Cuckoos."

Noah protested, outlining his respect, "The Triad's combined telepathy is ultimate; they pinpointed your location before I even asked them to help me. Yes, they're like the Stepford Cuckoos." A vague, confronted look rose in his face and then he queried, "Why are we quoting X-Men?"

Connecting to his own limited, custodian telepathy, the Triad's telepathy manifested as apparitions before Noah.

Pilar's voice licked up his neck, "Manipulate…"

Juliann appeared next at his right ear, "The probability…"

Siobhan at his left ear, "Of the magical atmosphere…"

Zane's telepathic apparition appeared in front of him, "And we shall attack with a mental strike!"

Together, to the side where the pine trees embroidered the clearing, the Triad stood superior and powerful. They looked upon the Vampress with such disgust; their mental strike would obliterate her instantly.

Hearing vague whispers, but not loud enough to fully understand what was being exchanged, Perry queried. "Noah, what…?"

~*~

Contorting his face with fear as he watched on – like a protective father – Noah then extended his arm. Gesturing his hand, he used his witch power, as insisted upon by the Triad, to manipulate the probability of the magical atmosphere surrounding the demon.

Instantly effective, Cayden was propelled back into the tree.

Stunned that it worked, Noah murmured, "Whoa!"

Perry cried as he shot backwards...the backfire of manipulating probability for personal gain. Hitting the ground hard, he raised his head and looked at his brother with a cautious glare.

"What the hell was that for?!"

As outlined by the bewilderment in his face, Noah looked back at his brother and then looked ahead at the vampire pinned against a tree. Getting to his feet, Perry brushed himself off and remarked sarcastically. "I love you, too!"

Peeling herself off of the tree, the Vampress landed on her feet. Turning her head, she growled at the Triad, sensing their telepathic power entering her mind. Reaching up, she tore a decent-sized branch from the tree and threw it at them. Shrieking as the branch hit them, they were knocked to the ground.

"Little bitches!" Cayden growled.

Widening his eyes, Noah quickly realized why she was not immune to his power.

"Cayden..." The slightness of his deep and masculine voice made her ears prick up, and she smirked. Flicking through his thoughts, he searched for mythology. "Caydit Packrem, 15th century."

Perry queried, "What?" returning to his brother's side.

Smirking as she continued to glare at him, Cayden's heightened hearing allowed her to hear what Noah was saying.

With a humble echo, "The Brothers Grimm…" slipped from her glossed ruby lips.

"Because she drank your blood," Noah revealed, outlining the effects of drinking the blood of a witch, "she is no longer immune to our powers!"

Confidently striding toward them, Cayden murmured to herself, "This is going to be fun!" and then in the blink of an eye, she was gone.

COME HOME WITH ME

The moon shone in through the bare branches, casting spectacular rays of light.

Set a yard apart, the towering pine trees – immortalized with their own shadows – gave the setting an imperial and aged feel. The branches began to rustle as the wind picked up for a moment and the delicate fog from Noah's teleportation power waved, unsettled, across the ground.

With baited breath, Perry – vamped out – slowly turned his head as he scanned their surroundings. Raising his nose, his heightened vampire senses allowed him to sniff out her scent on the wind.

"She is close…"

Cayden's confident voice reminded him, "I know she is!"

Turning his head quickly, Perry was greeted by his maker's astounding beauty. Giving him a dirty grin, she shoved him forcefully with one hand. He cried out as the force of the attack launched him backward into a tree, causing him to fall face first into the fog-blanketed dirt.

With a nervous gulp, as he stood on the other side of the regal Vampress, Noah uttered, "You are not immune to my–"

Her vicious eyes suppressed his blue sapphire ones as she grabbed him by the throat and began to elevate him from the ground. She stared right into his soul as he began to choke and gargle within her tight grip.

"You will be silent, you bubonic plague!" As she spoke with repulsion, Cayden rigidly tilted her head and sniffed his intriguing scent. "You smell nice…" She smiled, as though delighted, "Bvlgari; correct?"

Her lips curled and parted, showing off her white fangs. Looking over his charming facial features, she smirked coyly.

"It would be a pleasure to bite such a handsome specimen." Lowering him down, she let his feet touch the ground again, and then forcefully pulled him in for a passionate kiss. Gasping as she pulled her lips away, her eyes glimmered with a fierce lust.

"Your lips taste as good as you are handsome!"

Taken aback by the sudden kiss, Noah displayed a look that gave away his liking for spontaneous thrills. "I bet you say that to all the boys."

"Your brother didn't seem to complain." Cayden toyed with a beautiful smile as her vampire features faded back into a mortal complexion. "He thinks more with his penis than his actual brain." Noah raised an eyebrow with intrigue…it didn't surprise him that Perry would act in such a way, but to hear it from a lustful creature of the night made it even more startling. "He is my most prized creature."

In a bitter tone, Noah stated, "The transformation drove him insane!"

Cayden merely smirked, knowing too well of the side effects of turning a witch into a vampire.

In a brief flashback, Noah recalled Perry tied to a chair in the attic thrashing about in an insane, animalistic way.

"His witch DNA, fought hard against the vampire DNA, causing a chemical imbalance and an animalistic nature."

Cayden winked with one eye and said, "Does that surprise you?" He gave her an odd look of confusion. "All men are animals at heart." Reaching out with her free hand, she caressed the side of his face. "But every now and then, I come across the odd honorable man like you, Noah Pogue." Briskly pulling her hand back, she returned to their conversation. "The demon brings out the animal inside…" Sighing with delight, she spoke with the utmost respect, "I created an artist!"

To Noah's knowledge, if a witch was turned into a vampire, the potent DNA of both species caused a chemical imbalance, sending the host insane.

Noah protested, "The insanity made him bite and feed on his own blood. He was his own cure!"

Cayden turned her head slightly and narrowed her eyes conceitedly, "Yes, so I have noticed. It appears you Pogue witches are more unique than originally thought."

Much to his surprise, Noah realized he was having a civil conversation with the monstrosity before him. Being frank, he said, "Both witch and vampire came together as one hybrid DNA. You have no influence over him!"

Glancing to the side, and watching Isadora where she lay on the ground with the Triad, Cayden's smirk became sly.

"I can make him feed on her." And with that, Noah's sapphire eyes showed the fierce, protective side of him that not many people knew he had. "Mm." sensing his pulse race, she quickly glanced back, "It appears I have struck a nerve. She means something to you." Noah calmed himself, removing all forms of defensiveness from his face and eyes. "Ah…" she sighed as she looked deeper into his beauty; she had found the thing that made him so protective of his niece. "There it is…"

Caressing his face again, she ran her index finger over his lips and made a *shhh* noise with her lips. "I will let you watch."

Noah nervously murmured beneath the finger on his lips, "Wh-what?"

She smiled again, "I will let you watch Perry feed on her." Slipping her finger away from his lips, Cayden moved her head slightly and summoned in a harmonic tone. "Perry, my sweet boy…" Rising to his hands and knees, Perry — vampire in appearance — raised his face in her direction and then rose to his feet.

Acting as though he was under her influence, he walked over to his maker and halted directly behind her right shoulder. Magnetically, his eye met with Noah's, who trembled.

"Perry!" Noah roared, struggling under Cayden's physically powerful grip. Almost hysterical, he growled at his brother, "Don't you dare lay a finger on her!"

Suddenly he saw Perry give him a coy wink with one eye.

"Perry…sweetheart," Cayden gestured, without making eye contact with him. Her smile was breathtaking from Noah's view. "Feed on the girl." He nodded his head. "Why bite a custodian when you can watch him crumble at the sight of his innocent being killed by his own brother." Her beautiful, white teeth gleamed in the moonlight. "There is no greater pleasure."

Kissing her bare shoulder like a love-struck idiot, Perry acted in agreeance to her orders. Tracing his lips up to her ear, he whispered against her silky skin. "I will not do a thing!"

Her eyes widened with bewilderment.

Perry whispered against her neck again, "I am no longer yours to control!" Reaching open his mouth and revealing his fangs, Perry then sunk them deep into her neck and fed on her ancient, vampire blood.

Cayden raised her head, sealed her eyes shut and screamed out in agony.

She released Noah — quickly he ducked away — and then grabbed Perry by his hair as blood streamed down her neck and down the front of her blouse.

"Insolent little insect!"

Ripping his head free, Perry let out a mighty gasp of exhilaration. Turning around, she raised her knee, struck him in the gut and then launched him back into the shadows.

A voice from behind her cut her off in early sentence and stole her attention.

Isadora summoned, "Hey, Cupcake!"

Turning around, Cayden was struck across the face by the witch's knee-high boot as she used her power to levitate. Dropping back to the ground, Isadora strode toward the staggering vampire.

"You know better than to let your guard down!"

Regaining her bearings, Cayden instantly healed over her neck wound and then swung a punch at the witch…growling as she went. Taking a deep breath, Isadora, her pulse racing dramatically with adrenaline, channeled her power into her vocals to create a sonic scream that ripped the bark from the trees.

Throwing her head back as she clutched her ears, Cayden screamed out in agony.

The forceful ripples of Isadora's power launched the vampire into the darkness, where she slammed into the ground and then fled to safety.

Extinguishing her power, Isadora began to drop to the ground. In a gust of wind, as he appeared in a blur of green, astral energy, Zane caught her and held her against his body as she panted with exhaustion.

Zane murmured, "Your powers have advanced; that's all. In time, control will come." She nodded her head vaguely and almost dropped back to the ground again, but luckily he caught her again. "Easy, easy, I got you."

Walking with her over to a tree, Zane sat her down.

Ambling over, Noah was able to sense her aura – a blaze of clear flames – with his custodian powers, and realized that her new power required more energy than her body contained.

"This advancement requires more energy than your body holds."

Stepping out of the dark, Juliann – the blonde, Siobhan – the red-head and Pilar – the brunette, slightly battered and bruised, halted a little to the side. Battered and bruised himself, and with blood on the corner of his mouth, Perry halted and looked down at his niece with an impressed smile.

"That's a wicked power you've got there!"

Looking at Noah, who stood to the side, Perry nodded his head, intimating that his brother should step away, so they could talk in private. Walking off, they halted a small distance away, with the others still in their view. Standing with his arms loosely folded, Perry queried his older brother with a sense of seriousness.

"That was close."

Noah agreed by nodding his head, with a look of relief but also serious concern on his face. Striving for eye contact, he touched his brother's forearm. Gaining what he desired, Perry appeared curious, a question forming in his green eyes.

"Why are you here, Noah?"

"Can't I visit my little brother?" Noah replied calmly, playing coy.

Perry narrowed his humble eyes. "You're a terrible liar. Why did you come here?"

The two of them exchanged serious stares – neither one of them was going to budge with the truth.

Grumbling with dissatisfaction, Noah began. "Okay; busted. You caught me. I need your help. If you wouldn't–"

Perry threw him a sarcastic and narrow glance, raising his hand to interrupt. "Help with what?" He gestured his eyebrows seriously and gave another hard expression. "Sorry, but our family is broken. I have nothing to offer you."

He turned away and headed back to the others as they stood under the moonlight.

Behind him, Noah turned and watched his brother disown him, like their older brother Aaron had.

Emotion was evident in Noah's voice as he called out.

"You are just like Aaron!"

Touching the right nerve, he watched his brother abruptly halt and stand silent in the shadows for short moment. Perry looked over his shoulder and replied. "How dare you call me that name!"

Approaching, Noah turned his brother around, grabbed him by the scruff of his shirt and pulled him closer.

"I know our family is broken!" Perry, shocked and with a redeeming glint his eyes, remained silent as he saw the obvious sadness in his brother's face. "I don't want to lose you like I did Aaron. He abandoned us. You still have a choice; choose me, because I cannot keep doing this all by myself."

The Triad – Siobhan, Juliann, Pilar and Zane – with their ultimate telepathy, remained silent, keeping out of the argument as the brothers' voices began to elevate.

Pulling himself free, Perry gave his brother a cold stare. "I have always chosen you!" He turned away and ambled a few short steps. Turning back, he then hastily strode up to his brother until they stood face to face. "Our lives fell apart. Aaron chose mortal life…yet ironically," he looked out the corner of his eye, gazing at Aaron's daughter who sat beneath the tree, "he is surrounded by the craft. I left, not to abandon you, but to find myself." A glimmer in his eyes revealed how he understood his brother's pain. "I am sorry for the way life has turned out." and then Perry sighed, "I can never deny who I am. I'm a fricken vampire." He went on to correct himself. "At my centre, I am a good witch! I am a Pogue – a descendant of a powerful line of witches, like you and Aaron…even though he'd rather disown his lineage!"

Listening, Noah remained silent.

"I'll help you," he said, as he let down his guard. With a regretful and unhappy look in his face, he continued. "My Empathy is blocked. I haven't been able to read a person since…" Noah stared at his brother; with a pout that made it obvious that he too had a blockage of sorts within him. "I-I honestly cannot remember. It's been so long."

Noah sympathized. "My powers have been off, too. It would explain why demons haven't targeted you." A vague look of intrigue swam across Perry's wholesome green eyes as he nodded his head. "We'll have to see Maria and ask her to fix it for you."

"Noah," Perry snapped, ruining the caring mood, "I am a person, a witch…a vampire!" He made note with a loud emphasis that he was anything but something that needed fixing. "If I have learnt anything," his brother's sapphire eyes submitted, "it's that emotions have a lot of influence. The disconnection is tied to me and you…we've cut ourselves off subconsciously." The caring mood seemed to return as they both looked past each other and deeper to find a common understanding. "The block is emotional."

Moving his head off-center and dropping his chin a little, Noah spoke carefully, "You blame Aaron for this?"

Leaning his neck back and stiffening his posture, Perry, feeling like he was being cornered, narrowed his eyes with complaint.

"Are we really going to have this conversation?" He turned away again.

The air between them was so tense, you could almost see it warp.

Noah murmured, "Everything happens for a reason."

Sighing with irritation, Perry looked back, "Our mother was murdered. How do you get past the pain and the grief? It tore our family into pieces." His eyes again watched the moon capture his brother's aura. "I have never doubted your role, Noah. You have given up so much." He turned his head in the opposite direction as he put his attention onto Isadora again in the distance. "Aaron walked away without giving it a second thought."

From a passive point of view, Noah countered, "You walked away too, remember…"

Defensively, Perry growled back, "I kept my powers. I've always offered you assistance when you've wanted it. Aaron doesn't care if we live or die." Turning back to his brother, the dark cast its silhouette across his face, "I will help you with your…demon…"

"Indy," Noah summoned, as he approached her with Perry.

The Triad turned their attention to the approaching brothers. Rising to her feet, the young blonde-haired witch looked at him curiously.

"Be safe," Noah ordered, as she nodded her head with a contented look on her face. "You'll return her to Aaron?" he queried the Triad.

Pilar replied humbly, "As promised."

Watching her halt before the four witches, Noah gestured his hand and then swayed it, making the Triad and Isadora disappear in a rush of smoke – sending them back home.

Noah looked at his brother, who stood behind him, "Ready?"

"When you are…" Perry responded, placing his hand on Noah's shoulder before they too departed, vanishing in a rush of smoke.

Staggering out from behind a tree, having watched from afar, Cayden – clad in her vampire visage – stood in awe of the moon.

"You'll pay with your life, Perry Pogue!" she growled.

SUPERNATURAL STORM

The night across Treadwell, Deane County, was tranquil, as stars sparkled like fibre-optic lights on a canvas of black. The moon, guardian of the night and giver of light in the seedy dark, was full and luminescent as a heavy storm front moved in over the ocean. Picturesque lightning forked across the horizon in quick, momentary flashes.

Along the beach – between Hindley Jetty and Epstein – a visible stream of enchanted wind curled about as it drifted along, fiercely flicking up sand. Waves lapped the shore and the townhouse mansions along the esplanade stood bathed in street lights.

Atop the approaching Supercell storm, iridescent with a heavy purple tone, stood a beautiful being dressed in a tattered gown – her arms held out and fury in her eyes.

To the common mortal, a storm was just Mother Nature's fury. But to the entire magical world, a storm was an actual magical manifestation, occasionally referred to as a Tempo, but properly acknowledged as a Weather Being.

Tempo was an allusion to the volatile nature of the beings. They were remarkably beautiful humanoid-creatures – emerald green hair with marine coloured eyes – and it was extremely rare and honorable to be in the presence of one.

The storm's heavy shadow crept across the ocean – heavier than the normal black of night – as it made its way toward the shore. The size of thirty football fields, the outer limits of the Supercell quickly blanketed the sky over Hindley Beach. The street lights flickered.

Moving her arm and flicking her hand, the Tempo unleashed a different kind of fury. In an Italian tongue, she commanded a minion – a Cloud Being.

Considered to be a lesser level creature, Cloud Beings make up the cloud mass plateau around the Tempo herself. Like weaponry on an aircraft carrier, they are deployed to execute such menacing acts as creating low-lying fog, and in rare instances, form tornados.

The Cloud Being appeared before the Tempo as the cloud plateau waved like water, and a delicate yet distinguishable abundance of mist rose upward. She ordered it, "Go to the Port, form and strike hard! A tornado should do enough damage!"

The small mass replied in a crackly old accent, "Such damage will be done!" and then it vanished in a riveting flash of marine coloured light.

~*~

A small, rectangular radio sat on a fisherman's tackle box.

Wilde Green, DJ of THRIVE-FM, spoke over the playing tune.

"… and in other news, reports are flooding in right along the coast. The predicted Supercell has reached shore, bringing with it king tides, some of which have destroyed jetties and sand dunes." As the radio announcement played, the ocean dropped dramatically.

In Bedwell Harbor – bound in the darkness of the surrounding suburbs of Morse and Argyle – thunder rumbled, complemented with an array of lightning strikes.

A mist began to quickly manifest atop the choppy water, and it immediately rose up, taking on the form of a withered crone with long white hair.

The Cloud Being, known to be quite vicious in special circumstances, had large, reptilian eyes – an eerie green with black, slit pupils. She also had jagged teeth and wore a dress of tatters.

Lightning flashed again and thunder rumbled.

Glaring ahead at the bridge in the distance, the Cloud Being gave a low growl before raising her face and arms out to the sky. The water danced beneath her feet.

"FORMA!!! (Form)" she screamed out in Italian.

Instantly upon her enforcing word, she began to slowly rotate and then quickly gain powerful momentum. The still air violently ripped up, sending concussive winds across the water.

Above, the Wall Cloud of the storm began to churn. Quickly, some slithered downward in a circular motion and gathered around the Cloud Being.

Thunder exploded amongst the clouds.

Ferocious flashes of lightning persisted, and then heavy, pelting rain began to fall. Hail assisted in creating havoc, striking like bullets as individual pieces impaled the windscreens of vehicles, bringing the steady flowing traffic across the Argyle Bridge to a standstill.

The wind roared this time, howling like nothing any mortal had ever heard.

Lighting on both sides of the Port's canal flickered. The newly built New Port apartment complex cowered in the shadows; its entire power supply instantly cut off as power lines were torn from their fixtures.

With hysteria in his voice, DJ Wilde Green spoke again over the radio.

"And…just in, a rogue twister has formed in Bedwell Harbor. We're crossing live to Morgan, who is in the area.

Morgan, what's it like where you are?"

Exiting their vehicles that had queued across the bridge, mortals all bore witness to the formation of a tornado.

"Wilde," a terrified reporter replied over the radio, "what I am seeing is incredible, I am standing at the Vincent Street end of the Argyle Bridge. Just minutes ago, a tornado formed in the harbor…" Suddenly, he cried out as he witnessed something horrifying. "Wilde! The twister has destroyed half the New Port apartments, killing God knows how many occupants!"

Brilliant flashes revealed the raw electricity arcing off the partly demolished site.

Atop her plateau, the Tempo ordered in a firm tone, "Take down the bridge!"

Inside the tornado, the Cloud Being abruptly halted and fixed her glare in the direction of the Argyle Bridge.

"It will be a pleasure!"

The wind current abruptly changed its course, blowing its potent gale in the direction of innocent bystanders. Watching the tornado approach with unbelievable speed, witnesses began to flee.

The ocean rose up in front of the towering column of wind, causing a huge tidal surge. Pulling away, the wave continued to rise higher and higher until it crashed against the heritage-listed bridge. Buckling under the force, deep fractures ran up the concrete supports, making the bridge drop under its own stressful weight.

The fleeing innocents cried out as the bridge ducked beneath their feet.

The Cloud Being gave a foul glare, "Devasti! (Devastate)."

Upon her second commanding word, she shoved her arms forwards and gestured her hands rigidly. Tearing up from the water, the focused and devastating gale made the aged structure groan.

Mortals cried out, thrown back by the force of the wind.

"Ah, Lampo!!! (Lightning)" she commanded, throwing powerful bolts of lightning.

In a triumphant display of power, the bolts of electricity obliterated the small brick command posts, showering the bridge in debris and rock. Terrified, people fled back to the Vincent Street side of the bridge.

Wilde Green spoke again over the radio. "Morgan. What is it like where you are?"

Over the radio, a man replied, "Wilde; as we speak, Bedwell Harbor is in a state of chaos. Rarely does Treadwell even see a waterspout, but tonight a tornado has formed!"

The concrete supports disintegrated as the twister slammed against the bridge.

Screams of terror cut through the night as the solid support arches broke, falling into the river below.

Reporter Morgan continued with more hysteria in his voice, "Oh my God! Wilde, I'm not entirely sure of how many people were on the bridge but it just collapsed!!"

An eerie, disembodied moan consumed the roaring wind. The twister moved through the gaping hole where the bridge had once stood, whisking innocent, drowning mortals from the water and propelling them in multiple directions. It moved away to the right, tearing the barges from the wharf and the front of the Bedwell Harbor Market building.

"Oh my God!" Morgan's voice shrieked as he continued to report the ongoing situation. "The twister just ripped the red lighthouse from the docks!"

Whistling like a missile, the crumpled red lighthouse crashed onto the road – landing on cars as they passed through the intersection of Dyson Road and Vincent Street – bringing more traffic to an abrupt halt.

Amongst the chaos, the sound of mortals screaming continued to tarnish the atmosphere. Stunned, and in a state of disbelief, people vacated their cars in the street as they watched the twister rage around the harbor.

"Morgan Heist reporting there," Wilde credited the roving reporter. "What a phenomenon. Treadwell has had its first tornado. Here, I thought nothing exciting ever happened in this city." His serious tone was filled with subtle intrigue, "We will cross back to Morgan later and follow up on the unfolding chaos."

~*~

Approaching the Epstein Jetty, a beautiful woman walked across the water.

Elegantly – in a slow gesture – she raised her arms, aiming her motion at a wooden structure in her direct line of fire. Her long hair curled around her neck and flowed over her shoulder. Her stunning, marine eyes made her even more imperial.

Noticing the mesmerizing beauty walking on water, local fishermen murmured with bewilderment as they squinted with their eyes.

"What the...?"

"No way..." muttered another.

Beneath them, the bitter, growing ocean gave a disembodied groan, like the sound of something monstrous.

A heavy, black shadow crawled over the wooden planks. The imp-like lanterns shorted out for a moment, and then thunder, like an atomic bomb, suddenly tore through the sky.

"Hear my voice!" The being's sultry and heavenly voice had a strong echo as she commanded the ocean. "By the Force of Mother Nature, I beseech thee. Make the ocean come alive!" Moving her hostile eyes, the female then glared upon the shoreline and commanded in a booming voice. "Tuono!!!! (Thunder)"

Then along the shoreline – as far as East Lagoon to the left and Canford to the far right – the street lights shorted out from the explosion of thunder, and then they came back on.

The ocean trembled beneath her bare feet.

Music playing on the fisherman's radio turned to static.

The water dipped deeper, exposing the sand, before it suddenly rose back up with force.

"RUN!!!" roared a fisherman to a dozen others.

The water blasted up through the gaps in between the jetty's wooden planks, ripping the bolts free and sending some boards into the air. At the end of the jetty, underneath the shelter, a trapped man hugged a pole. Curiously, he watched the beautiful woman walk atop the deadly water.

Her hair blew about in the wind. She fixed her eyes onto him, and he could feel her fury.

He murmured vaguely, "Heaven…"

"I care not for mortals." Her uncaring voice slithered across the surface of the ocean. "Mother Nature!" With enough encouragement, the regal creature could easily advance from a mere storm to a cyclone.

Mother Nature spoke telepathically to her minion, "Do not try me, Séverine. I will not stand for your intolerance. I will dispose of you!"

The rigorous ocean blasted up in between the wooden planks again, tearing more from the jetty and catapulting them into the water.

Obliterated by the force, the trapped man cried out in his last moments of life.

Within minutes, the shadow of the storm had crawled over half of the suburbs and was headed for the bright lights of the city ahead in the distance.

The being's pupils suddenly enlarged, and then decreased abruptly as she sensed the presence of evil.

~*~

"Yo," a young man sat in his rich and stylish phantom-black Jaguar with black leather interior. He rested his arm on the window seal whilst speaking to a mate on the phone, "I'm all for Bel-laire Red tonight. Find some pretty little things to kill."

He smirked, his hazel eyes flashing orange and cat-like.

For a second, he idolized them in the mirror, and just as quickly, they disappeared.

Glancing into the mirror again, on the side of his car, he watched the dark storm clouds.

"Bro, are you above ground?" His friend replied inaudibly. "No crap. Hey, this storm is packing some wicked power." He glanced to the side, looking out of the window to admire the ferocious ocean.

Something in his headlights captured his attention, "Oh sh—!!"

Jumping in fright, he cried aloud and dropped his phone out of the car window. The beautiful Tempo stood before the car, her eyes fixated on him in the driver's seat.

She held her head in a rigid position.

"Philanderer Demon…Muck that claws its way up from the dirt." Her voice lofted through the stereo for him to hear. "A rotting, supernatural plague!"

"What the f…?" he glanced from the stereo back to the woman standing close to his expensive car. "Ah!!" He raised his hands to his face as she sent lightning bolts smashing through the windscreen.

Brilliantly displaying the ferocity of Mother Nature, the Tempo obliterated the stylish vehicle and vanquished the demon within. In a wicked explosion of orange, a fireball lit up the night.

~*~

The Pogue Book of shadows specifically stipulates, *Tempo's a.k.a. Weather Beings can be both male and female and are the physical manifestation of the deity 'Mother Nature'. They are under her command. Legend perceives that these temperamental beings are as immortally beautiful as an angel and are rarely physically seen. They are not to be considered the same because of the different intensity of each category given to a storm. They are neither good nor evil but biased at times. They are neutral and are situated as infinite on the supernatural echelon. They appear all year around like rain but it is believed they hibernate during the summer in Treadwell when the climate reaches its hottest.*

Cyclones, hurricanes, tornados, monsoons and typhoons are the most powerful of all Weather Beings because of the damage they cause. They speak only in an Italian tongue. Only the most powerful of witches, good or evil, can manipulate or summon one.

~*~

Sévérine as her name came to be, appeared to have a rugged nature due to her status as a Supercell storm. And with the status came the hazardous mentality – at any given moment, her state of mind could slip and unleash chaos.

"Steady rain, fall with grace."

Thunder rumbled amongst the harsh, charcoal clouds, and rain began to fall gracefully, reaching a full downpour quickly. Pitter-patter sounds outweighed the sound of the raging waves, as the rain slashed the corrugated roof of the shelter from the end of the jetty as it washed up on the beach. Behind in the dark, all that remained were the thick, wooden beams that held the structure over the water.

"Lightning, bring light to this black night."

"Sévérine," a divine and womanly disembodied voice summoned loudly on the howling wind. "Return to your plateau!" The being showed ignorance. "Must I remind you, of how short the life span of a Tempo is?"

"As you wish, Mother Nature," the beautiful being replied, as she rigidly tilted her head, glancing at the blackened sky. Growling behind her gritted teeth, Sévérine summoned, "Parta (Depart)" gesturing her arms like a ballerina.

Marvelously, she disappeared in a victorious pulse of energy, and the burning wreck of the car she had destroyed dissolved into the ground. Upon her return to the plateau – what the mortal weather bureau would call the anvil of the cloud mass – bolts of lightning forked across the sky.

BAD GIRLS

Clad in charcoal robes and marvelous large, black-feathered wings, four beautiful figures stood in the middle of the paved, Hindley Square...unseen to the mortal eye.

"Mother Nature," the British Angel-of-Death, Aloyus, queried as he named the earthly deity. "Give this Water Sprite permission to develop."

Looking into the thick darkness of the storm, Celestia had a displeased look upon her immortal complexion.

"Where credit is deserved, they strike evil where it stands. But this is so discourteous."

"No kidding." Everette, the rapturous blonde female growled. "She is nothing more than a short lived being, Celestia. As quick as she has manifested, she will dissipate. Perhaps the rudeness is what makes them, as a magical race, so imperial."

Thad, the second male of the group spoke, "Mother Nature," and then he looked at the raging waves that lashed the red brick retainer wall, "in her most ferocious form."

"It appears someone has already been allocated." Everette identified a young, platinum blonde girl standing at the opening of the brick retainer walls that lead out to the Hindley Beach jetty. "A Romani, I believe."

Thad queried, "How do you know that?"

"My quality is compassion. I'm empathic, remember." Everette's divine integrity was never questioned. "I'm able to feel her by the manner in which she exudes her presence." Her company watched as the tall girl, standing with her lanky arms out, eyes closed and mentally wielded the inherited Romani power of Nature Manipulation. The angel acknowledged, "Her will is strong."

"Sévérine won't bend to her will." Celestia's bigotry toward lesser beings was becoming obvious. "The Tempo will only be enraged."

Everette cut her off. "This Romani is strong. Sometimes, the quality of justice, Celestia, is blind. You too, are blinded at times by your need for retribution."

Atop the anvil of her storm mass, Sévérine swayed her arms forward and then moved them slightly out to the left and the right.

In a spectacular, booming voice she commanded the sky, "Thunder, bring life to the night!" Clouds began to erupt and rise up around her.

At the edge of the storm, Cloud Beings rose – slender, lanky figures made of cloud – like a line of warriors eager to engage in war; waiting for their leader's cue.

"Clouds, hear my words!" Her voice was radiant as it echoed. "Unleash thy fury!" Under her command, the Shelf Cloud beneath her opened up, unleashing more heavy pouring rain that formed a thick veil as it fell.

Below the storm, Treadwell showed off its aged beauty. Its wonderful churches were beautifully defined by lights. A classical city acknowledged for its gothic and modern architecture along King Gustav Boulevard. Beautiful beaches with a backdrop of picturesque, rolling hills...home of the legendary Rune Wine Valley.

~*~

*R*ed – the place to be in Windsor Way, Treadwell's Club-Hub, emanated a mystical appeal. Its brilliant redness was a glow in the night, and outside in the street, the heavy bass could be heard.

"Okay," the brunette spoke with caution in her voice. "We're all clear on what we have to do?" she turned, and her long hair swayed.

Her cocktail dress, coated in black sequins, glittered under the street lights, and her baby blue eyes became electric. The black, Jimmy Choo stilettos she wore added more height to her leggy figure.

"Okay," the lavish woman with long black hair commented in a tolerant tone. "Maddy; three times we've gone over this plan!"

Madelyn, a meter ahead, turned around and began to walk backward as she faced her three friends and her cousin, Ryder Romani.

The tall, opulent blonde of the group commented, "The plan is simple enough." She wore a white satin blouse and a high waisted skirt. "Unless there is more than one, then we're screwed."

Madelyn replied with a pout, "I'm not in the mood for nonsense, Dylis." There was deep concern in her eyes. "It's a Philanderer Demon." Her voice was serious. "They pick off the weakest-looking innocent."

Ryder interjected briefly, "Preferably female."

Madelyn gave her cousin an honest, understanding stare. "Lure them," she continued. "Spike their drinks. Rape or kill. The innocent's body is left in a deserted alleyway."

"Revolting bastards!" Dylis snapped vigorously.

Ryder commented again, "Saliva." Madelyn looked at her again, staring. "The saliva, if excreted during a bite, can turn a mortal into a Philanderer Demon. They feed like vampires, only they thrive on pheromones instead of blood."

"So, demonic sniffer dogs, almost?" remarked Dylis, interrupting again.

"Similar attributes, yes." Ryder, an intelligent and extremely powerful witch trained in demonology knew a lot about the demonic fiends. "I wouldn't say they're similar to dogs. Dogs can be domesticated, but Philanderer Demons are extraordinary predators, remember that. They have the ability to manipulate pheromones."

To the side of Dylis was another young woman, a witch of almost the same height and equally just as beautiful. Her whiskey brown hair draped down and spiraled into gathered curls around her neck.

She appeared worried as she listened to Ryder's factual knowledge.

Madelyn toyed with her, "Don't worry Layton, you're the lure."

"Oh, sure, don't worry." Layton remarked uneasily.

The others looked at her with odd expressions. They were surprised at Layton's sudden fear when usually she was flawlessly confident.

"It's only my life that we're playing with. If he turns me into a Philanderer Demon, I'm so coming back to kill you all!" Calming herself, Layton sighed, and they all stopped on the sidewalk. "Sorry, I just had to get that off my chest."

"Feel better now?" Ryder expressed subtle irritation.

Layton smirked, "Much. Thanks."

They continued to walk along Windsor Way. Madelyn turned back around, but quickly glanced over her shoulder and spoke. "I think you'd make a hot Philanderer Demon."

Layton replied, "I could so pull it off." Her confidence had been reinstated.

Saturday nights in Windsor Way were usually the busiest. Taxis crawled along at snail's pace as they eagerly waited for a fare. Enforcing security – police officers mounted on gallant grey horse – patrolled up and down the street, while police officers on foot made their presence even more felt as they moved amongst the crowds.

Her presence going unnoticed by all mortals, Sévérine's cloud mass had started to swallow the night sky over the city. But regardless of pouring rain or stinking heat, it would take more than the weather to deter club goers. Flattened by the pumping bass coming out of nightclubs, the loud explosions of thunder went unnoticed.

On the corner, where the footpath met a small street, the girls halted. A huge line of club goers had already formed. At least one-hundred hopefuls stood with displeased looks on their faces. The building was black all over with red along the front.

Next door was *Drum & Dancer*, a club equally as popular.

Crossing the street the five, twenty-something-year-old women were ogled by onlookers, their astounding, wiccan-fused beauty imperializing. The young men waiting in line watched, their eyes deep with enchantment and their drooling jaws resting metaphorically at their feet.

Intimidated women waiting in line offered the girls stale expressions, fueled by shallow feelings and inconsiderate eyes. Eagerly, as the young witches walked back onto the footpath, the mortal teens gripped their men tight around the arms...*possession is nine tenths of the law*.

If only they knew witches really existed, Ryder thought to herself as she looked at the envious young women in the queue.

Good witches who practice good witchcraft are duly noted to be in the possession of radiant beauty. Good rewards loyalty, whereas evil ages a witch quickly, reducing its beauty.

Along the sidewalk out the front of *Bel-laire Red*, the women waiting in line closest to the entrance offered more blatant glares. Those girls were provocatively dressed and stunning.

"Oh, is this where the bitches line up?" Dylis remarked, coy and sarcastic.

"Excuse me?!" one replied in a hostile tone.

"Jesus! You must be jealous!" Dylis remarked again.

The voluptuous, strawberry blonde in line continued to hold a stern glare.

In a deep boom, she replied, "What do I need to be jealous of?!" She stepped forward to engage in a war with Dylis, who'd be sure to win.

"Hmm," Dylis smiled wondrously. "Well, I will be leaving here," her confidence was undeniable. ".... with your man." She was not afraid to get up close and intimidate the woman, although she spoke calmly.

Abruptly, the woman abandoned her ferocious glare and slipped nervously back into the line, put in her sour place.

"That's what I thought," Dylis sighed happily,

Gracefully, the five women walked up to the bouncer who stood at the door.

Brian was the regular bouncer. He was built like the incredible hulk, but was the nicest guy to those who knew him. He had a shaved head and thin, straight black lines of facial hair. He was dressed in black suit pants, a white T-shirt and a black blazer. His eyes were a soft and gentle blue.

Madelyn halted before him, smiled and said to him, "Hello Brian."

He replied by flashing a smile, "Ladies." A rarity...even for him! But secretly, he knew Madelyn's bewitching secret. One fateful summer's night she'd saved him from a Succubus. "Painting the town tonight?"

Madelyn sighed, almost disappointed, "Strictly business tonight, B!" Her smile made him weak, and the iris in each of her eyes turned a glowing emerald green. Her cinnamon fragrance overpowered him with a sense of contentment.

"You're already on the list," he replied, taking in the smell with a delighted smile. He waved his arm in the direction of the open door. "Go right in. What is it tonight?" "...A Philanderer." Madelyn replied.

"I'll keep an eye out," Brian replied.

Layton laughed nervously as she went past, "Good luck with that, big fella!"

Dylis kissed him on the cheek, "Have a good night, handsome." She slipped past him.

Standing in front of him, Madelyn smiled, and her eyes glimmered with raw power. She was a powerful gypsy-witch; resilient, sharp and resourceful. She could bend nature at will and manipulate it to its fullest potential. Plants grew in her presence, and she was capable of hearing and understanding animals while luring demons with beautiful scents.

Brian smiled, and, she tore her wholesome gaze away, like tearing the rough side of Velcro from the smoother side. Gracefully, she then moved on, stepping into the dark passageway. Chantelle followed, along with Ryder.

Walking up the staircase in the poor light, Ryder, concerned about the misuse of magic and the karma of personal gain commented, "Your mother will kill you," a slight laugh was evident in her voice, "if she found out you used magic on a bouncer to get into a club."

Chantelle, a neutral natured witch, interjected, "What she doesn't know won't hurt her."

Climbing the stairs and leading the way, Madelyn replied. "It was used for all intents and purposes of finding the Demon." Although her tone was adamant, Ryder a powerful Empath and Telepath, saw through the guise.

"...Rebel." Ryder laughed in reply.

"Damn straight!" Madelyn turned the corner in the passage and entered the vibrant club.

At the foot of the staircase, Brian stepped in front of the open doorway, blocking it with his hulk-like body. He raised his hand to the crowd as the line pushed toward the door. Annoyed and bitter people complained aloud.

"ID! No ID, no entry!"

A bigoted male roared, "Ah, that's crap!"

Brian stepped forward. His intimidating eyes made the few front members of the line step back out of fear as he roared back, "Is that right?!!!"

~*~

At the end of the passage, where it opened up into the huge nightclub, the five ladies halted and looked about.

Madelyn gave instruction. "...Dylis."

Nodding her head once, Dylis replied. "I'm on it."

Slipping away, she took Chantelle's hand into her own. Holding a steady gaze at the DJ as he mixed his tunes, Dylis used her power of Thought Projection to bend his mind to her will. His pupils enlarged and he became entranced – under her influence. A seductive and sultry song played.

"All you bad girls," The DJ spoke over his head piece. "I want to see you get naughty on the floor!"

Standing in the doorway, Madelyn nodded her head, turned and went off to her position at the far end of the bar. She was the look-out.

Sighing, Ryder narrowed her eyes and then walked on, disappearing into the crowd as she went to dance. Weaving through the crowd, Dylis, with Chantelle in pursuit, halted in the middle of the disco-style, flashing dance floor.

Dylis pressed her lips against Chantelle's bottom lip and then slowly moved them down her neck as they danced up against each other seductively. She ran her hand up Chantelle's thigh in full view of every guy and girl.

"Ready? Let's show them how to be bad girls!"

Chantelle all but smirked as her eyes glittered under the lights. She appeared genuine as she looked lovingly into Dylis's eyes.

Under the brilliant light, Dylis ran her hand down her friend's chest, and in sync, they swung their heads clockwise and anti-clockwise, swishing their hair about.

"Whoa," the DJ called out, as he focused the lights on the two witches. "It's gettin' hot in here!!"

Grabbing at her companion's side with one hand, the opulent blonde raised one leg erotically up her side. Dylis gripped it tightly and then arched her back. Straightening back up, Chantelle lowered her leg, and the couple began to sway their hips as they danced provocatively. Abruptly turning away, Chantelle, all flustered and aroused, pulled a handsome man by the shirt toward her and began to dance with him. She swayed up against him and then began to lower down to a squat – seductively rising back up to give him a subtle kiss on his bottom lip.

She queried him, "Do you like bad girls?"

He gave a devilish smirk and began to dance with her. Dylis swayed her hips as she lowered down to the floor and then briskly rose back up. Then, she pushed her breasts together, released and swung her hair about.

Moving away from the door, Layton progressed toward the bar.

In the corner, a young, blonde woman made out with a man. He seemed to rigorously nuzzle at the side of her neck, making her writhe in pleasure, gasp and tightly grip the back of his dark brown hair.

ENTER THE DEMON

"Excuse me!" Madelyn made her way through the crowd as a clubber bumped into her. She shoved him back with an arrogant attitude, "Jesus, watch it mate!" Slipping out into an opening, she saw a guy friend sitting in a booth. "Daly!" she summoned, as she strolled up to the table and halted. "Hi!"

Her smile drew his attention, as well as his small horde of chauvinistic male friends, who did not know he was a witch.

Revealing his infatuation for her, he smiled before responding.

"MJ!!" he exclaimed above the loud music. "Hi!" He glanced to the left and right of her and noticed she had no company. "Alone?!"

Daly Kenneth was a typical, ruggedly handsome twenty-three-year-old guy. Blonde, surf-style dreadlocks, sky blue eyes, left eyebrow pierced, knee-weakening smile, square jaw and a small snippet of blonde hair under his bottom lip. On his right wrist was a tattoo of a pentagram embellished in a circle. A partly open shirt revealed a buff chest.

His active witch power was Euphoric Manipulation...the ability to manipulate endorphins in a person until the point of drunkenness – without alcohol – or to create a delusional sense of euphoria.

The male to Daly's right – obviously intoxicated – tried to flirt.

"Hi, Luke!" he and Madelyn exchanged a hand shake. "What a pleasure it is," he kissed her hand, much to her dismay. "...to be in the presence of such a beauty."

Madelyn snatched her hand back. "The pleasure ain't mine, trust me!" she growled, wiping her hand on another girls dress. "So what's the feat?" Her retort was full of obvious sarcasm. "Alcohol induced coma?" Confidently, she swayed her sight from each of Daly's six mates. "Drunk and disorderly?" She brought her stunning eyes back to the he-witch in the middle. "...Or abstinence?"

The down-side of Euphoric Manipulation was that Daly himself was immune to the effects of alcohol.

"What is your feat?" Daly growled sarcastically as he looked down his nose.

The air crackled with sexual tension. Daly wanted her, she wanted him...but neither wanted to admit it.

"Pleasure...?" he queried, both exchanging a sly smile of knowingness, "or hunting?"

Madelyn stared at him with blatant sensuality. "We—"

He interrupted her, "We?"

"Are...hunting a Philanderer Demon," She continued bluntly, not giving any information away.

With the risk of a Philanderer Demon being any one of them, a telepathic whisper suddenly moved through the young witch's mind.

"Madelyn..." the voice of her telepathic cousin Ryder had an angelic hum to it, although it was forceful. "This ain't a tea party. We have work to do. Play with the hot he-witch later!!" With a sigh, Madelyn smiled, batted her eyelashes and then walked away.

"Dude!" the idiot Luke remarked chauvinistically, as he bumped Daly in the arm. Both watched Madelyn's ass as she disappeared into the crowd at the bar.

"If you don't tap that, I will."

With a silent but very bitter look on his face, Daly used his power. Luke's eyes gave off a subtle green glow, and suddenly he was sober instead of completely drunk.

"Damn, dude! I'm sober!!"

Stepping in between two dancing clubbers, Ryder Romani curiously scanned Daly Kenneth and his friends with a highly suspicious look on her face. Her powers of Telepathy and Empathy identified a good witch and three docile mortals.

Standing with her back against the bar as she bobbed her head to the beat of the song, Layton appeared to enjoy the spectacle of handsome men around her.

"Hi!" a female voice caught Layton's ear. Casually, she turned and was greeted by the bartender. On her black satin blouse, her name, Natalee, was clearly displayed on a small name tag. "What can I getcha, Strega (witch)?!"

Startled by the term, an unsure Layton turned her head to the far end of the bar where Madelyn gave a stern look and moved her hand, insisting that Layton buy a drink.

Glancing back with uncertainty, Layton leant forward to reply in a low voice.

"You know I'm a witch?"

Natalee replied with a brilliant smile, "Course. Natalee Holm," she said, surprising Layton. "I'm a wood nymph. Clearly, this is a disguise, so no demons recognize me… especially Philanderer Demons. You do know they can read auras, right?"

Dumbfounded, Layton replied, "You're a wood nymph?" she stuttered with amazement. "I-I-I."

Natalee gave a vague stare, "Well, spit it out, cupcake."

"It's just I've never met a wood nymph before." Layton replied.

A flattered Natalee smiled back, "I'm honored. The storm outside…? It's a Weather Sprite. You do know that, don't you?"

Many magical folk, good and evil, gave Tempos different names…Weather Sprite, Water Sprite etc.

A confused Layton remarked, "Err…"

"How long have you been a witch?" Natalee queried.

Layton chuckled as she mocked herself, "Apparently, not long enough!"

Natalee turned her head away, and she glanced at the supernatural blonde in the corner with a suspicious look, before glancing back at the witch before her.

"What can I get ya?"

"Sex On The Beach!" replied Layton.

Liking the witch's taste in alcoholic beverages, Natalee nodded her head "Good choice." And then she turned away and went about her job.

Layton looked about purposefully, wondering what the Philanderer Demon would look like. Packed as it was, she could not make anyone out that looked remotely demonic or ominous. Along the bar as she looked around, it was at least four people deep in places. If you wanted a drink, you had to push your way to the front.

After a few minutes, Natalee returned, sliding Layton's cocktail across the bar in exchange for payment.

Natalee, a wood nymph and a hot bartender, had a certain rock star appeal and a hair style that matched. Across the bust of her black top it read: *Jealous? At least mine are real!*

Layton complimented her, "Cool top!"

Natalee replied with a coy smirk. "Thanks, love. Have a good night."

Her sumptuous, dark-chocolate hair had light brown highlights. Falling to her shoulders, the texture had smooth waves and it was blocked at the bottom, with special attention to the soft lengths that framed her face. Raising her drink as she turned away from the bar and took in the packed club, Layton toasted herself.

"What the hell!" She took a large mouthful of her alcoholic beverage. "If I'm going to be the bait, I at least want to have a good time doing it."

~*~

Over his microphone, The DJ commanded, "I wanna see you dancin'!!!"

Pressing a button on his laptop, he melded the song into another dance track. Going with the upbeat dance music, Ryder, Dylis and Chantelle danced provocatively in the middle of the floor. At odd intervals, the fellas put their hands in the air and clapped twice to the beat, and on the even interval, the ladies did the same.

Weaving through the crowd, Layton emerged, "Let's show them how witches get down!"

Chantelle strutted forward, and on the spot, she twirled fast, dropped to the floor, rose back up quickly and arched her back. Her power of Luminescence made subtle light emanate from the outline of her silhouette as she swayed her hair about.

The DJ cheered on the bewitching blonde, "Woo!"

Dylis and Ryder, in a sultry manner, danced up to one another and shimmied. Ryder swayed down to the floor, squatted for a moment and they swayed up as she traced her hands up her friend's thighs – showing how a real vixen danced.

Glancing at a watching group of handsome fellas, Ryder pulled Dylis in and kissed her passionately.

The men cheered, "Woo, Yeah baby!!!"

Meanwhile, in the corner of the club, the supernatural blonde still made out with the guy who nuzzled at her neck. Every so often. she shuddered from his sensual touch as he ran his hand up her torso.

~*~

Outside in the street, cabs still crawled along, and they weren't in short supply.

Along the footpath, heading from the Rosemount Hotel, a handsome young man confidently strode along.

His dark hair was styled. It was short at the back and sides with more length on the top. His enchanting, hazel eyes sat above a handsomely unshaven face. A fitted charcoal, short sleeve shirt defined his biceps, and immaculate, fitted black jeans heightened his sensual appeal. As he walked along, he turned and halted at the edge of the footpath and looked both ways before crossing.

The sound of horse shoes tapped on the bitumen as the Mounted Police approached.

The masculine, grey gelding moved its nervous eyes, carefully watching its surroundings. Its soft white mane and long tail swayed. Then, suddenly sensing the presence of something other-worldly, the grand steed snorted heavily and glared at a man.

"Whoa…" The officer tried to calm his horse, and he shot a glare at the youth. "Oi!!" In response, the young man gave the officer a cold and tyrannical stare. "Move it! Off you go.

Cross the street! Stop spooking the horse!"

~*~

Back inside *Bel-laire Red*, the dance tracks continued and the dance floor never seemed to empty. Dylis, Ryder, Chantelle and

Layton – the lure – continued to dance, oblivious to their surroundings.

Walking down to the far end of the bar, Natalee approached Madelyn, "Another! But you are Romani!"

An intimidated Madelyn remarked, "Excuse me?" in a blunt tone, as she then awkwardly glanced about, making sure no one had heard. The beautiful gypsy-witch leaned forward and curiously queried, "How do you–"

"Wood Nymph. Natalee," the bartender announced. She held her hand out for the gypsy-witch to shake. "All good witches and… Romani give off a scent…either cinnamon or pine. But you," the wood nymph gazed at the beauty with amazement in her eyes. "You smell like watermelon on a warm breeze."

Impressed and flattered, the gypsy-witch then shook Natalee's hand, "Madelyn R–"

"I know who you are." A sparkle appeared in the wood nymphs eye. "You're a descendant of Amedea Bonifacio and the Triad." Madelyn gave a stern look as Natalee named the immense power that she belonged to. "A hybrid, if I'm correct. A gypsy married a witch. You are well revered in magical circles…like the Pogue Witches. You and the Pogue Coven are two of the founding families of our humble city."

Madelyn smirked as she nervously brushed her cheek, "Someone's done their homework."

"No," Natalee smiled back. "Legends and fairytales as any mortal would put it." The gypsy-witch rocked her head, inclined to agree because she knew no mortal would ever believe that witches existed. The wood nymph then charmed her with an incredible smile, "So, what will it be?"

"I'll have a Blue Lagoon," Madelyn replied. Natalee nodded her head in favor, "My favorite!" "Mine too." Madelyn smiled.

~*~

Out in Windsor Way, stepping off the footpath as he walked past the two mounted police officers and their horses, the young man gave the horse an intimidating glare.

For a split second, the flow of time halted.

His hazel eyes and the horse's eyes met as his turned a demonic, electric blue. Reaching its head forward and tearing the reins from the officer's hand, the horse snorted ferociously and neighed territorially...and the flow of time regained its momentum.

The officer growled, "Move it!! Or I will arrest you for obstruction!!"

Ignoring the warning, the young man continued on, halting in the middle of the street. There, he turned his head enough to see that the horse was still watching him. There was something about the horse, and as he looked harder, he noticed a Therianthrope symbol: a *Celtic Sun*; branded on the horse's shoulder.

A Custodian disguised as a horse!

"Easy, Duke!" the officer calmed his steed by patting it on the neck.

With a swift movement of his hand, the young man used a Power Word charm.

His hand shone with blue, magical energy.

"Impennarsi...!! (Rear Up)"

Reacting to the attack, with a loud neigh, the gallant grey rose up onto its hind legs. Caught off guard and unprepared, the male officer was thrown forward against the horse's neck as its reins fell free.

"Whoa, Duke!!"

The horse struck out with its front legs making a wonderful spectacle. The gelding was magnificent, and the street lights captured his dark grey dapples.

Standing in the middle of the street, the young man with obvious magical attributes turned and walked out in front of an oncoming taxi. Slamming on the brakes, the taxi came to a screeching and abrupt halt as the driver sounded the horn. Behind him on the furthest side of the street, both mounted officers watched the young man with cold glares. He was clearly a disturber of the peace by his sly and blatant persona.

Leaning out of his window, the taxi driver roared, "Watch where you're walking, moron!"

With an egotistic swagger, the young man stepped up onto the sidewalk. Gesturing his hand as he walked along, he suddenly disappeared, becoming invisible to gain entry into the nightclub without having to provide ID. He easily slipped past the loudly chattering cue of club goers and the hulk-like Brian as he entered *Bel-laire Red*.

Brian roared at the queue, "ID!!!"

~*~

Madelyn stood poised at the bar and surrounded by men who tried endlessly to flirt with a brick wall. She resembled an angel under the soft ruby colored downlights.

Natalee queried, "Another?" She appeared to be playing favorites with Madelyn because of what she was.

A handsome, fair-haired young man, clearly drunk, interrupted, "Hi!" Before Madelyn could reply, he continued, "My name's Jarvis."

Annoyed, Natalee stared at the guy, "Hey, shithead!" With docile eyes, he vaguely stared back at her, "Bugger off!"

He stuttered his slurred words, "I-I'm-m T-t-talking," correcting Natalee as he went, "to her, not you!"

Ignoring the drunken man, whose name was apparently Jarvis, Madelyn smiled at the wood nymph and spoke, "Yes, please."

Nodding her head, Natalee understood, but for a moment before she turned away, she glared at the drunken idiot again.

Casually, as she waited for her refreshment, Madelyn's eyes glanced along the bar – staring in the direction of the entry that was directly ahead of her. Her line of vision then moved around to the dance floor, and she watched her friends. She halted her eyes on Layton, making sure she was using her charm to lure out any Philanderer Demons that might be present and unseen.

All the while, the intoxicated Jarvis failed to acknowledge that Madelyn was ignoring him. "Are you an angel? Because you've taken my breath away, baby."

One had to give him credit for his perseverance.

Hearing him use his pick up line, Madelyn turned her head and gave him the most undeniably, vicious glare.

"I swear if you don't shut your painted hole, this angel just might stick her fist in it!"

As much of an idiot as he was whilst drunk, he simply stared at her whilst trying not to lose his balance.

"I love fighters!" He smiled with a slurred look on his face. "Has anyone ever told you how sexy you are?"

He began to caress her hair. Out the corner of her eye, as she made the alcoholic beverage, Natalee watched him make a costly move.

Madelyn moved his hand away, "Don't touch what you cannot afford!"

Dismissing her, Jarvis returned his hand to her hair and continued, "I'm pretty sure I could afford you."

Natalee returned, sliding a Blue Lagoon across the counter top. "Mate; she said she doesn't want to be touched!"

Madelyn smirked at the wood nymph, "Oh, don't worry he'll learn...the hard way!"

"Oh, I imagine so." Natalee raised an eyebrow.

Idiotically, he continued to flirt and touch her hair, ignoring all forms of warning.

"You are seriously thick as a brick," Madelyn growled again, this time grabbing his hand and slamming it against the bar. He was beginning to get on her shortened nerves. She sarcastically spoke his name, "Jarvis?!"

"See, I knew you'd remember my name." he toyed.

Madelyn chuckled unpleasantly as she glared at him. "Not by choice, trust me!"

~*~

Climbing the staircase, the still invisible man magically reappeared in a ripple of energy in full view of the bar and crowd. Looking in that specific direction as she took another mouthful of her drink, Madelyn coughed and almost choked as she witnessed the abnormality.

"Bloody hell!" She coughed again and wiped her mouth.

With her eyes still upon the man, she knew that Layton wasn't going to grab the male's attention any time soon. In two mouthfuls, she finished her Blue Lagoon, put the empty glass down on the bar and began to leave.

"Okay." She pumped herself up.

Jarvis blocked her as she tried to leave.

"Can-can I get your-r-r number?" he slurred.

Madelyn did admit to herself that he was attractive, but there were more pressing issues at hand than to be stopped by a drunken idiot.

"Maybe we could go on a date sometime." He began to run his fingertips up her arm.

Finally, her fuse broke.

Grabbing him by the head, she roared, "for God-sake!" and forced his head down against the bar, making him head butt it before pulling him back. She released him, and he fell back, crashing onto the floor. "I said, NO!!"

Her bark was just as bad as her bite. It's what made her powerful.

A voice suddenly came from the floor, "Maybe next time then...?"

Confidently striding off in her glamorous, Jimmy Choo high heels and black sequin-covered dress, Madelyn deliberately brushed past the handsome and magical new arrival, drawing his immediate attention.

"Wanna dance?" her gentle and seductive tone stole his stone cold heart.

He replied in a deep, knee-weakening voice, "I won't say no."

FLIRTING WITH EVIL

Walking ahead of him, Madelyn slipped through the crowd as she made her way to the dance floor. Behind her, his eyes followed the curves of her body as the light reflected off her sequin dress.

Caught off guard, he blushed at her beauty.

Weaving deeper into the crowd, Madelyn came to an opening where Chantelle, Ryder and Dylis danced. There, they had drawn the attention of several single men, who seemed to be unable to defer their attention.

Madelyn spoke, using her thoughts. "He's the demon!"

Looking back at her cousin, Ryder then casually glanced at the man and gave him a smile as she used her telepathy.

Telepathically, he said, "Eisheth will be pleased," as he glanced at Ryder. Keeping up the pretence, he smiled back...she almost worshipped it. "I could easily have a threesome."

As though she had smelt something bad, Ryder screwed her nose up and quickly glanced away.

Ryder used her telepathy to re-engage her cousin, "Yes, he is!"

Madelyn gave her a subtle signal. Nodding back, Chantelle agreed.

Chantelle suggested loudly, "I need a drink!" and as she stepped past, she bumped an approaching Layton into the man.

"I'll come with you!" Dylis cried out, pushing through the crowd.

Turning as she collided with the man, Layton gasped. "Oops, Sorry!" she fell into his hazel eyes as they met. Both immediately made a devious connection.

Witnessing his smile, she immediately worshipped him too, "My, aren't you just handsome!"

He smiled, captivated by her beauty, "Want to dance?" "Sure," Layton smiled back.

As he danced with her, the man began to turn, and the flow of time began to slow to the point that the room stood still around him.

Halting with his back to the witch – frozen in time – his eyes magically changed to a stunning electric blue...his demonic, cat-like eyes. The skin around his mouth became dry and enflamed, with painful cracks appearing.

Growling, he parted his lips to reveal his jagged teeth.

His hairline receded, his ears enlarged slightly – like elf ears – and his brow protruded.

His hyper-sensitive powers allowed him to view human auras. The strong and independent innocent women were outlined with white, sparkling auras that glimmered like fireworks. They weren't worth pursuing. The average and intriguing women had purple auras. They too didn't seem to attract him either.

The humble, mellow and here-to-have-a-good-time innocent women were the most vulnerable...easily fooled because their guard was down. Their auras were a beautiful, electric green, but a good witch's aura was a lurid crimson.

After analyzing the entire nightclub, and noticing no easy women to target, the man began to turn around, only to notice Layton's glorious, electric green aura. Upon this acknowledgement, his horrid complexion formed a dirty grin and instantly his face morphed back to normal.

With a vicious hiss, he made a comment in Italian. "Carne Fresca… (Fresh Meat)" and calmly, he took a deep breath, exhaled and raised his hand to create a gesture.

Using a stolen witch power, he swayed his hand in a circular motion and made the entire club unfreeze. Time flowed fluently again, picking up exactly where it had left off. Handsomely, he – like all male Philanderer Demons – had the inconceivable ability to appeal to every woman's desire, and easily that weakness could be exploited.

Layton turned her back to him, put her arms up and waved them about as she danced up against him. All the while, he trailed his hands along and around her body. The strobe lights moved about and constantly changed colours.

He leaned his head close to her ear and spoke, "My name's Floren."

Layton replied with intrigue, "Oh, wow. That's an interesting name!" He teased her again with his brilliant smile. She enquired, "Is it Italian?"

Keeping up his pretence he said, "My parents came from the south of Italy. What's your name?" he enticed.

Fluttering her eyelashes, Layton said, "I never kiss and tell."

Again, he blushed. Her beauty astounded him, and she would soon become his greatest failure. Layton had the power of Telekinesis, and she could easily extend it to extreme lengths.

Cunningly, the five young ladies had opportunely cloaked their magical essence so as not to give themselves away. It was a complicated but achievable effect that could be easily reversed.

Layton walked the walk and talked the talk, dancing provocatively; she had, with ease, become the demon's prey. She was irresistible. As he danced with her, he licked his lips subtly, once and then twice, as she tantalised his taste buds.

Outside, the queue to get into *Bel-laire Red* appeared not to have moved in the past hour. In places, it was still ten deep as it snaked along the front of the building around and down Rosina Street, directly beside the club.

Standing in line in the side street, waiting to get into the nightclub, another young man began a conversation with an unsuspecting young woman.

His charm was very easily enticing, "Hi. Texas; but people call me Tex."

The girl smiled. "Visper; but people call me Vi."

Curling his lips into a daring smile, he replied. "Well, Vi," her eyes glittered as her heart fluttered from an overdose of fatal attraction, "you're looking very eye-catching tonight."

"Please," Visper smiled, flattered by his compliment. "You're a guy. Infectious flattery is a part of your genetics...anything to woo a girl and get into her pants."

"Well," he touched her hand with his finger, "you are infectiously beautiful." And with that very comment, Tex, a second Philanderer Demon, won over this prey.

Philanderer Demons, male or female, were not given to play the shy and innocent card; a cocky and confident personality always got the desired victim.

Her potent, electric green aura, visible to his hazel eyes, induced the most mind-numbing sensation. Visper had intentionally played vixen, though her better judgment had told her to steer clear of strangers. Flirting with the unknown often had dire consequences.

Out the corner of his eye, standing some distance behind him, Tex then noticed a young woman with blonde hair. He immediately dismissed her appeal and eagerly aimed his evil intent back at Visper.

~*~

In the middle of the dance floor, time seemed to slow around the group of witches as Dylis shifted her eyes back onto the DJ's. As they both met, a subtle, orange glow eclipsed each of her hazel irises as she used her power of Thought Projection again.

Time now stood completely still.

Projecting her power, she willed his thoughts. Mentally, she then began to move his hand across the keyboard on his laptop, scroll with the mouse-touch-pad and click the button to change the track.

Instantly, time reassumed itself, and swiftly she spun around.

Dylis murmured to herself, "Let's see what we have here…"

Then suddenly, by magic, she was able to see individual auras around everyone, and from their auras, she could see what they yearned for. The tangy taste of delight danced across her tongue. Instantaneously, people suddenly began to act lustful toward one another as their individual needs became amplified.

A devious yet harmonic voice faintly called over the speaker.

"I whisper to thee, command thy desire. Let lust burn like fire…"

Ryder turned, with a suspicious look in her empathic eyes. As she started to dance again, she casually passed a glance at Dylis, who seemed at first was preoccupied – vaguely staring into the crowd with a devilish suggestion in her face.

Ryder queried as she yelled above the booming bass and music. "Dylis?!!" using her telepathy. Dylis's head was occupied by a faint echo. "…Dylis!"

Placing her hand on the witch's forearm, Ryder felt a slight static charge, and she jumped from the sudden jolt. Pulling her hand away, both Romani and witch looked at one another.

Ryder queried again, but with an odd expression, "Are you okay?"

Dylis replied with a sigh, "Hm." Her smile was stunning, flattering to say the least. "I'm fine, sweetie. Just thought I saw someone I knew. I think I'm gonna go and get something to drink." Ryder's hand slipped down her arm, creating a faint arc of static as they brushed past one another.

Dylis walked on oblivious, leaving a curious Ryder alone among the crowd. Gasping aloud, a sudden surge of power overcame the Empath and Telepath. Her eyes rolled back and her hair blew about.

"Vecchio come tempo!!" The deep, fanatical voice was demonic.

Again, Ryder gasped. She gripped her head with both hands and she shut her eyes as a painful rush of thoughts from everyone in the club overwhelmed her mind. The powerful affliction had been brought on by touching Dylis's arm.

Pulling her hands away from her head, Ryder raised her painful expression to the ceiling and commanded in fluent Italian. "Give thee clarity, ease thy mind. Cease the burden of these sudden cries."

Purple static magically arced from her finger tips and eased her mental pain – a feat considered unachievable by any standards.

~*~

Casually walking through the crowd, Dylis approached the bar with Natalee the bartender in full view. As she watched, the wood nymph gave her a certain glare of acknowledgement.

Dylis smiled as she halted against the bar. "Hi. Natalee, right?"

Listening, Natalee nodded her head. Surprisingly, she didn't address this young beauty as, *Strega*, as she had done the others.

"Be a sweet Wood Nymph and make me a Black Russian. I'm feeling confident."

Natalee growled back, "Don't sweetheart me. I know what you are, Demone!"

Dylis smiled back, "I have no idea what you're talking about. I'm a witch, like my–"

Natalee cut her off, "I know a Strega when I see one! I can sense them by the scent they give off. You are rotted through. Your stench is worse than the disguise you so deceitfully wear. The smell of rotting meat is not a turn-on!"

Dylis's bright expression turned foul and ghoulsome,

"Watch yourself!"

Natalee growled, standing her ground, "Like I said, I know what you are, E–"

"Uh, uh, ah," Dylis immediately corrected her. "I wouldn't if I were you. You just might incur something you will regret, Wood Nymph!"

Natalee gestured her hand.

In an abundance of delicate green energy, a drink appeared, "Take your drink and piss off. I don't want to see you in my club again!"

Dylis took a sip and gave Natalee a sly smile.

Leaning forward, Natalee growled, "Shouldn't you be worried that the Telepath maybe on to you?"

Dylis turned her head to look at Ryder, who stared at her with a strange look from across the nightclub.

Natalee continued firmly. "You do know that she is a Superior Level Romani?" Dylis took another sip of her drink and smiled nervously. "Like I said, I know a Strega – or a Romani, when I see one!"

Running his hand up Layton's arm while they danced, Floren's hand gained a very faint green glow as he used his limited Empathy ability.

Sensing the activation of the power, Ryder turned her head and shot him a dirty glare. She noticed the green glow of his hand. Turning her head back in the opposite direction, she used her telepathy on the DJ.

Mixing his tracks on his laptop, the DJ called out over his Mic, "I want to see you get naughty!" and he began to play Beyonce Knowles' *Naughty Girl*.

Shoving at a dancing clubber, Ryder knocked him against Layton, pushing her back into Floren, who caught her in his arms. The sudden distraction deactivated the glow from his hand. For a moment, Layton's eyes showed a faint green glow as she succumbed to his magnetism. As they gazed lovingly into one another's eyes, Floren gently caressed her cheek as everyone around them danced – they stood still.

He spoke with convincing kindness. "Layton," "Yes…?" she replied, intrigued.

She had never told him her name, so how did he know it?

She appeared dazed as she looked into his hazel eyes.

"Can I buy you a drink?"

With a giddy, love struck smile, and a gentle nod of her head she said: "I'd love one. Thank you."

~*~

Passing through the crowd with difficulty, a young woman with long brown hair pulled back into a sleek ponytail, complained.

"Move it, dickhead!"

The young woman was dressed in a Matthew Williamson signature, coral pink, Valencia beaded cocktail dress. Slipping through the gaps in between dancing clubbers, the young woman came up behind the Romani and then tapped her on the shoulder.

Turning around, Madelyn acknowledged her with awkwardness, "Oh … Hey, Cerina!"

Cerina queried in a blunt tone, "Having fun?"

"Some," Madelyn replied. Quickly, her smile disappeared.

The unpleasant tone in Cerina's voice indicated the lack of progress in the mission.

"Tell the cronies…"

Unable to hear over the music, Madelyn spoke loudly.

"What? I didn't hear—"

Leaning toward her friend's ear, Cerina pressed Madelyn's earlobe in and spoke again, "I said…!"

Madelyn pulled her head away, "What? I can't hear anything!"

Grumbling to herself, Cerina rolled her eyes, "Ugh!! Screw it!!" she pulled Madelyn by the arm and they began to push through the crowd to move to a quieter place.

Cerina was an urbane beauty. Her figure was tall and curvy. She styled her long, dark hair up in a Mohawk, with a distinctive, single, copper streak adding a unique touch. The length of it hung down the back of her neck. On her wrist sat a distinct tattoo of her zodiac – Gemini.

For Cerina, associating with powerful witches was the same as being friends with a celebrity – it gave her status.

Madelyn Romani was the third eldest child of the recognized Romani Coven leader and high priestess, Pilar Romani. The Romani's birthright was a fitting gift from their ancestor, Louise Western, the great-great-great granddaughter of Benjamin Eastey of Salem Massachusetts, born 1669. The Romani Coven, otherwise known as the Triad, ranked as the second most powerful coven in Treadwell, behind only the Pogue Coven.

Through the crowd, Cerina led Madelyn to a quiet corner to the left of the bar and just up from the passage-entry of the nightclub. Stepping into the corner with her back flush up against the wall, Madelyn appeared attentive as she looked at her friend.

"What do you think you're doing?" Cerina demanded in a serious tone.

Uncertain, Madelyn shrugged her shoulders and yelled, "What?!"

"I said!" Cerina rolled her eyes and grumbled. "Screw this!" Turning her head to the side, her eyes gave off a subtly blue glow, and instantly the entire nightclub stood still.

One of her amazing powers, besides finesse, was Eloquence; the ability to slow the flow of time to the point that it stood still.

The words just slipped out of Madelyn's mouth, "My God!"

Clubbers stood frozen in peculiar poses. Dylis, Chantelle, Ryder and Layton looked about with confusion. Ryder's mind fell silent. Her powers of Telepathy and Empathy didn't hear any thoughts or sense any emotions.

Cerina yelled, "I said!"

Listening to her friend yell, Madelyn gave an odd expression, "Why are you yelling?"

With a blank expression, Cerina silenced herself and narrowed her stare.

"Ugh!" she growled. "What are you doing? You're not supposed to be having fun! The idea of this mission is to lure the Philanderer Demon out!"

Madelyn replied honestly. "We are."

Speaking perfect French, Cerina said in a curt tone, "Dancing around like hussies is not what I would call productively luring a demon out into the open, Madelyn!"

Insulted, Madelyn replied, "Did you just call me a hussy?!"

"He's not alone, you idiot!" Cerina revealed the obvious. "There are three Philanderer Demons. I have Dan standing guard outside watching one too."

Annoyed, Madelyn stepped forward. "You brought Dan! Why?!"

"Because I did!" Cerina suddenly became very sarcastic and mean. "Madelyn, he is a Pyrokinetic witch. Hello! Useful! Plus, he can shapeshift." There was an obvious emphasis displayed in her eyes as she continued... "and he is not even a Therianthrope!!"

Madelyn rolled her eyes. "Yes, I know how much of a rarity he is. A shapeshifting witch who is not a Therianthrope...you have to be a descendant of a Therianthrope to be able to shapeshift, blah, blah, blah. I've gotten the memo, Cerina, several times!"

Standing beside Ryder, Dylis overheard the conversation and appeared somewhat intrigued by the small talk. Ryder watched her out of the corner of her eye with a look of suspicion.

A sly and curious Dylis queried, "Dan can manipulate fire?"

Ryder replied in a blunt tone. "Yes. Legend dictates that the *Western Line* of witches, or Romani as we're properly known, are descendants of both gypsies and witches. We have a genetic power. All of us, in some shape or form, can manipulate a different aspect or element in regards to nature."

Intrigued, Dylis replied. "No wonder they're considered powerful."

Still suspicious, Ryder continued watching out of the corner of her eye as she explained.

"My manipulation of nature is Weather, but my superior powers are Telepathy and Empathy."

Revealing her connection to Madelyn, Dylis intervened. "She doesn't elaborate much at work. It's interesting learning about her lineage. She was relieved that there was another witch in the work place." Understanding, Ryder, in a fake manner nodded her head. "I have the power of Thought Projection."

"Clearly..."

Dylis turned her head, looking at Ryder oddly, "I'm sorry?"

"Sorry. I was thinking aloud," Ryder lied, with a coy look. "Cerina implies that there is more than one Philanderer

Demon. She is correct. I have heard thoughts from two other Donnaiolo – that's their true name. It is said that a Huntress, in the early 8th or 9th century, discovered the foul fiend."

"Where did these demons eventuate?"

Ryder's encyclopedia-like mind jumped at the opportunity. "They are said to be the children of Eisheth, the first Succubus. In *Zoharistic Kabbalah*, Eisheth Zenunim is one of a group of angels associated with Sacred Prostitution. She is–"

Chantelle interjected. "Eisheth is an Old One."

Outwardly confused about the term 'Old One', although secretly already knowing, Dylis continued her brief, educational talk.

"What's an Old One?"

Ryder quickly took the reins of knowledge. "They are the pure-breed demons of the Old Age. But on the contrary, there are good Old One's too! Atarah and Eliora a.k.a. Adam and Eve, Cleopatra..."

"You're kidding, right?" Dylis scoffed, as though she had met the ancient Queen of Egypt.

"Mortal history only sheds light on some actual facts. Cleopatra was deeply seated within the realm of magic. She gave so many witches of Ancient Egypt their powers. Uphara protected her from a Vampire Lord named Lazarus. Lilith, Eisheth, Hecate,

Anne, Apollo, Menrva, Bune, Lamia, Naberius and the Queen, Maria, are all Old Ones."

"Due to the decree of magic," Chantelle, offered, very knowledgeable herself, " Old Ones are refused power to interfere with the mortal world. Maria was allowed permanent passage and the key to cultivate good magic."

Intrigued, a sly Dylis beckoned for more. "Who are the evil Old Ones, then?"

"Eisheth is said to be the most beautiful of them all. Then there are Bune and Vine."

Layton, somewhat knowledgeable, added, "Legend depicts that in the Old Age, the Old Ones occupied the monumental plateau, Mauvaise. It's a seat of power."

"Are we ready?" Madelyn queried her associates.

"What for? Cerina replied.

"We're going to vanquish him?" Ryder interrupted

quickly with caution, "Right here? Are you serious, Maddy?"

Madelyn looked at her cousin strangely.

"What!?" Cerina glared at the Romani. "Please tell me you're kidding!"

Madelyn defended herself. "We cannot risk this demon escaping as soon as he gets Layton outside. Out in the open is too dangerous as it is! We have the vanquishing potions," Chantelle elevated her hand, showing off a potion vial, "so let's vanquish him here!"

The girls all agreed, although much apprehension was visible in their faces as they then proceeded to take positions around Floren as he stood frozen in time. Each of them held a small, glass potion vial in their hand and a small piece of paper with a vanquishing spell written on it.

"*Crave Pheromones,*" Ryder cast her part in Romanian,

Chantelle continued, "*From love to lust,*"

"*Philanderer Demon,*" Layton spoke her part in English.

Speaking in Romanian, Madelyn finished the spell, "*With you vanquished, your life is dust.*"

Throwing their potion vials at the same time, the poisonous concoction splattered against Floren's clothes and skin, causing him to unfreeze and cry out in agony.

Instantaneously, he exploded into nothingness, and a wisp of flames danced in the air where he had stood. It disappeared, leaving only a scorch mark to stain the floor.

Dylis stood back, silent and impressed.

LIGHTFOOT'S VISION OF GAIA

It had been two months since Noah had last ventured to Los Angeles to find and ask for his brother Perry's assistance in vanquishing a demon – one who still remained elusive to track. Perry had taken up residence in his brother's contemporary, two storey home in the small, country town of Chickerell Creek, Deane County.

The demon Noah was tracking had something that he wanted.

Downstairs, in the lounge room, Perry sat with his legs crossed on the coffee table, taking slow, deep breaths with his eyes closed and arms relaxed as they rested in his lap. Opposite him stood Noah, impatient and with his arms tightly folded. He tapped his foot on the carpet, eagerly awaiting an answer. Perry breathed in and then out, focusing his power of Sensazione.

"Well?" Noah blurted out.

Irritated, Perry's powers made the light bulb in the corner lamp explode in a flash of light. He opened his eyes and glared at his older brother.

Noah pressed impatiently again. "We need to find this demon now!"

"Our powers are still blocked, if you haven't forgotten. So must I remind you how hard it is to focus and make them work with you constantly–" He was abruptly cut short, midsentence.

He suddenly felt the Premonition ability aspect of his Sensazione power kick in. He let out a loud gasp and his eyes were forced shut.

Astral-projecting into his vision, Perry manifested elsewhere in a sparkling glow of green energy. As he turned around, he saw the Treadwell City Stadium from the north, with the stadium itself in the foreground of his vision. It was night time, and the Colonel William Lightfoot commemoration statue was at his side.

It whispered to him *"This city is the key to your power..."*

Its outline was ablaze in a magical white light, as though something emanated from within.

Released from the vision, Perry gasped and reopened his eyes.

"What did you see?" Noah queried, this time patiently. Perry, uncertain, replied. "Treadwell!" Both exchanged looks of confusion, "Are there any high points within the CBD that overlook a stadium?"

Noah paused and then spoke, "Lightfoot Hill."

"And where is that?" Perry asked, as he got up from his seat. "Specifically, I mean."

Noah thought for a long moment. "North Treadwell." "Grab your coat," Perry said, throwing his brother a cocky look. "I think we just found us a lead to your demon!" Stopping at his brother's side, Perry halted and revealed a small glass potion vial in his hand. It contained a pearly, white liquid. "I call this the traditional mode of transport."

Throwing the vial to the floor, it smashed, releasing a flash, and instantly, the two were teleported out of the house.

In prior decades, witches used potions as a form of teleporting themselves from place to place, long before teleportive genes began to manifest and offered witches and gypsies various forms of teleportation. It was only allocated to magical beings and demons.

~*~

In the depths of the Underworld, a small party of demons had gathered in Azazel's throne room – as she would happily refer to it. She was a powerful demon monarch who had risen to power sometime during the Industrial Revolution.

The ground was covered in dirt – a common furnishing in the Underworld – and rock face walls with modern light fixtures gave off a decent burn. To the side was a colonial style bar that was maintained and serviced by a demon bartender. Azazel loved her drink.

On the far side of the room, was a timber deck that sported a black conference table capable of seating fourteen individuals. To revel in her impressive intellect, Azazel had a wall-to-wall book shelf filled with books that listed everything from the mortal world to the magical world. Four modern sofas were positioned in the middle of the area, with a massive and creative pendant light-feature that hung down on a chain from the abyss of black above.

Azazel, a beautiful, tall woman with long, flowing dark hair entered her chambers in a fiery inferno that tore up from the ground.

"So, tell me," she summoned firmly, as she proceeded to walk around the sofas where her male demon minions sat, "did anyone find the Sundial?"

She was dressed in black leather leggings and a black-and white polka dot blouse with a red belt under her breasts.

"Yes, we believe we have found the location," replied a proud demon.

"Fascinate me," she ushered him with a hand gesture to continue. "My boss wanted it two months ago, and I'm sick and tired of vanquishing demons who return empty handed!" She grumbled to herself as she folded her arms, "it's not your arse on the line!"

A demon mumbled, "Pushy bitch!"

Flicking her hand out, she threw a fireball, vanquishing the demon.

"Does anyone else want to join our friend?" she demanded firmly.

"We believe," the male leader of the small party stepped forward, "that the Sundial is inside the Commemoration Statue at Lightfoot's lookout–"

Azazel interrupted with a smile, "Good work, Louis."

"I will deploy my men on your command, but I cannot verify if our foes have been made aware of our intention." Louis was a six-foot-tall demon, dressed in a black leather jacket, ribbed tank top and black pants. "May I be frank with you, my Liege?"

Azazel looked at him with humble eyes, flattered by the title used to address her.

"What is this Sundial worth?" he queried curiously.

Her humble expression quickly became unlikable.

"Forgive me," he continued, "but what does it represent to us? I have not heard any rumors about this relic until now."

With a sultry look, Azazel appeared humble again – not ready to vanquish him for his questioning, as she would to any other demon. She silently wondered whether to reveal the truth to him or not. What if he turned against her and went for the power for himself, to elevate himself along the demonic Echelon? She couldn't risk that.

"You're asking a lot of valid questions, Louis, but I'm not at liberty to reveal any information. Your job is to do as I order.

However, I will tell you that I am going to accompany you to the site."

Louis nodded his head as he accepted the rules of the proposition.

"Boss," another male demon approached Azazel. She glanced to the side as she listened to his soft speech. "There are two witches at the site. Do we attack them?"

Azazel moved her glance; she glared ahead at Louis and curled her lips at one end.

"Louis, gather your demons. We're going to kill some witches!"

~*~

As the later hours of the evening wore on, North Treadwell was quiet, with only a few motorists out driving. Evenly spaced street lights created gold glows along Maiden Hill Road and Pennington Terrace. The bitumen was still wet from the light showers of rain that had fallen at dusk. A breeze moved the branches of the big, old tree on the corner where the two streets met, causing the damp leaves to shower the pavement and grass with raindrops.

In the middle of the manicured lawns, segregated by paths and flowering garden beds, stood a towering commemoration statue of the man, Colonel William Lightfoot – the Surveyor General of Treadwell – which depicted him with his arm extended, pointing over the city in the view from its location.

Spotlights in three different positions cast an immortalizing glow upon the monument, making it distinguishable in the dark.

On the sidewalk of Pennington Terrace, in a flash of white light, Noah and Perry Pogue reappeared, tall and shoulderto-shoulder. Cautious as he was, Noah turned his head, looking about to make sure no one had seen the display of magic out in public;

the risk of exposure would be costly. Looking ahead, Perry analyzed the statue for a short moment, and then proceeded to move forward along the path toward it.

"You saw this," Noah queried as he began to follow, "in your vision?"

A curious Perry remained silent as he continued to observe the statue above the stone foundation, followed by the foundation itself. He felt compelled, pulled to it, as though it was magnetized. Curiously, he circled it slowly, taking in every detail.

"You don't feel that?" he queried, looking back at his brother as he stood side on to it, his arm extended and hand gestured as though he was feeling something invisible. "It's warm; like sunshine."

Cautiously, Noah replied, "I don't feel anything. I'm not the Empath. You are!"

"Come here," Perry summoned. "You seriously," he questioned with confusion, "cannot feel that?" As Noah approached, the radiating emission grew in sudden strength. "Whoa!" Perry withdrew his arm in an instant. "That was weird...a bit too weird even for my kind of strange!"

"This is hardly the time or place to discuss your sexual fetishes, Perry!"

Analyzing the monument with more scrutiny in his eyes, Perry witnessed it flicker like an old television struggling to maintain its picture and then appear normal.

"Stop!" He extended his arm at Noah, but Noah ignored his gesture. "Stop moving!" He lowered his arm back to his side.

"I don't like the feel of whatever this is..."

Behind Noah, some distance away, a blur of energy rose up from the ground, and Louis teleported into the location. His evil intentions were given away by the look on his face. *Attack the witches and procure whatever the statue possessed.*

Turning his head to look back at his brother, Perry acknowledged the demon's presence.

"Demon!" he identified aloud.

Noah remarked amidst confusion, "What?"

"This is our power," Louis growled loudly. Upon hearing the voice, Noah turned around and saw the demon. "We," Louis said, waving his hand as six other male demons appeared, "are under orders to kill any witch, Pogue or not, should they intervene in the procuring of this relic."

Perry murmured curiously to himself. "Relic?"

Louis created a ball of fire in his gestured hand, throwing it at Noah.

Using his power of Probability Manipulation, Noah extended his arm and gestured his hand. His fingers glittered with gold as he snapped them, causing the fireball to explode and then extinguish. Flicking his hand forward at Louis, he caused him to cry out in a pit of agony and explode into a fireball before it extinguished.

"We are Pogue!" Noah scoffed. "Idiot! Who did you think you were dealing with?"

A female's voice sounded. "Me!" Atop the stone ledge that looked out over Treadwell, Azazel stood confident and modest. "Azazel!"

An intimidated Perry stepped back as he observed the stunning spectacle. He knew who Azazel was; his father, Greg, had told him stories about how enchanting and beautiful the demon was. He knew her as cruel and cunning, and that her history was colourful; she had infiltrated many witch and gypsy covens and slaughtered them by killing and then assuming the identity of a prominent member.

Instinctively, he assumed his vampire visage and proceeded to swing his arm, using his power of Telekinesis to attack her.

Moving her hand out, a loud bang resonated as she caught the attack and then crushed it.

"You're a Superior Level Demon!" Perry acknowledged, nervously. "Why would you even bother revealing your presence? Most demons of your stature manipulate from the shadows."

Azazel smirked. "Trying to flatter me with your diehard tongue?" She was clearly immune to his flirtatious nature. "Pretty Perry the vampire-witch!" She swung her arm, throwing him backward with her power of Telekinesis. "You're an idiot!" Instantaneously Perry slammed against an invisible wall of energy that flashed green on impact. Ripples of a glittering, apple-green spread to the left and right, revealing a magical barrier.

"What?" Azazel murmured, looking about her surroundings with caution. "Rafaela?" she queried aloud, believing her superior to be the invisible presence.

Spontaneously, Louis's six demons cried out in agony as their bodies were pulled into the ground and vanquished in eruptions of intense flames. Wisps of glittering, green energy floated for a moment as the flames of defeated demons faded.

A glowing, green figure stepped out of the commemoration statue.

"Who are you?" Azazel growled territorially,

The glow around the figure faded to reveal a woman with two-tone blonde hair held aloft in a loose bun. She wore a modern, moss-green shawl and a brown, long-sleeved top underneath, with camel coloured pants and a red scarf for a belt. "I am Gaia!" she announced territorially, as her eyes gave off an intimidating glow. "Goddess of the Earth! This land is my pantheon!" Using her divine powers, Gaia read Azazel, "The Sundial does not belong to you, Azazel. It is—"

Turning her head, she acknowledged Noah where he stood behind her right shoulder. She watched Perry get back up onto his feet. Her power as a god allowed her to sense that the two brothers were a part of a powerful dynasty.

"Azazel," spoke another, deeper woman's voice. "Kill the goddess!"

Turning her head, Azazel looked to the right, acknowledging a black figure clad in a heavy, hooded cloak. Drawing the light to it given off by the moon, the demonic individual felt more and more imposing as it stood motionless on the grass.

Hearing and acknowledging the orders given to her by her superior, Rafaela, Azazel turned her head and attention back to the goddess standing before the monument. She moved a hand out, created a ball of fire and then threw it – using her telekinesis to enhance the attack's speed.

"I am a god!" Gaia protested with insult. "You ought to know your place, Demon!"

Using her power of Superior Nature Manipulation, Gaia activated her barrier again. Hitting the invisible ability, the fireball's impact – before extinguishing – made it glitter green and then disappear.

"I'll have you know," Azazel said, extending her arm and gesturing her hand in an attempt to wield her power of Paralysis, "Gaia, goddess of Earth, I am a Superior Level–" Cut off in midsentence, she screamed as the goddess's barrier slammed against her, throwing her back from the stone wall she stood upon.

Banished from the location, Azazel fled in an eruption of rich, red flames.

"The Sundial belongs to me," the cloaked woman declared with a hiss. "Its power is mine, Gaia. I can and I will kill you if you keep me from it!"

Turning to face the demon, Gaia spoke. "Nothing in this dimension belongs to you, Rafaela. You have no power here; the Old Ones will find a way to banish you back to your hell dimension!"

"The Old Ones have had no success, yet." The cloaked and hooded figure began to slowly approach, "No one has the power to stop me, not them, not you, no witch!"

Extending her arm and feeling threatened, Gaia swayed her hand. Both Noah and Perry vanished from where they stood in flashes of light, and then magically reappeared on different sides of the monument. She then manipulated their bodies, making them extend an arm each and reach out to touch the stone.

"Reveal!" she commanded.

Before Noah and Perry, energy surrounding the stone monument of Colonel William Lightfoot warped and moved. In its place sat an aged, limestone sundial with the four compass points N, S, E and W.

"You need to be stopped." Gaia stood firm against the evil before her, "If neither God or Old One is capable of stopping you, then maybe they can!"

Standing face to face, all that prevented the demon from smiting the goddess of earth was the barrier she had put up to protect herself and the monument she swore to guard. Gasping as her lips trembled, Gaia witnessed the identity of the figure beneath the hood, without Rafaela removing it.

A set of gazelle horns emerged as the hood moved back a little, while piercing red, glowing eyes surfaced in the black underneath.

"In my demise," tears fell like diamonds from the corner of the goddess's eyes, "the Pogue Witches shall be this world's last defence against you, you foul– ARGH!!!" Gaia let out a scream as she burned up in a rage of red flames.

"Holy…" Perry exclaimed with shock, "shit! It just vanquished a god!"

In her vanquishment, Gaia's barrier became completely visible to the naked eye, and it quickly began to dissolve toward the ground like glittering, green rain.

"Touch it," a frightened and instinctive Noah gasped, knowing that the same fate would become theirs. "Touch the sundial!"

A reluctant Perry replied, "What? Why? Are you kidding? we don't even know what it does!"

"That Sundial is mine!!"

Raising its arm up from beneath its heavy cloak, the demon used its power of Telekinesis as it approached, emitting a wave that tore up the ground as it went.

"I said," Noah ordered his brother firmly, "bloody touch it! What other option do we have?" Together, they each placed a hand onto the octagonal shaped surface before them.

Perry touched the symbol representing east, and Noah touched the symbol for south.

Bringing forth its power, the sundial gave off a glow that enveloped the two brothers. Withdrawing back into itself as the light disappeared, the brothers and the relic vanished ... teleported away.

Agitated as it watched the object of its obsession disappear into the hands of good, the cloaked demon with horns let out an otherworldly roar that caused the fabric of air around it to warp. Seconds later, four red-cloaked demons appeared behind it, shoulder to shoulder. Each had a symbol embroidered on their front – N, S, E and W, just like the Sundial had.

At the moment of their arrival, the roaring ceased. "They took the Sundial!" the cloaked demon revealed with irritation. "This is what we–" It was cut off mid-sentence.   "You abomination!" A familiar and nasty voice spoke in a Greek tongue. "You are not entitled to the powers of this reality!

...Rafaela!"

A vortex of green energy wrapped itself around the fiend, burning away its cloak and revealing a gorgeous, tall and slender woman with long and thick-flowing, black hair. Her gazelle horns were complemented by an impressive gown of gold, adorned with rubies and emeralds.

Rafaela, revealed to be the cloaked demon's name, wore a fantastic, black gown constructed with different materials of varying textures.

"Gaia!"

The goddess of earth had returned, unharmed and without a scratch or a mark from her blazing vanquish just minutes prior.

"I am a primal god and this is my relic!"

Rafaela replied, "No one has to get hurt. I can tempt you to my side, give you power! Like I did to Neptune!" she revealed her evil grin.

"It has been my duty since the Old Age to protect this relic!"

Rafaela questioned, "Who said you had to take on such a stressful role?"

"So far you claim to be Avatarian Demon, demi-goddess from Alestra with no power, but instead a heavy, choking shadow!" Gaia extended her arm at Rafaela, and twisted her hand into a fist. "I am immortal, capable of resurrection! You—" She released her clenched hand and flicked it out at the demi-goddess, using her power of Annihilation, "are not!"

Screaming, a brilliant green glow instantly shone out of Rafaela's body, and abruptly, she was gone. The harsh light faded. Behind, the four individuals in red cloaks vanished swiftly to avoid a painful demise.

~*~

Treadwell, 1835...

*I*n the distance, from a hill – to be named Maiden Hill – which overlooked the country plains, a man, Colonel William Lightfoot, the Surveyor-General of Deane County, witnessed the rising structures as the city of Treadwell rose from the soil.

With his hand above his eyes, he blocked out the sunshine to admire the view.

Behind him, two men stood at a table, poring over blueprints of the new city's layout. To his side was a sundial, untouched and as though it had been there forever. Vines coiled up from the ground, curling up the column and stopping at the octagonal shaped top. At its centre was an impressive sized crystal.

"What is this…?" the Colonel asked, his intrigued spiked. On closer inspection, he silently acknowledged what it appeared to be with a, "Hmm…"

He traced his finger around its octagonal edge as he walked around it, and then stopped to touch the crystal at its centre point. It glowed simultaneously, and he quickly withdrew his hand.

"Argh!!" – "Ah!!"

Behind him, his men cried out in agony.

Turning around immediately, he saw the bodies of his butchered fellow men, with three native, tribal demons standing over them.

"Who," his voice squeaked as his body trembled in fear, "are you?"

The three male, human-looking demons had russet skin with scars over their bare bodies, and small pieces of cloth covering their front male parts. Ceremonial pieces of leather decorated in bird feathers and teeth crisscrossed over their chests. They had piercing orange, crocodile-like eyes that enabled their power of Binocular Vision – they were shrouded in heavy grayish black shadow and discolored, jagged shark-like teeth.

One wielded a handcrafted spear, another handcrafted daggers and the third a whip with razor sharp teeth down the length of it to the hilt.

Spontaneously, they cried out in pits of agony as their bodies erupted into rigorous green flames and they were finally reduced to smoking piles of ash.

"Colonel," an endearing female's voice sounded behind him where the Sundial was, "you are safe." He turned around to be greeted by an immortal beauty. "I am Cynthea Houston."

"Huh?" He was too shocked to know any different.

"What was all that about?"

She replied, "Please, do not fear me. They were demons, and truthfully," this woman revealed, "I am a goddess; Gaia, of Earth, sworn protector of the Sundial, and now, the protector of you and your city."

"Err?" he was stumped.

"Are you aware that you have built your precious city, of–" she gestured him to reveal its name.

He replied, "Treadwell."

"–Treadwell..." she said, with curiosity. "on what we gods, deities and apparently the Portuguese call, Boca Del Inferno, meaning Hellmouth, the whale-monster Leviathan? "she continued.

"I will call it Treadwell; the city of churches. Sanctify it against evil."

Gaia smiled. "The city of Witches!"

"Witches?"

"They already live amongst you to protect it! These tribal demons, are only just the beginning!" she replied.

WILL BE WELCOMED

*O*n a farm to the South of Stiles Pond, Boxford Essex –

Massachusetts, ferocious lightning idolized a two storey manor; portraying it in bold light and blacking out its surroundings.

The stormy night brought a low-lying fog about the land.

Rain lashed against the house as thunder erupted behind the hostile clouds that blanketed the sky.

The date was November 19th 1685, the year that Nathaniel Eames was born to his mother, Rebecca Blake, and father, Robert Eames. He would be their eighth child. They had two daughters, and he would be the couple's sixth son.

In an off-white flannelette night dress as she lay upon her bed – under the coaxing, scarlet candlelight – Rebecca Eames was delivering an ordained baby.

"Argh!" the familiarity of labor was something she was used to, after having had seven children already. "Argh!" she panted; tensing up with anguish as tears streamed down her cheeks.

Perched up with pillows, she sat with her legs arched and parted.

"Argh, I cannot!" Rebecca halted for a moment, partially exhausted.

"You're almost there, Rebecca," her friend and midwife encouraged her. "The baby is crowning. Just a little more!"

At her side, gripping her hand tightly, doting husband Robert offered compassionate aid – something unheard of in their community.

"I am here, wife; you are almost there." With a towel, he sponged her sweaty forehead. "Just push," he urged, knowing nothing of pain beyond comprehension...he had no words to describe what he witnessed. "One more push, Rebecca!"

"Argh!!" she cried out, screwing her face up in agony as she hunched forward, gathering additional strength. "Urgh!!" she let out an almighty groan and then sighed with relief as the sound of a crying baby quickly filled the room.

Wrapping the newborn in a towel, the midwife smiled joyfully. "It is a boy."

Robert smiled with pleasure – another son added to his growing family.

"He is beautiful, Rebecca." Carefully, the midwife rose to her feet and carried the crying infant around the bed to his waiting mother, who lay recuperating.

Taking the child into her caring and loving embrace, Rebecca kissed his forehead, caressed his little cheek and smiled at the little life she and her husband had created.

"Nathaniel." Rebecca could sense his destiny by the touch of his forehead. "Nathaniel Eames."

As a witch herself, her innate power was psychometry...an ability that allowed her to both see and sense the future of an object or a person when she touched it.

Standing flush against the bed, Rebecca's friend and midwife frowned. She had noticed a little, distinct but faint, birthmark upon his little arm. "Is he?"

In Salem, many had been condemned to death because they bore a birthmark. It was an honest birth abnormality, but of course, the people of Salem referred to it as the mark of a witch...a symbol of Wiccan Heritage.

Penny, the midwife, immediately regretted her question – she would have said nothing had it not been for the fact that, like Rebecca, she also was a witch.

"Is he what?" Rebecca replied. "A witch?" Penny gave her a subtle stare and Robert sat silently, curious for the same knowledge. "Of course, he is. Like me, my mother and my grandmother." Raising her child and looking him over, her eyes sparkled with wonderment. Her loyal friend passed a glance at the doting yet concerned father, but Rebecca dismissed them both. "I wonder what power he will be blessed with."

"If he is," Robert began, "we must keep it secret. Who knows what scrutiny he may suffer? None of our other children have powers."

All their children were squibs…non-magical, but Rebecca was not disheartened. She loved them all the same.

The morning sun rose high in the sky on that wonderful Fall day as Rebecca watched her newborn child sleep. She was enthralled to have a child that would carry on the same birthright she had been given.

~*~

36 years later – 1731

The venomous words spoken by a foul rival licked up Rebecca's neck.

"Reap what you sow, witch!"

Pressing through the gaps of the window…the cold winter's breeze gave the important occasion a certain, future altering attitude.

The chill of the night outside the rickety attic windows had iced them up. In the candlelight of the room of the Eames' wooden house, Rebecca Eames engaged in battle with a beautiful and powerful demon.

A devil – a woman in appearance but eternally a succubus – her name was Carissa Estherbridge.

Appearing as a true enchantress, she wore her long, black, shimmering gown, her curled hair complemented with a lace veil that drooped across her shallow and empty eyes. The lustrous wreaker-of-havoc wore striking red lip-rouge, and her attire was less than conservative for the times, leaving little to the imagination...inappropriate for a woman of Salem. Considering some were being hung or burned at the stake for witchcraft, it was dangerous.

"So shall I perish by the flames of purification?" Rebecca growled back, territorially defending her ground and honor. "At least I shall have rid the world of you, Succubus!"

"You know what I am?" Carissa appeared smug and impressed.

With words as sharp as a knife blade, Rebecca said nastily, "A whore of Salem is what you are, Carissa." The sexually ambitious demon gave her a foul look, insulted by the word used to describe her. At Carissa's feet, Rebecca's husband had fallen victim, dead on his side. In the candlelight of the attic, the witch's beauty was seamless. "I know what your husband is; an Incubus!" The Succubus morphed her tense lips into a smirk.

Standing in the doorway of the attic, Nathaniel, now a thirty-six-year-old man, watched what would soon become his weekly or even daily routine.

"Ma!"

Sharply shooting a glare at the man, the hundred-yearold Carissa, immortally gorgeous as a twenty-year-old, formed an outrageous grin with her alluring lips.

"Come now, boy. Do as I say—"

Swiftly extending her arm out and firmly pressing her palm against the air in the direction of the Succubus, Rebecca used her newly acquired power of Energy Manipulation.

"Slur your words in my presence no longer. You don't have any power over him!" The air violently pulsated around the demon. But she was truthful; the Succubus had not affected Nathaniel. "Your havoc ends here. Making women leave their husbands so that you can seduce them. It is because of you that my friends are being burned!"

Smirking, Carissa shifted her gaze from Nathaniel and placed it back onto the witch before her.

"Come now," a bold, fierce tone and foul stare swelled in her face. "I only encouraged what the morbid citizens of this town do not."

"What is that?" Rebecca barked.

"Sex, of course," Carissa sneered devilishly. "After all, I had your husband, didn't I?"

Approaching as she swung her arm, Rebecca slapped the woman across the face.

Beyond the windows of the attic, the glowing flame lit the torches of the growing crowd and shone a bold orange. The prejudiced and fearing folk of Salem were coming to collect their criminal;, a witch.

"Oh, what is that I hear?" Smiling, Carissa completely dismissed the slap across the face and the redness swelling on her cheek. Startled, Rebecca gasped as she staggered back. Her eyes widened with fear as she heard it too. "I believe the townspeople are coming to arrest their witch!"

Entering into the room, Nathaniel, displayed bitterness upon his adult face.

"Your truculent nature is not welcome here." Extending his arm as he charged, Nathaniel used his telekinesis. From the table beside his mother's sacred, tree-green, leather-bound Book of

Shadows, an Athame with a swirling blade shot away and painfully impaled the succubus in the abdomen. (An Athame is a double-edged ceremonial knife with a black handle often used by witches in their rituals. They are more often than not, used by demons to steal powers of other magical beings.)

"Nathaniel, no! Leave!" Rebecca ordered.

Stunned by what she saw, she turned and seized the moment before death came knocking on her door as the Succubus cried out in agony.

Unfolding a piece of parchment, she cast the vanquishing spell that would consume her last moments with her loving son.

"Evil of the night, no longer shall you blight. Take this evil, flame of hell. She shall know no love, only the PAIN OF THIS WITCH'S SPELL!!!"

Raising her head to the ceiling, arching her back, flailing her arms out at each side and rising onto her tip-toes, Carissa's scream was absolute.

A brilliant glow of golden sunshine shone out of her mouth and hands.

In an incredible display of witchcraft, ecstatic flames rose up from the floorboards – appearing out of thin air – and raced up her body, consuming it like a snake would its prey. And then, with a triumphant explosion, Carissa was vanquished and the flames instantly disappeared in a blinding glow of orange.

Rebecca's Athame clattered on the floor until it lay still.

Turning, with watery, emotional eyes, Rebecca kissed her adult son – first on the forehead.

"Always remember that I love you, Nathaniel." Attentively, her son wiped a tear from her cheek. "Remember what I taught you,"

"Our magic is a secret."

He repeated what she had so strongly enforced upon him his entire life.

Choking on her tears, Rebecca smiled, proud of her boy. Bringing him in close, she held him tightly in her embrace for the last time.

"I love you."

Innocently he said, "I will protect you!"

Moving her head away from his shoulder, Rebecca wiped her watery eyes, sighed and then spoke to him of the truth, in a desperate hope that he would understand.

"Nathaniel, you cannot. You too will be burned if you do.

I cannot have that!"

He stared at her.

"Some people have seen me use magic, and they have reported me. That woman," she turned slightly and pointed to the scorch mark on the floor in the middle of the room, "she was a—"

"...She was a demon, I know," he acknowledged.

She looked at her son, "Yes, darling, she was. But now, I must pay for my crime."

He found it hard to understand the evil nature the townspeople said existed in witchcraft, when his mother solely used it for good to protect them.

"Ma; witchcraft is hardly punishable if you are protecting people." Nathaniel raised his hands, looked at the soft texture of his palms and then looked back into his mothers eyes. "Surely they must know that," he said.

Bringing him in close, Rebecca did not discourage his power or instincts as an adult witch.

"Darling, they act out of fear. They hate what they do not understand." Moving away, she gave him a stern look. "Nathaniel; I want you to hide the book. Keep it a secret and make sure it remains safe. It is yours now." He tried to interrupt her, as he

mouthed a word of protest. "No buts, Nathaniel. You know how to use it, and I know you will do me proud." Her eyes glittered with joy, knowing that her son would be the one to carry on the Eames line of witches. "Go. Quickly." He left her side.

At the waist-high, dainty timber book stand, Nathaniel snatched the book. Watching him, his mother saw the book give off a glow as he grabbed each side.

"Destiny..." a proud smile curled her lips.

Nathaniel paused as he turned to her, looking for his next direction. Out the corner of his eye, he saw the blade of his mothers Athame glimmer in the candlelight. Taking one hand from the book, he moved his arm and held out his palm to the knife.

Curiously, Rebecca watched.

In an instant, the knife shot away from the floor and abruptly halted within his grasp. Again, he looked to her for direction.

"Nathaniel; go." Rebecca insisted. "Find a place, and hide it now!"

Nodding his head, he did as she said and quickly left the room.

"Watch over him." Rebecca turned around. Behind her, a much younger version of a woman named Maria – approximately the mortal age of nineteen – magically appeared out of thin air, as though she had been standing there the entire time. "Please."

Maria, dressed in colonial attire, smiled peacefully. "I know his future, and his legacy will lead to greatness." Rebecca smiled gratefully. The angelic young woman's long, golden blonde hair framed her face and accentuated her hazel blue eyes. "Thank you, Prudenza," Rebecca praised.

Flattered by the speaking of her name, Maria replied, "Please, call me Maria." Understanding, Rebecca simply gave a contented smile.

Below, two floors down, the sudden rap at the door caught her attention. "I do not fear my fate. I served good." Rebecca said.

Maria gave a subtle smile and gave a silent nod as she agreed.

Rebecca continued, "I do not care for their condemnations. I have come to realize that mortals fear anything they do not understand. What they envisage as work of the devil, is the evil work of their own self-conceited doubt!"

Some hours later, upon the mound of sticks located in the town center – in the brilliant light of the flame-lit torches held by the fearing citizens of Salem – Rebecca stood, bound with twine to a tall, wooden stake: a fearless witch full of virtue.

To her left and right, were the women of her coven.

Telula Ledger and Olivia Charity had also been found out and condemned to death.

The front of the imposing timber homes, buildings and church of the town square, looked paralyzed in the orange light.

Around the three women that were to be burned, the town's people, consumed by their own self-conceited fears, murmured and wished death upon the women. They all hoped that hell would welcome the three blasphemous women with open arms, and that heaven would reject them willingly.

The town's mayor stood before Rebecca, eager to light the pyre.

"The Elders of Salem hereby declare you guilty of practicing witchcraft. Have you any final words, Rebecca Eames – witch of Satan?" She stood silently proud of what she was and what she did – fighting and vanquishing evil, protecting people. It was hardly a punishable crime. "Well?" he forced upon her.

Mayor Winston Estherbridge, born in 1671, was remarkably handsome for a fifty-year-old – he appeared as youthful as a twenty-year-old and did not seem to age at all. He was built to be striking in appearance. Often glowing, his eyes were the most magnetic and eerie blue.

"Burn, witch!" an eager and fearful man cried out.

Rebecca proclaimed, "The only thing I wish to say is that I protected you from evil. A Succubus plagued our town and I vanquished it. I have served no one but the Divinità!"

Outraged, the mayor ridiculed her. "The Divinità does not show pity toward the foulness that is witches!" His stern, yet fearful eyes became captured in Rebecca's honest and loyal ones.

"Heaven frowns upon you!"

Amongst the crowd, Maria stood silent in the glow of the flame-lit torches. Telepathically she praised the woman before her. "Do not be afraid. You will be welcomed."

Behind the parting clouds in the black sky, the stars glittered brightly and the full-moon shone its gaze down, consuming Rebecca within its glow and causing the town's people to gasp in disbelief.

With her head raised and eyes closed, Rebecca breathed in and then exhaled.

"I will be welcomed." Looking down, she reopened her eyes. The amulet that hung on a chain around her neck glittered and gave off a beautiful, amethyst glow. "It is your self-conceited doubt that is evil. I served the greater good and I shall die with honor, like the other witches who have died before me." Sighing with a proud smile, she recited a verse in Italian. "Oh heavenly moon, wrap me in your embrace. For I serve you and light. Take me, this sacred night!"

"Turn away your ears and minds," the mayor ordered, "for she speaks verses of the devil!"

"Hardly...!" a woman mocked, murmuring to herself.

"She ain't no witch of mine!"

WITCH IN THE WOODS

Carefully hidden amongst the frightened folk of Salem, a woman – rapturous like the Succubus that Rebecca had engaged and effortlessly defeated – watched with only evil intent in her stone cold heart.

Her long, fiery-red hair fell straight, framing the sides of her face.

In the glow of the moon, resistant against the light of heaven, she revealed a small portion of her true nature.

As witness to her existence, Nathaniel coincidently looked in her direction, and he now knew the face of all things evil. The moon's glow forced each of her irises to change colour, brown to striking red; the legendary Potentate god-king of all things evil.

"Let the witch burn!!" the woman roared in a deep, booming voice.

With the flame-lit torch in his hand, the mayor threw it onto the pyre, and it immediately ignited the dark night with a ferocious roar and wondrous glow. As she awaited her fate, Rebecca looked at the devil from behind the veil of dancing flames.

"From beneath the ground, where evil dwells, I banish you, demon, out of this world!" Gathering all the spit she could muster in her mouth, she reached forward and propelled it through the fire and onto the woman's face.

A brilliant light shone out from the woman and she cried out in agony. Screaming in fright, the townspeople drew away from her and watched.

"Witch!!" a bystander cried out in fear.

Magnificently, the area around the woman rippled, and she was gone – swallowed by the fabric of air.

Turning back to the pyre, the fearful folk were greeted by an extinguished mound.

The sturdy, scorched, wooden stake that Rebecca was bound to was all that remained. The amulet she wore, that protected her, lay in a pile of ash – a reminder to Nathaniel of her honorable death. Content with the killing of a witch, the townspeople and mayor returned to their homes.

In the same year of his innocent mother's death, Nathaniel married his beloved Beatrice Maidus, a mortal who did not believe in killing witches, but who was instead a silent activist for the rights of good witches.

Some two years later, in 1723, witches had been banished from Salem, into the night to live in the woods.

Along a deserted road, just outside of Salem, tightly hugged by overhanging trees, a cloaked figure rode a gallant, black steed.

Nathaniel narrated as he rode through the fog, "Those who were outlawed to hide in the night," the horse's heavy feet pounded the gravel as it galloped along, "shall have the most magnificent beauty; by day and by night."

Coming to a narrow path off to the side of the road, he slowed his horse to a complete halt. Alert to something unseen ahead, his horse and Wiccan familiar neighed wildly and reared up high.

Gripping the horse's thick black, wavy mane, Nathaniel's hood fell back and revealed his mature face.

"Whoa," he calmed his stallion with a soothing tone. "What is it, Hudson?"

A wind tore along the road, howling like a ghoul; the horse feared what was approaching from behind the thick fog.

Nathaniel's witchy senses frightfully warned him, "Witch Hunters!" Squeezing the heel of his boots into the horse's sides, he insisted it move on.

The stallion reared up in refusal.

Nathaniel clicked his tongue, and with another sharp kick, the horse ducked off down the narrow trail.

Coming along the road, three distinct neighs echoed beautifully. A large chestnut, a grey and a golden palomino with striking red eyes, cantered side by side. The three heavily cloaked Courtmen Witch Hunters made eerie other-worldly squawks. Halting their devilish steeds, the middle rider, and leader of the three, rigidly and swiftly looked about the woods at each side of the road.

"Do you smell a witch, Akeisha?!" the hunter on the Palomino asked in a spine-tingling voice.

Their faces were concealed beneath their baggy hoods.

Identified as a female, the lead hunter sharply turned her head to the left. Beneath her hood, a set of red glowing eyes glared into the woods. Her vision turned the world to red as she sought out white figures that she would identify as witches...but her power revealed nothing.

She sniffed like a depraved dog, "I smell!"

Raising her head, the moon cast its faint light onto her horrid, demonic face. All of their faces were disfigured and coloured an eerie, hammer-tone grey. Their heightened sense of smell was credit to them not having the skin or cartilage over their noses...you could see the inlets of their nostrils. Their full lips were black, and they had jagged, dog-like teeth and long, pointy chins. Their hands were brittle, with long, lanky fingers sporting brown, razor-sharp fingernails.

Clenching her brown leather reins, Akeisha replied rigidly. "There was a witch here," irritated, she continued to look about, "but it is gone now!"

The third Hunter, Matais Courtmen spoke in the most unhinging voice. "Let us ride to Salem! Winston is expecting us!" The wind whipped up ferociously around them, their steeds reared, and with fierce growls, the riders galloped off into the night with their cloaks flapping behind them.

Walking along the dark trail, weaving throughout the tangling trees, Nathaniel, unable to see properly, raised his hand and commanded a Power Word Charm.

"Luce!! (Light)"

His palm shone a brilliant, momentary blue. Magically, three white-glowing orbs appeared and began to spiral in, out and around one another as they cast light for him.

~*~

*I*n an opening, some thirty kilometers into the woods, an old and dilapidated shack with golden light burning in its dirty windows and smoke curling out of its brick chimney caught Nathaniel's attention.

Inside, alone and isolated from the town and banished into the night lived the renowned Clairvoyant, Janae Rose.

She was an alluring woman aged in her early thirties, and many believed her to be a siren because men were easily attracted to her…amongst her tricks of clairvoyance, she could also hypnotize.

Dismounting from his stallion, Nathaniel led it to the front porch, where he looped the reins around the wooden banister.

"Wait here, Hudson." His insisting eyes and the horse's cautious ones met.

Understanding his master, Hudson snorted loudly and gestured his head up and down.

Turning away, Nathaniel walked up onto the timber deck. His pulse raced, a sweat glittered across his brow and his throat swelled as he gulped nervously. Extending his arm out, he went to knock on the slightly lopsided door made of planks of wood.

Pulling the door open, a beautiful woman stood in the way.

"Well, strike me dead; a witch!" She looked him up and down with her alluring blue eyes. "Nathaniel Eames, as I live and breathe; knocking on my front door."

"Janae...?" he replied, uncertain of her character.

She was the most entrancing beauty he had met, next to the astoundingly beautiful Succubus that his mother had vanquished three years earlier.

Janae was not like the conservative women of the town.

Her attire was a lot more straightforward than a humble woman under the thumb of her husband and her religious leaders.

She wore her long, midnight blue hair in a style of her choosing. It cascaded down one side of her oval shaped face. The front part of her hair was braided across her forehead and blended into the rest of her hair at the side. The corset she wore asserted her breasts – little wonder every man in town wanted her. It was green, while the rest of her gown was sky blue. The sleeves were made of an expensive-looking, opaque fabric unknown to the women of Salem.

Behind her, the crisp smell of sage and cinnamon brought Nathaniel to contentment. A relaxed sigh escaped his pursed lips.

Most people perceived the witches of Salem to be dirty old hags, who lived in filth but ironically, Janae's shack in the woods, alight with a warming glow, was clean and immaculate with a large black cauldron in the middle of the immediate area behind the door.

"I saw you coming," she revealed, looking over her meticulously perfect fingernails. "I am clairvoyant, am I not?" Lowering her hand, she met his gaze again. "I see Mayor Wankshaft!" She spoke as any bitter witch would call him - she disliked him very much, seeing him as misogynistic and woman hating.

What innocent townsfolk saw as a law enforcing mortal, she saw as a demon. He was the suitor of the woman who Nathaniel had seen reveal herself as the Potentate on the night that his mother had burned. Mayor Winston Estherbridge was an incredibly attractive Incubus in the guise of a mortal.

Janae continued. "Winton Estherbridge has summoned the Witch Hunters to our honest town; ghastly creatures, they are! Their bite is worse than their bark!"

Nathaniel admitted, "Hudson sensed them."

With a satisfied smile, she said, "Isn't that what all good

Familiars do; warn their witches of approaching evils?" She gazed over his body, around which energy raged like ecstatic flames. "I know what you seek." Stepping aside, she allowed him entry into her humble home. Contently, Nathaniel entered through the door and halted just inside as she closed it behind him. "But with respect, Nathaniel, you should be able see for yourself. You have the required power."

He was bewitched by what he saw. Shelves upon shelves lined the back wall; jars filled with herbs and ingredients. The list was countless — wolfsbane, belladonna, and cupids dart, thistle, sage, dandelion and more...

"I-I found a sundial," he uttered. Turning, he removed his gaze from her witchy ingredients. "...In the woods."

Surprised and partly taken aback, Janae batted her eyelashes and replied.

"Not what I was expecting to hear. A sundial, you say?" He nodded as she walked past him. "Describe it to me," she finished curiously.

A certain, uneasy look consumed his mature face. In the glowing scarlet light, his stubble gave him that extra sensual and masculine appeal.

"Uh, grey stone base with an octagonal plate on top, four points embellished in gold with a diamond at its centre." He looked to her with brilliance in his eyes. "May I draw the symbols for you? Do you have any parchment?" It was fairly obvious that every woman in Salem desired him; solely based on his sex appeal and content, happy-go-lucky charm. It was his wife, Beatrice, who made sure no one touched her man.

"Here." Janae pulled some loose parchment off the shelf and casually handed it to him. Then, she dipped a quill in a bottle of ink for him to scribe with. "Symbols, you say?" she queried again.

Upon the small, circular table, he fussily drew in detail the four symbols that he had seen on the sundial; the same ones revealed in futuristic dreams.

"This one looks like N, for North, the S for South, E for East and the W for West."

Sliding the piece of parchment across the table, Janae gazed over it. Sharply, she raised her eyes and fixed them on the male witch opposite her.

She queried him cautiously, "Nathaniel; this is what you see in your dreams?" Quietly shocked, he tried to reply, but she cut him off. "I see in your aura that you have the power of Premonition, as well as Telekinesis."

Turning away from the table, she filed through the books on the shelf until she came across one titled Symbols, in a fancy font.

"I have read about these symbols before," she acknowledged.

Opening the book, she closed her eyes and magically made the pages turn as she cast her thoughts upon it, searching for the intended symbols that Nathaniel had shown her.

"Here," the pages instantly halted and fell flat, "it is. The Compass of Power." She raised her eyes from the book, looking at him eagerly. "I knew I had read this before!"

"The Compass of Power?" Nathaniel said with confusion. "Surely it could be anyone's sundial. I often see Cynthea Houston, my neighbor, wandering into the woods. Is it not her possession?"

Giving a bigoted stare, Janae laughed sarcastically, "Ha! That old toad is as far from being a witch as she is from being human." Nathaniel stood with his eyes wide at his friend's sudden outburst. "Come on, Mr. Eames. You have not noticed anything peculiar about that old crone?" He gave her a suspicious look. "She is the Goddess Gaia disguised as an old crack-pot. I found it out by accident, coming across her frolicking naked in the spring just past on Old Man Jerkin's farm."

As he listened, Nathaniel put all the images together to create the fantasy. He queried more why she was out there, instead about Cynthea Houston, "Why were you out there? You know he shoots first and then asks questions later."

"It's the only place I can find saffron, fennel and ginseng in this area." She deferred from the subject and glanced back at the page. "Your symbols are governing powers. Like the triple goddess that the Triad wield."

Nathaniel appeared confused, "The Triad...?"

"Yes," she replied vaguely. Janae appeared stunned that he did not know of the neighboring coven of quadruplet sibling gypsies on the other side of Salem. "The Triad is a rising power. Oddly enough, there are four of them...instead of three." her eyes conjured a perplexed look. "Three brothers: Carson, Jordan and Brian, and their sister, Zara." She drew their symbol of power on the piece of parchment.

First a crescent moon, a joining full moon and then another joining crescent moon.

Focusing back to Nathaniel's symbols, she began to trace them with her index finger and then suddenly gasped, receiving a premonition.

Concerned, Nathaniel queried, "Janae. What do you see?"

"Your legacy, your fortune and," she paused as she looked deeper into the vision, before a sudden, broad, deep grin morphed her lips. "Your incredible power! "Turning her head in his direction, she reopened her eyes. "This is fate, right there." "What do you mean by that?" Nathaniel queried.

"This Compass – Sundial, whatever you want to call it, is yours. Each point or symbol, as you would have it, represents a power, a trait. North – The stubborn power of Deflection, South – The instinctive power of Probability. East – The lurid power of Sensazione and West, appears to me as – a tangible power, strong willed and impulsive."

Awkwardly uncertain and suspicious, Nathaniel replied,

"But I don't have those powers. My daughter, Una–"

"Ah, yes, it all makes sense," she interrupted him, the broad grin still upon her face and the pristine glimmer in her eyes. "Una has the gift of Teleportation. A witch like her father. But. All this...these symbols. It all begins with you." She closed her eyes again, focusing on the vision some more. "I see a long and very, very powerful line of good witches – which you are the creator of. Una is only the first–"

"First of what?" he interrupted her with concern evident in his voice.

"Many generations of witches."

~*~

*T*hat night, returning to his warm and comfortable house in Demuth Street, a two-storey wooden house with a flame-lit street lamp in line with the front gate, Nathaniel sat beside his young daughter as she lay asleep in her bed.

As always, the moon shone its heavenly glow upon his house. The town always missed its entire focus.

In the candlelight, his incredible handsome appearance — fatherly, sapphire eyes, dark brown hair and defined facial features, were what Noah Pogue would look like some few hundred years into the future.

That same fateful night, under the full moon, the three Courtmen Witch Hunters, maliciously vanquished Janae Rose and burned her shack to the ground.

Chapter Twelve

VISIONARY - PART ONE

In the present day, deep within the Underworld, Rafaela stood at the edge of her elevated platform and gazed upon the panoramic view of the ocean floor – crystal clear water, mermaids, sharks, dolphins, fish and whales just behind a pane of glass magically fused to withstand the gigantic pressure.

She wore a black gown of chiffon, her long, dark locks up in a bun of dangling curls.

"They have the Sundial," she grumbled aloud and unsatisfied to all her minions that were present or hiding in the shadows of her imperial lair. "This frustrates me!!"

Using her powers, she made the earth around her tremble, causing gravel and dust to fall from the ceiling somewhere above in the dark, and the water against the window to ripple.

"What do we know about the Pogue Witches?" she queried.

A minion with small knowledge of the Pogue Witches' powers slithered out from the shadows and presented herself.

"Prometheus Pogue is the visionary. He has the power of Sensazione."

Rafaela responded without turning her head. "You're not telling me anything I don't already know, demon!" The irritation was strong in her voice.

"Um," the demon's voice trembled nervously, "Noah Pogue is a Custodian–" Abruptly, she screamed as her body combusted into flames, telepathically vanquished by Rafaela.

"Anybody," Rafaela turned her head slightly as she glanced over her shoulder, "else? For the past," turning around fully, she glared upon the seen and unseen minions present in her chambers, "copious amount of years, we have watched and studied the witches. The Vampires watched Perry in Los Angeles, the Warlocks stalked Noah in Treadwell and Aaron – well, who the hell knows where he is. Their circle is weak because of their broken relationships, so how is it they are still powerful enough to thwart any demon attack we send?" The shadows fell like silk around a set of feminine legs as someone moved out into the gloomy light. An object of desire, she was dressed in a skimpy, long sleeved, low-cut white dress with a brown leather corset that hugged the bodice area and accentuated her breasts.

"Leave the visionary to me," the woman said, confident and smug.

"And you are?" Rafaela queried.

"I am Kamenwati," the woman replied, as the Avatarian demi-goddess looked her over curiously. "Some call me Kamen.

You've not heard of me or my kind?"

The silence was enough for her to know that Rafaela had no recollection.

"I am an Incubo; a Nightmare Soldier."

Rafaela replied "Fascinating," she said, abruptly and unenthusiastically.

"We are demon Sandmen."

Rafaela processed the information and then spoke. "Okay. So prove to me you're different to any other demon I have sent after Prometheus Pogue." Kamenwati stood proud, with evil lust in her eyes. "You have your opportunity to prove your worth to me. Prevail, and your race shall be reimbursed with unimaginable power...fail me," this time Kamenwati appeared slightly nervous, "and your race will literally be sand!"

Kamenwati composed herself. "It would be an honor to prove myself, my Liege!"

With a proud smile, she levitated from the ground and assumed her horrific, ghostly, wraith form before disappearing in an abrupt flash of dark blue light.

"Yes," Rafaela murmured to herself with no faith, "…honor!"

~*~

In was warm in downtown Los Angeles, and a smooth breeze kissed bare skin and caressed it like silk. The skies were clear and blue. A city as busy by day as it was by night - the only thing that slept were the lights of the *Hollywood* sign.

South of the Los Angeles CBD, in a park on Ladera Park Ave, Perry Pogue appeared in a pulse of energy. Some character displacements lingered in the air around his outline before vanishing.

Beside him, a burst of blue flames rose up from the grass.

Dantalian Romani stood tall with a confident stare.

"So," Dan queried as he looked about their surroundings, "this is where you lived?" Perry stood silent as he acknowledged the homes on the opposite side of the street from them. "A bit," he created a hand gesture to express his uncertainty, "plain… even for you, Perry."

Perry listened as he stared at the house across from him.

"No, not me," he replied. "Friends; the Sognare Coven."

Dan understood the Italian word. "Sognare means Dream."

Gypsies possess the innate ability of Omnilingualism: to understand, speak and read any language, whereas some witches may only speak a second language due to cultural upbringing.

"They are a group of Witches who specialize in constructing dreams."

Dan made a curious and impressed facial gesture. He was not familiar with such a power, or with witches who could do such a feat. As far as he was aware, there was the ability of Dream Manipulation – used by either good or evil, to bend visions in sleep into nightmares, dreams or prophecies. Dream Weaving however, was classified as being the most benevolent form of the manipulation power.

At the front door of a modern, open plan house, Perry knocked three times. On the third knock, the door, revealed to be unlocked, moved inward. Perry looked through the gap in the door, while Dan Romani made a silent evaluation of what he could see.

"Hello," Perry called out, "Aislinn?"

Peering through the gap, Dan acknowledged what looked like a blonde-haired female lying on her side in an open doorway in the hallway. Her arm was extended across the floor with her head resting on it.

"Um," Dan murmured with caution, "I think we might have a problem, Perry!"

Pushing the door inward until it stood completely open, Dantalian revealed the blonde deceased woman.

"...Aislinn!" Perry gasped.

Attempting to enter and assist his friend, Perry triggered an invisible force by stepping across the threshold. In a flash of light, he and Dan cried out in fright as they were thrown backwards onto the front lawn.

"Oh," Perry raised his head from the grass, "what the hell was that?"

Raising his head and reaching his arm forward, Dan ignited a ball of fire in his hand and threw it at the open front door. Quickly rising to his feet, he swung his arm briskly once, created a hand gesture just as fast, and commanded his own power of Pyrokinesis with a P.W.C. – Power Word Charm.

"Isolare! (Isolate)" he spoke in Italian.

He proved himself to be a powerful individual.

Passing over the threshold, his fireball exploded, creating a raging inferno that engulfed the doorway as he instructed it to isolate the unseen power. Closing his eyes, Dan focused, telepathically finding the obstruction. Flicking his eyelids open, each hazel iris was consumed by blue flames as he isolated and then used his power to break down the barrier.

"Annientare! (Annihilate)"

Reacting to his magic, the unseen, protective force keeping him and Perry out created an explosion that blew out all the windows in the house and tore a gaping hole where the front door once was.

Rapidly extending his arm out in front, with his hand gestured at the house and the noise, Perry commanded his own P.W.C.

"Silenzio!! (Silence)" his hand gave off a watery blue shine.

His attempt to immediately silence the noise of the boom and shattering windows was successful. The last thing he wanted was to expose witchcraft and it powers to the mortal world.

"Are you stupid or something?" Perry queried Dan. "You

Romani might be powerful...but you're so bloody reckless!" Extinguishing his powers, Dan raised an eyebrow.

"Excuse me?"

"What if someone," Perry shoved Dan in the arm, glaring at him for his inappropriate action, "saw you, you idiot child!" Both exchanged hostile stares. "Clearly, you need to learn more about what it means to be a witch!"

Dan corrected him abruptly. "Gypsy-witch!" "Pft...hybrid moron," Perry growled.

Turning their attention back to the front door, a six-foot tall, masculine and naked male stood in their way on the steps of the front porch. His wavy-brown. shoulder length hair moved as a breeze stirred.

"Who…?" Dantalian queried curiously,

Perry remained silent and looked away to avoid the sight.

"You attacked me," the naked male grumbled cautiously. "Why?" Abruptly, he moved with accelerated speed across the lawn and halted before the Romani and the Pogue Witch. "You dare to bring harm upon my witches?"

Dan appeared awkward, although he blushed a little – revealing his homosexuality – he tried to keep steady contact with the man before him. The set of piercing blue eyes were so captivating and hypnotizing.

"You're witches?" Perry questioned cautiously,

Dantalian let out a sigh of relief, his tense posture becoming relaxed.

"I can feel your desire for my body," the male smiled desirably at Dan, "You are homosexual, are you not?"

Perry, already knowing and not caring about his ally's sexuality, simply stared at the man before them. All gods, goddesses and other divine beings possessed the innate ability of Soul Reading to feel another being's aura and desires, as well as to determine their fate.

Perry's reply was sarcastic. "He's either a straight gay or a gay-straight. What they call a *John Citizen* gay. I forget!"

Generally, Dantalian gave off a *straight* body language, although to those who knew him, he was content being gay.

Acceptance, comfort and confidence was his motto.

"I am," this time the male turned to Perry, "Morpheus,"

Perry replied with knowledge. "Some witch circles call you a Daemon…"

"Others call me a god of dreams." Revealing himself to be the god named Morpheus, the male explained, "The Sognare Coven draw power from me and I protect them."

A remorseful Dan spoke. "I apologize for attacking you." He watched the very painful third-degree burn on Morpheus's abdomen area magically heal itself. "But you expelled us."

Morpheus stared back with regret, having originally believed them to be evil.

"Will you grant us passage?" Perry asked politely. "We believe this coven to be in terrible danger."

Morpheus gave a look of acceptance, lowered his head respectfully and then vanished, as his body turned into a wisp of smoke before disappearing entirely.

Returning to the front door, Perry paused, cautiously looking about the framework for any more hidden enchantments that might block their entry into the house.

"What," Dan queried his friend as though he had lost his mind, "are you looking for?"

Perry remarked sarcastically, "clarity!"

"Which is usually found that at the bottom of a wine bottle; correct?" said Dan.

Turning his head as he passed through the doorway, Perry gave his Romani friend a sour stare. Dan followed not far behind. Not too far down the passage, Perry knelt down on one knee as he observed the deceased blonde female lying in a doorway to the right.

"Aislinn," he mourned in a low voice. "She's been dead," he felt her neck for a pulse and found none, but using his vampire side, "for four days," he was able to determine when death had occurred. "What happened to you?"

Dan stood just behind his shoulder, observing the deceased witch.

"What happened here?" he then queried.

Perry rose back up and looked into the large dining room adjacent to them through the square archway. The furniture had been disturbed, thrown and broken. Looking into the room across from where he stood, Perry then walked through the doorway into the ruined dining room, observed it, halted and then closed his eyes to access his vampire senses – to identify any lingering scent of blood or any echoing rhythms of a heartbeat that would be beyond to the average level of human hearing.

In the middle of the room, he could feel the living, magical energy of the place ripple and warp around him as it made itself visible to his supernatural senses. The Sognare Coven had been teaching him how to connect with the Equilibrium. It was well-regarded that the feat was only achievable by a few skilled witches.

The all encompassing, Supernatural Equilibrium connected all magical creatures and is repulsed by evil. An invisible, primordial force that existed even before the Old Age – before the time of man, or even the dinosaurs – that also hemmed and stitched all dimensions and worlds to the mortal world.

"There was something here." Perry said, with his eyes closed. He turned and followed the echoing voices of the house's previous occupants.

A female's voice echoed, *"Aislinn."*

Through the unclear and hardly observed Astral Echo, he saw his friend killed by an invisible foe. She was thrown at the wall and her neck broken. A second apparition of a female ran through the house.

"Gaia," Perry identified her, his eyes still closed.

Observing the Astral Echo some more, he saw a black shadow swoop through the room and emerge screaming from a back area of the house.

Abruptly, he reopened his eyes with a fearful look in his face.

"Dan," Perry turned to his friend, "you go check the back of the house,"

The Romani nodded his head as he agreed, departing through the doorway and venturing to the rear part of the house. Behind him, as he left, Aislinn's body was silently dragged into the darkened room by an unseen evil presence, leaving a small trace of sand in its wake.

Moving around the room and observing the damage, Perry tried to make out what had happened to his friends. What ill fate did they succumb to?

Behind him, a watery portal manifested on the floor, and through it, a sinister individual silently levitated upward, disguised as the deceased Aislinn. Standing close behind Perry's left shoulder, she opened her mouth to reveal vampire-like fangs.

Feeling a cold breath on his neck, Perry stiffened his posture, and his fate was suddenly decided.

VISIONARY – PART TWO

The floorboards creaked beneath Dan Romani's feet as he moved cautiously and hesitantly toward the rear of the Sognare Coven house. His ash-blonde hair was cut short around the sides, with some length on top to create a Mohawk.

Ahead of him at the end of the hallway, the left side of the double-door entry to a room was left ajar, leaving him to speculate what may lie behind it as a shadow moved about.

"Hello?" he called.

A shadow shot past the partly opened door and Dan suddenly hesitated. He gulped nervously. Behind him, shadows swirled in the hallway. Gathering into a mass, gangly arms and hands with long lanky fingers moved out in an attempt to grab him by the shoulder.

It was an Incubo; a Nightmare Soldier Demon in its shadow form.

Subconsciously wielding his power of Pyrokinesis, the air around Dan rippled as his body radiated a heat, creating a protective barrier from evil. Singeing its hands, the entity's gangly arms quickly withdrew back into its shadowy mass, and the Incubo vanished before its presence was given away. Sensing something, Dan turned his head quickly to glance over his shoulder, and then turned it back to return his focus to the doorway ahead of him. Approaching it, he extended his arm. Gesturing his hand, he manipulated the temperature of the atmosphere, making the air ripple and the doors swing open.

Crossing the threshold, he lowered his arm back down to his side and entered cautiously; unsure of what he might encounter.

He entered and then paused. Cautiously, he scanned the room to the left first. On the right side of the room, out of focus, the body of a deceased individual was dragged silently into a darkened closet. Before him, the furniture in the room, the floor, walls and ceiling, were vandalized with thick, black scorch marks from an onslaught of demon fireballs.

The windows that overlooked the back courtyard were broken and the drapes casually flapped in a vague breeze.

"What the hell," he murmured to himself, becoming disturbed, "happened here?"

Behind him on the right side of the room, a ghostly black figure manifested as it rose up through the white tile floor. Hovering for a moment, it then shapeshifted into a slender woman dressed in jeans and a blouse, her short, brown hair styled like a pixie's.

Using magic, tears appeared in her clean clothes and bloody wounds on her body.

"Help me," she whimpered, quickly placing her feet down on the floor before he noticed her, "please!"

Startled, Dan jumped and gasped. Quickly, he turned around and acknowledged her, but he felt cautious and remained where he stood. Tilting his head slightly, he curiously analyzed her.

"Who are you?" he squawked abruptly.

She replied with sadness. "Thalia. I am a member of the Sognare Coven."

"Where is Aislinn?" he pressed her, forgetting for a moment that Aislinn's body lay in the front of the house.

"Who is Aislinn?" she replied, appearing convincingly confused.

Dantalian moved his arm, gestured his hand and made flames spontaneously combust.

"Oops!" Caught out, her entire persona changed from whimpering and scared to confident and evil. "I should have given a different answer. The dumb bitch, sorry, witch is dead!" Magically, the tears and wounds vanished from her clothes and body. "The entire coven no longer exists!"

"What are you?" Dan questioned cautiously.

She smirked. "What do you think I am, handsome?" revealing a beautiful set of canine teeth. The pupils in her eyes enlarged to fill each iris, and her skin turned a pasty, ill-looking shade of grey. "I am your worst nightmare!" Extending her arm, she gestured a hand and manipulated the air around Dan, revealing the barrier of heat that his power radiated to protect him from her — just as he had done in the hallway. "Intriguing! You're a gypsy and a Firestarter?"

Her hand glowed. Using her demonic powers, she syphoned the rippling, heated air across the room and into her gestured hand.

"I am Mangiare!" she boasted.

Dan smirked sarcastically. "You are Eat?"

Insulted, she clenched her fist and then opened it, firing an attack at him. Without a shield to protect him, he felt a heated, telekinetic force slam against him and then launch him backward across the room. Slamming into a buffet adorned with precious photos, the timber structure broke and the frames shattered.

Without effort, she had proved she was powerful enough to overthrow and subdue anyone — mortal, witch or magical creature.

"Mangiare Essenza Sogno!" she articulated in the most passionate Italian tongue. "Eat, Dream, Essence. But we have many names." Overconfident, she continued. "Dream Eaters, Dream Devourers. I am a part of the sub-sect of the Incubo, Nightmare Soldier species. I might not be as superior, but I am still deadly enough to kill a pathetic Gypsy."

Sitting slumped against the wall, Dan swung his arm around as he conjured flames into his hand and threw a ball of fire at the demon across from him.

Using her mind, she evaded the fireball by changing its course and causing it to strike the wall, setting a large part of it alight. As it extinguished, a black mark scorched a large portion of paint.

"Pretty pathetic, aren't you?" she huffed, displeased. She grabbed him by the throat and elevated him from the floor. "To call you a Romani would be an insult!"

Drawing back, he then spat in her face.

"You," she screwed her face up in repulsion, "disgusting insect!" with her free hand, she wiped the saliva from her cheek. "Now," flicking the spit to the floor, she then elevated her hand back to the side of Dan's head where she made it glow a magical red by activating her power of Dream Sensory, "let me see what you dream of..."

Feeling searing pain obliterate his brain cells, Dan cried out in agony.

"I see what you dream of," she smirked with tantalization.

Abruptly, the Mangiare Demon was sent flying with unforgiving force out of one of the broken windows. Outside, she crashed into the metal dining setting, knocking it over and becoming entangled.

Dan dropped into a heap on the floor, disorientated and weakened.

"I think," said another woman's voice, "you don't know a damn thing about what people dream about!"

Standing in the doorway, a beautiful woman stood with long, flowing blonde hair with caramel highlights. She had a narrow face with kind, immortal features. Her ocean blue eyes appeared territorial, full of strength and pride. She wore a pair of sophisticated, high waisted dark 70's pants and a pink button up shirt beneath a brown leather jacket.

She was very much like Jill Munroe of *Charlie's Angels*.

Walking into the room, she halted by the young Romani, and revealing her strength, effortlessly lifted his dead weight body from the floor and stood him upright.

"My dear," she turned his face to look into his dazed eyes, "you are not powerful enough yet to take on a Mangiare."

Dan, as he regained his faculties, murmured, "Who-who are you?"

"A Guardian Angel," was all she said to him.

Stepping back, she elevated her arm and gestured her hand at him, magically manipulating his Pyrokinesis power to teleport him in an eruption of flames back to Treadwell, Deane County.

Outside, Thalia telekinetically threw the chairs of the outdoor dining suite out of her way as she levitated across the courtyard, approaching the broken windows. The woman standing in the room turned her head; her long hair fell across her cheek, and her blue eyes became more intimidating as she stared the demon down.

"What do we have here?" Thalia commented curiously and without caution as she walked around the room to face the woman head on. "Another filthy Romani?" Her eyes sparkled as she smirked modestly. "A witch?"

The woman followed her with her hard stare around the room.

"You don't want to get on my bad side," the woman responded with a cold and confident tone. "I am more than you're capable of comprehending!"

Thalia extended her arm out in front of her, attacking quickly with telekinesis.

"Bring it on, goddess!"

The woman elevated her chin slightly, revealing her pride.

Confidently she ruined the demon's speculation. "I am not a god!" Revealing her potency, she made her power appear as flames in her eyes. "I am something worse," Thalia screamed, as her body spontaneously combusted into flames. "I am Tempest Pogue!" In a fiery explosion, the demon was vanquished. "Did your sovereign not warn you about me?" Her question went unanswered.

~*~

In the dining room at the front of the house, Perry stumbled about; clutching his neck as blood wept from a wound. Across from him, the vision of Aislinn levitated in midair, smirking, canines drawn, pupils dilated and long hair floating about. Her long, black rags swayed around her body.

"You crazy bitch!" growled Perry.

Quickly raising his arm, he crossed it over his chest and then continued to swing it, attempting to attack her with his power of Telekinesis. His foe turned herself incorporeal, and his power passed through her and the cold fireplace exploded, blowing soot and debris into the air.

Perry shielded his eyes and mouth from the smoke, coughing as it filled the air.

"Oh, you poor possum," the demon mocked him sarcastically as she chuckled, turning corporeal again. "We Incubo are immune to the powers of a witch. You are," extending her arm, she gestured her hand at him and blasted him with black lightning, "miniscule to me, Pogue Witch!"

Elevating to the tips of his toes, Perry arched his back and held his arms out as he cried aloud in pain, electrocuted by black magic.

In the back part of the house, Tempest Pogue turned her head toward the doorway. Hearing the sounds of Perry's fight drew fury to her calm complexion. The air around her body warped violently as her power of Advanced Pyrokinesis became wildly aggressive.

Radiating from her feet, flames swept across the floor. Unharmed, she casually walked off through the doorway, heading for the front of the house. The room behind her was a blazing inferno.

Walking along the hallway, the floorboards warped and buckled from the heat that she emananted.

Reaching the doorway, she watched Perry Pogue being electrocuted and lifted from the floor by black lightning that would surely kill him very shortly. Compared to the regular power of Electrokinesis, the Black Lightning of an Incubo was far worse – it had the potential to corrode in a good witch, either gradually or quickly turning them evil if not stopped.

Behind the Aislinn imposter, the charcoal logs in the fireplace spontaneously combusted with a roar. Startled, the Incubo demon became distracted and released Perry from its dark power. Shrieking, she shielded her face as the heat became intense.

"I smell a witch!" she shrieked, moving abruptly as she expelled a pulse of energy through her power of Paralysis.

Hit by the energy as he recovered from being electrocuted, Perry dropped to his knees. Paralyzed, he then fell sideways onto the floor. Crossing the threshold into the room, Tempest was struck by the pulse and she too was unexpectedly paralyzed and unable to move. Elegantly, Aislinn's apparition dissolved as a faint breeze brushed past the demon and she resumed her beautiful Kamenwati visage.

"Grandma," Kamenwati smirked with cocky body language, "I presume?"

Tempest grumbled with dislike. Closing her eyes and elevating her face toward the ceiling, she silently and secretly exercised her great power to summon other beings – a power that only a select few possessed. It usually belonged to divine entities or powerful demons of the upper or superior levels of the echelon.

Moments later, a gold shimmer moved down from the ceiling. Gathering in mid-air almost beside Tempest, the manifestation became a woman with long brown hair pulled back in a ponytail.

Elsewhere on Wilshire Boulevard in Downtown L.A, reacting to the magic of Tempest and her accomplice's presence, the Le Brea Tar Pits spontaneously ignited.

Tempest spoke. "We will ask the questions." Telepathically, she made the air throughout the entire house suddenly warp as she manipulated the temperature to a stifling heat.

On the floor, Perry coughed, breathing in a short flame as he felt his insides begin to roast.

"Philomena," Tempest acknowledged the other woman beside her. "Crush her!"

Kamenwati, looked fearlessly at the brunette woman, eagerly waiting for a hand or a body movement. Suddenly, the gravity surrounding her became strict, and she screamed in pain.

"How-how!" she beckoned, groaning uncomfortably as she dropped down to one knee. "I will not stand this–"

Closing her eyes, Philomena summoned the sun's glare to amplify Tempest's Advanced Pyrokinesis with her gravity manipulating power. A disembodied groan was heard throughout Los Angeles, and a 5.0 magnitude earthquake disrupted the county. Traffic came to a screeching halt as explosions resonated and manhole coverings along Hollywood Boulevard were sent rocketing up into the air. Unseen by the human eye, the sun's rotation was revealed as its rays became a single beam. A slight shadow, as though the sun was hidden behind a cloud, was cast over California.

The air warped as the glare of intense and focused heat of the sun made the roof of the house groan and browned the lush, front lawn. Two trees and all of the cars parked in the street spontaneously combusted into flames.

"Helios, god of the sun!" Tempest elevated her arms, revealing her own immunity to the demon's paralysis power, "Hear me!–"

A disembodied male voice replied, "I hear you," from the heated air, "witch!"

"Lend to me," her long blonde hair began to elevate into the air, "enhance my fire!" The illusion of flames manifested in her eyes and her aura warped with heat. "You want to see what a Firestarter can achieve, Kamenwati?"

From her feet, flames swept out across the floor, setting it alight. The fiery effect was kept distant from Perry, creating a small, safe area in which he lay. Flames poured down the walls from the ceiling like water. Unaffected, Philomena continued to telepathically manipulate the gravity so that the demon was unable to move.

"They are Gamma Witches!" Perry murmured.

Kamenwati appeared frightened by the revelation and decided to flee, but with arrogance, she said, "I refuse to bow to witches! The Visionary is mine!"

Letting out a painful yell against the harsh gravitational force bearing down upon her, she made her body change, and she resumed her black shadow form. Moving across the room amongst the flames, she wrapped herself around Perry, and in an instant they were both gone.

Outraged, Tempest yelled, activating her power to its fullest.

The tops of the palm trees along Hollywood Boulevard spontaneously ignited, reacting to Tempest's Pyrokinesis. From outside in the street, the house was annihilated in a massive inferno. Walking through the flames, out into the front yard, Tempest, followed by Philomena made their way to the bitumen.

Casting her gaze to the sky, Philomena released the sun from her manipulation.

"Oracle's of Phaedra!" Tempest summoned.

Three distinct and individual disembodied voices replied. "How may we serve you, Tempest Pogue?"

"Find me Prometheus Pogue!" her facial expression revealed determination.

Philomena queried, "Where are we going?"

"We need Noah!" Tempest acknowledged. "We're going to Treadwell!"

Together, they both vanished, teleporting out of Los Angeles in a ripple of heated air. Upon their departure, the earthquake and flames stopped, leaving the City of Angels in a slight state of chaos.

~*~

I t was late in Treadwell, Deane County; darkness pressed against the glass windows of the modern airport departure and arrivals lounges. Outside light could only keep night at a certain distance, but it cast enough delicate light to outline buildings, aircraft and airport machinery.

A female voice called over the intercom. "This is the last call for Flight CX974 Cathay Pacific to Hong Kong." Behind a column, a fiery torrent rose up from the floor and Dantalian staggered for a moment, regaining his balance. Revealing herself to be a pyrokinetic witch also, the extreme extent of Tempest's power proved she could manipulate another's power of the same element and was capable of transporting Dan back to his hometown.

Turning around as he stepped out from behind the column, Dantalian murmured to himself as he took in his surroundings.

"How the hell did I end up here?" Turning some more with his eyes to the ceiling he queried, "P–" Abruptly, his words were cut short as he bumped into another male. "Perry," he thought aloud.

Quickly, the male's hot, take-away cup of coffee fell from his hand.

"Gelare! (freeze)" Dan gasped out a P.W.C.

The hot coffee abruptly froze in time from the Power Word Charm, along with everyone and everything else around the young male Romani – except the male that Dan had rested his arm on.

"Shh–" Dan tried his best not to swear he scooped up the cup and its contents in midair. "I am so, sorry–" Returning his eye contact, he acknowledged that the male in front of him was not still in time. "Oh – this is awkward…"

The male replied apologetically. "No, I apologize; I should have been watching where I was going. It's not your fault. I'm a klutz at the best of times, mate!"

Dan just stared, hoping that the male wouldn't notice his still surroundings. Quickly, he snapped his fingers, breaking the active enchantment. Everything began to move again. Gasping again, a new, untrained power that Dan was growing into glimpsed an insight into the man. Linking, the infant stage of Mind Control as his power came to be, allowed him to access another's thoughts like Telepathy but was able to view them like a Premonition.

He saw the man shapeshift into an impressive Lion that roared as it leapt at him.

Gasping, Dan ripped his hand away in fright of what he had witnessed.

"Are you okay?" the man queried him.

An uncertain Dan replied, "Um. Yeah… I think…"

The man moved his hand out to offer a hand shake, "My name is Aiden."

"Dantalian," He grasped the hand and shook it politely, "Dan, for short."

Aiden smirked as though he knew more, but he kept quiet and departed.

THE MEAT LOCKER

It was rather crisp at midnight and there was hardly any traffic on Norvard Boulevard in Treadwell. A faint drizzle brought a commanding supernatural presence to the glow given off by the street lights.

Some weeks had passed since Kamenwati abducted Perry Pogue. A desperate Noah struggled to grasp the idea that all his leads, good and evil, were coming up empty. The Nightmare Soldiers had done an impressive job at cloaking their location.

The sound of a pair of high heels pounded the footpath as a woman ran frantically toward the east end of the city, past Royal Treadwell Hospital. Her breathing was shortened, long hair flapping in a headwind and heart racing in her chest as adrenaline sped it faster and faster. Changing her course, she ran through the open gates and into the city's Botanical Gardens.

Her short, unfit breathing became louder as she made her way along a bitumen path hugged by dark, wet vegetation. From the darkness, a fireball shot through the air. Ducking as she ran, the woman evaded the attack from an unidentified person.

"Why–" a telepathic voice moved through her head. "Why are you running?"

Startled, she turned and almost tripped over her own feet. Continuing on, she veered to the left as she came to a T-junction in the path.

From within the foliage at the bitumen's edge, a slick chain of silver energy wrapped around her leg and as she screamed, the woman was flipped up into the air. With a grunt she hit the trunk of a tree and groaning, she fell onto her stomach on the wet ground.

Raising her head from the grass, she brushed her brunette hair from her face and watched a slender, platinum blonde, seventeen-year-old girl emerge from the foliage.

"Addison," she beckoned.

The young woman, named Addison, gave a cold and unfriendly expression. A sudden wind blew her long blonde locks about. The street lamp with the addition of the fine rain, gave her white dress a subtle glow. Over the top she wore a long sleeve charcoal fly-away cardigan and suede thigh-high boots.

Lifting her arm to the young blonde, the woman summoned, "Sister, please!"

"Who are you calling sister?"

Flicking her left hand to the side with a brisk gesture, using Telekinesis, Addison threw the brunette woman away.

Crashing onto the grass, the woman picked herself up and scampered off in fear across the lawns of the gardens.

Turning her head, Addison's long blonde hair fell down the side of her face; putting a stronger emphasis on her dark glare.

"You can run all you want, but you cannot hide!" she said.

Running across the wet lawn, the terrified mortal woman saw security in the building ahead of her. Her breathing quickened again, her hair flapped behind her in the wind and the fine rain felt like sand whipping across her face.

She grunted uneasily, a hand grasped her by the throat and then she was suddenly thrown down on the ground.

Madelyn Romani stood over the woman, "So I see you are wearing me as a disguise!" using her Nature Manipulation power, she elevated the woman from the ground with tree roots and held her at eye level. "I wish I could say I am flattered but unfortunately I am very pissed off!"

"Oh," the woman sighed, "your reputation precedes you!"

Madelyn growled, "Oh, please! Shut up!" her long brunette locks moved in a sudden breeze, "I've worked pretty damn hard on my reputation! So don't think riding my coat tail is going to win you brownie points in the Underworld!" the beautiful Romani remarked with strict sarcasm, "I've spent 3 fing days in police lockup. The District Attorney Noah Pogue arrested me because I killed three witches." The fierceness in her glare acknowledged the hate Madelyn held within about the killing of good individuals, "Crimes I know I did not commit. So now, you're one screwed demon!"

The female scolded, "Filthy Romani scum!"

Madelyn, wearing the demon's saliva on her cheek, held her head to the side with a portion of long brown locks blocking the imposter's view. Turning her head back rapidly, the brown locks elevated and her soft eyes blazed a sparkling emerald.

Wielding her power, she dealt the demon a devastating blow.

Screaming in agony, the body of the woman was torn apart by tree roots; vanquished in a display of red and gold flames.

Behind her, out of focus, a second individual emerged from the ground as the air warped. Lunging forwards, it attacked Madelyn from behind. Sensing and evading to her right, she used magic to speed up her movement and then abruptly halted. She struck back hard and sharp, throwing the Athame from the male's hand. Grabbing him by the arm she pulled him forwards and flipped him over. Grasping the weapon as it fell toward the ground, Madelyn impaled her attacker in the chest.

In an outcry of agony his body combusted and he was vanquished.

Turning around, she screamed as a stray fist came straight at her face. In a flash of purple, the hand collided with a barrier of energy. The structure held, but all the bones in the hand broke.

Whipping his hand back, the demon whimpered as he cradled his limb.

To the side of the clearing in the Botanical Gardens, under a street lamp, Brady Romani stood with his hand gestured at his side as he wielded his ability.

"You broke my," the male cried in pain, "hand!"

"Suffer pain, demon bane," a female's voice cast a vanquishing spell in Romanian, "vanquished with a searing flame!"

The male's skeletial structure groaned and buckled. Letting a strained cry of agony he was vanquished as his body combusted into rigorious flames. Stepping into focus, Addison Romani revealed herself as the superior.

"Don't get too comfortable," Madelyn cautioned her sister, "There will be more." turning her head she looked over at their young brother as he remained beneath the street lamp. "Philanderer Demons are the same as Vampires when it comes to nesting and hunting in packs!"

"Salutations," a woman greeted in French,

Turning around, Madelyn was struck by a telekinetic attack. Thrown, she crashed into Addison; knocking them both onto the grass.

A woman stood sophisticated in her high-end designer attire. Her long blonde hair, in thick, loose hanging curls blew about as the wind picked up again.

"The children of Gaia," she spoke in such beautiful French as both Madelyn and Addison seemed to understand what she was saying. "Filthy Romani!"

Letting out a cry, Madelyn, as she sat on the ground, reached her arm forwards at the blonde causing the ground to explode and tree roots to strike her, hissing like snakes.

"Bind my victim," Madelyn commanded in Romanian.

Wrapping around the slender female, the tree roots crunched and hissed.

Madelyn gestured her hand at her target, "Zdrodi! (Crush)"

Giving off a green glow, the tree roots abruptly restricted their victim, breaking every bone in her body. Pulling her sister up to her feet, Madelyn brushed her hair from her face as she watched her magic kill the demon.

"How do you feel?" she queried Addison.

Addison replied, "Like you landed on top of me?" A sarcastic and confused look appeared in her youthful face.

"Why?" she queried, cautiously looking about.

Giving off another glow, the tree roots binding the female demon began to creak as they expanded.

Madelyn murmured, "Huh?"

The tree roots shone a mysterious green and in a burst of sparkling particles the woman emerged, appearing rather irritated.

"Oh," Addison's eyes widened, "Houston we have a problem!"

Madelyn grumbled irritably, "Gaia, give me strength!" extending her arm at the female demon, she cast a spell in Romanian, "Beneath the ground, roots I command you, strike with force!"

The blonde female smirked modestly, "this ought to be a treat!"

Around the botanical gardens a disembodied groan moved and the ground between Madelyn and her aggressor exploded as massive tree roots tore up. Rising fast and lurching forwards abruptly they hissed like pythons.

Extending her arm and gesturing her hand, the woman projected, "Geler!! (Freeze) in beautiful French. Magically the serpent-like tree roots halted and turned to ice. "Faire Sauter! (Explode)"

Swinging her arm, fast, she used her demonic telekinesis to project the broken and jagged pieces of tree root back at the two Romani sisters.

Madelyn and Addison let out a shriek.

Reaching forward between the two sisters, Brady used his power of Barrier Projection. Whistling like missiles, the swift moving weapons recoiled off an invisible dome that flashed purple with each individual impact.

"VIA!! (Away)" Madelyn commanded.

Letting out a scream, the blonde female was ripped backwards by tree roots and vanished into the dark and seclusion of the trees across the way.

Madelyn smirked confidently, "Don't piss off Mother Nature!"

~*~

The humble and sleepy city of Treadwell was situated over a Hellmouth. Being positioned over such a powerful focal point, it was also Witch Territory — a ceaseless and watchful guard against any evil that may try to rise and claim it.

To have more than one coven of witches located in one place was called a grove. New Salem was located outside of Treadwell in a dimension out of phase with this reality that had full peripheral view of Deane County.

Under the rule of Queen Maria, numerous low level covens occupied different provinces around city, outer suburbs and rural townships.

The Cavallo: A Coven of Therianthrope Witches guarded the Rune Valley.

Potenza watched over Victor Harbor.

The Dynasty Glamazon, super model-esque witches situated in Sandhurst, Hoxton County. While the Pogue Coven ranked superior to them all and the Romani Coven ranking second occupying residency in Treadwell and the surrounding Treadwell Hills.

Teleporting into the open area of the park, a male demon roared as he threw three consecutive fireballs at the Romani sisters.

Reaching her arm up as she gasped, Madelyn projected a green mist from her open palm; extinguishing the fiery attack with the Poison Projection branch of her Nature Manipulation power.

Levitating down through the air, he came to land heavily on the grass with a thud.

"Texas!" Madelyn snarled,

He replied nastily, "Madelyn Romani!"

"Blow it out your ass!" she hissed,

He replied, "Bitch!" and he threw an Athame at her as he extended his arm. "Die Mischling!" he named her magical species in German.

Using her telekinetic power of Chain Reaction, Addison Romani mentally sent the knife flying in another direction. It bounced off the trash can, rebounded off a tree and as a male Philanderer Demon teleported into the opening he was impaled in the back. Gesturing his hand to conjure a ball of fire, the demon accidently struck a second demon that suddenly appeared beside him with the lethal fireball. Crying out in agony both their bodies erupted into flames and were vanquished.

"Brady let down the barrier!" she requested bluntly,

Gesturing his hand, Brady Romani made a glittering wall of purple energy appear and then disappear.

Amongst the wind, Madelyn's long dark hair that framed her long face lifted about. Her stern scolding glare was picturesque. Both the demon and the Romani waited with anticipation. Who would be first to strike and annihilate their foe?

Quickly swaying his hand, Texas conjured a rotating ball of fire. Pulling his lips up over his sharp demonic teeth he gave a deep, territorial growl.

"Maddy," Addison hissed under her breathe, "You cannot be serious!"

Madelyn queried, "Does it get you off?" as she accentuated a broody confidence.

He growled again, clutching his rotating ball of fire in his hand.

Her firm lips moved again, "Killing innocent women who do nothing wrong!"

"I," he began, steadily keeping firm eye contact with the Romani, "am the hunter and you are the hunted!" Madelyn narrowed her eyes nastily. "Women deliberately dress to tease. Lead by desire and fueled by their ambitious hormones. How can men refuse the taste of something so fine?"

"You pathetic, insolent little man!" Madelyn growled back.

He grinned, describing the sensual pleasure he felt from killing innocent women.

"The feel of their silky skin within your hand when you're about to break their neck," Her eyes ignited with ravenous fury. "The ecstasy," he clenched his fireball tightly as he tensed his body with pleasure, "When you drain their life and feed on their pheromones. You were made for us to feed on. Like cattle!"

"Is that what you did to Visper?" Addison queried, "the woman you abducted, and killed I imagine by now!"

Outraged by his disgusting small talk, Madelyn growled with ridicule, "You weak excuse of a man!" Her eyes began to blaze with impressive green. Tree roots rose up behind her, hissing and striking like snakes. "You dare to speak so ill!" With a brisk swing she moved her arm out in front, projecting her attack onwards. "It is you who shall feel the life drain from you!"

The tree roots made whip cracking noises as they surged at their target.

"No way, Xena!" growled Texas projecting a forceful wave of telekinesis. "Go back to the Amazon!" and in sync their powers collided; her power launched him back and his telekinesis catapulted her through the air.

Addison and Brady evaded to each side while Madelyn somersaulted and crashed heavily onto the grass.

"Ugh…" she lay there for a minute as she regained her clarity but mustered enough muscle to grumble, "Son of a…"

Amongst the trees and shrubs of the gardens, Dylis stalked a Philanderer Demon as he waited in the wings for his summons to join in the battle.

"Hey, Princess!" said a familiar voice.

Turning his head, his chin met the rough end of Dylis's fist.

With telekinetic propulsion, Dylis threw the young Philanderer Demon at a large tree.

She growled very displeased, "You know better."

As the two made eye contact the beautiful witch's eyes magically turned from hazel to teal. He appeared to relax as a certain look of familiarity consumed his face and then a look of confusion followed.

Grabbing him by the throat she retorted, "A gentleman should never hit women!"

Crushing his wind pipe he managed to murmur, "Eish—"

"Uh-uh ah!" she fiercely corrected as she submitted him into silence. In a deep voice under her breath as she maintained a foul stare, she ordered him, "Don't you dare speak my name you ill-mannered muck!"

He nervously nodded his head once, understanding perfectly.

Telepathically she commanded in fluent French,

"Séjour… (Stay)." Lowering her arm, his body magically stuck. Dylis kept full eye contact, stepping back she continued in eloquent French. "I am Eisheth, Old One and creator of your kind."

Hiding amongst the shadows of nearby bushes, Ryder's eyes glittered as she used her telepathy to listen in on Dylis.

Dylis narrowed her eyes as she gave him a cold, hard look, "You will leave. The Innocent is lost, the witches have won."

A suspicious Ryder stepped out from the shadows to reveal herself. Out the corner of her eye, Dylis noticed the

Romani and then quickly glanced back to the demon before her.

"Waste not, want not." Dylis smirked, giving him a devilish stare. "Your services are no longer required!"

Spontaneously he arched his back and he cried out in agony. Exploding before her bewildered eyes, Dylis stepped back. Marching up beside her and abruptly halting, Madelyn's friend Cerina touched Dylis on the shoulder.

"You okay?"

Dylis's eyes magically reverted back to normal before she replied, "He, uh," she pretended to be somewhat traumatized. "Tried to compel me, seduce me with his demonic powers." Glancing back at the tree, all that remained was a thick black scorch mark.

Texas spoke chauvinistically, "I will break you!"

Bringing his masculine arm around and in front of his torso, he then swung it back around as he used his demonic power. Using her power of Empathy, Ryder accessed his telekinetic power and used it against him.

Instantly he shot sideways and with brutal force crashed into the ground where he stayed, unable to move.

Approaching him, Ryder halted with her arm extended and her middle finger pointed at him.

Firmly she ordered, "Stay!"

Irritable he slandered her, "Make me, bitch!"

She replied in a calm voice, "Watch your tongue with me boy!" Ryder was the superior in this situation. Her power of Empathy had taught her how to work with emotion instead of against it, enabling her to manipulate a hostile opponent. "Swear again and I will cut it out." she was confident, absolute and regal. Standing away from him she simply stared at him...telepathically unhinging his mind and controlling it, "I want you!"

He repeated, "I want you..."

"Who are you?" Ryder queried.

Again, he repeated under her control.

Now out in the opening a surprised Dylis watched; impressed that this simple Romani could achieve such a feat while Cerina went and helped Madelyn up off the grass.

Ryder moved her lips again, her voice still so placid, "I've been waiting for you."

He repeated, "How could I hurt–"

Ryder reinstated his suppressed conscience, "...an innocent woman?"

Suddenly his body began to shudder as he fought back...or so it seemed.

He said, "This is guilt I feel..." Ryder forcing the words against his will.

A single diamond-like tear appeared in the corner of his demonic eye.

Closing his eyes, he suddenly arched his back away from the ground and then slammed it back down as he reopened his eyes.

In a manic tone he oppressed her power, "You cannot control the words that spill from my lips, Mischling!"

Behind, slightly out of Ryder's focus, Dylis inaudibly moved her lips – this time she appeared to be controlling him. Positioning her head on a slight tilt, Ryder, unafraid, looked at him curiously and encouraged him to say more.

"Go on. They are only words…" And then suddenly she sighed with contentment. "The best way to destroy a Philanderer."

Instantly Dylis stopped moving her lips and listened.

"Give them a mortal conscience. Their thirst for desire is their own undoing and a conscience is designed to install morals." Ryder said knowingly.

He suddenly cried out and flames ignited at his feet.

Racing up the length of his body the flames left only a lick of black on the grass. In a ripple of energy, another Philanderer Demon appeared.

Terrified Dylis called out, "Behind you!"

His unique scent of Blueberry moved past Ryder's nose and drew her immediate attention. The scent was his manipulation of her desire to do good.

His deep mellow voice was heart melting, "You shouldn't be walking these dark gardens alone."

Turning around she almost died from his charming features.

"Whatever will I do out here all by my lonesome?" She implied sarcastically.

At that key point he assumed a demonic visage different to that of Texas. The canines in his bottom row of teeth protruded like bore tusks. Thorns protruded from the sand cracks around his mouth, the veins in his protruding brow were more dominant and his cat eyes were smaller and more evil.

Opening his hands, his fingernails magically morphed into talons. Petrified and unable to move, she used her telepathy to find his name amongst his disturbing and malicious thoughts.

"Hyson," she announced his name, creating aggravation within him. "That's an interesting name. Charming too."

He realized, "Romani!" speaking aloud in his charming voice. "You will die!"

Using her power of Empathy, Ryder gained control of his body paralyzing it so he could not move.

"Oh, mate." She sighed comfortably. "Shit before the shovel, I'm afraid."

An abrupt look of intimidation moved in his stiff expression.

Watching from afar, Dylis gave a sly smirk and then suddenly disappeared in a pulse of clear energy.

Staring into his ravenous, cruel and demonic eyes, Ryder was able to hypnotize him. Each of her pupils enlarged to the full size of the iris in each eye and then returned back to normal as she activated her power.

Running across the grass, Madelyn halted and called out,

"Ryder!"

Standing before him, gazing into one another like an intimate couple, Ryder took a deep breath and then exhaled as she prepared for what she would find within his mind.

"Unhinge the mind, so I shall see; reveal the pleasures of this evil entity."

Instantly the tortuous cries of victims pierced her mind.

She cringed and the Botanical Gardens around her filled with a disorientating black. Amongst the dead void she could hear her own strict breathing.

"Who are you?" murmured a vulnerable voice.

"Have you come to save us?" said another fearful voice.

Startled Ryder beckoned, "Hello?"

"Are you a demon, too?"

Raising her arm – toward what she thought was the sky – Ryder commanded in a superior voice.

"Luce! (Light)"

Exploding from her body a brilliant light blew away the dark and beyond it was something even more horrifying.

She gasped, "Oh my God!"

Raising her eyebrows in horror and covering her mouth with her hand. She stood inside an enormous Meat Locker.

Lining all four walls was every victim ever slaughtered by a Philanderer Demon.

GAMMA WITCH

There was an outcry of agony...

The attic of Noah Pogue's house was in darkness beyond the partly opened door. Suddenly, flames began to spontaneously ignite until a large circle of white candles was revealed by the warm golden glow.

A woman's scream resonated. Plummeting down from the ceiling, inside the circle, Isadora crashed onto the floor. The impact with the floor flicked up a breeze that made the flames atop the candles sway.

"Ugh..." she groaned uncomfortably, getting up onto her feet, "that bloody hurt–" Distracted, she began to turn her head and look about the room. "Hello?" she called out.

Another voice replied, "Hello?"

Startled, she gasped and spun around.

"Whoa!" both said at once, intimidated by what they saw. "Who are you?"

Opposite to her, on the outside of the candlelit circle stood a second Isadora Pogue. But this one was dressed in short white denim shorts and a pink blouse. Her long blonde hair pulled back in a ponytail. The Isadora inside the circle wore black leather leggings and fitted corset that emphasized her breasts. Her blonde hair styled.

"I know who I am," the more innocent looking Isadora outside the circle smiled, "but you, I think, are confused?" Inside the circle, the other smirked cautiously. "Imitation," with a jolt of her hand, the real Isadora made the air ripple and she used her power of Energy Manipulation to throw her imposter backwards, "Is the greatest form of flattery!"

Crying out in pain, the imposter crashed against an invisible barrier that trapped her inside the circle and then magically shapeshifted back into a male as he fell onto the floor.

Isadora continued briefly, "But you Genderling Demons ought to just pick a gender and stick to it!"

She watched him get up onto his feet again, "Do you like," she gestured her hand at the form of his imprisonment, "our nifty invention? No?" they both gave each other a dark glare. "This is what we call a Spirit Prison."

"I know what a Spirit Prison is," he growled back arrogantly, "you stupid woman!"

She ignored him and continued, "We mostly use it to summon the spirits of our ancestors. But tonight, we've trapped your essence inside of it." Her expression glowed with sarcasm for a moment, "You cannot teleport out and none of your frenemies – demon friends – can summon you to them. They're literally going to have to come barging in here to free you!"

Roaring at her, he reached his arm forwards in an attempt to grab her. Reacting, the flames atop the candles reached up aggressively and created the same barrier he rebounded off prior, but this time it was scorching hot and scalded his hand. Ripping his hand back he cried out in pain.

"Tsk, tsk, tsk," Isadora mocked. Clicking her tongue as she gave a dark and vicious stare, she waved her index finger and cursed at him in Italian, "Sticks and stones, may break your bones."

Suddenly, both his forearms twisted. He cried out as the sound of bones breaking moved about the candlelit attic.

"Who did you think you were dealing with, Soul Devourer," they both exchanged a stare, "Genderling Demons have always fascinated me. You're able to switch between male and female while maintaining a constant psychic connection with one another. You can read auras and have perfect accuracy when telling the future. How many mortal souls have you stolen?"

Moving her arms forward, she gestured her hands at him. Manipulating the energy around his body she crushed him. He cried out in agony and was vanquished in flames.

~*~

Gasping, the male demon opened his eyes and found himself sitting on a chair inside the same circle except now the room was lit by the lights in the ceiling and walls.

He had witnessed his demise via illusion.

Maneuvering at each ear was a hand connected to an invisible arm. The fingertips gave off delicate strands of white electricity that penetrated the left and right temples of his brain, creating visions of things that were not real. But he did not know this.

A deep growl moved about the room.

The grey, cougar form of Noah Pogue roared as it leapt out of the shadows in between the old couch and cupboard. Landing on its front paws, it rose up onto its hind legs. Arching its body, both front legs were extended forwards and its mouth was open wide – showing off its beautiful white teeth. Releasing its large eagle wings, it flapped them with force.

In a human voice it roared, "TELL ME WHERE MY BROTHER PERRY IS!!"

Terrified the Genderling Demon, shapeshifted into Isadora out of fear and the hands at each side of her head disappeared. Screaming, she was projected backwards while still bound to the chair by the telekinetic waves emenating from the cougar's bellowing roar.

In the proper reality, Bermuda Pogue stood behind the demon while he sat bound to the chair. She held a hand at each side of his head, articulating her power of Illusory to mentally unhinge his mind.

The power of Illusory allowed the wielder to create faultless illusions compared to the power's infant form, Illusion Casting.

She proposed, "Are you ready to talk now?" smirking as she moved her hands away. "I think I scared the crap out of him enough. I showed him his vanquish!" she revealed as she stepped out of the circle.

Bermuda Pogue — Burke, as called by her sister Isadora — was a tall woman with an individuality all of her own. She is outspoken and honest. This Pogue Witch does not care much for cosmetics, always trying to keep it natural or as minimal as possible. Long blonde hair, in what she calls, styled tangles because she hates brushing her hair, she prefers it messy but pretties it up on occasion.

Her emerald coloured eyes are deep. A statement to her nature because no one would dare provoke her.

"What's wrong?" Isadora summoned as she walked around the outside of the circle, "Witch got your tongue?"

Noah intervened, "We have other methods," as he sat with the families *Book of Shadows* on the old couch across from the demon. "There is a thing called a truth spell that we could always cast on him!"

"I say," Isadora and Bermuda turned their attention to Shane, Noah's son, as he spoke, "I say, I electrocute it out of him!" and his hand gave off sparks of green electricity. He queried arrogantly, "How would you like a thousand watts coursing through your body?"

Sitting silently, the demon absorbed all the small talk. But then, spontaneously screamed out in pain as orange light shone out of his eyes and open mouth. His aura rippled with such immense heat that the candles creating the Spirit Prison melted into a ring of white wax on the floor.

Shrieking, Isadora and Bermuda turned their heads away, shielded their faces with their hands and were forced backwards until they halted where their cousin Shane stood.

After a moment of his insides roasting, his body combusted and all that remained was a thick black scorch mark on the timber floor. Quickly the intense heat settled and the room resumed a comfortable temperature.

"There will be no need," said a mature woman's voice from the doorway, "to use a Truth Spell on him." Tempest Pogue and her sister Philomena Beaumont stood proud.

Noah, bewildered by the demon's vanquish, sat forwards on the couch.

"Grandma?" he queried with surprise,

Isadora, Bermuda and Shane looked at the two seventies-era fashioned women and then turned their stares back to Noah.

Tempest appeared stern in her facial expression, "Hello Noah, sweetheart," and then relaxed enough to reveal a humbleness to see her grandson. "The Genderling Demon possessed no knowledge of Perry's whereabouts!"

Noah queried with caution, "How do you know that?"

"Because we, Philomena and I, fought the Incubo Nightmare Solider who abducted him." Tempest revealed as she stepped toward the middle of the room where the melted circle of white candles was.

Noah rose from his seat, he appeared irritated, "You're telling me that three months of dead ends and you knew the entire time who took him?"

"You're angry," Philomena spoke, trying to sooth him, "and we respect that."

Noah barked at her, "you bet your Gamma Witch arse!" as he returned the *Book of Shadows* to its position on the book stand. "I am pissed off! You-you," he chuckled awkwardly, "you have some nerve to show your face here!"

Listening to the term, Gamma Witch, a confused Isadora interrupted.

"Just a quick question, but, who are you and what exactly is a Gamma Witch?"

Noah spoke abruptly, "This is your Great Grandmother, Tempest Pogue and one of her sister's Philomena. My mother's mother and aunt!" Isadora appeared vague, listening to her uncle and then turned her head as she gazed upon her ancestor. "As for the term, Gamma Witch," Noah began again, "it is the highest and most powerful status a witch can gain. The power of a Gamma Witch surpasses all."

"There are four of us," Tempest continued to reveal the definition of her status, "myself, Philomena, Patrella and Darla. You need four to become Gamma Witches, to have not only full possession of the Pentagram and its power but also the compass points!"

"North, South, East and West," Bermuda murmured with realization.

Tempest smiled, impressed by her great granddaughter's knowledge, "That is correct. Not all witch lineage can bare the power. We fused our blood with our family magic–"

"We needed the power to battle Troupeador," Philomena interrupted, "he was our destined final battle and it was that battle that cost us our lives. We died just as he was also vanquished. He ruled the Underworld during our generation's time of power. The Queen of Magic, under the orders of the Divinita rewarded us with wings–"

Bermuda interrupted, "Aaron, our father,"

Philomena made a confused look with her face. "Would tell us bedtime stories about the four powerful witches who became archangels!" Philomena and Tempest gave a certain look of reasurruance that Bermuda's fable was in fact about them. "You are them. You are those witches!"

"Enough!" Noah grumbled, unsatisfied that he was hearing things he already knew. "Get to the point, Grandma!" Tempest gave her grandson an odd look. "If you don't have any useful information for me, regarding my brother, then you can get the hell out of my house!" Isadora blurted out, "Noah!"

"It's okay, Isadora!" Tempest calmed the young blonde witch, "I get where he is coming from." She turned her sight to Noah this time, "We have much to discuss, Noah. But you know the rules. We – Mena and I – cannot be in these corporeal forms for long. Our stone state will resume and we will be forced to rest for twenty-four hours–"

Philomena added, "Just being here, the two of us, is creating weather anomalies, global disruptions. Increased Gamma Radiation."

Noah gave a narrow stare.

"Sweetheart," Tempest approached and then halted, "What can we assist you with?"

Noah turned his head. Out the corner of his eye he saw the stone Sundial outside the window of the attic, positioned in the front garden below.

"I don't know what is more important. My wife leaving me, finding my brother or protecting that stupid Sundial. What does it even do, that Sundial?" he turned his head and resumed eye contact with his grandmother. "What is its purpose? Perry and I touched it. It has power. We felt it!" Tempest was attentive. "Rafaela sent Azazel to procure it. She doesn't just send Azazel after anyone or anything. It's a very powerful chess piece in this war machine she is driving."

Tempest folded her arms loosely and thought for a moment. Her long blonde hair framed both sides of her face, giving her eyes extra depth as her mind ventured into the past for something that validated his questions.

"The Sundial," she stared off to the side of Noah, her eyes fixated on the book, "we can worry about later. Discuss its purpose when you're all united, here under the one roof." Noah raised an eyebrow with intrigue but also gave a look of caution. "I know how we can find Perry," she continued, moving her gaze back to her grandson.

"Yeah?" he questioned, smug in tone, "what Ace does the great Tempest Pogue have up her sleeve?" Philomena gave him a stern glare, she was not pleased by his attitude.

"Don't bite the hand that feeds you."

Noah gave her an odd look and then continued speaking, "All my Custodian and Magical Community contacts have all come up useless. No one knows anything!"

Tempest spoke with reassurance, "You haven't contacted the Mangarap Biyahero!"

"Who or what is the Managarap Biyahero?" queried Isadora.

"It means Dream Traveller." Noah gave a strange look to his two nieces and son, "Liliane and Mylane. They're a Filipino Coven but they are too far to reach..."

Turning his attention back to his grandmother, his voice dropped to silence as he gazed upon her and Philomena's white stone statue forms.

"That—" disappointment imposed on his chance of finally getting some answers, "that is just bloody brilliant!" he raised his index finger to his grandmother's face, "You always were a cow!" and then he abruptly turned away, venturing back over to the *Book of Shadows*. "Ugh!" he grumbled with frustration running his hand through his hair, "Where do I begin?!"

Moving across the room, with a serious look on her face, Bermuda approached a small cauldron sitting in the middle of a round table with a few moss-green candles around it and old jam jars filled with different herbs and potion ingredients.

"Onto the winds, I call too thee, Philippine Goddess Anagolay of all things lost." She began to cast her spell as she picked up Perry's watch, "Stolen witch come to me. Tell me where to find he!" and dropped it in the cauldron.

"Anagolay?" Isadora queried,

Bermuda's spell reacted, creating a bang and a flash, smoke bellowed upwards and formed a cloudy, full colour image of the flag for the Canadian province of British Colombia.

"I know that flag. It's the provincal flag for Victoria–" Shane acknowledged.

Isadora appeared confused.

"British Colombia, Canada. Victoria is the Capital."

Shane turned his head, he looked at his father who stared curiously at the cloudy vision. "Do you think the Demons have him in Vancouver?"

Noah lowered his head and focused his attention on the book as he turned the pages.

"First Nations!" he spoke aloud.

Bermuda turned and replied, "Do you think the Indian tribes would help?"

Noah closed the book and began to make his way across the room toward the attic door. Shane, Isadora and Bermuda silently observed as he walked past his grandmother Tempest, and then her sister Philomena without the slightest care.

"Dad," Shane called as he began to follow, "where are you going?"

Noah halted just before the door, "going to Canada to save my brother!" he did not turn around.

"What about, Tempest?" Isadora queried,

Noah waited for a moment, turned and looked back at his grandmother, "Inform her of my whereabouts when she returns. Gamma Witches can locate anyone on this plane in a second. I don't think Perry is on this plane, which is why they came here.

They cannot sense his presence."

Bermuda seemed confused, "but a locating spell can?"

"You called upon a god, which amplified the spell's directory. Besides, she is technically back on the otherside, unable to contact us. The stone acts to preserve the spirit's vessel, allowing her to return to it when the veil between this world is thin enough. Hence, the reason there is Santo Cathedral in Monument Valley. If the vessels and effigies are left out in the open, Evil can possess and exploit them!"

Isadora saw some vague sense, "Midnight and midday, is when the veil is thinnest. Right?"

"They are the between hours. The crossing of A.M into P.M and vice versa. When the sun is at its highest. Just like the moon," said Noah. "Ask Bermuda. Like Perry, they can both see ghosts due to the Mediumship branch of their Sensazione Power."

"In the house between those two points, I've had ghosts spiritualize. Move things, make noises, make the hair on the back of my neck stand up because they cannot take a corporeal form," Bermuda entertained her theory, although it could be proven wrong.

Shane left Isadora's side and approached his father, "I am coming with you! You are not going alone!" he showed bravery to the man who stood in front of him with uncertainty in his face. "Dad. Let me help you!"

"Tell your great-grandmother," Noah spoke as he looked past his son to acknowledge Tempest and then he focused on

Bermuda, "she failed to save my mother, but I will do anything in my power to bring my brother back alive!"

Together, Noah and his son, teleported out of the house in a rush of white smoke.

Left alone in the attic, Bermuda and Isadora exchanged uncomfortable looks.

"Let's place some crystal's around the house," Isadora walked across to the old cupboard, opened the doors and pulled out a polished, wooden box with six white and six amethyst crystals inside. "I don't want any unwanted guests popping in!" She turned, closing the cupboard door with her shoulder.

"Two female witches," Bermuda gave her sister a smug look, "in their early twenties? I reckon we can handle a few demons, if they're stupid enough to attack!" Isadora gave a modest smirk.

DESCENDANT OF ROMANI

Raising her eyebrows in horror, Ryder Romani covered her mouth with her hand. She stood inside an enormous Meat Locker. Lining all four walls was every victim ever slaughtered by a Philanderer Demon.

Innocent men and women hung on butcher's hooks – between the approximate ages of nineteen to forty – their bodies were clothed, their skin was pale and preserved. Some were dressed in rags, presumably killed in ancient Egypt with many dressed in modern garments.

Centuries of different attires.

"Hello?" Ryder's voice echoed on and on.

The dead replied telepathically, "You cannot save us..."

Confused, she stepped forward. "What?"

"This is their domain," The distinct and unique voice of a young woman moved through her mind. "This is where all their victims are kept." Ryder looked about from where she stood in the vast catacomb. "You're a witch. A supernatural being. You should be able to feel the scent."

Focusing and lengthening her power of Empathy she was able to catch the strangely comforting sweet scent that lingered. "I smell it."

The voice did not reply, but listened.

"It-it, smells like melon and pineapple." Ryder revealed,

The telepathic voice informed, "Pheromones."

The voice, stricken with emotion spoke again, this time firmly, "You must go, Strega!" feeling with her powers Ryder suddenly felt scared. "You are not safe here. Eisheth will—" the voice immediately silenced.

Ryder called out aloud, "Hello?" but received no response. "Who...who is Eisheth?"

A smug chuckle came from behind her. "Hello, Ryder!"

Turning around she was greeted by Dylis, confident with her hands on her hips.

Dylis retorted sarcastically, "You're a long way from, Treadwell!"

Acknowledging the pretentious young-looking woman, Ryder gave only a look of repulsion.

Dylis spoke again, "You knew the entire time who and what I am."

"...Eisheth," Ryder addressed her by her real name.

Eisheth smiled brilliantly. Her magical glamour washed away like smoke on water.

She had long fuchsia coloured hair with thick pastel pink and teal highlights that complimented a set of small horns that protruded from her forehead. Her perfect French manicured human nails turned into brown talons.

The cocktail dress turned into a pink oversized men's shirt with a red sequined, halter neck top underneath. A dainty black belt around her waist, a pair of maroon short shorts and black thigh-high stiletto hooker boots with a six-inch heel.

For an Old One, she was surprisingly very stylish.

"You manipulated my power!" Ryder growled angrily. "Turned it against me, but lucky for me I knew how to reverse the effects!"

Eisheth sighed contently, "Evil is coming." For an Old One she seemed somewhat cautious. "I, myself am evil. I was created like the others out of the order of balance: light cannot exist without the dark. But this coming evil will destroy everything." A subtle hint of fear twinkled in her eyes for a second...enough time for Ryder to acknowledge it. "I like what the world has become. It's self sufficient and strong willed. An improvement to say the least. I watched the Neanderthals as a child. The human race is more intelligent today, put it that way."

Confused, Ryder hit back out of sarcasm, "You're evil, what care do you have?"

Swinging her arm out, Eisheth struck Ryder, throwing her afar with great force.

"I really do not like the quick of your tongue, I may cut it out." She remarked, irritated. "I have created the Philanderer Demon." Eisheth expressed a sense of happiness over her achievement. "But when you're as old as I and tasted it all..." she gestured her hand indicating the hanging bodies, "the world tends to grow boring. Your queen, Maria is my cousin, just like the rest of the Old Ones – but I am not purely evil like the rest; I've...what's the word you mundane people use?"

"Ugh..." Ryder groaned as she raised her face from the floor as she lay on her stomach. "adapted?"

"Yes," Eisheth glanced upwards with a sly smile as though proud. "I've adapted."

"You're a moron. Once evil, always evil!" Ryder then queried, "What is this place?"

She revealed the title of her domain, "The Meat Locker. My home. A demon dimension!"

At Ryder's side, an apparition of the woman – not much older than thirty who had been conversing with her telepathically before – appeared and began to whisper.

"I was a child," keeping steady eye contact with Eisheth, Ryder listened as though oblivious. "When Napoli was young in the 9th or 8th century BC."

The talisman hanging on a chain around the woman's neck – a large diamond embroidered with small pieces of amethyst – created a sudden burst of glorious light that blocked out everything.

Ryder queried, "Who are you?" Using her telepathy she found the answer within the void. "...Amedea."

~*~

*T*he woman's voice started again, "Father told of a woman named Eisheth–"

A gentle and warm European sea breeze suddenly picked up. The blinding glow faded revealing a rickety bedroom set in the era of the 9th century BC.

Before Ryder, in a wooden, box-like bed, wrapped in a cloth, Amedea, a child, was read a bedtime story by her father.

Amedea's father spoke for a moment, "–Who came down from the clouds... But do not be mistaken child, she was no angel." Amedea's voice returned, "Father was not magical, that I know of. But little did he know that his mere fable was but a premonition."

Suddenly the facade morphed as it moved steadily ahead through time.

"This is how the first Philanderer came to be."

The sun shone overhead. The edges of the towering clay brick buildings were sharpened by shadows. Ryder, now clad in 9th century clothes, glanced about the structures.

Intrigued and bewildered she acknowledged, "Is this Napoli?"

Beside her the woman appeared clad in rags, "Yes Strega. Watch." Both raised their heads to the stunning blue sky scattered with partial clouds. "The cloud changes." Before their innocent eyes a large cloud turned a fierce charcoal as it rippled like water and a portal opened within it.

Amedea pointed out, "The Old One descends." And through the portal came an abundance of sparkling fuchsia, the length of a fully grown human body.

Ryder murmured, "Eisheth."

"See," Amedea tugged at Ryder's arm as both looked ahead at the handsome young man as he walked along the dirt road oblivious to what was above. "That is your enemy Hyson that challenges you in your own time."

The sparkling fuchsia touched down on the road, instantly revealing the most gorgeous woman with long flowing fuchsia coloured hair that was decorated by pastel pink and teal coloured highlights.

She smiled wondrously "Hello," her alluring teal eyes sparkled in the direct sunlight.

He halted abruptly and greeted her suspiciously, "Ciao. (Hello)"

"What is your name?" eerily she hovered toward him and as she halted, she caressed his marvelous facial features. He trembled in her presence. "Do not fear me," her smile comforted him. "I've come to fulfil your destiny." the words just rolled off her tongue. "Tell me. What is your name, boy?"

He exposed against his will, "Il mio nome è, Hyson."

Eisheth pressed him again, "How old are you?"

"Venti... (Twenty)" He gazed lovingly into her eyes as he questioned, "Che cosa è il vostro nome? (What is your name?)"

She sighed in the most delightful way, "Il mio nome è (My name is) Eisheth."

Gracefully she caressed his defined jaw line again as she amplified and awoke his lust. His eyes glowed with red energy.

Bound by lust, he still gazed into her eyes and then he lunged at her, passionately kissing her warm, wet lips. The warm Napoli breeze swirled around them as it tried to force them apart, blowing her long fuchsia hair about her face.

"Ugh," she gasped as she moved her lips away.

Consumed by lust he murmured, "Dovete essere un angelo… (You must be an angel)" as he began to kiss her soft neck.

Glancing away her eyes became scheming and misogynistic, "Your mother should have warned you," magically her teeth morphed, turning jagged and sharp. She continued firmly, "that not all angels are good!" and forcefully she sunk her teeth into his tanned neck.

He cried out in horrific agony. Feeding on his lust and pheromones, Hyson gripped at her hair and pulled it in an attempt to pull her away. But the more he tried, the more force she used to effortlessly overthrow him.

Quickly his mortal strength waned and he became limp within her grasp.

"Hyson!" a beautiful, female European voice came up the dirt road.

In the most beautiful manner Eisheth elegantly reopened her eyes and they gave off a momentary glow of teal.

"This was how I died." The woman informed Ryder.

Amedea, a tall and regal brunette with porcelain features, dressed in tatters came up the road.

She queried, "Hyson…?"

Halting some distance away she watched Eisheth remove her teeth and place the dead man at her feet.

Amedea whimpered, "Che cosa avete fatto? (What have you done?)"

Standing proud and regal, Eisheth gave the innocent woman a stuck-up glare and remained silent.

Amedea approached.

Eisheth smirked pleasurably, "Hm," Swinging her arm, she struck the woman, throwing her back. "Ragazza stupida (Stupid girl)"

Heavily in a cloud of dirt, winded by pain, Ryder gasped as she looked up from the ground. She had taken on the role of Amedea as she watched the historical moment.

~*~

Back in the real-world Ryder still maintained her power, as she stood body-to-body with the demon named Hyson, hypnotizing him as she gazed into his eyes. Curiosities led her to see how the mind of a demon worked.

Madelyn called out, concerned for her cousin, "Ryder?"

~*~

Back within the demon dimension, Ryder continued her in-depth history lesson as she lay on the ground. Getting to her feet, she abruptly realized something peculiar about Amedea. Looking at her hands, turning them over and looking at the lines, she saw something within them.

Her eyes glittered with empathy, "Amedea Bonifacio…You're a gypsy."

The innocent, now revealed to be a gypsy, smiled kindly with a superior look in her porcelain complexion.

"I am where your power comes from, Ryder. I am your ancestor!"

Not entirely bewildered by the revelations Ryder replied, "But..."

"Salem is where we were acknowledged; the same as the Pogue Witches." Amedea switched back their bodies. "Father is a Romani. Mother is a witch. She can manipulate fire and he, water." Ryder's eyes widened with intrigue as she realized where the genetic trait of the nature manipulating power came from. "We are a line of hybrid gypsy witches with whom individual descendants can manipulate a different aspect of nature. My daughter Fiore can manipulate earth – make flowers grow, grass green, hear and talk to il animale."

Mesmerized Ryder replied, "Y-you can even speak fluent English."

"Si," Amedea responded. "I understand all languages."

"Omnilingualism is unique to Romani." said Ryder stunned by her own acknowledgement. "You can understand and speak any language." Amedea flashed her beautiful European smile. "Why are you showing me this?" she looked back at the Old One and deceased young man that were now both frozen in time. "What is so important about this, the 9th century?"

Amedea gave a concerned stare, "She distorted his perception and turned him into a demon. The first Philanderer Demon. He is my husband. Eisheth told him, to survive you must feed on pheromones. Such a demon can amplify the lust in innocent women or men, appeal to their needs and be what they desire. The Donnaiolo are as ancient as the Vampiro! They are our rival, our nemesis! They must be stopped!"

Annoyed, Ryder replied, "You avoided my question." Amedea simply stared at her. "Why did you bring me to this specific time?"

"To give you this, Ryder Romani..." Moving her hands behind her neck, she undid the thin chain made of small diamonds.

The Talisman within sight was most breathtaking.

At its centre was a large oval cut diamond embroidered with dainty pieces of amethyst. Inside the centre piece, a pearly liquid rocked like the ocean and in the sunlight, it gave off a heavenly glow.

Amedea presented the object, "This is our family's sacred talisman. Luce solare liquida."

Around the outside, the individually embroidered pieces of amethyst gave off a subtle glow. Mesmerized, Ryder cradled the piece with care, resting it in the palm of her hand.

In amazement, she said, "Liquid Sunlight..." it glimmered in her eyes. "H-how though?"

"A Seraph," Amedea paused briefly as she let the object of pure beauty bask in the past. "Gave it to father. The diamond..."

Ryder accidently interrupted, "This is an object of legends..." she gazed at it with the most believing look in her eyes. "The liquid within the diamond itself is said to give off a light so strong that it is capable of vanquishing, banishing and eliminating all evil at the command of the beholder. The ring of amethyst is said to create a force field of protection around the witch who possesses it."

In her European accent Amedea continued, "You are well educated."

Ryder asserted her qualifications, "I am proficient in Metaphysics, Epistemology, Witchcraft and Demonology. I studied at Oxford to become a Paleontologist."

A proud smile formed on Amedea's face.

Ryder replied, "I live to learn, to grasp, read, absorb and understand the nature of things."

Amedea sensed the level of power in her descendant, "I feel that you are a Superior Level Mischling." Glancing away and then looking back, she curiously questioned. "Who leads our line..." hesitation appeared in her expression, "in your time?"

The 21st century Romani replied, "My aunt. She is a member of the Triad."

Amedea gasped with shock, "The Triad!" Ryder gave an odd look. "Father foresaw the arrival of three powerful gypsies." "Gypsies..." Ryder remarked in a vague tone. "Wait...did you say three?"

Amedea replied eagerly, "Si. Three."

"The Triad has four members." reading her greatest ancestor with her empathic power she suddenly realized something else...a motive. "You think I can vanquish Hyson in my time, with this...?"

"Si." Amedea replied but then her eyes scanned Ryder's body language. "Who is Pilar?"

"Huh...?" Ryder murmured.

Amedea smiled again, "Where do you think your empathy came from?" suggesting she possessed the power of Empathy herself. "You are able to manipulate the weather to a small degree, yes?"

Ryder, silently impressed replied, "Erm, slightly...it's a work in progress." Confused, she then touched base on her aunt's power. "Pilar possesses the power of Paralysis."

Stunned Amedea replied with a gasp, "Paralisi is a remarkable power!"

"I agree." The 21st century Romani smiled, holding the highest respect for her aunt. Her ancestor listened with intrigue. "She vanquished Pandora," Amedea's eyes suddenly widened with terror as though she knew of the horrendous creature.

The Romani Book of Shadows elaborates that Pandora was an evil witch of Napoli; a modern knock-off to the mythical

Pandora who, too, had a sinister box of horrors. She hunts magical people ripping out their hearts and feeding on their mystical life force to suppress the aging process and retain immortality.

Curiously Ryder queried, "Not the mythical Pandora and her box of ugliness? You know her?"

Amedea paused again as she read her descendant. With an impressed look of realization she confirmed her own theory.

"She survived so long...?"

"She tried to kill Pilar's husband," Ryder revealed.

Analyzing Ryder she curiously pouted for a moment and then continued, "But if he is mortal, Pandora has no reason to hunt him." She glanced away and then looked back. "How proficient is your aunt?"

"Superior Level," The 21st century Romani was proud.

Amedea raised an eyebrow.

She said with emphasis, "Pandora is a supreme level witch!"

Ryder went on to narrate her aunt's abilities, "Her power allows her to manipulate the physical structure of a person...or object. Crippling it with immense pressure until the point at which it implodes."

Amedea gulped uneasily.

Sternly, as she watched the golden sunlight idolize her ancestor, Ryder brought their conversation back to the pressing situation behind them.

"Now, back to Hyson..."

ORIGINAL DEMON

9th century Napoli

Even though only a jumble of clay brick buildings – was beautiful in the imperializing sunlight. It was a natural place of magic having been home to the sirens in the Greek poem Odyssey.

The golden rays of light glimmered around Ryder's figure as the gentle, warm wind toyed with the hem of her dress. The sun captured and revealed her brilliant aura.

Amedea, a gorgeous daughter of a male Romani and beautiful witch, turned her head and she looked at Eisheth again.

"You must rewrite history," she said.

Behind, standing out of focus, Ryder appeared grim at the idea, knowing too well that one should never change the course of history...under any circumstance.

Amedea pressed her, "Hyson is to kill me. He will take my talisman and give it to her." Turning her head slightly she gave a stern glare to her descendant.

Her eyes glimmered. Forming a smile, she reached out to the Romani, knowing that she would understand the effects evil had.

"If in evil hands the liquid shall turn to black giving it the capabilities of restoring any evil. Regardless what power and shape."

A confused Ryder replied, "What could she possibly restore?"

The young 9th century woman knowingly stared back at Eisheth, "Something ultimate and powerful. Six-Six-Five." And on its own authority the talisman magically vanished from Ryder's open hand and then reappeared around her neck.

Amedea began again, "Jamal Bole," naming a powerful Seer that lived in secrecy in Napoli. "Is what the Romani call, Sgombro. A Seer." Oddly enough Ryder already knew what the word meant. "She came to my father Adone. Jamal told him of an evil. An evil so great."

Ryder raised an eyebrow, struggling to foresee what kind of evil could be greater than Lucifer.

"It is not as evil as the devil in the ground," she referred to the fallen angel in hell. "This...evil is more powerful. Whoever dare speak its name..." a grim look quickly appeared in the young woman's glittering eyes again. "is swallowed by the air they breathe."

Finding it hard to believe, Ryder implied, "Swallowed by a portal...?"

Amedea gave her a vague look, "You do not believe such a thing to be?" she took a step forward, closer to her descendant.

"Six-Six-Five."

"Why do you keep saying that?" Ryder questioned firmly.

A stern look washed the fear out of the ancestor's eyes, "Change the five to a six." The 21st century Romani's eyes widened slightly. "You saw the Meat Locker, Mischling." A look swum in Ryder's face. "Eisheth plans to offer a sacrifice. You looked into the demon's eyes, seeking what he hides. She is going to—" suddenly her voice dropped out as something stole her attention.

She turned as Hyson reopened his eyes revealing his new demonic quality. Levitating up from the ground, he turned and faced Amedea and time unfroze.

Taking a deep breath as she looked at her future – her descendant and imminent death – Amedea cast some words into the sunlight in her European accent. "Return her from whence she came."

Fading into the sunlight, Ryder touched the talisman around her neck acknowledging both its origin and the Romani Coven.

"Uccidala!! (Kill her)" Eisheth said in a booming voice.

Lunging at her, Amedea screamed as he sunk his teeth deep into her neck; drawing blood as it cascaded down her neck, covering her clothes. Her body fell limp in his tight grasp.

Pulling his blood covered mouth away he threw her to the ground and reached his opened mouth to the sky. He roared as every fibre of his being became electrified with ecstasy.

"Ugh! What power!!!"

Eisheth ordered in a booming voice again, "Take her talisman!"

Under her command, he tore Amedea's dress revealing her breast and acknowledged that there was no talisman.

"There is no talisman!"

He turned and looked to his rapturous, fuchsia-haired maker.

~*~

Moving through time and space without even realizing, Ryder, in the blink of an eye, had returned to the Meat Locker that Eisheth called home. Shocked and uneasy she gasped as she reacted to the deceased bodies hanging along the walls...all six hundred and sixty-five of them.

Eisheth growled, "Now," narrowing her glare as she watched the young Romani. "What the hell did you just do?" cautious with a fearless look in her eyes, Ryder glared back. "What kind of magic was that?"

The confident Romani replied humbly, "I never kiss and tell!"

"Be careful," Amedea's voice whispered in Ryder's mind.

"Be on your guard. She will take the talisman from you!" Eisheth's teal eyes widened with disbelief. "Ugh! And where did you get that from?!" She clenched her fists, giving off raw undiluted energy. "Gone through my possessions have we?!"

Covering the talisman with her hand Ryder stood her ground.

"It was never yours to keep. Luce solare liquida belongs to the Romani Coven. I am a descendant of the woman you had Hyson kill the day you turned him into the monstrosity he is today!"

"Amedea Bonifacio," the Old One raised an eyebrow with curiosity. "You're a descendant of her. The Romani Coven originates from Amedea?"

The superior Telepath/Empath stepped back, protecting the family heirloom.

Eisheth chuckled manically for a moment, "Well this is something. No wonder she hovers around you," Ryder gasped and her expression went grim. "I am an Old One, Mischling. I have tricks you couldn't even begin to imagine." She extended her arm straight out in the direction of the Romani, her immense power cracked loudly like a stockman's whip.

Protecting the beholder, beneath Ryder's hand the amethyst in the talisman gave off a subtle glow and a slight ring of lavender glimmered on the ground around her. The protectiveness of it forced the attack to recoil back at Eisheth. "Argh!!" she shot backwards, flipped up off the ground, into the air and landed back on the ground crouching like a tiger. "Disrespectful," the Old One rose back to her feet, "Give me back the damn talisman!"

"Why?!"

Eisheth growled irritably, "Don't be stupid girl!"

"Six-Six-Five," Ryder announced, with her free hand gesturing to the deceased bodies on the meat hooks. "You plan to offer all these bodies as a sacrifice. With this," she moved her hand away from the talisman. "you plan to restore this, supposed, coming evil."

"Dear child!" the Old One roared, "You're the idiot who gazed into the creatures eyes!" Ryder suddenly had a spell of realization. "Six–Six–Five is going to become Six–Six–Six!" leaping away from the floor, she soared through the air in an attacking position. "You will die!"

Gasping, Ryder suddenly felt compelled to close her eyes.

In her head, via her power of Telepathy Amedea spoke to her again, "Activate the Talisman! Banish her!"

Paying attention to the advice, she took a deep breath and briskly reopened her eyes.

~*~

Back in the real world, incredible dark blue flames blasted through the dark as they roared across the manicured opening in the Botanical Gardens toward Hyson, still hypnotized by the majestically beautiful telepath.

Tex chuckled, "This is our playground, Mischling!" opening his hand he conjured a ball of fire, "No one plays fair and no one gets out alive!" and then he moved his arm to throw his attack at Madelyn Romani.

Raising an open, upward-facing palm to her chin, Madelyn blew a breath and from her hand glittering green poison spores became airborne. Surrounding the fireball, her magic made a sizzling noise and it extinguished the fireball.

"Piss off," she growled.

Swinging her arm and hastily gesturing her hand, she made tree roots rip up out of the ground around Tex. Wrapping around him, they bound his arms to his body so he could not launch anymore attacks.

"Up!" she commanded in Romanian. Catching a glimpse of the fiery attack, Madelyn screamed, "DAN," reaching her other arm forward slightly, "NO!!! YOU'LL KILL HER TOO!!!!"

~*~

*I*nside the demon dimension, Ryder activated the Talisman…"By the power of light," the pearly liquid inside the large diamond at the Talisman's centre gave off a stunning, imperial glow, "Displace this blight!"

Triumphantly, the stunning warm glow turned into a golden ray of sunlight. Screaming out in horror as she continued to lurch toward the Romani and unable to veer out of the way of the oncoming attack, Eisheth, exploded into a plume of thick fuchsia smoke, banished by the power of the simple, yet powerful device.

~*~

Back in the real world, watching the fiery attack approach Ryder, Brady Romani took it upon himself to become involved and protect those around him from his brother's devastating power. Standing behind his sister, Addison, he closed his eyes, lowered his head, elevated his forearms and gestured his hands upward and cast a spell.

"Extend from me," he muttered in Romanian, breathing in deeply and then exhaled aloud, "power in me," raising his head again, his eyes sprang open and gave off a brilliant purple glow, "protect me and all Romani!"

Perched on a street light a black crow cawed as it watched the happenings.

Entranced, as they both stared into one another's eyes, the tide of colossal fiery power wrapped itself around Ryder and the demon Hyson. In a display of how devastating it truly was; an explosion instantaneously pursued. The structure of the fiery vortex curved inward and then blew outwards.

Standing little chance against this immensity, the shadows of the Botanical Gardens were completely blown back as the costly light engulfed the sprawling opening in its entirety with Madelyn and her cohorts vanishing.

~*~

Reaching up into the sky, the marvelous glow drew the attention of Zéphyrine the imperial Weather Being as she loomed overhead on her plateau of clouds.

Her glaring eyes shone with power, "Sorcières! (Witches)"

Raising her gaze, she watched the plume of light morph into a mushroom cloud and then fall back down to the ground. It could have easily drawn unwanted attention from the mortal world.

Zéphyrine then murmured in English, "Reckless buffoons!"

Madelyn was welcomed by a male's voice as the glow disorientated her.

"Sorry I'm late."

Blinded, she narrowed her eyes, managing to gain a small perspective of a tall, medium built man.

"Who..." as the glow faded completely, she was able to acknowledge him. "Dan! What?"

Madelyn and Dan exchanged an electricity fueled glare.

"What the hell—"

Dan growled back, confused, "What?"

"Desecration? You used an aspect of your Pyrokinesis that you have no control over, on our cousin," Madelyn's humble green eyes had turned a deep emerald with anger, "you could have killed her! Not to mention wiped out this entire city block!

You cannot always call upon Sagittarius to increase your strength!"

Dantalian narrowed his eyes with anger at this sister.

She knew too well that, as a witch or Romani grows from child to adolescence, and then into adulthood, that their power advances and branches into new techniques. Some which are potentially deadly to not only the possessor but others around them.

~*~

Intrigued by the continuing spectacle below, Zéphyrine adjusted her microscopic vision and zeroed in on the power being given off by the talisman around Ryder's neck as it emanated light.

"This power, I must have!"

Turning to swoop across her cloud plateau, an abnormal echo sounded and she suddenly recoiled back.

"I cannot allow that!" said a firm, unpleased voice. "Your mission is only ever, to find evil and destroy it. Not siphon power off Witches or Romani!"

Levitating abruptly back to her feet, the regal Weather Being roared, "Uncharted territory you are in, Connemara Preston!" and thunder exploded marvelously in a display of Zéphyrine's anger.

"Leave the witches to me," The shady woman instructed. "Continue your course and then dissipate back to mother, or I will end you!"

Reading the adept woman, endorsed with magic, Zéphyrine curiously replied; "Your essence is fragmented. You are not who you claim to be!"

Giving a smug smile, the woman used her Therianthrope abilities to turn into a crow. Hovering, she flapped her wings, crowed and then flew off.

~*~

Watching the growing white glow, a confident Brady stated modestly, "If I wanted to I could extend the barrier protecting Ryder to the entire city block."

Bitterly, Madelyn glared out the corner of her eye as she sneered at his comment.

"Cockiness is what gets a witch killed!" looking a little further she acknowledged the small piece in his ear, "I see you decided to wear your hearing aid."

Brady, Madelyn's second younger brother, aged eighteen was almost a twin to his older brother. He stood the same height but had a lanky build, yet to fill out, mature and become a man. The boy was a thing of intrigue to say the least with his daring blue eyes, high cheek bones, messy surfy style blonde locks and the sly curl of his lips made him a chick magnet.

But his attitude sang a different tune. The boundary pushing teenager ignored his peers and enjoyed being different and his own person – inexhaustible, honest, charismatic, ambitious, and confident.

As an infant, he suffered from spinal meningitis. Given only three outcomes of being left blind, deaf or to die, he survived with becoming deaf. With an innate stubbornness, he developed the power of Barrier Projection.

Resonating brightly, the glow withdrew back into the large diamond at the centre of the talisman around Ryder's neck. Blinking as she gazed into Hyson's eyes, Ryder broke her power of Hypnotism.

The 2,500-year-old demon staggered backwards, gasping as he suddenly slipped back into reality. Shaking his head, he abruptly halted with an obvious look in his face. He gave a hearty growl and then revealed his demonic visage again.

In his deep voice he asked, "Did you find what you needed to see?" Ryder gave him a smug stare. Flicking his hands, Hyson's fingernails turned into talons. "I will rip that talisman from your warm neck!"

Holding her arms out and showing no sign of a struggle, she insisted he try and steal the family heirloom.

"If you want it, come and get it."

Madelyn, Addison, Dantalian and Brady watched with anticipation. Growling behind his gritted teeth, Hyson took a step forwards.

Taking a deep breath Ryder allowed the power of the talisman to flow through her. Raising her closed eyes to the full moon beyond Zéphyrine's storm clouds, she invoked in beautiful

Italian: "Grace of light!"

Magically the storm clouds swirled and the moon's glow pierced through and illuminated the talisman. Magnifying its power again, a sudden flash of light erupted and Hyson slammed against an invisible barrier as he tried to strike the Romani.

He growled, "What is this?"

He slammed his raised fists against the barrier over and over. Adapting to a new power, her voice deepened as an eloquent breeze tousled her short blonde hair.

"By Osiris!" her pupils dilated, "Hear my plea!"

The fabric of air began to distort around her as the talisman revealed a small portion of its power as it connected with an unseen, godly force.

Brady raised an eyebrow as he passed comment, "Did she just...?"

"Dear God!" Addison's bewildered eyes glimmered and her parted lips trembled, "...Osiris?"

An impressed Dantalian stood silent.

Extending both her arms out, Ryder commanded in a deep voice, "Taketh this demon! Banish this evil!" with her hands rigidly gestured the energy surrounding her violently surged.

Swarming around him, the ancient demon failed. Spontaneously in an agonizing scream his body exploded into nothingness leaving a wisp of flames that dissipated instantly.

Immediately her pupils returned to normal.

HER MASTER'S VOICE

From the seclusion of the dark shadows, an unseen individual

threw an Athame at Ryder Romani.

Turning, at the last minute, the weapon sliced through the air; narrowly missing Ryder Romani's blonde hair and ear. Noticing the ripples in the air and a glitter of silver, Addison knocked her older sister out of the way.

"LOOK OUT!!"

Extending her arm upwards and gesturing her hand, she used her telekinetic powers to halt the knife in the air and then with a swish of her hand she sent it upwards. Impaled, Texas – the Philanderer Demon, cried out in agony as he lingered overhead, suspended by Madelyn's tree roots. He met his vanquish, his body erupted into flames and then exploded into nothingness. The tree roots withdrew back into the ground.

Shrieking, Ryder was thrown by an unexpected wave of telekinesis. Moving through the air, she then crashed onto the grass with a thud.

In pursuit, multiple fireballs shot across the opening. Glimmering as the flames rotated, Ryder raised her dirty face from the ground. Noticing her cousins were unaware of the approaching attack, she placed two fingers to the side of her head and used her power of Telepathy.

Reacting, Brady turned side-on to the approaching attack, a flat palm facing forwards, as if to block.

A fireball, ahead of the rest exploded against Brady's invisible barrier, making it ripple like a stone thrown into water.

A French spoken voice moved from the dark, "Arrêtez! (Stop)"

Coming within a few inches of the invisible barrier, the remaining fireballs suddenly stopped in midair. Brady gave an odd look at the strange happening.

"Réagir! (React)" said the same French, feminine voice,

Suddenly and spontaneously, the fireballs caused a large fiery explosion with enough force to throw Brady, Madelyn, Dantalian and Addison backwards onto the grass.

"Oh God," Ryder gasped like she was going to vomit, she brushed her blonde hair from her face as she muttered anxiously, "Shit–Shit–Shit!" getting to her feet she ran over to her cousins. She feared for their lives when they did not stir nor return to their feet. "Get up!" she growled upon approach.

Startled, she was forced backwards a few steps as Brady's barrier still remained active.

"Are you guys alright?" she queried nervously,

Unbeknownst to Ryder, she did not see the suspicious woman, with long red hair, as she walked out of the dark and into the light of the opening.

"Our master who is not in heaven," the woman spoke in beautiful French.

Ryder stiffened her posture, "Our master?" her ears pricked as she heard the voice, "Who?" she questioned curiously.

Turning around she saw only the empty open area of the Botanical Gardens. Madelyn opened her eyes and sat up on the grass. She rubbed the back of her head, feeling a slight headache from the impact with the ground.

"What the hell was that?" Madelyn queried aloud.

Ryder turned her back to the opening as she acknowledged her cousin.

"A demon attack," she said.

Behind her, the suspicious red-haired woman reappeared, this time in the middle, where she had engaged Hyson and vanquished him.

"Hallowed be his name, his kingdom come," the beautiful French accent came again.

Gasping, Ryder spun around, "Who are you?"

"Visper," the red-haired woman revealed her name. "former mortal, turned Philanderer Demon!" moving her head she inhaled, "Impressive!"

Ryder gave her an odd look, "What is?"

"You," Visper exhaled, "Mischling, who smells like peaches and mangos!" she took her attention away from the beautiful scent of pheromones that lingered in the air and then placed it on the Romani, "Pheromones smell incredible. But you, you smell completely different!"

"What is it with this Mischling?" Madelyn grumbled,

"What the hell does it even mean?"

Ryder explained, "It's German for half-breed!"

"If we're a Mischling, what do you call Noah and Perry Pogue or River West?"

"A Nefas," Ryder revealed, giving a look of stupidity,

"Do you even read your family's *Book of Shadows*?"

"Enough!" Visper protested with a demonic growl, "of this bullshit banter!" and with a sway of her hand she effortlessly threw Ryder to the side with Telekinesis. "I have to kill you!" Accelerating forwards in a blurred motion, the Philanderer Demon halted and then struck an invisible wall as she attempted to attack Madelyn. "What magic is this?"

Rolling over on the grass, a disgruntled Ryder sat up. Brushing some strange blonde hair from her face, she quickly extended her arm and pointed her index finger at Visper.

"You're a dead bitch!"

Clenching her hand into a fist, she then flicked her fingers. Using the Donec Laoreet – Latin for Mental Strike – branch of her telepathy power, she caused Visper to grip her fingers into her head and scream aloud in excruciating pain.

White strains of electricity began to emerge at Visper's finger tips as she pulled the pain out of her head.

"Ah," Ryder scrambled to her feet as she gave a look of confusion, "That's new!"

Withdrawing static from her head, Visper brought her glowing hands together, closed them and then reopened them to reveal a tennis ball size orb of white, electrified energy.

Visper turned her head, "You, Telepath!" she gave Ryder a scolding glare, "are really beginning to–" maneuvering her arm, she swung and threw the orb at the Telepathic Romani, "piss me off!!" Striking Ryder, the power flung her across the gardens. "My master–"

Abruptly Visper was struck by a blue fiery attack and launched backwards.

"Your master is a moron!" Dantalian yelled.

Visper crashed into the ground right where Ryder had vanquished Hyson. Could lightning strike the same spot twice? Pushing herself up with her hands and forearms, Visper began to rise back to her feet. She paused with her back to the small group of Romani and made a rather evil smirk as she thought unimaginable acts of cruelty in her head. Modestly she elevated her head a little, like all Philanderer Demons, she saw Romani as small and insignificant. After all, they are sworn enemies.

She looked back over her shoulder, "It appears the Firestarter would like to rumble."

Extending his arms out in front of his body the tattoo on Dan's wrist, his Sagittarius zodiac – half man, half horse with a bow and arrow – began to move as it came to life. In his open hands blue flames spontaneously combusted.

He commanded his power in Italian, "Gather around!"

Pouring off his hands, the blue flames touched the grass and quickly rose up around him. The fiery embodiment hissed, snarled and crackled as it swooped around the entire height of his body and over his head.

"Sagittarius…" his voice, suddenly deeper than normal, was filled with power, "Fuel this Romani fire." From inside the fire he growled resolutely, "You have no idea what this

Firestarter is capable of!"

With a bellowing roar, the flames lurched forward as he mentally projected his power.

Swooping across the ground, the fiery spectacle morphed, taking on the form of the mythical centaur as it began to gallop around the perimeter of the sprawling opening. The creature of fire neighed as it made sure Visper knew she was its target.

"He has big King Kong balls," Visper smirked as her cat eyes filled entirely with black and then turned an eerie red as something else took over her body, "I like that!" her voice deep and manly.

The fiery creature moved behind the Philanderer Demon in the distance. Its vibrant blue glow lit up the tree line. Raising its bow, it arched it and fired two arrows at once. Swaying her hand, she summoned two more Philanderer Demons into the botanical gardens.

Impaled, both demons cried out in pain as they were vanquished by the fiery creature.

"Ugh, you're all the same!!!" it became apparent that a male presence spoke through Visper, "I am the fire of hell! Sagittarius cannot hold a candle to the power I have!"

She vanished as the creature came up behind her. Reappearing behind it, the creature dug its front hooves into the ground, skidded to a halt with its back hooves and then quickly spun around to attack her.

In Italian, Visper commanded, "Arrestare! (Halt)" she raised her hand causing the fiery thing to instantly still. Narrowing her vicious eyes, she roared, "Meddle elsewhere!!!" and under her thrall the centaur exploded.

Effortlessly, without making a move or gesture, Visper – possessed by her overlord, Saxon Preston – twisted the power and sent it surging back in the direction it came from.

Madelyn murmured uneasily, "Oh crap!"

"I'm on it!" Stepping forward and halting beside his older brother, Brady shook his hand and then briskly gestured them forwards like he was going to catch a large ball. Awkwardly with a nervous gulp, he requested, "Pray I'm strong enough to counter

Dan's power!"

~*~

Standing away to the side, Ryder observed as Visper bombarded Brady Romani's barrier with ferocious blue flames that had begun to turn black and grey as the demon's evil gained control over Dantalian Romani's power of Pyrokinesis.

Terror crept into her mind instead of letting the calm and collected Tyro Custodian nature inside of her rise to the surface. Her hands began to shake slightly, which increased the more she let the worry consume her.

"Oh God!" her trembling voice choked, "Come on Ryder, do something, she's going to kill them!" she coaxed confidence back into herself.

Catching a glimpse of the moon as an opening in the clouds passed overhead, an idea struck. But then a memory echoed in the back of her mind.

"Those who have a wealth of knowledge," Pilar Romani's voice spoke, *"know that you need to possess substantial power to summon the assistance or will of a god to aid you in your craft. If your gut instinct deems it's too risky, then it's too risky! An inexperienced Romani could unwillingly become a conduit!"*

In Romanian, she summoned the Triple Goddess, "Hear me, feel my power, triple goddess aid me in this sacred hour!"

Hearing her call, the moon shifted noticeably in the night sky and filtered its glow down onto Ryder, capturing her in a beam of light. Behind her, unbeknownst to her, three ghostly apparitions manifested – the Maiden, the Mother and the Crone.

Each reached an arm forwards, placed a hand on both Ryder's shoulders and then collapsed into a mist that lingered around her. They made her the new conduit, removing the status from her father Zane.

Again in Romanian, she continued to cast her spell on Visper, "Onto you I do impart, to banish your master, now depart!"

Letting out an otherworldly roar, a black mist was expelled from Visper's body.

"Go to hell," Ryder grumbled irritably, "Saxon Preston!" she coughed for a moment and brushed some straying hair from her face, "You're not killing our coven today!"

Wincing, Brady struggled to maintain his power as his brother's fiery power, manipulated by Visper, continued its relentless assault against his barrier. Increasing its validity, he made it turn from clear to a periwinkle colour.

With obvious distress in his voice he said, "Dan, you're going to get us killed!"

Dantalian complained, "I cannot control it anymore. She is!" With his hand rigidly gestured he failed to show any form of manipulation. "Brady, we need this barrier to stay up!"

"Oh," Brady protested loudly, "You don't think I'm bloody trying!"

Addison interjected, "If I could see her, then I could throw her with my telekinesis!"

Bringing her left arm back, as she enjoyed her menacing attack on the Romani, Visper manoeuvred her hand, and then flicked her fingers, creating a blast. A large explosion against the barrier caused it to flex as Brady struggled even more to maintain it.

"Ugh," Madelyn grumbled irritably, "enough of this!" Gesturing her hand at the ground she used her power of Nature Manipulation and cast a spell at the same time: "From the ground rise up tall, tree roots make a wall!"

A groan moved through the Botanical Gardens again. The lawn glittered like an emerald and then, bursting up through the ground, thick tree roots intertwined and formed a wall that took the full brunt of the fiery blast.

"Connecting with nature, clever little–"

Madelyn remarked, "Connect with this, bitch!"

Turning around, Visper took a punch in the face and was knocked to the ground.

Visper snarled with repulsion. Throwing her hands up in a gesture of surrender, she projected Dantalian's replicated power of Pyrokinesis up at Madelyn as she stood over the demon.

Visper remarked, "Time for you to burn, Gaia!"

~*~

Standing over Visper, Madelyn shielded her face with her arms and screamed. Lowering her arms she revealed a smile as her long brunette hair fanned for a moment in a breeze.

"Thank you!" Magically absorbing the flames into her abdomen, Madelyn then shapeshifted back into Dantalian, "for giving me back my fire!"

Scrambling to her feet, Visper, now substantially weakened, turned and attempted to flee. Looking back over her shoulder at Dantalian, she slammed into an invisible wall and was thrown backwards onto the ground.

"Going somewhere?" Brady remarked, lowering his arm and barrier.

Rising back to her feet, a flustered Visper moved her arm, gestured her hand, and conjured a glimmering ball of fire.

"You'll never defeat us—"

With a brisk sway of her arm, Addison sent Visper sideways, "We'll see about that!"

Smashing into another invisible wall, the Philanderer Demon crashed into the ground, her hand scalded from her failed fireball.

"You're new and you're stupid." Using her power of Nature Manipulation, Madelyn made tree roots slither up through the grass and wrap around Visper's ankles. "You see," Madelyn made green energy sparkle in her gestured hands, "we are the Mischling and we are Romani!" A hateful Visper struggled to fight her binds. "Our stubbornness and durability comes from nature—"

"The Romani," Addison interrupted.

Madelyn continued, "And our power... it comes from the witch within us!"

"Half witch," Dantalian interrupted, "Half Romani!"

Brady finished, "Mischling!"

"Admirable," Madelyn gave a smug stare as she admired the Philanderer Demon's strength, "you are, sure. You came here to fight us, test our strengths and powers. But you know what you left here with?" Madelyn named her sarcastically, "Visper?" "All your heads as trophies!" Visper boasted.

Madelyn shot her down, "WRONG!" she then pointed her finger at the demon, "It will be your demise!"

Visper suddenly paused upon seeing the seriousness in Madelyn's glare.

"Shall we?" Madelyn gestured with a smirk.

In sync, the four siblings cast their vanquishing spell in Romanian.

"Since ancient times, the demons came, to desire the Romani but not to claim, with our will, strength and might, we vanquish you on this all hallows night!"

Visper screamed in agony and as she was vanquished in a glimmer of flames, the air rippled and the fiery spectacle disappeared.

"So, this is how you Romani spend your Halloween?" queried a female voice.

Gasping, as Madelyn Romani turned, her long brunette hair floated and fell around her face and shoulders. Addison moved one foot backwards and clenched her fists. Dantalian made blue flames combust in his hands and Brady revealed his Barrier Projection power through his aura, making it give off a purple glow.

"Who are you?" Addison question cautiously,

Madelyn narrowed her eyes, "I know you! You attacked us earlier!"

"I am Riel Preston," the platinum blonde revealed her name. "There is movement in the Underworld. I simply wanted to taste your power!"

Brady used sign-language as he spoke, "What do you mean, taste our power?"

"Hmm," Riel's eyes sparkled with pleasure, "a deaf witch! How did I miss this?"

Taking a step forwards toward Brady, a whip-cracking noise echoed through the air; instantly she stopped and glared at Madelyn Romani.

Madelyn ordered, "Stay away from him!"

"You Mischling amuse me!" Riel smirked,

"Why?" Addison questioned territorially, "What is so amusing about us?"

Dantalian's flames roared, "Get to your point about 'movement in the Underworld'!" Riel, impressed by his tenacity, smiled at him lovingly. "You would not have told us, if you didn't think we needed to know; considering we're arch enemies!"

"I enjoy our species' life-long war! Philanderer vs. Romani! It's something I'm not prepared to handover so the Avatarians can have dominion over all!" Riel relaxed her demonic aggression and adopted a civilized approach, "Like I said to the local vampire Sovereign, Treadwell is built on a Hellmouth—"

"Yes, Yes, the Whale-Monster Leviathan!" Addison rolled her eyes, already knowing, "the earliest settlers were warned by the local tribes. The churches here are gargoyles, sent to guard and act as safe havens for the witches sent here to protect the lands and citizens from the—" Addison gestured her hand at Riel as she implied, "evils, that may crawl up from the Underworld or venture here!"

"Oh," Riel remarked humbly, "blondie-bear, we don't crawl! We have elevators into buildings and portals that transport us up and back from the dark below your city!"

"ANYWAYS!" Dantalian growled irritably,

Riel smirked as she narrowed her eyes, "And they," she gestured to the sky, implying Queen Maria and her ensemble of divine individuals, "thought they conquered the evil in Sunnydale, California. But the point I'm trying to make is, be prepared! The Avatarians are building an army. My girl Visper, was a Épreuve de la puissance–"

"Why?" Madelyn queried at the stupid notion.

Addison interrupted, "She said 'Test of Power' in French."

"I know," Madelyn hissed at her sister, "I am not stupid, thanks!"

"Impressive, by the way," Riel looked at Dantalian. "Dantalian Romani, with the making of a flaming Sagittarius with your Pyrokinesis! You're my favorite! You all proved that you're ready for the reimbursed demons that will come your way!"

Dantalian seemed more cautious than arrogant now, "Whoa, wait, what do you mean reimbursed demons?" Riel gave him an odd look; it became obvious these four Romani were unaware. "What is the difference between them and a normal demon?"

As Riel turned away to depart she revealed, "The Avatarians reimburse anyone, good or evil, with power to gain their allegiance in their coming final attack!" Madelyn's eyes widened, "I thought your Custodian had already informed you of this? Au revoir!"

KILLER IN VANCOUVER

"**B**onjour 911," a frantic, French Canadian woman made a telephone call, "Police, s'il vous plaît!" her heavy breathing echoed in the speaker, "I would like to report a murder!"

Under the light of a telephone box near Canada Place, Vancouver, a man was actually magically mimicking the female voice.

"Yes, officer, there is a deceased male. Where? On the wharf of Canada Place!" he paused in silence for a moment as he listened to the police officer on the other end of the phone line. "You want to know my name?"

The man turned his head. He looked at the dead body of a young male, aged approximately in his late twenties. The male was lying face down with a bloodied stab wound in the middle of his upper back. A second male, knelt beside the body. He rose, wiping his Athame with a cloth as he removed the victim's blood. "Hang up the damn phone!" the male growled.

In his mimicking French female accent, the male on the phone replied, "My name is–" and then he quickly hung up the phone. In his normal, manly voice he queried, "Did I sound convincing enough?" he grumbled irritably to his companion who was obviously the one who was in control of the situation. "Was it to your standard?"

"Are you talking back to me," the other domineering male questioned, "I am the hunter and you are the Romani under my control!" Reaching his arm out he quickly grasped his weaker and not very independent companion by the throat. "You kill the Romani filth, as per my request." He turned and looked back at the deceased male, "That way you take the fall and I go undetected!"

"Why do you do this to me?" the easily manipulated male replied, "Isn't it enough to control me and my life, but to make me the one responsible for murdering innocent Romani?"

The domineering male glared into his companion's eyes, "I use you because you are a Romani! Consider this your punishment for you ending our relationship. We could have been happy together for eternity. I am bent on destroying you until you agree to return to me!" Releasing his companion, he threw him to the ground, "you'll never be free of me and my Mind Control powers!"

In the distance, police sirens echoed through the downtown city streets of Vancouver.

"Go," the domineering male ordered, "meet me back at the Sutton Place Hotel!" and then magically he vanished in a bolt of lightning.

Standing nervously for a moment, the weaker of the two males fidgeted with his hands, quickly looked about and as he turned on the spot departed in a glimmer of emerald flames. Stepping out from the shadows of an adjacent building, a female, the deceased male's girlfriend revealed her silent presence.

"I am so, sorry," she mourned as she knelt down beside him, "that they thought you were a gypsy, Jesse. I should have told you my secret, I am a Romani!" revealing her true magical identity she wiped tears from her eyes and caressed the back of her dead lover's head. "I am so sorry—"

"I killed a mortal?" said a male's voice,

Shrieking, the startled woman quickly rose to her feet and spun around, greeted by the Romani who killed her partner.

"It's you," she wailed at him, pointing out of anger. "You're the one killing the Romani in the city!"

Showing signs of being deeply shaken by the revelation that he had killed a mortal, the man covered his mouth as tears began to well in the corner of his eyes.

"What have I done?"

The woman swung her arm, throwing the man with her telekinesis. Groaning, he hit the ground heavily.

"Tell me your name!" she growled at him as she approached, "TELL ME!!!" holding her arm up, and in a gleam of copper energy she conjured an Athame into her hand. "Tell me why I should not smite you where you lay, you murderer!" Turning over, he surrendered, placing his hands up in defence.

"M-my name," he choked on his emotions as he answered her, "is Aiden!" the sleeve of his shirt dropped down his arm, revealing a Therianthrope birthmark. "My name is Aiden Mercier!"

The woman stopped herself from attacking him with her Athame as she came to realize something about the man below her.

"Wait... Aiden Mercier?" she withdrew her knife in another gleam of copper energy, "I know you! You're in my coven's Grimoire!" letting her guard down she curiously scanned his appearance. "Leonardi! I am Briallen, of the Forêt Romani Coven."

Losing composure, Aiden broke down crying, succumbing to the agony of his crime. "Please help me!"

The woman hesitated for a moment, long enough for the man before her to quickly alter his mood.

"Pompous bitch!" he growled up at her.

Magically his visage morphed into the domineering male of the two that murdered the woman's mortal partner. Screaming she staggered backwards to evade his hand as he attempted to grab her.

"I knew you were still here!" he revealed, "You Romani have a certain stench!"

Letting out a startled scream, she felt the hot blade of a knife penetrate her in the back. Turning her head, she caught a glimpse of the real Aiden Mercier as he murdered her from behind.

"He is the hunter and we are his to control..." he whispered to her.

Feeling the knife remove from her back, she let out another scream and her body burnt up in a fiery glimmer. In a dwindling flame, Aiden Mercier showed a colder and more dominating nature in his eyes compared to his submissive persona before when ringing and alerting the police.

"Good work, Aiden," said the domineering male,

Aiden replied modestly, "All for you, Jon Chasseur de Gitan," naming his superior.

Jon appeared uneasy at the use of his name and with a sway of his hand he manipulated Aiden Mercier's Romani power of Therianthropy to make him shapeshift into a beautiful fully grown adult male lion.

"In this form," Jon looked down at his minion, "your senses are heightened, sniffing out any Romani in this city is as easy as snapping your fingers," Aiden in his lion form made a chesty growl, "Just like Treadwell, Salem, and New Orleans, this city is a magic haven!"

Obviously, Jon Chasseur de Gitan failed to remember that, unlike the cities he mentioned, in this city and the country of

Canada, hiding in the forestry fringes were the First Nation Clans that could shapeshift into bears, deer, bison, elk, bald eagles, raccoons and Canadian geese.

"We've been here for three days, killed nine Romani and gone undetected!"

Vancouver, in the province of British Columbia, Canada, was a city of brilliance. Turn one way and you see skyscrapers and then turn another to see temperate rainforest and mountains.

It's a city of nature and antiquity, like New Orleans in Louisiana. The historical neighborhood of Gastown, in the city's colourful west end was where it all began, as Vancouver's original downtown core.

It is here that one of the city's local Romani Covens known as Sol (French for Ground) lived, hidden in secrecy on Carrall Street. Forêt, the Forest Romani Coven was situated in Ladysmith on Vancouver Island; Eau, the Water Romani Coven was situated on Pender Island and Ciel, the Sky Romani Coven was located on Grouse Mountain.

Stanley Park – 1,001 acres in size; ten percent bigger than New York's Central Park 840 acres but only half the size of London's 2,360-acre Richmond Park – was beautiful at night, as a steady breeze moved the branches and leaves enough on the trees to make them rustle.

In a small clearing, flames spontaneously combusted atop white candelabras as they hung in the trees. On the ground, a small pond of water rippled as it manifested; catching the candle light its delicate surface shimmered. Rising up from the water, a figure in a baggy blue cloak appeared.

At the same time, amongst the trees a tall figure clad in a baggy green cloak entered through an archway made of vines and roses that manifested upon the person's arrival.

There was a clap of thunder and beautiful veins of lightning flashed as they struck the ground. In the fading glow, a figure emerged clad in a baggy white cloak.

Flames reached up from the ground in a roar and as they faded, a sophisticated man dressed in a business suit emerged with an ice-cold glare on his face.

"Welcome, fellow Romani Leaders!" he said.

Removing their hoods, another male and two females revealed their identities to one another.

"Why have you summoned us, Siôr?" growled the male in the white cloak, "What is of urgency at this hour?"

"Someone," Siôr spoke angrily, "is killing Romani!"

The woman in the blue cloak revealed, "Four were killed from the Eau Coven!"

"Detective Kathryn Penthal informed me that four unclaimed Romani," the woman in green spoke with knowledge, "unclaimed meaning they had not joined any of our covens, have been found murdered! Their bodies were found in the west end of Vancouver. At first she thought they were just a part of the homeless colony, but she found gypsy talismans on each victim." "Do our affiliate covens," the woman in the green cloak began to query, "In New Orleans, Treadwell or Salem know about these murders?" she gazed about her fellow Romani leaders looking for an answer. "Do we know who might be responsible?" Siôr spoke as the four Romani leaders fell into silence.

"We must be vigilant but first and foremost, we need to follow protocol. To keep the death count at nine, I am enforcing a countrywide lockout!"

The woman in the green cloak protested, "You cannot be serious? How is issuing a lockout, going to protect us? Innocents will be at greater risk. The witches of this country alone cannot fight all the demon attacks."

"It is the rules, Siôr!" The other male honored the magical code of conduct, "All witches and Romani must share the load; protect mortals, fight the demons and serve the greater good!"

The male in the white cloak spoke: "Karrye," he looked to the woman in the green cloak and then to the woman in blue, "Leighan, I think it is best that your covens keep out of the city. Keep to the forests and the waters and I will keep mine to the sky. Maybe we don't need a lockout. Perhaps we can lure the attacker into one of our domains. Take him or her out of their comfort zone!"

"Morgan," Karrye agreed with the leader of the Ciel Romani Coven, "Vancouver offers sanctuary. Have we heard any news about the Leonardi Coven?"

Leighan revealed what she knew, "The Leonardi are still missing in action. Aiden Mercier and his coven apparently never made it home."

The four local Romani leaders of Vancouver all had a look of alarm.

The towering skyscrapers and hotels' abstract outlines formed a menacing backdrop as police cars with their flashing lights crowded the street of Canada Place. As a cruise ship terminal, the Canada World Trade Centre, The Pan Pacific Hotel and Vancouver Convention Centre; Canada Place was a bustling tourist and business district. On the wooden boardwalk down the left side of the building, police had tended to the crime scene and covered the deceased body with a sheet.

Pulling up at the curb, a tall woman exited a charcoal coloured four-wheel drive. Shutting the door, the force fanned her long honey blonde, caramel-highlighted hair. She wore suit pants, a dark blue satin blouse that brought out her teal coloured eyes and an open blazer.

"Detective," said the officer guarding the scene.

She revealed her detective badge and went under the police tap.

"Kathryn,"

"Geoff," Greeted by a constable, she queried, "What do we have?" as they both approached the deceased body,

"Do we have any witnesses?"

"Err," the constable consulted his notepad, "It's a Caucasian male estimated mid to late thirties with a stab wound to the upper back. The only apparent witness was a French speaking woman that phoned it in—"

"Have forensics done a full sweep of the crime scene?"

Geoff replied confidently, "Yes!"

Stopping at the feet of the covered body, Kathryn analyzed the crime scene. Brushing some stray hair from her face she identified the public phone used to phone in the deceased male. Moving around to the upper torso and head of the body she knelt down. Ushering a forensic officer over, she was given a set of latex gloves. Reaching out, she pulled the sheet back to observe the victims wound in his back as he laid face down.

"Did forensic," as she investigated the wound she queried, "find any forms of identification on him?"

Geoff ushered another police officer to him who had the victim's possessions.

"Victim's name is Jesse Volden."

She replied, "Is he Canadian?"

Quickly glancing up to observe how close the police officers were to her, she, with her free hand, activated her supernatural power of Extra Sensory Perception. Moving her hand, it gave off a soft red glow. On the back of his neck, partly covered by his dark hair, Kathryn's power revealed an invisible tattoo of the 'Tree of Life' symbol of Forêt Coven of Romani. "Hmm," she murmured curiously and quickly deactivated her power, "can I have a U.V. light! I think I might have found something!"

"What is it?" Geoff questioned.

Gesturing his hand, he summoned the woman from forensics over to the body. Removing her phone from her pants pocket, Kathryn dialled a number and then placed it to her ear as it began to ring.

"Detective Noah Pogue?" she queried as she received the U.V. light, "Detective Kathryn Penthal of the Vancouver P.D. here. How are you?" pausing she heard his response, "Look, I am sorry to disturb you on your first night here. But I am at a crime scene and I have found something that might be of interest. Care to meet with me?" there was another pause and then she said rather abruptly, "Now would be preferable!" Hanging up she placed her phone back in her pants pocket.

Carefully and slowly she began to move the U.V. light over the invisible tattoo on the back of the victim's neck. Suddenly the object in her hand froze. Confused, Kathryn removed her hand and looked up, noticing the police officers around her completely still.

"Kathryn Penthal," Noah's – deep and soothing – voice as he approached, "It's been a while!"

Rising up, Kathryn curled some hair behind her ear and acknowledged the broad-shouldered male as he came into her direct line of sight.

"Noah Pogue," she gave a heartfelt smile, "It has been a while!" Glancing past his shoulder she noticed that he had a companion. "Who is this?"

Halting at his father's side, Shane extended his arm, "Hi," he shook her hand as he introduced himself, "Shane Penthal. I'm Noah's son!"

Kathryn looked at Noah as she shook his son's hand.

Noah raised an eyebrow as he gave a slight smirk.

"I-I," she stumbled through her words, "I'm your aunt.

Your mother Connor – sorry, Connemara – is my eldest sister!"

Shane queried aloud, "The Grey Witch?" he looked at his father out the corner of his eye whilst keeping Kathryn within his peripheral vision. "I have heard about your legend!"

Kathryn gave Noah a smug look, "And what legend might that be, huh?"

"Oh," Shane murmured awkwardly, but corrected himself, "Just that you've been good and you've been evil. You're a Grey Witch. You're feared by both sides!"

Noah smirked, "Oh, yeah, feared by most!" mocking her sarcastically. "Anyways," he assumed a serious attitude, "what do we have that might be of interest to me?"

Kathryn looked at Shane, "You know how this goes right? Deceased body, crime scene, etc!"

"Don't touch anything!" Shane remarked nervously.

Kathryn gave a cold stare, "He's a smart boy, Noah!" Returning to the body, the three of them knelt around the deceased male. "I think there is a Gypsy Hunter here in Canada!"

By coincidence the U.V. light had frozen directly over the invisible tattoo, revealing it in full.

"And you're certain of this?" Noah queried as he looked up, "last I heard Jon was entombed in Israel by the Israelite Romani!"

Kathryn stared at Noah, "This is the ninth victim in three consecutive days! If it had been two victims with invisible tattoos sure, I'd call it a night. But nine?" Noah remained silent, unable to counter her evidence. She looked across at Shane and then back to her brother-in-law, "The entire magical community here in Vancouver is whispering."

Shane's intrigued was pricked, "Whispering about what?"

"Something about Avatarians..." she looked at the two witches opposite her for clarification. "What the hell is an Avatarian for starters?"

"They're taking over the Underworld," Shane revealed, "Rafaela, their leader is reimbursing demons with power. Good folk are turning evil for the sake of not being slaughtered!"

Kathryn sensed something in Noah, "What is it?"

"The Incubo, Nightmare Soldiers, took Perry. I was visited by Tempest and Philomena!" Noah revealed to Kathryn.

Startled, she raised an eyebrow, "You were visited by Gamma Witches? That's big business, if they left Santo Cathedral in Monument Valley. How do you know Perry is here, though, in

British Columbia? Canada has ten provinces and three territories. Locating him with scrying or spell would be like closing your eyes and dropping a pin somewhere on a map!"

"Bermuda did a locating spell," Shane revealed, "and the provincial flag for British Columbia was revealed!"

Noah analyzed her with his limited Custodian power of Empathy, "You're hesitant..."

"Noah," she spoke as though frustrated, "There are many things here. Not all magical things respond well to witches treading onto their territories, whether you're good or evil!"

"This place is Paradise." a naïve Shane queried unknowingly, "What could be here that does not take kindly to witches?"

Kathryn spoke with caution, "First Nations!" Shane and Noah both raised their eyebrows in surprise, "They are solitary people. They don't take kindly to witches of any kind stepping foot onto their lands. I recommend you consult the Tribe Elders before you go walking into a situation where you may not come out of the same way you went in!"

Chapter Twenty

VISIONARY – PART THREE

Sunlight broke on the horizon, washing over the snow dusted peaks of the Coastal Mountains of British Columbia, Canada, with warm golden rays.

Out on the balcony of his penthouse suite at the Hotel Vancouver – a château style hotel in the heart of the downtown sector – Noah Pogue, dressed only in casual suit pants sipped a hot cup of coffee.

The lost look in his eyes as he watched the sunrise revealed the contemplation of his life this far; although seemingly full of ambition he felt a distinct lack of direction.

Emerging onto the balcony, Kathryn Penthal, dressed in Noah's shirt, a bra and panties wrapped her arms around his waist and placed a kiss on his neck.

"That sex last night–" she smirked.

Noah stared out at the scenery, "Was emotionless, a quick fix!"

"Don't worry," removing her arms, Kathryn walked to the balcony's edge, "I won't tell your wife!" Looking back at her brother-in-law, she snapped her fingers. Magically, her attire glittered in the sunlight and suddenly she was dressed in white denim shorts, a pink tank top, thin cardigan and brown western boots. "My darling older sister left you, remember!"

Noah cleared his throat and placed his cup down on the small table, "I'm a family man. I have dignity to uphold–"

Kathryn cut him off, "Don't be so considerate of others! It's annoying!" Noah gave her a glare, "You're too goodiegoodie, it's revolting!"

"And you're a bitch!" he growled angrily,

Kathryn smirked, as though flattered, "I tell it how it is! Now get your shit together," her hostility made her stride even sexier as she walked past him, "we're leaving for Squamish!"

After driving through the city streets, Kathryn, Noah and Shane made their way along the motorway through Stanley Park. In the backseat of the BMW four-wheel drive, Shane, looked out over the Burrard Inlet and Vancouver Harbor to the right as they crossed over the Lions Gate Bridge toward the North Shore of Vancouver.

Nowhere to Run by the Commitments played on the radio.

On the side of the road, invisible to the human eye and apparently witch, a trio of women stood clad in black robes. Fixating on the vehicle as it passed them, their eyes turned black and their mouths reached open revealing shark teeth.

They were Incubo, Nightmare Soldiers, hiding on the threshold where the Spirit Realm met the human world.

Travelling for some time along the Sea-to-Sky Highway, feeling the effects of drivers fatigue, Kathryn placed her indicator on and turned off onto another road to her left. Leaving the bitumen road, she drove into a parking lot that overlooked a scenic bay at the Porteau Cove Provincial Park.

Moving along a small roadway, Kathryn turned, crossed a train line that ran alongside the sea-to-sky highway and then drove into the car park. Adorned with trees and picnic tables the picturesque location had a backdrop of mountains and a wonderful view of the ocean.

Turning the car off, Kathryn sighed aloud. Running her hand through her long hair, she then turned her head and acknowledged

Noah asleep in the passenger seat beside her. Looking a little further back, Shane was asleep and slumped in the backseat.

"It wasn't that long of a drive," she appeared confused and then looked to the left to the ocean view, "was it?" Removing her seatbelt, she opened the car door and exited out into the Canadian wilderness. "Mm!" although close to winter, she felt a warm breeze sweep across her face as she closed the door behind her, "I forgot how beautiful it was up here!"

"It's such a pretty picture!" said a croaky old voice.

Grabbed by the throat, Kathryn shrieked as she glared at a Nightmare Soldier Demon in the eye. Black hood covered its hair, but its eyes were an abyss of black and its teeth looked like it would strip human flesh from the bone.

"You're in trouble," with a hearty groan the demon threw Kathryn against the car, "witch!" Waving her arm, she made two more demons appear in clouds of black on either side of her. "You crossed the threshold into the Spirit Realm! There are things here that you don't really have the power to fight!"

"Ugh!" Kathryn groaned, getting up to her feet, "like you? Please! You ugly bitch! What could be possibly more horrible than you? Oh wait..." taking a deep breath she let out a sonic scream.

"I'm immune to your powers!"

The concussive pulses given off from the power suddenly caused the demons to grip their heads and buckle under severe pain. Throwing its arm out, one demon succumbed to being vanquished as it burnt up in flames.

"ENOUGH!!" yelled the Nightmare Soldier, "Cram it Goldielocks!"

Extending its arm, she began to electrocute Kathryn with black lightning. Venturing around the passenger side of the car, the second Nightmare Soldier pulled the car door open and attempted to attack a sleeping Shane in the backseat. She glanced ahead noticing Noah still asleep in the front.

"Mm," she was tantalized by Shane's appearance, "such a handsome witch! It shall be a delight to devour such a specimen!"

Reaching into the car with her arms and claws, the door was slammed shut on her, severing her right arm from her body.

Screaming in agony, she turned around and was greeted by Noah himself.

"Touch my son and it will be the last thing you ever do!"

The demon growled, "What? You were just—" turning her head she saw that he was still asleep in the car, "Astral Projecting! Clever!"

A confused Noah replied, "Huh? How?"

The Nightmare Soldier smirked, realizing she suddenly had an advantage over him. She could destroy the vehicle with his body inside it, leaving him unable to return to it. Bringing her remaining arm in close, she then quickly pushed it forwards, throwing Noah back onto the ground with telekinesis.

"Hello friend," said a woman's voice in Filipino.

Turning, the Nightmare Soldier looked into the car. Seeing nothing, she then began to magically elevate upwards until she stopped, staring a beautiful Filipino woman in the eyes who stood upon the car roof.

The demon named her, "Aryan!"

"Do not bother," Aryan, the Filipino woman gave a confident smirk, "You are not powerful enough to counter my power!"

Looking up as he lay on the bitumen, Noah observed the Nightmare Soldier hovering off the ground beside the car, incapacitated by the power of the young Mangkukulam: Filipino Witch.

"You know that coming into the Dream Dimension is treason!" Aryan wagged her index finger from left to right. "The

Dream and Spirit Dimension are one in the same. Do not think for a second you are granted passage here!"

The Nightmare Soldier grumbled her response, "I will devour you once I have devoured the other witches, Mangkukulam!"

Placing her index finger on the demon, Aryan cast her vanquishing spell in Filipino. "Flames shall take the rest!"

Letting out a scream, the demon was vanquished in a ravenous fire that began from its feet all the way to its head, before disappearing in a small wisp of smoke.

Arching her back and screaming Kathryn continued to be electrocuted by the Nightmare Soldier around the other side of the car.

"You'll never find Perry!" the demon revealed.

Hearing those words made something snap inside Kathryn's mind. Silencing her screaming she channelled her Energy Manipulation power through her entire body instead of her hands and vocal cords. Forcing her hands forward she created a glittering barrier around herself to absorb the electricity.

"Don't worry," said a second voice in Filipino.

Distracted, the Nightmare Soldier turned and immediately collapsed onto the ground as another Mangkukulam held her gestured hand at the demon's face, using her power of Sedation, she lowered it with the demon.

"We will find the male witch," she revealed looking over at Kathryn quickly and then returned her focus back to the demon at her feet. "The ground shall swallow you whole!"

Using her power of Portal Creation, she made the ground ripple like water and sent the demon into another dimension. In the blink of an eye the ground was solid again.

"Thank you!" Kathryn thanked her savior.

The Filipino woman looked at the witch, "You are a Grey Witch! You of all people know it is deadly travelling to this dimension, the way you did!"

"I don't need a lecture on Astral Projection, thanks!" Kathryn leant against the car for a moment as she regained her faculties. "Are you the one they call Liliane?"

Liliane replied humbly, "Yes, I am Liliane. The Mangkukulam over there is Aryan!"

"We would have been safer to Astral Project from our hotel room!" protested Noah as he came around the car, "How long ago did we cross the realm threshold?"

Liliane replied, "You crossed the threshold back at Magnesia Creek!"

"That was eleven kilometers back down the bloody road!" Noah quickly leapt at the chance to be sarcastic, "What, so they make cars with auto-pilot now?"

Another Filipino Witch emerged, "We guided you here with our magic! We have great power here in the Spirit Realm. Unlike you Mr. Pogue, we can exist here in a full physical form like the Nightmare Soldiers. You can only maintain existence here via Astral Projection!"

"This is Mylane," Liliane introduced her fellow Mangkukulam, "I've seen your brother, Mr. Pogue! I know this because a premonition some days ago revealed it to be the only question you would ask me."

Mylane announced, "The Nightmare Soldiers have him!"

Liliane continued, "But before we venture deep into this realm, we must be granted permission by the First Nations. They are the power here, second to the gods and won't take too kindly for uninvited travellers!"

Aryan revealed, "They are what you would call, The Care Takers!"

A frustrated Noah sighed aloud. He impatiently ran his hand through his thick hair. In front of him, some meters away, the three Mangkukulam deliberated how they would travel to Squamish from here.

"It could be treacherous," Aryan stated with her arms folded, "the slightest foot off the track and who knows what pocket dream they could fall into!"

Liliane replied, "How else do we get them there if it is too hazardous by foot?"

"We ask the gods for safe passage?" Aryan queried curiously,

Mylane interrupted, "We could summon Morpheus and ask him for his blessing."

Noah queried, "The naked God of Dreams?"

"That would be him," Aryan remarked with a sparkle of praise in her eyes, "his naked form represents how much desire is actually in our dreams!"

Morpheus was one of the three overseers of this realm — along with his siblings Phebotor and Phantasos — and implied to be the most powerful of the trio.

Eavesdropping on the conversation, Noah turned to the side to admire the view of the glorious sunlight over the water. Startled, an apparition of his brother Perry stood before him.

"NOAH!!" Perry demanded, reaching out to his brother with clenched fists, "FIND ME!! SAVE ME!"

Startled Noah cried out, "PERRY!!" reaching forwards he touched his brother's hand and felt an electrical charge, "Ouch, PERRY I'M HERE!!!"

In an unknown location, as he lay in an induced slumber, Perry's body gave off an electrical charge. Startled, three figures clad in heavy black robes staggered backwards.

Aryan queried Noah, "You're absolute that you can see your brother?"

"Don't you see him?" Noah insisted, as he held his sight on Perry, "Tell me," a look of confusion swelled in his face, "tell me you see him!" Heartbroken he turned back to the others for clarification. "Is this some cruel trick?" Perry simply stared at him.

Liliane replied, "The Dream Realm and Spirit Realm overlap one another. It is said that's how spirits are able to come to people in their dreams."

"What you are seeing is Perry's subconscious," Mylane forced Noah to acknowledge the magical effects of this realm he had ventured into, "reaching out through this world. You can see and hear him. But he cannot see you; he can merely sense your presence!"

Noah announced firmly, "I touched him!"

"Pardon me?" a shocked Aryan questioned.

Noah continued with clear certainty, "I touched him and I felt an electrical charge!"

"It's not physically possible here, you must be mistaken!" Mylane dismissed the allegation, "Only kindred spirits are able to touch one another in this world!"

An intrigued Aryan raised an eyebrow with suspicion, "awakening their kindred spirits could turn him corporeal!"

"How can being kindred help?" Kathryn asked bluntly.

Mylane replied, "A kindred spirit is the soul calling to its soul mate. It would make pinpointing Perry's location easier! But we don't possess the kind of power to awaken slumbering spirits!"

"We need to summon Morpheus!" Liliane declared.

~*~

In an unknown location, in a void of white, lying on a grey stone altar, Perry remained in an induced slumber as the three heavily cloaked figures moved cautiously toward him after being jolted back by an electrical charge.

They talked inaudibly amongst themselves.

A burst of dark blue light at Perry's feet and Kamenwati, Nightmare Soldier superior, appeared. Her long hair pinned up in a bun, with curls gently falling about her face. She was dressed in a short white dress with long sleeves, hugged in a brown leather corset that accentuated her breasts.

"Mangiare, have we access to his mind?" she asked in a blunt tone.

Revealing a partial silhouette of its face and big ram horns to its superior, the lead Mangiare standing behind Perry's head spoke: "The Sognare Coven put a lot of barriers in his head!" Revealing itself entirely, the Mangiare was an elderly woman in appearance, "I am able to break through them. However, one at a time! That coven was strong, but I am stronger!"

"For a thousand years old, I expect you to be powerful, old lady! Get back to work! Rafaela wants to know the secrets he possesses about bringing Alera back!"

In flash of dark blue light Kamenwati entered Perry's body and mind.

Trapped inside his dream world, Perry sat in the sand dunes of Aldinga Beach, looking out over the crystal blue water as the sun beamed down overhead.

He sighed, believing in the content he was feeling, as he listened to the sound of waves crashing onto the shore.

VISIONARY – PART FOUR

"**P**ERRY!!" Noah's voice called on the wind.

Startled, Perry gasped and turned his head; quickly glancing about to see where the familiar voice came from. Rising from the sand where he sat, Perry saw a ghostly figure of what he thought was his brother Noah down at the water's edge.

He called out, "NOAH!!"

"PERRY!!" the voice called again.

Running down the sand to the figure, Perry passed through the apparition and stumbled into the water as it lapped over his feet. Turning around sharply he saw no one but his own footprints in the sand.

Confused he ran his hand through his hair, "Huh?"

Suddenly from behind there was an explosion in the water and Perry was thrown through the air and crashed into the loose sand. Rising up from the ocean, a figure made of water walked onto the shore. It shone a dark blue as Kamenwati assumed her beautiful form. Then using her power to Shapeshift, she turned into a middle-aged woman with long blood-red hair that fell in styled curls down to her waist. She wore a long white Grecian gown with a heavenly aura that was amplified by the sunlight.

Face-down in the sand, Perry groaned as he raised his head and began to turn his body around to see his attacker. Wiping sand from his face, his blurry eyes adjusted and he caught a glimpse of what looked like his dead mother.

"Mum...?" he murmured with confusion, "How?"

Kneeling down, she smiled at him and caressed his cheek, "Hello my son!"

Moving her arm around behind his back she brought him close and they hugged.

~*~

Noah, Kathryn and a sleeping Shane had not moved from the Porteau Cove Provincial Park, the place where they were ambushed by Nightmare Soldiers and rescued by a trio of Mangkukulam. Their adventure into the Spirit and Dream Realm to find Perry had stalled involuntarily. Seeking a blessing for safe passage from one of the three reigning gods of the dimension – so that the three travellers could be granted their true physical forms instead of astral projections – Liliane, Mylane and Aryan sought to summon Morpheus.

"Hear our words." The three Filipino witches held hands and cast a summoning spell: "Morpheus, Dream God, we summon you into our sacred circle, humble are we by your power! Blessed we are in your presence!" Some minutes of silence passed.

"Well," Noah reacted sarcastically, "that went splendid!"

Abruptly he was silenced and lost his balance as a burst of light and energy knocked him back into Kathryn. Making his entrance, the light faded revealing a fully naked man with an olive tan, toned body, masculine arms and long dark hair.

"Liliane," he spoke, "why have you summoned me?"

Intrigued, Kathryn eyed the god up and down, admiring his well-sculptured behind. The muscles in his back became defined as he moved his posture.

"A... god!" she murmured with lust and disbelief,

Turning his head, he looked over his shoulder, "I see you brought a Grey Witch into my dimension!" Analyzing her, he then turned his attention back to the three Mangkukulam. "You wish for me to bless them safe passage?"

Mylane nodded her head, "Yes. We need you to make

them corporeal. It's not safe for their bodies to be left here while they venture through this world as Astral Projections!"

Noah murmured to Kathryn, "Surely he must be cold?" his eyebrows raised curiously, "I grew up with two brothers. I'd like to think I can handle a naked guy…!"

Turning around, Morpheus acknowledged Noah.

"Another Pogue?"

Noah's eyelids pulled back, "Ha…" he remarked awkwardly, "It's just hanging there!"

"That's the gayest thing I think I've ever heard you say," Kathryn remarked bluntly, "The first thing you acknowledge," She crafted a sarcastic gesture with her face and made a hand motion at the god in front of them, "is his penis and masculine body? Yeah, you're totally straight, Noah Pogue!"

Noah growled at her, "You do realise that you're such a bitch, right?"

"I am what I am!" she retorted very calmly, "Bitch is just one of many things!"

In an inspired moment of thought, Noah turned his attention back to the god in front of him. He gestured his hand to verify what he had heard although his attention was placed on Kathryn Penthal.

"Whoa, wait! You said another Pogue?"

Morpheus replied, "Did I stutter?"

"You've seen my brother, Perry?"

Morpheus spoke again, "More like monitoring him with my two other siblings. He is being held captive by the Nightmare

Soldier Kamenwati. They have substantial power here for some reason…" he appeared lost in a moment of confusion, "They have him inside an impenetrable bubble of magic."

Noah gave a confused look, "You're a god. This is your dimension. Surely you have enough power to vanquish this Kamenwati and her minions?"

Morpheus's eyes turned a daring blue out of frustration, "EXCUSE ME!" his voice bellowed and the ground shook for a moment. "I will have you know," his voice and eyes returned to normal as he calmed himself, "We deities, like the Old Ones, tend to keep out of the Fate's business!"

Noah raised his eyebrow out of ignorance, "The Fates?"

"Atropos, Clotho and Lachesis," Kathryn interrupted for a moment to explain, "the three sisters of fate. They are very big on everything happening according to a timeline. It's punishable by vanquish or incarceration for Old Ones and Deities if they intervene in the destinies the Fates have woven!"

"You're still a bitch!" Noah growled under his breath,

Kathryn smirked as she kept her eyes on Morpheus's face, "I still think you're gay!"

"Enough!" Morpheus interrupted, "There is chatter amongst the spirits that venture here to visit their loved ones in dreams. The Nightmare Soldiers are trying to access something in your brother's head. He knows a secret, something about resurrection? That is First Nation business!"

Noah's eyebrows rose, "I don't know what Perry would know about resurrection?" he turned to look at Kathryn, "Maybe how to get an erection; he gets laid a lot! But resurrection, nah I think that's a load of bull—" Noah turned his head and lowered it as a surging pain moved throughout his body.

"Noah?" Kathryn queried cautiously,

Noah groaned, "Ugh, oh God!" throwing his arms out, he yelled and his aura burned bright as his eyes became eclipsed with white, "ARGH!!!"

"He is a kindred spirit?" Morpheus leant back cautiously, "He can quite literally feel his brother – mentally and physically!" quickly extending his arm and gesturing his hand at Noah, he used his godly powers. "I will grant him a permanent form; I will put him back in his body. Or–"

Kathryn blurted out firmly, "Or? What the hell does that mean?"

"Or," Morpheus glared at her for a second, "His soul will die, killing both Astral Projection and Physical versions!" Magically his hand gave off a sudden glow and he spoke an incantation in Latin, "In all realms he shall have a form."

Dropping to his knees in agony, Noah fell onto his side as his aura continued to burn. Although an Astral Projection, the kindred spirit in him was whisked away in an abrupt flash. Noah was gone and Kathryn gasped in shock.

~*~

Opening his eyes and letting out a gasp, Shane Penthal awoke in a different location within the Dream Realm to his father and aunt.

The gentle sunlight shone down through the canopy of the pine trees. Looking around he found himself standing in a Canadian forest. Turning around on the spot, he halted and caught a glimpse of an old stone crypt overgrown in vines and fauna.

"W-where..." he queried, "am," he observed the three tall cloaked, bronze guardians, "...I?"

A male's voice moved past his left ear, "Are you lost, boy?"

Startled, Shane spun around to his left and was greeted by the endless forest.

"He must be!" A different male voice moved past his right ear, "He has to be a Visionary!"

He abruptly halted and trembled with fear as a woman stood in front of him.

"P-Persia?" he stumbled over her name, apparently knowing her by appearance, "What—"

"Shh—" she extended her arm and pressed her finger against his lips, "The more you speak, the more attention you will draw to yourself!" Withdrawing her arm back to her side, a male appeared at either side of her. "In the human world, you know our physical selves…"

The male on her right spoke, "but here, we are an entirely different consciousness—"

"Together," the male to the left of her spoke but interrupted, "subconsciously, we are the Old One."

"Known as the Morrígan!" said Persia.

Shane spoke nervously, "The Morrígan is an Irish Deity of Battle, Strife and Sovereignty that has often been depicted as three…" he acknowledged that in this incarnation the Morrígan was two males and a female, "sisters. But I know you as the triplets Dantalian, Persia and Mars Romani!"

"Oh," Persia smiled, "sweet, sweet Pogue Witch! They are our reincarnation. Our original names are Badb, Macha and Nemain!"

In front of the Pogue Witch, the triplets levitated above the pine needle-covered ground, shoulder to shoulder. The sunlight that shone in through the canopy glittered as it was absorbed into their individual auras.

Dantalian interrupted, "Like Prometheus, you are a Visionary!"

"You're going to free the Romani from the Hunter!" said Mars.

A shocked Shane replied, "Come again?"

The triplets stared at him with shining eyes.

~*~

Still feeling startled and a little helpless as she watched her brother-in-law drop to the ground in agony, Kathryn, on the spur of the moment, turned around and looked into the car behind her only to see that Noah's body had also disappeared.

Morpheus had given him a physical form in the unpredictable realm that can change, pending one's perception.

He, his deity siblings or the Morrígan have the ability to turn that unpredictably into stability.

On the secluded beach – within the Dream Realm – where Perry Pogue's Astral Projection loitered, his older brother Noah manifested in a flash of light; their kindred spirits brought them together.

A shower of sand fell around him as he turned around on the spot, admiring the incredible blue ocean and the sound of waves crashing onto the shore.

"Where–" he murmured curiously, "the hell is," turning around some more he witnessed his brother being attacked by a woman with long red hair, "this? PERRY!!" he blurted out abruptly out of shock.

Moving his arm out, he gestured his hand to utilize his power of Probability Manipulation. Achieving the result he was hoping for, the woman electrocuting Perry with black lightning had her power suddenly turn against her and was thrown backwards into the sand, where she vanished in a ripple of energy.

"PERRY!!" Noah cried out as he ran up the beach to his brother lying in the sand, "PERRY!!!" he came within meters of reaching out to touch, "I am here–"

Abruptly an invisible presence threw black lightning at the Pogue Witch and catapulted him backwards into the shallow water that lapped the sand. A black ethereal mass began to manifest as it crawled over Perry's body. It began to take a humanoid form; first a head emerged with beaming red eyes complimented by a mouth with shark-like teeth.

Long red hair grew out of its scalp and cascaded down in a single flop.

Arms reached outwards toward Noah as he pulled his wet self out of the water. He coughed and spat sea water out of his mouth. He groaned, turned and gasped as an otherworldly noise rang out and black lightning struck the water causing an explosion.

~*~

Deep inside the Canadian forest, Shane Penthal carefully walked up the steps of the Romani Crypt. He paused for a moment to analyze the three bronze figures that stood on either side of the iron door entry.

"This place is really..." glancing over his shoulder he cautiously noticed the Morrígan levitating above the ground some distance back, "creepy!" Turning his attention back to the iron door he extended his arm, moved his hand in a swaying gesture and cast a Power Word Charm, "Aprire! (Open)" in Italian.

The deadlock unlocked with a clunk, the large door groaned uncomfortably and at a snail's pace swung inwards. Pushing against the door it opened wide and beyond the door was a large ceremonial room. On entering the crypt, flames spontaneously combusted upon white candles that lined the walls and adorned the stone altar.

"What is this place?" He queried as he strolled about and curiously touched things he probably shouldn't. In a broken piece of mirror that hung on the wall, he caught a glimpse of an old rickety wooden door.

"I feel like I have been here before," he could feel the history in everything he touched, "What's behind the door?" He turned and looked at it, curiously compelled to open it. "Why does this place feel so familiar?"

Macha, who looked like Persia Romani, began to reveal things to Shane about himself that he never knew: "Centuries ago, in one of your past lives, you were a Romani–" "Your name was Amias," Badb interrupted.

Shane made his way to the old rickety door. Carefully he began to extend his arm but cautiously halted as he went to place his hand on the handle.

Nemain spoke, "You, Ba'al, Meydad, Moss and Nevo were known as the Israelites, a powerful coven of Romani that lived in Eilat, in the Middle East. You – they – encountered Jon, the Gypsy Hunter and imprisoned him inside this crypt–"

Shane traced his hand over the door handle as he vaguely recalled something, "The Haus of Romani was a place where all Romani gathered for rituals and celebrations." Angrily he ripped the door open and another, pantry size room was revealed, "He perverted that–"

Throwing a bolt of lightning into the small area, Shane's power struck something and the sound of smashing glass reached his ears. A white mist went unseen by Shane as it escaped.

~*~

In a hotel room, somewhere in the Coal Harbor sector of Vancouver, Jon Chasseur de Gitan – the Gypsy Hunter – and his partner Aiden Mercier had killed another Romani, but not before having a sexual encounter with him.

The deceased lay naked and sprawled out over the bed with Jon standing close-by and analyzing his achievement. While in the washroom of the hotel suite, Aiden looked at himself in the mirror, wondering who he was. Suddenly, he felt a white mist possess him.

Chapter Twenty-Two

SOMETHING IN THE WATER

It was a still spring night. The sky was clear, stars twinkled and the full moon illuminated the calm ocean. Not far off Aldinga Beach in Treadwell, Deane County, sitting in his small dinghy, a fisherman had fallen asleep. The swaying water was hypnotizing. He waited for something to take the bait and pull on his fishing rod.

An odd, otherworldly noise moved around the boat beneath the water's surface, but the man did not stir; he continued to snore. The dinghy suddenly rocked uneasily and the man abruptly awoke. Obscured to him by the dark, he did not see the collection of hungry, glowing green, marble-size spectacles under the water's surface.

He turned to observe his surroundings. The eyes beneath the water suddenly vanished. In the distance, the man could see the lights of Aldinga Beach, but was too far out to even consider calling for help should he come into any kind of trouble.

Sighing, he overcame the fatigue that had plagued him, stretched and went to reach for his fishing rod. But upon his grasp it was pulled from the boat and into the water.

"What the...?" he murmured cautiously.

Behind him, a mysterious shadow rose up from the water and levitated midair with hungry green eyes like the ones that stalked the mortal from below him. It expanded its arms and seemed to sway in the air, revealing a mermaid-like tail as the moon's glow glittered on its scales.

"I say," said an eerie female's voice, "dear sailor–"

Startled, the man turned and was greeted by a horrific looking mermaid with pitch black eyes, void of life or good, shark-like teeth and a very gaunt face, like she had been starved for a millennia.

She continued, "There is a very bad reason why the ocean should not be journeyed alone at night."

"Why?" he queried her sheepishly.

"We Undine," she reached out, caressed his cheek and paralyzed him, "devour those who dare to venture into our watery graves. Don't worry about the sharks, worry about the Water Dwellers!!"

A bloody cry rang out over the quiet ocean as the man was murdered.

Undine or Ondine, are the evil counterparts of Mermaids and Mermen. They are cold-blooded killers who prey on sailors and lure them to their death; they are confident enough to venture aboard cruise ships to devour victims. Perry Pogue was turned into one but later saved by his brother Noah before he could kill anyone.

Four days after the vicious attack and having gained the unintentional attention of the Romani, the local government labelled the incident as a 'Shark Attack' in an attempt to cover up the supernatural occurance.

Standing at the far end of the Brighton Jetty, a teenage girl admired the clear sea water several feet below as she contemplated her position in the world. In November, the weather in Treadwell is unpredictable; it's warm or it's grey and miserable.

The sea breeze blew her long hair and the sunshine kissed her tanned skin. Raising her head, she admired the clear blue sky and closed her eyes to take comfort in the warmth with a smile on her face. Her lack of attention lead to not sensing the black mass that moved in under the jetty in the water below.

"Hello," a female's voice came from behind, "sweet girl!"

Startled, the girl turned around and acknowledged an ethereal woman with long aqua coloured hair with a decorative crown of ocean coral. Her apple green eyes sparkled as they captured the sunlight.

"Who-who," timidly the innocent mortal girl queried, "are you?" she quickly looked about the deserted boardwalk and wondered where this woman had come from. "Where did you come from? There was no one here a moment ago!"

"I am Salacia," the woman revealed her name as she took a step forward, "consort of King Neptune, of the Ocean!" in a split-second she was gone, but then reappeared behind the girl. "Don't fear me child," she whispered against the girl's neck, "you smell so sweet, like mangos..." and she proceeded to slowly and sensually wrap her arm around the girl's waist. "Don't resist—"

"What-what," the girl looked out the corner of her eye, "do you want from me?"

"Step away, Salacia!" A male's voice stole the focus of the life-threatening situation.

Salacia shot her stare ahead and acknowledged the man, "Gregory Fox!" she narrowed her eyes, "I should have known the Government Supernatural Bureau would be monitoring mine and my king's domain after I killed that fisherman!"

"No one has to get hurt." The man with neatly styled blonde hair and dressed in a suit – obviously a white-collar worker – stood with his arms folded, "Let the girl go, Salacia!" Salacia laughed, "The great and powerful, sophisticated and..." she seemed to lose herself in a moment of lust, "desirable, Gregory Fox! One of the G.S.B.'s finest agents!" abruptly her attitude changed, "How revolting." She swiftly snapped the girls neck and let the body fall to the jetty.

The woman from the water stepped over the body and began her approach toward the confident man. With his stiff posture and stern expression, he did not fear evil or anything potentially more powerful than him.

Greg rolled his eyes. Revealing his great power, he mentally wielded his inherited abilities. He watched Salacia bump into a wall of energy that flashed white upon her touch and then disappeared the moment she stepped back.

"Clever," she taunted him, "aren't you, Fantastic Mr. FOX!!!"

He replied, "Do not approach me! You are below me, water dweller!"

"I am a goddess! It is you who is below me, Sentinel!" she growled.

The hierarchy of the G.S.B. went: The CEO, Sentinels, Custodians and then Tyro as the entry level. It was designed by the Old Ones to monitor the human world for low and significant evil supernatural threats, but to also offer protection to good witches.

"You have drawn some attention in the mortal world," he revealed as he mentally began to make her body contort, "The G.S.B. wants the "Something in the Water" case dealt with."

Three large and heavy shadows moved beneath the ocean behind Salacia.

"The Oceanic Kingdom does not kneel before the CEO!" she showed repulsion toward the G.S.B. "We answer to our liege; to Rafaela!"

Otherworldly groans were heard, followed by explosions that sent water shooting into the air. From the torso up, three giant water deities, who were aligned with Salacia, emerged with dark expressions in their faces. They attempted to intimidate the Sentinel.

She remarked modestly, "I hope you don't mind," he continued to give her a sour stare, "but I brought company just in case I was set upon! Brizo, Palaemon, Rán."

Brizo was the Greek Sea Goddess who protects sailors and fishermen.

Palaemon was a Greek Sea God.

Rán was the Norse Sea Goddess of love who collects the drowned.

Gregory Fox, Sentinel of the G.S.B., raised his arm away from his side and gesturing his hand, vibrant green electricity began to arc within his palm. His gentle blue eyes strengthened to an intimidating deep sapphire.

"Negotiations with the Oceanic Realm," he spoke aloud to his higher power that listened remotely, "were of no success. King Neptune and all who consort with him are now enemies of the magic populous and the G.S.B."

Salacia remarked nastily, "From Custodian to Sentinel... Sentinel to deceased!" Moving her arm, she gestured her hand and in a glow of light she conjured a Trident into her possession.

"Someone ought to clip your wings..."

Aiming the three points of her weapon at the agent of good, she gave it a jolt to activate it and projected bolts of lightning up the Brighton Jetty. Retaliating, Gregory yelled and reached his arm forwards, throwing his bolts of lightning down the jetty at the water deity.

"Rise and fall," a firm and unseen female voice spoke in Italian, "ocean water, create a wall!"

The water beneath the jetty receeded to reveal the sand and then rushed swiftly back. The force of tide, combining with magic, caused an eruption that drove the water upwards. Blasting up in between the wooden planks of the jetty, a towering wall of glimmering water was created.

Both electrical powers were absorbed by the watery obstruction.

In a clap of thunder the water dispursed, revealing the presence of the Acqua Coven. A small and lucrative group of witches who were water deities in a past life and have been reincarnated, this time bound in a corporeal form. Their power over all things water and the weather is not as immense but still very much potent.

The coven leader – a powerful hydrokinetic witch born Dimitra Summers, daughter of Gretchen Summers and granddaughter of Darla Williams the sister of Tempest Pogue – was Amphitrite, a sea-goddess and once wife of Posiedon eons ago. Second in charge was Benthesikyme, reincarnated as a witch by the name Tracy; then Calypso, reincarnated as a witch named Sara and lastly was Cymopoleia who was reborn as the witch named Kara.

The four of them stood about the Jetty and close-by to Gregory Fox.

"Huh," Salacia grumbled unpleasantly and deactivated her power, "Well, if it ain't Dimitra and the scuba sqaud! You were worshipped and adored all those millennia ago! Now look at you, goddesses who reincarnated themselves as witches in order to survive when Paganism was overthrown by Christianity!"

Calypso growled, "Are you stupid?"

"I am a god! They ought to worship me out of fear!" Salacia smirked confidently, "I could always snatch them as soon as they step into my water!"

Calypso continued, "You could have exposed us! Not to mention the existence of magic! You will not gain worship by inducing fear, Salacia. As of now, there is an Illusory hiding us from human sight!"

Dimitra Summers' eyes filled entirely with a sapphire colour, "Salacia," her voice sounded deeper as she revealed a small portion of her power, "you were going to attack a Sentinel? Really?" her voice was full of acid toward an old friend as her eyes returned to normal, "Stooping to such a low, as to become evil?"

Salacia hardened her facial expression.

Dimitra continued, fueled by sarcasm, "Did you think Neptune would make you his equal? Share his power? Offer you a seat beside him on his royal altar?"

Sparked by her anger, Salacia made thunder rumble in the clear blue sky and caused clouds to quickly manifest, casting a harsh shadow over the Brighton Jetty.

"I am his equal, I am his–" Salacia was cut off.

Dimitra spoke abruptly, "Rafaela is his equal! He worships her like she is his wi–"

Salacia shouted, "LIES!!" and expelled a pulse of kinetic energy and then proceeded to reach her arms forwards, projecting powerful bolts of lightning from her trident. "Death is your reward for your betrayal to the ocean throne, Amphitrite!"

Calypso interupted, "The only betrayal Salacia, is you choosing evil!"

"From sea to sky," Dimitra extended her arm, magically halting the lightning bolts in their approach, "royal sprite, water deep, riptide!"

Letting out a scream, Salacia was pulled down into a watery portal and banished back to the Oceanic Realm along with the three other giant water dieties in the water. The lightning frozen in the air dispersed into glittering particles.

"War is coming." Greg revealed uneasily,

Dimitra replied bluntly, "It's already here!"

~*~

Later that night, on the Hallett Cove beach – down on Treadwell's South Coast and a thirty-minute drive from the CBD –

a large group of youth had come together for a twilight beach party.

Down on the beach, some meters offshore, a black shadow moved beneath the water, progressively making its way toward the sand. It first raised its head above the water revealing itself to be of female gender. Elevating a little more it revealed its torso while beneath a beautiful pink mermaid tail.

Raising her head she closed her eyes, sniffed the air to find the delicious scent of humans and then reopened her eyes. They turned from placid teal to a malicious black and her teeth became jagged like that of a shark.

It was a quick transformation from a mesmerizing being to an evil, water dwelling creature, void of anything attractive. Leaving the water, her mermaid tail began fading from sparkling hot pink to light grey, charcoal and then finally black before turning into a pair of human legs.

She turned her head, her long wet hair hung around her face; away to her side further down the beach there was a large group having a celebration.

"Hey babe," said a male, staggering about the shallow water, "how come you're all the way over there?" He stepped towards the female in the water, "Ah who cares, I'll show you a good time!"

Through reading his aura, she could see his intentions were not innocent; he would soon discover she was not as human as he originally thought.

She smiled at him rather eerily, "Yes." Her voice sounded low and uncaring, "Show me this good time!" Abruptly, wrapping her forearm around the back of his neck she pulled him in close. "But I know your libido will quickly wane!"

Pressing her lips against his for a passionate kiss, she then pulled away, smiled at him again and began to lower herself down to his groin to please him orally. He moaned with pleasure for a few minutes, elevated his head in delight and caressed her head with his hands.

He murmured uncomfortably, "Whoa, baby, ouch!" He tried to pull her off, "Baby, baby! Stop, ouch... you're hurting my d—"

Turning his head, he tried to call out for help but every time he did he would gargle on water and spill it from his mouth. His strength waned as he began to struggle in her tight grip.

Quickly, she filled his lungs with water as she removed all the testosterone and semen from his body to sustain her Shapeshifting power and to reproduce.

Some moments later she exited the water appearing beautiful with a slight glow to her skin, while behind her, her male victim lay face down and dead in the water with his pants down around his ankles.

"I need a meal." she touched the corner of her lips with her fingertips, "not a snack!"

~*~

Revelling in teen angst, disobeying his mother and father's orders that he was too young to be battling and vanquishing demons, let alone going out and partying, Brady Romani danced amongst the harmless mortals who were oblivious to the magic within their close proximity.

"Hi there," the woman from the water batted her eyelids at the guy serving beverages, "Can I get a drink?"

The mortal guy went about making her a beverage, unaware he could be the next victim of this evil woman's choosing. Standing at the makeshift bar of wine barrels, planks of wood and large ice-filled coolers, waiting patiently, she looked around at the partying mortals and set her sights on making a handsome blonde male her next victim.

SOMETHING IN THE WATER
PART 3

The attic in the Romani house was gloomy, with shallow light shining down from the ceiling onto the cauldron that sat over the small flames of a camp stove. Around it, scattered across the table's surface were jars and bowls of herbs and other ingredients for concocting a potion.

Madelyn Romani stepped around the table, "She will be hungry!" Captured by the light, she brushed her long brunette hair from her face and her eyes showed strength. "The Oceanic Realm has been...is now, an enemy of the state."

"Madelyn," Addison spoke casually as she stood opposite her sister, "we have other demons to worry about than a mermaid!" The two of them exchanged a stare. "You heard Riel."

In the weeks since Halloween, the Romani siblings had increased their vigilance toward the woman Philanderer Demon they had encountered in the Treadwell Botanical Gardens. Instead of just referring to her as 'Demon-Bitch' for her ability to test Madelyn's power or 'Philanda-Woman', because she was the only female Philanderer Demon they had encountered in a demon species so dominated by the male gender.

Addison continued, "She was testing our power, your power. Next to Mum, you're the most powerful individual."

Madelyn replied, "Yeah, true. Maybe," she picked up some poppy seeds and played with them in her hand. "Or she could have been surmising our power in an attempt to gage how powerful the current Triad: Mum, Siobhan, Juliann and Zane are. Your caution, Addie, is out of fear. You're inadvertently giving Gabriel Preston what she wants - fear! And, it will disarm you!"

"I suppose," Addison agreed with uncertainty.

"Anyway, let's focus on the Undine, shall we?" Madelyn threw the poppy seeds into the cauldron, "Those mortals are sitting ducks down there on that beach if we don't cast this spell to lure her to Brady."

Addison speculated, "Why all of a sudden are we naming her Undine?"

Madelyn gestured a hand at the *Book of Shadows* that levitated beside her, the pages turned and then halted at a page titled 'Undine, Beauty & Devourer'.

"You have a general classification of mermaids, right? They are beautiful and immortal creatures that inhabit water; not specifically the Oceanic Realm because, considering the current situation, that is when we start allocating them a place and a side. Beings are not evil or good by nature. They are technically neutral first, then magical before any general loyalty. It is an action of their free will that decides what becomes of them."

Addison tested, "But a demon is a demon?"

"I am theorizing here, shush!" Madelyn rebuked.

Entering through the door and then making his way down the five steps into the attic that was situated above the four car garage, Dantalian Romani entered the room. Against his ear he spoke to his twin sister Persia over the phone as she observed their youngest brother Brady without being noticed.

He hung up his phone, "Persia said that she found a deceased male in the water."

"So, she is either hungry, or finding a mate to fertilize her?" Madelyn splashed some salt water into the cauldron. "If it were a female, she'd just suck the life out of her. Deceased male mean's to reproduce!"

"And you're certain of this?" Addison queried.

Quoting the book Madelyn stated: "'Undine will, through oral sex, withdraw a male human's testosterone and semen. So, the testosterone would help increase her immortality, her beauty as such and the latter to reproduce."

"It's every Mermaid, Merman and Undine for themself now," Addison theorized.

Dantalian spoke again, "Did you want me to call Isadora or Bermuda Pogue?"

Madelyn looked at him, "What for?"

"What if she is too powerful for the four of us?" Dantalian speculated, trying not to damage Madelyn's pride. "If Persia uses magic or her Stealth Powers–"

"Bermuda and Isadora won't be able to help; they are guarding two Gamma Witches." Addison reminded her siblings. "Noah is out of the country and Perry is M.I.A."

"I know, I know!" Madelyn grumbled, throwing a pinch of sand into the cauldron, "Mum will sense Persia and know she is wagging boarding school. Fricken triplets," she and Addison gave each other a quick look, "always able to sense and tap into one another's powers. The three of you," she pointed her finger at Dan and remarked sarcastically, "always got the rest of us into trouble with your extrasensory triplet–"

Addison cut Madelyn off as she questioned their brother, "Do you have the spell?"

"Yes," Dan replied. He and his eldest sister exchanged a dirty glare as he handed Addison a piece of paper with his incantation on it, "I have the spell. Perhaps you should not have brought the boys home."

Madelyn's mouth dropped and she pointed at her sister, "They were always yours!"

"Don't point its rude!" Addison smirked,

Madelyn growled, "You little witch! No wonder I was always—"

"Bitch later," Dantalian interrupted as he halted at the table, "four pieces of coral," picking up four pieces of coral out of a bowl and dropping them into the cauldron. "We need to lure this Undine or else we're going to have a lot more dead innocents," he reached across the table, "some Cupids Dart for attraction," he dropped the ingredients into the pot, "and a few strands of Brady's blonde hair because he is going to be the object of her desire!"

"From ship to shore, is the Mermaids lore," Addison began to read the spell before handing the piece of paper back to her brother.

Dantalian spoke a sentence, "No mortal safe, for she will chase," and then he continued to pass the piece of paper over to Madelyn.

"For those are pure, will be her lure."

There was a bang as all the ingredients reacted inside the cauldron and it gave off a brief glow before it returned to normal. The spell was active now. Together the three of them made their way up the few steps to the door and exited. Downstairs, they snuck out the front door. Down the driveway they drove off into the night with no headlights on so not to give themselves away to their parents.

~*~

On the beach at Hallett Cove, people danced as music played loud, laughed as they socialized in small clusters, and drank. At the makeshift bar the woman from the ocean sat on a beer keg barstool and observed the men at the gathering but inconspicuously watched a certain blonde haired male off to the side out the corner of her eye.

"Hey," said a male as he came to the bar to get a drink, "how are you babe?"

She grumbled, "Go away!"

"Fine," said the male, lucky for him he walked away with his life, "cow!"

Under the influence of the spell cast by Madelyn, Addison and Dantalian Romani, the woman suddenly felt as though she was swaying. Her aura glittered, her eyes began to roll back as though she was getting high and as she turned her head to observe her next victim, she felt herself pulled back around in a circle and like a magnet drawn to Brady Romani.

~*~

Casually walking along the beach, his shoes in his hand, the young Romani observed the moon's glow over the ocean. It seemed to bring comfort to him, relax him. The sound of the waves breaking was silent to him.

A shadow moved up behind Brady.

"Hi there," said a female's voice. He halted after feeling a tap on the shoulder. "I'm Deidre. You're Brady, right?"

The entire time he only saw her mouth move, not hearing a word she had spoken.

"I'm sorry," she apologized, seeing the startled look his eyes, "I didn't mean to scare you."

Closing his eyes for a moment he activated his Enhanced Hearing ability that he had suppressed due to the loud music.

"You did not scare me…" he spoke in his deep voice, revealing he had lip-read her, "…much. Yeah," he smiled, shaking her hand and making her weak in the knee, "I am Brady,

Brady Romani."

"Do you want—"

Cut off midsentence she was suddenly thrown away to the side. Shocked, Brady looked a little further back to see the woman from the water lowering her arm, revealing she had used telekinesis to push an innocent girl away from the object of her desire.

"Hi there," she flashed her beautiful smile, "how come you're all the way down here?" The woman came back alongside him and halted, making casual eye contact before looking him over. "Parties aren't my scene either…"

Brady could sense magic in her, a feeling of compulsion, being seduced by every word she spoke to him. His own supernatural essence reacted, turning him off of her and deactivating her power of Vernacular Persuasion otherwise known as the ability of Luring.

"Who," he growled, narrowing his eyes, "are you?"

Sensing that she was not able to persuade him or lure him with her charm, the frustrated woman revealed her gritted teeth, growled and then reached her arm forwards. Touching him in the middle of his chest, she launched him backwards onto the sand with telekinesis.

"You think you can elude my charm," she growled, approaching him as he lay in the sand, "Who do you think you are, God? No one can resist me!" Reaching down, the woman grabbed him by the collar of his shirt. "I am a mermaid!" "Thunder Javelin!!" yelled a female's voice.

The dark section of the beach was lit up brighter than the moonlight. Struck in the back by powerful bolts of electricity, the Undine let out a scream. Dropping Brady back into the sand the creature arched her back and shark fins rose up the length of her spine to absorb the electricity. She morphed into her horrific form, turned and let out a scream into the night.

"Oi," said a female voice, "sea-hag!"

Turning back around to face Brady, the Undine was struck in the face by a fist and thrown backwards, crashing into the sand. Scampering around her brother and helping him sit up, Persia Romani, a Stealth Witch took over the fight.

A Stealth Witch was more powerful than your common Witch, but not nearly as powerful as a Gamma Witch. To be Stealth was to have lived three or four not necessarily consecutive lives in the one family tree; Persia for example had lived three individual lives within the Romani family. She had permanently, through a ritual of powerful magic, summoned each of her three past lives, absorbed each of their essence to achieve the Stealth Level. A process that has a eighty-five percent chance of killing the host.

One would have better chances of winning lotto than becoming a Stealth Witch; it's very uncommon.

"Let me handle this sea hag!" Persia placed her hand on her brother's shoulder, "the others will be here in a moment!"

Brady let out a groan of relief as he watched his older sister walk off to engage the Undine. Persia pulled her sleeves up to her elbows, pulled her hair back into a ponytail, puffed her cheeks and then exhaled.

"Let's go bitch!"

Swinging her arm, she threw a bolt of lightning from her gestured right hand. Sand was sent into the air and the Undine rolled over to avoid the attack and magically propelled herself back up onto her feet.

"Confident little..." the creature revealed her sharp teeth, unsure of what she was dealing with, the woman sniffed the air and identified Persia, "Filthy Romani!"

"Like you have room to talk," Leaping up off the sand, Persia levitated, spun around and kicked the woman in the torso, knocking her to the ground again, "you fricken Walrus!"

Landing back down on her feet and funnelling her Electrokinesis into her open hand she crafted a ball of glittering purple electricity combined with energy. Turning her head quickly, the Undine glared up at Persia.

"I am desirable!" she hissed and began to rise.

Persia scoffed, "Oh honey!" and rolled her eyes, "please. I'm going to kick–" abruptly she was catapulted by a pair of big arms and crashed into the sand. "Ugh!" she groaned, lifting her head.

"About time," said the Undine.

Holding her arm out, a rather masculine and imposing male Undine helped her back up. He turned his head. With impressive red eyes he captivated Persia, she found herself murmuring a 'whoa' as she observed his charming face and wet brown hair.

"The boy," the woman brushed the sand off her clothes, "he is immune." Pointing out Brady Romani to her partner she had become lost for words upon noticing he had disappeared.

"Where did he go? The brat escaped!"

Her partner queried, "What do you mean, immune?"

"Exactly that!" she replied angrily, "He was immune to my power! Only..." they both looked at one another with curiosity, "Only," she repeated herself as she began to speculate, "You don't suppose he is a siren?"

Turning her around abruptly, Brady glared into her eyes, "Let's find out, shall we?"

Pulling her head close to his, he planted his lips firmly against hers.

To her dismay and before she could scream to her brother, Persia felt herself being pulled by her feet down toward the water. Without her knowledge, a third Undine, a second male, had crept out of the ocean and was going to drag her into the depths of the ocean to drown.

"I am going to enjoy," the water lapped at his feet, "watching the life leave your body!"

Reaching around she grabbed him by the leg, "Moron!" he halted instantly and glared down at her, "Water conducts electricity! and I do love deep-fried calamari!"

Crying out in agony he felt her thousand volt power surge through every fibre of his being and in an abrupt end he exploded into glittering purple particles that quickly disappeared.

Persia turned quickly to observe Brady with caution written in her wet face. "But, how? Undine saliva is poisonous!"

Holding her firmly in his simple grip, the Undine screamed and convulsed as she felt her insides incinerate from his powerful kiss. According to mythology, a Siren's kiss was hot as flames and burnt its victim from the inside-out. Swinging a punch, the male Undine struck an invisible barrier of energy that Brady had projected and was thrown backwards. Removing his lips the youngest Romani watched a puff of smoke escape from between her parted lips as she spontaneously combusted in a glimmer of flames. A fascinating vanquish to those who had seen it.

"Brady!!"

Running down the walkway from the parking lot to the beach, Madelyn, Dantalian and Addison called out their brother's name in an attempt to scare off an attacker that might be harming the youngest and hearing impaired Romani.

"Brady!!"

They caught a glimpse of him standing alone on the sand by a scorch mark. Moving her gaze, Madelyn saw Persia standing down by the water. Startled, the three new arrivals halted and shielded their faces as the male Undine made a territorial growl and used his telekinesis to throw a veil of sand at them.

A glow of light quickly manifested behind him without his knowledge.

"Isadora?" Persia murmured in confusion.

The male Undine told Madelyn and the others, "This boy... this Romani of yours is in actual fact a siren! And I intend on killing–" turning around he was abruptly greeted by Isadora Pogue who boldly stared him in the eyes.

"Apollo, Diana, Juno, Luna," she quickly began her spell by summoning Luna deities, "By your might," out over the ocean the moon's glow began to noticeably move toward the shore and turn into a narrow beam, "by will of your light," using her power of Photokinesis she brought the moonlight to her, "paralyse this blight!"

The Undine groaned uncomfortably, suddenly he realized he was paralyzed as the moon fixed its entire glow solely on him.

"What have you done to me?" he questioned her.

Isadora smirked, "You're nothing but a speck of light!" and with snap of her fingers she reduced him to exactly that – a tiny speck of light. Manipulating the little particle she then made it explode into a small firework, vanquishing him. "I must go," she spoke calmly, looking ahead at Dantalian. "I cannot leave Bermuda alone for too long, you know what we're protecting!" and in a flash of light she was gone again. The moon's gaze returned to the ocean where it danced atop the waves.

"Remind me to thank her later," Dan said to his sisters,

You could tell by the tenderness in his eyes toward her that Dantalian Romani and Isadora Pogue shared a very intimate past. But by the tone in which they addressed one another, you could sense there was a lot of heartache between them also.

Standing in silence for a moment they observed their brother, but it did not last for long. Another voice came from behind them in the dark. Turning around, the three of them were greeted by a familiar and unpleasant face.

"Well, well, well," Riel Preston flashed her smile, "fancy seeing you here!" Her long hair whipped about her face in a sudden wind. "A bit far from home aren't we?" The sarcasm in her voice burnt Madelyn's ears. "I told you we'd see each other again." Moving her arms and gesturing her hands, she projected Addison and Dan backwards onto the sand with telekinesis. Reaching her right arm forwards she grabbed Madelyn by the forearm. "I didn't say I would be friendly either!" And then pulled the beautiful Romani toward her.

HOUSE OF ROMANI

The country road was dark. At the bend in the road a wide driveway came into view. A pair of iron gates and a seven-foot stone wall guarded the entry into a prestigious property. Dictating 'House of Romani' the left gate displayed a 'Ħ' symbol, an 'ф' was in the middle where both gates connected and a 'R̲' symbol on the right.

Atop the high point of the wall was a Victorian lantern illuminated with energetic light. Behind the wall, thick and towering pine trees set the wisdom of old power. Arriving at the gates, the headlights of Madelyn's black Alfa Romeo shone against the dark. Beside the car, in a gleam of green, a handsome male elf guard manifested.

"Evening Maltin," she lowered her window and turned down the radio.

He nodded his head.

In his manly voice he spoke, "Evening Miss." Madelyn's bewitching eyes glittered with lust. He questioned, "Your code please?"

Lowering his window in the backseat, Dan looked at the masked owl as it sat perched atop the lantern right next to the gate and the large white tiger that sat below it. They were a second and a third elf guard, both in their Therianthrope forms.

Considered highly desirable — to evil — because of the incredible power it held and magic, the one hundred-acre Romani

Property was under twenty-four-seven guard by elves, an invisible shield and an Illusory.

Madelyn replied with a serious look, "Fluffy."

"Fluffy!" laughed Addison from the passenger seat.

Leaning down, the guard gave her a stern glare.

Addison apologized nervously, "Sorry, Sir."

Straightening up, he swayed his arm to the gates and they magically opened.

"As you were," he said, allowing them to pass.

Placing her hand on the gear stick, Madelyn moved the car from park and into drive as she took her foot of the brake and allowed the car to move forward. Passing through the gateway the invisible shield glittered.

~*~

The large pine forest known as, Soglia di autunno, which in English translated to 'Threshold of Autumn' hugged both sides of the narrow, dirt drive. As the car crawled along, there was nothing but silence. Scattered amongst the trees were lanterns on tall poles. A small gazelle grazed beneath one. A centaur galloped across the drive and disappeared into the woods on the other side.

"Evening Miss!" called a small voice.

Glancing out the window Madelyn saw a dwarf gathering brushwood who had taken the time to greet her. Her response was a kind smile and slight wave as she continued on. Amongst the woods, as Dantalian looked about, he saw a portal of shimmering light. Surrounding the portal was a small iron fence complimented by harvest pumpkins, brown and golden autumn leaves and straw. It was the portal to the 'Autumn Forest' realm of the Elves.

Two beautiful wood nymphs, one blonde and the other brunette, giggled as they frolicked at the side of the drive. They waved to Dantalian who waved back. Coming to the end of the five-minute journey, Madelyn drove between another set of tall stone fences.

~*~

The flat one hundred-acre plantation property sprawled out before the car against the back drop of a black, cloudy sky. To the immediate left was endless pasture. Encroaching on the tree-lined boundary was a historic stone barn with large timber doors. Inside were horses with their Pegasus Stallion.

Both sides of the driveway glittered with magic as the Illusory remained in place.

Ahead, the dirt circled a large piece of lawn. There stood an old stone, two-storey English-style cottage. All four of its front windows, upstairs and downstairs, were ablaze with a warm golden light. It barely looked big enough to raise eight Romani children. Maybe humble enough to house two people.

Addison, Dantalian and Brady stood on the porch. Turning, all three of them waited while their older sister locked her car by remote while walking toward them. On the front door was a beautiful and large, handmade Christmas wreath.

Tomorrow would be Christmas Eve.

"You go first," Addison shoved her sister to the front.

Dantalian jumped at the thought, "I second that!"

Brady protested as Madelyn looked to him, "Shotgun not going first!"

"You little shits! Make me look like the bad guy why don't you!" Madelyn narrowed her eyes.

"Hey," Dan raised his hands in defense. "you're the one who located the demon. Not us. Easily lead is my excuse." Madelyn's eyes bulged out of her face with insult.

"Yeah…" Addison agreed humbly with a sly smirk. "I'm with him. We saved your incompetent arse." Madelyn's jaw dropped.

Brady smirked, "I'm sensing at least four months being grounded."

"Oh you would!" growled Madelyn as she gave him a glare full of daggers. "You're just gutless wimps!"

Dan nodded his head as he replied sarcastically, "For sure!"

Moving her head to glare at all three of them, she promised, "I will kill you all while you sleep for betraying me!"

Addison thought for a moment as she twisted her lips,

"Pretty sure it's not betrayal. I call it protecting my assets."

"You don't have any assets you twit!!" Madelyn replied.

Addison remarked modestly, "You have no idea how much people would pay for my arse!"

Reaching for the rickety brass door handle, Madelyn turned it and pushed against the timber door.

Inside the home, the bold glow faded to reveal the cottage's impressive and luxurious interior. Outside it appeared old and rickety, barely big enough for a modest size family…on the inside it was an affluent ten bedroom, modern three-storey plantation mansion with classic antique and modern features.

Pilar Romani, a very powerful gypsy-witch, had cloaked the extraordinary estate. Outside, the stone cottage visage dissolved into an enormous piece of modern architectural grandeur. Blunt squared walls with large modern windows.

A curt voice rose in the foyer, "Where have you been?!"

Halting, Addison, Brady, Madelyn and Dantalian jumped slightly as the front door telekinetically slammed shut.

The foyer was notable with an impressive double height ceiling, extravagant two-door entry and grand cedar staircase to the left. Fittingly, the ceiling to floor windows, made of expensive leadlight, gave the foyer a cathedral feel. Hanging in the middle of the ceiling, on a lengthy iron chain was a large crystal detailed chandelier. The floor was slate.

Christmas garlands decorated doorways and staircase; the windows were frosted and decorated with twinkling clear Christmas lights. In the middle of the area was an antique marble table with an elegant vase filled with pink, purple and red tulips.

In the corner, sleeping upon its perch was Pilar's familiar *Julius*, a gallant dark brown wedge-tailed eagle. To the right in the middle of the wall was a square archway, decorated with a lavender garland, which led through to the gourmet kitchen.

Above the double-door entry, in an iron fixture, was a large red object called a Buonosenso Crystal. A device that warns when there is an evil presence near the house of a good witch...or in this case, Romani. On the wall above the staircase was a large handpainted, mounted portrait of their greatest Romani Ancestor Amedea Bonifacio.

Ahead, dividing the foyer from the imposing lounge was an inspired terrace boardwalk lined with columns decorated with sage garlands and potted ferns. Atop the small step, their mother and High Priestess of their promising coven stood picturesque.

Her figure was tall and slender with a long narrow face.

Pilar's attire was sophisticated and figure distinguishing.

Her long hair was pulled back while her stunning and bewitching green eyes captured four of her children. They were usually so loving and deep, but now, they were angry.

Although aged in her late forties, the power she possessed made her look in her mid thirties. Occupying a mortal job, she was both an accredited and esteemed head of Pediatric Surgery.

Pilar gave her eldest daughter a cold stare.

"Care to indulge?" Gesturing her hand, Julius leapt from his perch and flew the short distance to land on her shoulder. "Madelyn Joyce Romani!" Once Pilar used a child's full name, you knew you were in serious trouble. "Why you were out hunting an Undine?"

Stepping down into the foyer, she then looked at Addison, then Dan and then Brady, the one son who was always innocent in her eyes.

Using sign language Pilar addressed her boy.

"Brady…" He sighed as he prepared to hear another belittling argument about why he wasn't allowed to engage in threatening situations, "you know I do not like you fighting demons."

The smothering was what made him feel incompetent at times.

"I am, old enough, to take care of myself." Brady signed back with an upset look in his eyes. "I am a Romani too Mum! I am a man! I am entitled to my powers."

Pilar remained silent and attentive, this was not the first time she had watched her son demonstrate…no, confirm his independence. Although deaf he could articulate his feelings better than others.

This time he spoke like a normal person, "Do not treat me like an accident prone child who cannot take care of himself!" she tried to interject, "NO!" he shouted.

"Brady, do not raise your voice to your mother!" Emerging out from the hallway, Anthoni, a loyal husband and loving father intervened as he halted at Pilar's side. "She just cares too much to see any of you get hurt!"

~*~

A̲nthoni wasn't a pretentious man but always content with a broad shoulder and masculine build. He had short dark hair, sharp jaw line and piercing blue eyes. As a legal aid for the Prime Minister, he was hardly home to be the rule enforcer, but when home, like now, he made sure that his disconnected and somewhat dysfunctional family ran smoothly. He was in his mid forties, averagely handsome and always dressed in his usual work suit.

Anthoni, like Pilar, was born into magic. Much to his family's dismay, he was a squib – born with no magic whatsoever. His family has this objective about consolidating their power...if you could call it that. If you had power, they wanted to induct you into their bizarre and promiscuous world eclipsed by a heavy shadow.

Intimidated by the power Pilar possessed and her children and line she descended from; the Modestos – Anthoni's family, minus his brother – had their particular ways of interacting with their squib sibling. It could be perceived as love but a whole lot of others saw their meddling actions for what they really were.

Having been born into power, not money, Pilar Romani and her husband were hard workers. Money was something they had by means of working; it was not something they desired as indicated by the dysfunction of their family. He had a company car. She drove a modern SUV. Discouraged by money, Pilar believed that you work hard to build a life and reputation.

Anthoni ordered, "Upstairs...!"

"Why!" Brady glared at him in protest.

Breaking the tension and conflict, Madelyn questioned politely, "Mum. What do you know about a Riel Preston?"

Shrugging her shoulders and narrowing her eyes with thought, Pilar then glanced back at her daughter.

"You'd have to ask Renae. I have heard of her," she seemed standoffish about the topic, while husband, Anthoni stood quietly to the side as he kept out of the witchy discussion. "but, I do not intend to challenge her. Philanderer Demons are degraded things. Although I have fought a couple myself and they were considerably powerful for low level demons!"

The interrogation about their whereabouts was snuffed out as the conversation veered in another direction.

Raising her head Madelyn summoned aloud, "Renae!" calling the family's Custodian and a look of anticipation followed. "I have a question!"

On the step behind Pilar and Anthoni, white smoke swirled up from the floor. An enchanting layer of delicate fog lingered for a brief moment over the slate foyer floor.

Beautiful, Renae Valore, the twenty-year-old looking Custodian of the Romani Coven was a gift to the powerful Pilar and her husband on their wedding day from the Queen of Magic.

"Evening," The young woman greeted her charges.

Her long white blonde hair was placed in a messy ponytail.

A trait that set her apart from her male counter parts, Renae had distinguishable amethyst coloured eyes.

"My apologies for being late," Renae apologized.

Brady gave her an odd look as he thought to himself,

'Late? It took you all of five seconds to arrive.'

In Renae's hand she held a brown folder. Every time she spoke, the atmosphere seemed to warm. "I was just at the Eiffel

Tower negotiating with the Fairy Republic."

This time, Addison gave her an odd look, *'Fairies are a republic?'*

"They refuse to share a portal to and from the mortal world with the Gnomes."

Madelyn paused, taken aback by the custodian's revelations.

"Uh," Renae then placed her unyielding eyes on the eldest Romani child. "What do you know about a Riel Preston?"

The Custodian's eyes immediately widened with caution, "You encountered Gabriel...the Philanderer Comtesse?"

Confused Madelyn remarked, "Gabriel?"

Pilar interjected as she appeared almightily pissed off, "Apparently tonight. They all snuck out. I found a bubbling cauldron in the attic." Both she and Madelyn exchanged a dirty look as Pilar identified her eldest daughter as the ring leader. "You left the candles burning too!" Addison felt her body paralyse with fear. "Heaven forbid that the house had burnt down, we'd be homeless!"

Turning her attention back to Madelyn, Renae cleared her throat. Expressing concern she revealed a small portion of knowledge.

"Riel is a Superior Level Demon," she glanced across, assuming all four of the children had survived the confrontation unharmed. "Impressive how you all survived her wrath..."

Addison appeared proud, while Pilar made a loud noise of disappointment.

Acknowledging the tension, Renae turned and gestured at the lounge room. In the distance, a massive nine-foot pine Christmas tree stood bold beside the grand fireplace in the lounge room.

Swirls of white smoke rose up from the floor as Triad members Juliann, Siobhan and Zane teleported into the room. They stood beside the imposing classic fireplace. Associate Jayme Kristo, leader of Il Cavallo Coven, manifested and took a seat on the lounge. While Pilar's niece Ryder Romani, Congraga Della Tomba Coven leader Stephani, a powerful witch with Necromancy powers,

Laura Mitnell, and two more witches all manifested in swirls of smoke.

THE GATHERING

Renae looked back, "Come, we must talk."

Pilar beckoned, "Renae. What is this?" upon noticing the members of her coven present in the lounge room before her.

Renae replied, "I will explain."

Addison murmured under her breath, "Something's up…"

"Must be…" whispered Madelyn,

Brady grumbled to himself. Looking to his youngest son, Anthoni ordered again.

"Upstairs. Now please. I will not ask again!" It was hard to separate loving father from rule enforcer. "Madelyn," he looked to the others standing by the front door, "Addison and Dantalian lounge room, now." he glanced back to Brady as he firmly pointed to the top of the staircase. "Go!"

Addison protested, "Dad!" in defense of her little brother.

Storming to the staircase Brady climbed to the first landing before it turned and rose up. There at the landing he stopped and glared back.

In sign language he said rudely, "You're an arse!"

Anthoni signed back, 'A hard arse!'

Grumbling, Brady then turned and stormed up the stairs to his bedroom. In the far distance a door slammed shut with force.

Addison growled angrily, "Well done!" as she passed her father bumping him deliberately.

Madelyn, Dantalian and Addison followed Renae as she led Pilar into the contemporary lounge.

Anthoni paused in the foyer as he watched Julius retake his position on his perch. With a heavy sigh, which almost sounded like remorse, he turned and looked up at the top of the staircase as he pondered his young son's independence.

~*~

Along the country road, hugged on both sides by groves of blackberry bushes, a drizzle began to fall and a gale blew.

The Grove (a grove being where several covens lived closer to one another) or New Salem, was a gated community for the most powerful covens and good witches in the country. Various portals in many parts of the country allowed wiccans access to this realm of sanctuary from the mortal world.

Directly opposite the main gates of the Romani Estate was a set of towering gates coupled with a modern glass fence. Beyond it in the dark, the moon idolized a new and desirable mansion that was in the process of being constructed. On the glass fence was engraved 'Eredità' – Italian for Legacy.

In the middle of the road, two men suddenly appeared before the unguarded gates of the Romani Estate. Not making eye contact with one another, they both grinned, held out a hand and conjured balls of fire. Throwing their attacks, the fireballs made the magical shield react, making it give off brillant flashes.

"Come out Romani!" crowed the demon on the left.

Materializing as it leapt out from the shield, a white tiger roared in midflight. Landing on its paws, its body magically rose up and took a human form. The elf arched her bow and fired.

Impaled, the demon on the right screamed and his body exploded into flames as he was vanquished.

Atop the wall the owl hooted and shapeshifted into an elf, "Be gone demon!"

The remaining demon remarked, "Excuse me," and he conjured another fireball. "How…?"

The male elf replied, curling his lips with repulsion. "Your stench gave you away!"

"Now, now," an invisible woman's voice intervened, "we don't want any trouble." In the middle of the road, beside the young man, the outline of a body glistened as the womanly individual then fully manifested. "We're just here to collect our brother!"

Passing through the gate, Maltin halted beside his female warrior.

Politely, he stated, "I shall summon the head witch."

Sarcastically the woman replied, "You do that." "Who may I ask is calling?" Maltin queried.

Behind her, four other females dressed in black with different signatures of maroon on their attire manifested in red glistening auras.

"Ragel Modesto." She identified herself. Maltin raised an eyebrow in suspicion. "Head Witch," Her eyes ignited with ego and superiority, "of the Modesto Coven."

Turning his head slightly, remaining suspicious, Maltin spoke to the female elf who clutched her weapon.

"Keep an eye on them," Ragel smirked as she listened. Giving a cold stare, Maltin instructed his warrior, "Banish them if they become a handful!" Still glaring at the visitors, Maltin turned and passed through the gates.

~*~

Walking around the lounge room, Renae spoke wholeheartedly and truthfully.

"I have been made aware of some vital information," All sat and stood silent and attentive. "A bounty has been put on this Coven."

Outraged, Pilar sat forward in her chair, "Excuse me?"

"I'm sorry Pilar. But it's the truth," Renae looked to her charge like a loving mother would at her child. "Inside intelligence forwarded me this information."

Intrigued, Addison murmured accidently, "Connor…" Renae looked at her quickly.

"Sorry." Addison apologized for interrupting. "Continue."

"Pilar. I have been your liaison for twenty-five years. I am taking every precaution necessary to make sure the safety of this coven is upheld. It has become clear that in the dismantling of the Pogue Coven, the Avatarians view you as a threat."

Everyone began to whisper amongst themselves as fear set in.

"Settle, please," Pilar ushered in a silence. In protest she looked to her Custodian and replied, "I will not take this on the chin, Renae."

Renae protested, "Neither will I. I have been informed that preparations have been made."

Confused, Pilar interrupted, "Preparations?"

"Yes. That is all I'm allowed to divulge." Renae appeared calm…though her eyes glittered with something else. As she continued, Maltin manifested in the passage. "I have spoken with Serene. Your Elve Guard is going to be—" Renae looked to him, "Maltin?"

Moving in her chair, Pilar looked to him for an explanation.

Guiltily he apologized, "My apologies for interrupting."

Kindly Pilar replied with a humble smile, "No it is fine, Maltin. What is it?"

A nervous look curled his lips, "A Ragel Modesto is at the gate."

Madelyn, Addison and Dan's eyes appeared startled as they widened.

Anthoni intervened momentarily, "My sister?"

Rising from her seat, Pilar appeared irritated by the unwanted presence. She did not like the Modesto family and they did not like her. But because of her husband, she was forced to draw a line.

Pilar looked to Renae, "I shall go to the gate. Continue on without me."

Renae replied with a nod, "As you wish."

Looking at her coven members and associates, Pilar excused herself. Turning away she walked up the steps, crossed the passage and ventured off into the foyer.

Putting on her thick wool coat, she fixed the sleeves as she said. "This should be interesting!" The irritation and repulsion was crisp in her voice.

~*~

Passing through the gateway, Pilar greeted her unwanted guest.

"Ragel Modesto," she hugged herself to keep warm. Nastily she finished with, "Of all people to be grovelling at my feet. Wow...you really look old for sixty!"

Stepping forward, Ragel retaliated like a depraved guard dog, "Filthy Romani bitch!"

"I'm sorry." Pilar replied humbly and unaffected. "Did you actually want something?"

Ragel gave a foul glare as she took a moment to silently relieve her pent up anger.

The young woman, Ragel's daughter, stepped forward as she stood to the right of her mother.

"Do not incur our wrath."

Looking to the woman, Pilar chuckled aloud, "You are kidding, right?" the woman gave a cold stare. This time showing no care or patience, "What do you want?" Pilar addressed the evil witch in a formal manner. "Àtrella Suntory?"

Patricia Modesto, Ragel's youngest sister intervened as she tried to mediate. "We've come to collect Anthoni." Pilar looked to her and gave a harsh look of repulsion. "It is all we ask."

Pilar queried, "You want me to hand over my mort–"

Lytton, Àtrella's teenage son interrupted in a rude voice, "Squib!"

Pilar gave him a nasty glare and then continued, "*Mortal* husband to you." They stared at the powerful Romani with anticipation. If they had to they would take the estate by force...but the shield would incinerate them before they even got past the gate. "I do not think so!"

Sharni, Àtrella's teenage daughter, dressed provocatively, stepped forward as she interrupted: "There is a bounty on your coven! We wish to save what is our own and–"

Three of Pilar's children halted behind her, causing Sharni to silence herself. Both she and Madelyn exchanged a dirty stare of repulsion.

"Oh please," a sarcastic Madelyn insisted. "Don't stop on

my behalf. I'm dying to hear what—" her sarcasm strengthened as a hostile look consumed her beautifully calm face, "you've got to say Sharni!"

Egotistically, Lytton opened his hands and ignited his black and silver flames.

"Little insect!" Becoming defensive, Dantalian did the same. His incredible blue flames provided greater light unlike his cousin. "Let's go, Princess!"

Dakela Modesto, the second eldest of the coven interrupted, "Enough!" she approached and halted at Ragel's side. In protest she said, "Give us what we want or we will take it by force!"

The hair on Addison's neck stood up out of anger, "You can try!"

Insulted, Ragel clenched her fists, Sharni growled and Lytton strengthened his flames.

"You're in my grove. Modesto." Pilar took control of the confrontation. "Twelve covens live on this road. Your attack will initiate war. We're not afraid to walk on your turf in Eris!"

"Give us the Squib," Ragel, in a sick and egocentric way, tried to initiate a peaceful exchange. "and no one gets hurt."

Pilar smirked sarcastically and then resumed her cold glare, "Funny, isn't it?"

"What is?" Ragel remarked bluntly.

"You are pure blood witches," Pilar identified the obvious as she continued with mild sarcasm. "Yet a filthy Romani, such as me, is greatly more powerful than all of you combined."

Obvious despise swam in Ragel's dark eyes. The mentioning of power and descendants infuriated her. To be outpowered by a half-blood fueled her fiery ego and bruised her pride.

"So," an unafraid Pilar stepped forward, "here is my suggestion to your predicament. You will not touch my husband

and you can shove your rescue mission up your arse!" They all narrowed their eyes furiously and prepared to engage in battle. Stepping back as she ushered her children back, Pilar turned her back to the evil coven. But as she halted she stirred their last evil nerve: "Anthoni is more intelligent than you give him credit for! He will not align himself with vermin such as you!"

Aggravated by the short comings of the confrontation Ragel and her cohorts each conjured a fireball into one of their hands as they prepared to attack.

Ragel remarked almost happy, "So you shall die!"

All at once, all six of them launched their fireballs.

Intervening, Madelyn projected her power. Vines shot past her and extinguished the approaching fireballs.

"Go home!" Addison remarked.

Facing her hand to the group, they shrieked and shielded their faces as Addison used her power of Chain Reaction to banish the group back to the evil village of Eris.

~*~

Back inside the house, manifesting in a delicate glow, Madelyn retook her position on the modern lounge and crossed her legs in a ladylike manner.

Renae said rather startled, "That was quick."

Madelyn replied sarcastically and fueled with hatred, "Nothing warms you on a cold night than a run-in with your evil relatives." Glancing about she noticed everyone had left. "Where is everyone?"

Renae informed, "I sent them home."

Madelyn nodded her head accordingly, "Oh. Fair enough..."

Addison manifested beside her sister and then Dan.

Dan queried, "Where is everyone?"

Madelyn replied, "Gone."

Dan nodded accordingly, "Oh. Fair enough…" Addison queried amongst the confusion, "How come?" "Renae sent them home." Madelyn replied again.

"Oh." Addison remarked.

Pilar manifested in her classic style white leather armchair, "I need a stiff drink after that!"

Renae politely arbitrated, "I think you need to keep a level head, Pilar."

"True. But have you not met my evil in-laws?" replied Pilar uncomfortably.

With a sour look Renae scratched the back of her head uneasily, "Once too often for my liking."

Shifting herself on the comfortable lounge, Addison curiously watched her father as he stood in awe of the impressive family portrait that hung above the fireplace. Empathy swirled in her eyes.

He did not know what family meant, its value or its love until he met Pilar.

The portrait itself was a substance of magic.

1986 was marked in the bottom corner, a young Pilar and Anthoni were newlyweds with Anthoni's two children from his previous marriage. Fair haired twins Serene and Jayson were ten years old.

Expressing its magic, it morphed again.

In the bottom corner it said August **1987,** and Madelyn was cradled in her mother's arms. The twins were older now and had now grown into their teenage years.

The portrait morphed again and still Anthoni watched it, infatuated by its essence of a loving family. In each time frame, twins Jayson and Serene appeared inseparable as they stood side by side...so close as brother and sister they were practically joined at the hip.

1988   Addison was born.

1989   triplets Dantalian, Persia and Mars were born and then finally in **1992** Brady was born. In the bottom corner, a fancy scribe revealed a new milestone. **2005**, the year Jayson married his wife Sloane and also the same year that he suddenly passed away.

At this moment and this caption of history, a single tear rolled down Anthoni's cheek as he remembered his beloved eldest son.

December **2005** Serene married Denver Rein, an Elf Prince of the Autumn Forest Kingdom. Not believing in traditions of marriage she had her first child Dustin in **2004**. In the portrait, on her hip was her youngest son Rome whilst husband Denver held their eldest, Dustin.

From the bottom of the staircase, Brady curiously watched the inaudible conversation taking place. Not wearing his hearing aid he relied on his skill to read lips to understand what they were talking about.

At the top of the staircase, a slender mass of shredded particles slinked down from the ceiling. Touching the floor the mass abruptly materialized into a tall, slender and curvy woman aged thirty-five.

It was Sloane.

She queried in a considerate voice, "Brady...?" as she quietly came down the stairs toward him. "Sweetheart, what are you doing?"

He replied in sign language, '*Watching them...Dad sent me to my room.*'

Halting beside him, his sister in-law gestured her curious expression accordingly as she signed back.

"Why, what did you do?"

Brady signed again, *'We tracked and vanquished an Undine.'*

She raised an eyebrow cautiously, "I see." Sloane never looked disappointed although having been through a turbulent life herself after losing her husband. She seemed to relate accordingly and understand the young teen. "Well don't frown. You're an independent young man."

Brady's expression suddenly became more relaxed. Unknowingly to him, whilst he spoke to her, she had used her power of Pathokinesis – mentally, she could connect with a person's soul and heal their emotions as they spoke.

"Give them time," she signed. "They always come around when you prove how confident and limitless you are." Sloane brushed his mop of golden locks and brought him close to kiss his forehead and then continued on into the foyer. But quickly she halted and looked back to him, "You better go back to your room."

He smiled in response as he lingered for a moment.

Sloane casually walked away, up the steps, across the hall and halted at the edge of the lounge room. She had worked with Pilar at the Women's and Children's Hospital in the city as a paediatric surgeon up until her husband passed away. Coming to terms with the turbulence and her grief she went back to university and achieved honors in Psychology to become a Psychotherapist. To have succumbed to such a trauma, she ventured through the darkness of her emotions. She lost herself and then found herself again to emerge on the other side a stronger and more resilient woman.

"Sorry, I'm late." Sloane apologized.

Turning her attention, Pilar smiled and greeted her daughter in-law.

"It's okay, we're just," she turned her eyes back to her children, "discussing certain discipline options!"

Sloane said courteously, "So, I've heard."

Pilar formed an uneasy smile. Quickly raising her gaze, her attention was drawn to Brady as he peered through the banister of the upstairs balcony that overlooked the lounge room.

"I concede defeat. I tell ya."

"It's not my place," Sloane said with consideration. "but perhaps, the example has already been set for them…?" Pilar appeared curious and attentive. "They live to be admired." Her empathy picked up their thoughts and emotions. "You, as a powerful gypsy and a witch is who they aspire to be. Locking them up, unable to express their abilities is not going to teach them to defend themselves against demons and god knows what else is out there in the world."

Renae interjected, "Is that psychology talking?" she felt her guardian nose being pushed out of joint.

Pilar quickly interrupted, "You're both superior in your own individual fields."

Turning her gaze, Sloane gave a confident smile. "No, Renae, it's their emotions. Serene is their mediator. As she is not here she asked that it be my job."

Pilar expressed appreciation upon her perfect face.

Sloane continued, "I'm sure if you and I were not here Renae or Serene, this," she gestured her arms accordingly to imply the situation before them, "would be a lot more hostile and there'd be a lot less understanding."

Chapter Twenty-Six

ALLURE

The golden rim of the sun pierced the dawn on Christmas Eve.

Golden light elevated up the small parting of the curtains in Brady's bedroom window. Moving across the room, the sun halted across his face and caused him to stir. In the distance the cockerel crowed...over and over...and over and...over.

Raising his head from his pillow, Brady looked to his alarm clock. It read 5:55am.

"Ugh!" he slammed his hands against his pillow, "Shittin' bloody rooster!" he sat up on the edge of his bed and rose to his feet as he began to move toward the square window. "I swear to God!" he tore back the curtains. He turned his head away from the harsh sunlight as it flooded into his room, "Ugh!" his eyes adjusted and then he looked back.

Unlatching his window, he pushed the panes open and glared down at the rooster as it scratched around in the front garden.

"Early wake-up call my arse!"

The rooster crowed again and exploded in a plume of feathers.

From his bedroom window, Brady laughed to himself, "See how you like it," he turned slightly and telekinetically closed the window.

Some moments later, give or take an hour, Brady came downstairs.

The foyer, lit by the sun and nothing more, was in all its wondrous shades of muted whites, slate and classic timber.

At the foot of the stairs, Brady paused as he heard music playing from the kitchen. Across the foyer he entered through the small doorway opposite the staircase where the unoccupied kitchen lay.

Asuka, the Romani's wood nymph housekeeper, prepared the empty marble counter with a variety of foods for breakfast. Plates of towering pancakes, another with sausages, bacon, scrambled eggs, toast, fried sundried tomatoes and fruit salad all appeared in individual gleams of gold.

She danced around the kitchen to the rock song.

Curiously as he scratched his blonde mop, Brady, infatuated by the twenty-five-year-old woman, remarked. "Take it off…?" He halted at the side of the counter.

She gave a smile, "Kesha." As she twirled, using her powers to make a bouquet of wild flowers appear in her arms.

"Huh. Never knew wood nymphs listened to music."

She gestured her hand, making a crystal vase appear on the counter. "Are you kidding? We wood nymphs love music!"

Reaching across the counter Brady took a bagel and placed some bacon, scrambled eggs and sundried tomatoes on it.

"You put on a good spread Asuka."

"I take my job seriously," She replied as she arranged the flowers. "Your family is a promising power. To work for you is an honour!"

"Where is everyone?" queried Brady,

Asuka replied, "Your mother has five surgeries today and your father has a 7:00am meeting with D.A. Noah Pogue."

Brady gave an odd look of conspiracy, "D.A.?"

Asuka appeared vague as she tried to remember the details, "The Prime Minister put him on a case involving a magical situation developing in Treadwell?"

Brady took a bite of his breakfast, "Well—"

Bringing the young Romani to silence, Madelyn's boyfriend Marc turned the stereo off. Both Asuka and Brady looked at him as they stood with stiffened postures.

"Not my kind of music. Play something I like next time." He had this thing about influencing control in a house that was not his own. Marc remarked as he ridiculed the maid, "Is this it?" "Excuse me?" Brady replied standoffish.

Marc looked about the smorgasbord of food and then shot a glare at Asuka.

"And you call yourself the help!" and with that comment, as hurtful as he had made it, Asuka vanished in a sparkling aura of green.

Putting his bagel down on his plate, Brady confronted his nemesis.

"Shut up, Marc!"

Walking around the counter, Marc, in an attempt to flaunt his mortal strength tried to intimidate Brady by getting close to his face. "Make me," and he grabbed him by the throat. "Want another black eye that you've so conveniently covered up?"

With a forceful shove, Brady projected his bully backwards into the fridge.

"Don't touch me. You're such a prick!"

Casually and unsuspecting Madelyn walked into the kitchen and Marc put on his genuine guy charm.

He remarked, "Morning baby," as he held her close and kissed her forehead. Both he and Brady exchanged a fierce glare. "Asuka has arranged breakfast."

Marc Veluda-Ackerson, the son of a mortal high profile socialite, met Madelyn two years ago. Comfortably she revealed her magic and he was most accepting.

"Mm," Madelyn took in the smell of everything as she approached the edge of the counter. "Look's delicious! I love Asuka." Looking at her brother she reached out and touched his throat where a red mark remained. "Are you okay?"

Brady remarked territorially, "Yeah. Course. Why wouldn't I be?"

Madelyn apologized, "I'm sorry. No need to get hostile Brady. I just noticed a red mark on your throat."

Brady nervously touched it and glanced back to his bagel, "Sorry. It must be shaver's rash or something."

When Madelyn's attention was placed on something else, Brady shot Marc a cold glare. As he began to leave the kitchen and venture back to the foyer area, Madelyn stopped him.

"Aren't you having breakfast with your big sister?"

Brady hesitated behind Madelyn and Marc gave him a threatening stare.

"I've already had breakfast."

A disappointed look curled her lips into a slight frown, "Oh. Are you going to see Burke?"

A suspicious look swarmed in Marc's face as intrigue rattled his cage, "Burke Pogue?"

Becoming defensive, Brady replied, "Yeah. What's it to you?"

"Brady!" Madelyn unwittingly defended her boyfriend.

"He was just asking a question."

Brady quivered at the thought of having to apologize but instead just remained silent.

Madelyn informed her boyfriend, "Yes Marc. Brady and Burke dated but are just good friends now." "What she said." Brady replied.

"Brady," Madelyn figuratively cornered him with a question. "what is the matter?" He gave a blank expression which made understanding even harder. "Is this still about Mum and Dad not treating you equally?" He sighed deeply and she appeared concerned. Using sign language – something Marc did not understand – she said, 'don't worry about them. They're just being naive and overbearing.'

Brady pouted as he felt hard done by. He shared a deep connection with Madelyn; she always found ways around his barriers to bring him out of his shell.

He replied, using sign language, 'I will see you later.' then he signed 'Love you' and before she could sign the same thing back he had disappeared into the foyer.

Acting coy, Marc queried, "I wonder what his problem is?"

Madelyn shrugged her shoulders as she ate a blueberry. Using his power of Mental Projection before shutting the front door, he pissed Marc off by turning the stereo on again but this time played *Bad Medicine* by Bon Jovi. The front door slammed shut in the distance.

~*~

Under the midmorning sun, Burke – a nickname of Bermuda Pogue – drove along Pulteney Street in her Suzuki Grand Vitara.

Her long honeycomb blonde hair was messy and hung over her right shoulder. Sunglasses shaded her eyes; fingernails coated in melon pink polish. Surf beads around her neck that complimented a shell pink top, white denim shorts and western boots.

Burke emulated her favorite musician Kesha.

Slowing down at the traffic lights, with her window down, she lowered her sunglasses to ogle at three men who crossed in front of her as she sang along to the song that played over the radio.

"Hey baby!" they whistled.

She sighed to herself. Bermuda was obscenely honest.

Her power of Sensazione – a remarkable power consisting of Intuition, Mediumship, Foresight, Empathy, and Telepathy – sometimes left her with emotional side effects so honesty was an enforced policy.

Leaning her head out the window she called back, "You wish. My taste buds aren't on the bottom of my shoes, shit lips!"

One of them grabbed at his heart, pretending to be offended. "You break my heart baby."

She replied with the quip of her tongue, "You actually need to have a heart in order to have it broken. Moron!"

"Womanly must be a swear word in your vocabulary!" Isadora Pogue, the snobbish sister, remarked as she flipped through a clothing catalogue.

A horn bellowed behind her. Quickly Burke looked to her side mirror.

Raising her head, Isadora looked at the traffic lights and then turned to her older sister: "The light has been green for almost two minutes."

Giving a quick glance to the rear vision mirror, Burke turned the steering wheel, indicated and then turned left off King Gustav Boulevard and onto Windsor Way.

Down a little she turned left again as she drove into the multi-storey car park next to the Windsor Way Police Station.

~*~

*T*heir freedom from babysitting their Gamma Witch grandmother had come after several demon attacks on the house just the night before. But the last one to attack was the demon Azazel and her brother Alistair...

Downstairs in the house, Isadora stood in front of the window that overlooked the backyard as she sipped a mug of hot tea. Behind her, a black figure materialized in a blur and upon assuming full form, it created a ball of fire in its hand. Feeling the shift in energy in the room –a technique from her power of Energy Manipulation– Isadora sighed, glanced to the side and accidently let the mug slip from her hand.

She turned around and acknowledged the male.

"Give me the Gamma Witch," he growled.

Swiftly swinging her arm, she projected her falling mug of hot tea with her Energy Manipulation power. Splashing him in the face, he shrieked from the scolding pain and extinguished his fireball. The mug smashed into pieces against the wall. Raising her hands, she briskly gestured them and caused him to explode in a fiery vanquish by manipulating the energy in and around his body.

"Burke!" she gasped. Looking up at the ceiling she vanished in a flash of light, teleporting upstairs to the attic.

~*~

*D*riving up the ramp to the rooftop level of the parking complex, Burke turned to the right and pulled into a vacant space. The low levels were completely full with the current level only occupied by three cars.

"This is stupid!" Burke complained. Turning the key in the ignition she turned the car off. "I hate the rooftop!"

"Why?" Isadora replied as she proceeded to take her seatbelt off. Sarcastically she halted before opening the door, "Because you have further to walk to the elevators?"

Vacating the car they both shut the doors and Burke used her key to activate the central locking. Together, under the midmorning sun, they began to walk away from the car. Rising up from the concrete a low level demon appeared in a blur of black. He blocked their way as he stood before the elevator.

Acknowledging the demons presence, Isadora gave a sour look.

Burke complained, "That is why!" as she prepared herself.

Isadora hooked her handbag over her shoulder "Don't they ever take a day off?"

The demon with dark hair in dreadlocks approached, clad in the usual black attire. He moved his hand and created a ball of fire. He groaned, throwing his attack at the two witches.

Diving to the side, Isadora crashed onto the ground, grunted and then protested angrily.

"All I want to do is to shop and not worry about a fricken demon attack!" With a brisk and fierce gesture of her hand she fired her power back.

The demon evaded the attack and energy exploded against the elevator door, leaving an impressive dent as the metal crumpled.

Still standing, Burke swayed her hand as it shone a delicate gold and she used her power of Deflection to deflect a second approaching fireball. Recoiling, the fiery attack shot off in the opposite direction where it hit a rubbish bin and it exploded in an inferno.

The demon asserted his orders, "Raffaela says you must die!" as he created another fireball.

Burke growled territorially, "You can tell precious to go sit on a fat one!"

Suddenly stiffening up, his face contorted with pain as he let out a bellowing scream. Instantly his body exploded into a fiery plume and Brady came into view as he stood behind the demon.

He remarked calmly, "Morning."

Isadora sighed aloud with relief. Burke raised her sunglasses to reveal her implausible eyes as she identified her exboyfriend. "Brady."

They had mutually ended their relationship and they remained very good friends.

Some minutes later, at the corner of Windsor Way and King Gustav Boulevard, the two witches and Romani waited patiently for the pedestrian lights to change. The traffic stopped and then they crossed as the little red man displayed above changed to green. Isadora walked ahead as Burke and Brady lingered behind.

Stepping onto the footpath on the opposite side of the street, the three of them entered City Mall.

~*~

*U*pstairs in the attic, Bermuda maneuvered her hand as she swung her arm. Magically her hand gave off a delicate gold glow as she deflected fireball after fireball. Out the corner of her eye she caught a glimmer of silver; a knife lay on the table.

"VIA!!" she commanded.

Magically upon her Power Word Charm the knife shot off the table and impaled a female demon in the chest. Screaming, the demon exploded into flames and was vanquished. Teleporting into the attic, Isadora reappeared in a flash of light. Swinging her arm, she threw a slender light dart from her hand, vanquishing a second demon.

"Be a good witch..." said a female voice. Abruptly struck and thrown, Isadora crashed into the wall and then fell onto the floor. The female emerged by the window, "...and give us the

Gamma Witches!"

"Who are you?" Bermuda growled.

The brunette woman replied, "I am Azazel! My brother Alistair and I are under orders to procure the effigies before they reawaken!" She threw a fireball at Bermuda who in return deflected it. "Our boss has big plans!"

Alistair knelt down at Isadora's side as she began to get up, "This one is very pretty!" he caressed her blonde locks, somehow preventing her from getting up. "I want to keep her, break her, and turn her evil!"

"STAY AWAY FROM HER!" Bermuda roared, keeping

firm eye contact on Azazel while trying to watch Alistair on the other side of the room with her sister. "How did you break through our protective charms on this house?"

Reaching her arm around, Isadora placed her hand

against the side of Alistair's face. She gave a beautiful smile and then, activating her power of Photokinesis, burnt his face. Staggering back he cried out in agony and clutched the side of his face. Swiftly she levitated herself up into the air in a rolling motion and then landed back on her feet.

"I'm not a dopey blonde, or a damsel in distress!"

Reaching her arm back, she spun around on the spot and kicked him in the abdomen, throwing him into a table that broke under his weight. "I am a natural red head and I can be a fierce bitch!"

~*~

In the middle of the open outdoor mall in the heart of the city,

was Buskers Restaurant. Behind the glass windows that had a full view of the mall, six women dressed in corporate attire eagerly eyed Brady as he strode past.

Were they Socialite Demons?

They are a race of demons that have the innate ability to blend into the mortal world without being detected. Their only visage was their sensitive pink eyes that were always covered by heavy black sunglasses because the sun could scald their eyes to the point of possibly being vanquished.

Some hours later, the two witches and Romani found themselves in the Prada store. Isadora held a garment to her body as she looked at herself in the mirror. Bermuda was away to the side, filing through garments hanging on a rack.

Sitting on a comfortable chair, Brady softly sung along to the Mark Ronson song *Uptown Funk* featuring Bruno Mars as it played over the stores intercom.

At the counter the female sales clerk –off in her own world of fantasy as she went about her work– raised her head with intrigue as the mundane tune Brady sung reached her mortal ears. Her eyes sparkled and she instantly became bewitched.

Ambling around the counter she appeared to be in complete awe of Brady as she approached.

Isadora turned in the mirror, "So Brady,"

He stopped humming and the sales clerk snapped from her trance.

Turning his head, toward the blonde witch, he replied, "It looks good."

Isadora gave a sarcastic stare, "Thanks but that's not what

I was going to ask."

"Oh," He looked perplexed and confused. "What were you going to ask?"

Isadora enquired, "How is Madelyn?" She stepped away from the mirror and returned the garment to the rack only to pick up something different. "I haven't seen her in a while."

"She's good. Marc snuck in during the night...as usual." He remarked, showing obvious signs of irritation and dislike. "He thinks he is superior." He implied Marc's self-assured attitude and the way he carried himself was so modest and proud. "Even for a mortal."

"Now, now we're all technically mortal. The wit–" Bermuda hesitated when she acknowledged the closeness of the female sales clerk. "The wittiness is just an added bonus."

Confused by the comment, Isadora turned to her sister with an odd look and then she acknowledged the sales woman.

"I was wondering what the hell you were going on about."

A puzzled Brady looked at the woman and then continued.

"He bullies me," and a disheartened look rose to the surface of his face. "constantly and no one believes me."

Bermuda removed another garment from the rack as she replied, "Want me to vanquish him for you?"

Isadora barked, "Bermuda Pogue!" in such a stuck-up manner as she called her sister by her formal name. "Remember where we are!"

Bermuda growled back very viciously, "Shut up!" Brady turned his head as he couldn't help but snicker to himself.

"Isadora Pogue!"

"I do love the jovial display of love between you two." Brady remarked with a smirk.

Isadora targeted him with a curt tone, "Shut it Romani!"

"Ouch..." he teased, "That almost hurt. Maybe try harder next time."

~*~

*I*n the attic of the Pogue house, Azazel reached her arm forwards and projected a torrent of flames at Bermuda. Gesturing her hand, she activated her power of Deflection. Behind her a robed individual appeared in a gleam of red and gold energy. Instantly she vanished in a flash of gold light and reappeared in the hallway outside the attic.*

Gesturing its hand it turned Azazel's fiery power to ice. Falling onto the ground, the frozen flames broke, scattering chunks of ice across the polished timber floor.

"Cool parlor trick!" she smirked.

The figure replied, "I am the guardian of Santo Cathedral! These Gamma Witches belong to me!"

Realizing how weak she was in comparison, Azazel hesitated. Out the corner of her eye she noticed a piece of paper on the table that detailed Azura Pogue's location and phone number.

"I have an idea!" she smirked as a devilish idea sparked in her mind. Magically, she made the piece of paper disappear and reappear in her hand. "Alistair, let's go. The Santo Cathedral Guardian has reclaimed them! I'm not prepared to die for an effigy of the Madonna!"

Fleeing the Pogue house both demons vanished in bursts of flames.

"Hey!" Isadora yelled at the robed Guardian, "who are you? Don't you dare—" instantly she was forcibly teleported out of the room and then reappeared out in the hallway with Bermuda. "H-how? Huh?"

Kicking the door open, Bermuda and Isadora burst back into the room.

"Hey!!"

Using her powers, Isadora threw a light dart at the Guardian. Deflecting the attack, the powerful being sent it at a cupboard to the side of the room that exploded into pieces on impact. Stepping between the two stone figures it reached its arms out and placed its hands upon them.

"I am the Guardian of Santo Cathedral!" the robed individual told them, "these belong to me!" and it, along with the stone figures vanished in a quick flash of red and gold energy.

"Huh?!" Bermuda remarked curiously.

Chapter Twenty-Seven

SECRET SIREN

In 1899, Eris Valkof, fled into the countryside of Treadwell from the city after word rose about witches living amongst the citizens. After the Salem Witch Trials, the puritan people drove out anyone who might have been different. He was born to convict parents who had fled their home many years before.

Into the wilderness, he ventured up into the Gorge of the Treadwell Hills.

He forged a refuge, a housing dimension for people like him, people who were witches, evil witches. In the future of the Deane County State, the same location would become the site of the Kangaroo Creek Reservoir. He used magic to create a portal accessible only by evil individuals.

The town of Eris was established; a sprawling medieval city whose lantern lit cobblestone walkways adorned the sheer cliff face.

Today, overlooking the flourishing evil city of Eris, on top of the hill was a grand Edwardian-era manor, home to Morgana, a promising evil power and leader of the Modesto Coven after overthrowing Ragel.

~*~

Still browsing through the Prada store, Isadora made an irritated noise as she returned to the mirror. She seemed to be frustrated that she could not find the right garment. Nothing was appealing today and that is strange, even for her, because normally she could walk into a store and walk out with more than she originally intended to buy.

"What do you mean by no one believes you?" confused, she enquired. "Your mother is a powerful woman. Even as a mother she should be able to sense when her child is being bullied."

"I swear he can manipulate perception," Brady rose from the chair and then walked up behind Isadora to stand before the mirror. Curiously Isadora watched him as he waved his hand over his right eye. She gasped and a startled look stole her curiosity.

Nervously he told her firmly, "No one can see this."

Isadora could not comprehend what she saw, "He did that? And got away with it?"

Halting at his side, Bermuda placed her hand on his cheek and turned his face to her to gain a better view.

Caressing his cheek like a loving girlfriend she displayed a stern glare.

"Please tell me you hit him back, Brady!"

Content by his ex-girlfriend's touch, he muttered, "No he knocked me flat. Who would believe that he did this to me?"

Isadora turned away from the mirror, "Err us. We're your friends Brady. We believe you. Why didn't you have your Custodian report him to Maria?"

"I swear to God," Bermuda removed her hand but she still held her stern glare. "If I see the toss bag I will not hesitate to serve him a smack in the face!"

Isadora enquired again, "What is his reason for bullying you?"

"I'm the deaf, dumb and stupid child." Brady's self-worth appeared to be very little and this shed a light on why he protested so much against his parents' wishes. "I am the easy target in his eyes."

Isadora grabbed him by the forearm, "How dare you even devalue yourself Brady Romani!" Abruptly she brought his arm up to draw an emphasis on his uniqueness. "You might be deaf but that does not make you dumb, stupid or any less of a person than me. With these hands, you project barriers. That is your power. That is your strength. I could not give a rat's arse if he is mortal or the son of a millionaire. Use your damn power to defend yourself!"

It was obvious that Isadora cared for him a little more than she let on.

The sales woman lingered close by.

Isadora encouraged, "Let's go to menswear." Her indigo coloured eyes glittered under the store lights. "It's my treat."

"I-I—"

Isadora pulled him by the arm and ventured off through the Prada Summer collection with a vintage off white trench coat hanging over her arm.

"Don't care. I always find shopping to be good therapy."

~*~

*I*n the dining room of the grand Edwardian-era mansion in the

medieval city of Eris, sat Morgana, a mature woman with long black hair and a gaunt face. Evil hollowed out her once remarkable beauty. To the left of the prominent leader sat a second woman, her right-hand-man or woman, who was similar but had layered chocolate brown hair just down past her ears. On the right sat a male – broad shouldered with styled blondish red hair.

Estelle was her name and his, Sheppard.

At the foot of the table, the Modesto group had gathered. Ragel was front and centre with the others behind her clad in black as they eagerly waited for their master's orders.

"Where is the boy?" Morgana questioned.

Àtrella Suntory replied, "He is out in the open!"

Morgana replied, almost enthusiastic for a moment, "Good," and then she turned her chair and sat side-on to the table with her legs crossed as she contemplated her task. "I cannot risk them finding…" she moved her eyes and acknowledged the man and the woman, "us, me, out."

~*~

Jovially Brady begged, "Isadora…" Isadora ignored his name calling and his feet skidded along the polished tile floor as he tried to resist. In the end, he caved under the peer pressure. "Fine you win!"

Isadora smirked as the three of them strode off through the store.

"I always do," she remarked modestly.

In the change rooms, Brady removed his shirt and bared his very developed swimmers physique. As he tried on designer clothes he, again, sung along to the chorus of the song *1983* by Neon Trees as it played over the store's sound system.

Outside, an unsuspecting Bermuda Pogue filed through racks of men's clothing; her ears suddenly pricked to Brady's enchanting tune.

"What is that?" she remarked at first, whispering to herself as she looked around. "Where is that coming–" her eyes sparkled as she became bewitched by the alluring tune.

Removing a T-shirt from the rack, Isadora held it up, "What about this one...?" she requested her sister's opinion only to find her absent from the immediate area. Glancing around she called out, "Burke?"

Entering into the area of the men's change rooms, Bermuda threw the clothes she had collected into the male sales assistant's hands.

"Ah, excuse me you can't–" he beckoned.

She replied vaguely, using magic on him, "Be silent."

Behind the door, Brady continued to sing along to the song, unknowing that he was suddenly able to bewitch females with his voice.

Telekinetically unlocking the door, Bermuda shoved it open.

"Whoa!" Brady covered his bare torso with a garment. "Burke. Wh-What are–" she pushed him back into the small area, shut the door and proceeded to kiss him passionately. "Whoa..." he moved his lips away for a moment as he tried to catch his breath.

She grabbed his jaw and ordered lustrously, "Shut up!" and she leapt up, wrapping her legs and arms around his body.

Somehow acquiring a new ability to lure via song, Brady made her lose control of most inhibitions.

Throwing her hair back she paused to say, "Right here!" as she read his thoughts of sexual innuendo.

Appearing at the entry of the men's change room, Isadora queried the silent assistant.

"Did a Kesha look alike just come in here?"

He nodded his head eagerly as she curiously acknowledged the slight glitter of magic across his lips as he spoke but nothing came out.

Bermuda undid Brady's belt. She gasped as he firmly gripped her thigh. He passionately kissed her neck and she climaxed.

Suspicious, Isadora replied to the sales assistant, "I see."

Walking onwards she halted at the door that she believed her sister and Brady were behind.

Turning slightly, Isadora looked back at the man, "This one?" he nodded again. "Brady?"

Behind the door their passionate make out had quickly started to turn toward sex.

Removing his lips for a moment, Brady hollered, "Occupied!"

"Oh, I bet!" said Isadora to herself with a narrow stare. Shoving the door open, her startled expression responded quicker than her words. In a shocked high pitch voice she remarked loudly, "What the hell are you two doing in here?!"

Bermuda leapt down from Brady and gave an awkward look, "Nothing!"

A sarcastic look swelled in Isadora's face as she said, "Oh sure. Miss loose lips!"

"How..." A confused Bermuda questioned aloud, "did I end up in here?" she turned to Brady, noticing him wipe his wet lips with his hand and his naked torso. She gasped, "Oh God."

Covering her mouth she questioned again, "Did we?"

Brady said awkwardly, "Have sex? Not quite!"

Isadora gave Brady an odd look accompanied with a blunt tone, "You're disappointed?"

~*~

Almost an hour later, riding the escalator down to the ground level that exited back out into City Mall, Isadora looked uneasy as she stepped off first. Directly ahead, in the middle of the mall, was the renowned and iconic City Mall Silver Balls.

Isadora grumbled aloud in Italian, "I cannot believe you two!"

Brady and Bermuda followed, there was an awkwardness between the two. They didn't know how to look at each other without being reminded of their seven minutes in heaven in the men's change room.

"You almost had sex in the men's change room!"

An old Italian lady that walked past shrieked upon hearing and understanding Isadora's Italian lingo.

"Shame on you!"

She wacked Brady with her handbag before continuing on along the mall.

Isadora gestured her hand at the woman, "I rest my case!" she gave an obvious smirk and continued to walk ahead.

Their conversation continued as they walked on, passing under the Gawler Place canopy.

A forty-year-old man stood at the phone box close by, chatting away inaudibly. Catching a glimpse of him out the corner of her eye, Bermuda was intrigued by the delicate slithering strings of electric pink and teal energy around him. Slipping away from Brady's side, she halted and looked on curiously. Her stare strengthened as a gentle tune, sung by a woman, touched her ears like soft silk.

She murmured, "What...?" both captivated and enthralled as a warm combination of melon and pineapple moved beneath her nose. "So..."

Out of phase with reality, the illusion before her of the man at the public telephone disintegrated and six good mythical sirens revealed their presence to the prominent Pogue witch. They were ethereal women; their only physical magical visage was their individual lurid hair colours.

The one with long purple hair said, "Hello Bermuda." Her stunning opal coloured eyes glistened under the sun.

Bermuda acknowledged, "Sirens…" her power sensing their essence.

"Empathy is a rare quality in a witch." the siren with the apple green pixie style hair said. "You're aware of our notoriety?"

The six of them, dressed provocatively, eyed off the young witch with lustrous eyes.

"Your notoriety…" Bermuda repeated vaguely. The light bulb switched on in her head, "The Siren Sorority." Quickly she looked for Isadora and Brady with a frightened look in her round face.

"You fear us?" remarked the siren with long hot pink hair that fell in tangling curls. "Pogue. We are your allies, not your enemy."

Clearing her throat, the second in command stepped forwards, "A formal introduction is in order." The way she spoke and exuded herself was very much stuck up and superior to those lesser than her. "Clartra Patil," standoffish she did not even offer the witch her hand to shake. "I am second in command of the Siren Sorority."

The siren with the blue hair in a Mohawk gave a slight wave, "Tigris Macaria."

"Lark Eavan," said the woman with pink curls.

The apple green pixie introduced herself next: "Donovan Lavi."

"Ryanne Frae," said the snobbish siren whose left side of her head was shaved with the right side free-falling to her shoulder at different lengths.

"Akira Chang," the Japanese-Australian siren informed confidently with her hands set firmly on her hips. "This is business." Her persona changed to become rather rude, "You're a Pogue, renowned and highly respected. But do not get in our way, Bermuda!"

Bermuda remarked, "In the way of what?" as she, herself, became standoffish. "Are you threatening my life?"

The only humble and nice member, Lark, intervened. "We wish to collect the siren you are currently protecting."

A confused Bermuda replied, "Come again?" Lark appeared confused herself. "What siren am I protecting?"

"Clartra the witch does not appear to know?" revealed Lark.

Clartra spoke again, "You do know what the boy is," Bermuda remained silent as she struggled to comprehend the situation. "Don't you...?"

Speechless, Bermuda made the silent, mental connection as she put two and two together that made up the answer to what the siren was going on about.

Lark's voice started to become distorted, "He is a..." and then it was inaudible.

~*~

"Bermuda," Isadora shook her daydreaming sister's arm.

"Burke?"

The mythical sirens were gone. The public telephone was vacant. Had the entire revelation been a figment of her imagination?

"Hello, are you in there?" Isadora roused her sister again.

Snapping back to reality, Bermuda sighed and blinked several times as she re-acknowledged her surroundings again.

Brady enquired, "Where did you go?" as he stood at Isadora's side. "What were you daydreaming about?"

Giving him a sharp look of intrigue, Bermuda could see the sudden difference in her ex-boyfriend; something had long lay quiescent. A different aura exuded from his body, no longer was it periwinkle, but a cherry red that gave off the most incredible and enchanting scent; enough to make the Pogue Witch momentarily giddy.

"So…" Brady gave her a vague look of suspicion and then asked them both a question. "Where do you want to go for lunch?" Still she looked at him as though mentally undressing him. Gesturing his expression accordingly, he snapped at her,

"What the heck is the matter with you?"

Bermuda queried, "Boxers or briefs?"

Brady raised an eyebrow as he listened to her question.

Isadora looked to Brady and then to her sister, "What relevance does this have?"

"Do you still go commando?" Bermuda queried again.

Isadora raised her eyebrows with intense shock. "Are you kidding me?"

"Erm…" An awkward Brady began. "Boxers. Why?"

Bermuda gave a sly smirk whilst still maintaining eye contact with him.

Isadora suddenly realized, "Oh my God, are you mentally undressing him?" she gave her sister a hardy shove in the arm breaking Brady's Luring ability. "You sicken me!"

"Why do your thoughts sing?" Bermuda remarked with intrigue as she pressed her fingertip against Brady's scalp. "It is most unusual…yet…very alluring."

Isadora gave an awkward look, as though her sister was delusional and possibly a complete nut job.

"Seriously...Burke..." Her smirk brightened with her fierce sarcasm, "shut up!"

Brady repeated himself, "Where should we go for lunch?"

"First Restaurant," Isadora looked to Bermuda as she spoke, "At the Hotel Richmond, down the mall."

~*~

Morgana still sat side-on at the far end of the long conference table in the dining room of her Edwardian-era manor. Three evenly spaced chandeliers hung over the table. The gloomy gold light shimmered over the heavy black curtains of the three windows to the left side of the long rectangular room.

Àtrella Suntory spoke, "Pilar is only a Romani!"She found it hard to believe gypsies could possess enough power to pose a threat to evil. "We witches are more powerful than gypsies. They're only a sister tradition!"

"That bitch," Morgana, frustrated, slammed her hands down on the table as she rose from her chair, "has our power – my power! You're an idiot. Clearly uneducated! We Romani are an amalgamation of power. It was our only means of survival against the Hunter some hundred years ago! Our ancestor Kizzy D'hôte married a male witch named Favian Tsura."

Ragel queried, "What does that have to do with the boy?"

"We're going to use him has leverage," Morgana smirked confidently, sitting back down, "Sister, dearest, will relinquish the Triad power over to us and we will finally get what was rightfully ours!"

~*~

Standing atop the canopy of Gawler Place an ethereal woman with shoulder length black hair, as irridescent as the mythical Morgana, watched the two witches and Romani below.

Sixty years old, she looked not a day over thirty.

Her sunken eyes were shrouded in charcoal eye shadow with lurid emerald green detailing. These subtle ornaments provided much evidence that her essence was innately evil...whether expressed or not.

Several blowflies circled around her head, "Is everything in place?" the flies replied to her telepathically. She gave a sly, egotistical smirk as her eyes darkened, "Excellent. I shall send the Romani to you. Fail me..." Her eyes glistened and they turned from humble hazel to a lurid glowing blood red, "and I shall rip your wings off!"

Instantly the flies disappeared in black orbs.

The woman waved her hand feverishly. Beside her, emerging in a ripple of energy, she made a teenage girl appear hovering with her hands bound behind her back. Silver tape covered her mouth as tears streamed down her cheeks.

"I will be replicating your power." Turning her head, the aged woman curiously queried, "What is your power, witch?" using telepathy she sighed aloud with a sour expression. "Animal Control...how pathetic...but I guess it will do." Her aura gave off a black glow as she replicated the witch's power.

SOMETHING EVIL

"**H**ELP ME!!"

A girl's scream tore through Brady's head as his power of Enhanced Hearing kicked in on its own. Startled, he threw his head about, looking up, down and around to see where it had come from.

He queried his friends, "Did you hear that?"

"HELP ME!!" the voice screamed again, "SOMEBODY!!"

Isadora replied vaguely, "I didn't hear anything..."

"HELP ME," The voice came again and this time Brady turned, looking back in the direction of King Gustav Boulevard. "SOMEBODY PLEASE!!"

Isadora looked at her older sister, "Use your power! Hear his thoughts!"

"Is that wise?" Bermuda remarked cautiously.

Isadora appeared confused, "Why wouldn't it be?"

Bermuda gave her sister an odd look, "Err. Hello! He is somehow able to bewitch me with them, that's why!"

Isadora gave her a superficial glare, "You're an upper level witch. Get a grip! Block all influences and zero in on what he is hearing."

"Wow. You're such a bitch!" growled Bermuda.

"It's a gift," Isadora smirked confidently.

Bermuda rolled her eyes, stepped forward, placed her hand on Brady's shoulder and not only felt his incredible power but instantly her sight shot forwards as her own power gave her a premonition. Reacting to the incident she gave a sharp, loud gasp.

"Meddling witch!" the woman atop the canopy viciously growled as she gestured her hand, raising it up into the sky. "I cannot have you knowing!" Closing her eyes, she projected her newly acquired, replicated power.

Isadora gasped as she grabbed her sister's forearm, "Bermuda?"

Summoned by the replicated power, the eyes in a flock of pigeons on the grass of the Treadwell Museum on Norvard Boulevard flashed a glittering red and then they all, in a hurry, flew up into the sky. The flock of thirty birds soared high over the buildings and then swooped down as they rounded the corner and shot along Gawler Place.

Isadora queried, "Burke?"

Upon Isadora's touch, deferring the vision away from Brady for a moment, Bermuda gasped louder as a vision of her sister, wrapped in white with six magnificent angel wings ignited in her mind. Feeling the sting of magic as static zapped her hand, Isadora pulled away and took a few steps back; glancing around she wondered if any mortals were watching.

The disruption of pigeons suddenly made Isadora shriek and cover her face with her hands and forearms. Hassling Bermuda, the pigeons forced her hand to retract from Brady and fall back onto the ground. Flies swarmed around the Romani. He waved his hands about to deter them.

Isadora stepped forwards, "Brady!" but restrained her power due to the significant presence of mortals. "Brady!" And it quickly came to her knowledge that the situation was out of phase with the mortal realm. "Brady!" projecting her power of Energy

Manipulation the glass in the Gawler Place canopy stressed and shattered, showering the people below it with glass fragments.

Seeing no more use for her abducted witch, the woman atop the Gawler Place canopy swayed her hand and the young witch screamed, falling to her death.

Mortals screamed in terror, some scattered, running for safety while some ran to the dead girl's aid as she lay on the paved ground.

Isadora gasped, "...Oh God!" and quickly lowered her hand.

Disappearing inside the swarm of flies they teleported Brady elsewhere.

~*~

*I*n the altar room – otherwise known as the attic – of the Modesto

Manor, in the black, faded light, misery, dirty windows and cold drafts, Morgana, Estelle and Sheppard stood around a large cauldron that levitated over a pile of rocks and flames.

"Artemis, Orion and Neith," Morgana added ingredients as she concocted a hunting and locating spell, "deities of the hunt, aid us evil of the underneath—"

Estelle interrupted, "A good deity is not going to assist evil, Morgana!"

"Shut up," Sheppard growled, "she summoned them because they are deities associated with hunting. Their attributes will enhance the spell!"

Morgana added a few strands of Brady Romani's hair, "Show to me, Brady Romani!"

The liquid in the cauldron suddenly gave off a glow. Swaying her hand Morgana used the power of Voyeurism to reveal the subject in real-time and his current location.

"City Mall," Estelle revealed the location. "He's in the city!"

Morgana smirked, "I will go! Prepare the barn; we're going to have a guest!"

~*~

The sun shone down and all appeared good in the world...for less than a second.

Atop the multi-storey car park on Windsor Way, the spiral of flies reappeared with a glowing spectacle in the middle. In the sun's direct gaze, its rays intertwined with the glow, making it give off intriguing shimmers.

"Ugh!" Brady protested as he waved his hands about, "What the hell?!"

The flies moved away and abruptly took on humanoid forms. Five individuals stood in a guarded circle around him.

They all wore different variants of black and charcoal with a small signature of golden copper with the eerie complexion of compound eyes, like a fly.

Disorientated by the travel, Brady ordered loudly, "Who...or what are you?" They did not answer but simply watched him with thirty grins on their faces. "What do you want with me?" the world spiraled around him as he turned on the spot.

The ordeal had disabled his Enhanced Hearing leaving him deaf. Overwhelmed, his heart raced and his blood pressure dropped dramatically, making him collapse into a heap on the ground.

"Well done," the firm and invisible voice of their superior moved. Using a borrowed, replicated power of Voyeurism, the woman's eyes appeared first with a glow around them and then her entire being manifested in the same manner. "Success." Ambling across the concrete as she approached, the cruel woman made her plan obvious: "I guess none of you are being tortured today."

Moving a hand out from behind her back, in a gleam of light she made Brady's hearing aid appear. Clenching her fist, she then crushed it into a fine granule.

"What now?" Comfortably, a male stepped out of her shadow dressed in a thick black hoody and charcoal track pants. Shadow shielded his face and identity. "My kind has served you well."

"Yes." She remarked, uncaring. "For a mute race that has no proficiency you certainly do a job efficiently." Turning her head to the side, she looked over her shoulder to say to the young male, "Please tell me you are not developing feelings for the Romani girl."

His deep voice replied, "No. I am doing as you instructed.

I am a fly on the wall."

She gave a smug, confident and rather pleased smile.

She reminded him firmly, "Remember. I gave you your charm, a voice and the power to manipulate perception."

"How come they do not know what you are doing?" he named her respectfully, "Morgana."

She turned her head back to idolize the bounty that would extort power from one of the most renowned covens. "Easy." Her lips curled with evil intentions. "I can replicate powers. Sometime ago I copied Bermuda Pogue's power of Sensazione. I use it to block the Custodians' powers."

"Custodians?" He repeated in a startled voice that became curious and cautious. "There is more than one?"

Morgana informed him which Custodian she had magically impaired, "Noah Pogue. But then there is that meddling prefect, Renae Ketch and her husband Basset." "Basset?" he replied again, just as vague.

"But I also block Bermuda herself from reading me." She folded her arms as she glared at Brady with a conspiring look on her face, "It seems our Brady is more than what he appears to be!"

The male queried, "What more could he be, besides a Romani?"

"A siren." The woman remarked bluntly, but also rather intrigued by her own revelation. "We must be careful that the Sorority does not come looking for him. Is the hideout ready?"

"Yes. We await your command," the hooded male remarked.

Behind, some distance away, a brisk whirl of bedazzling light rose up from the ground as Bermuda and Isadora teleported in with her power of Photokinesis. Their presence went unnoticed for a moment. Ahead of them, two people, a man and a woman stood with their backs to them while five individuals stood in a circle around Brady who sat slumped in a heap on the ground.

"HEY!!" Bermuda roared.

"Ah..." the woman gave a sigh and a sly smirk. Keeping her position, "We have company."

The hooded male remarked modestly, "Leave it to me!" unworried that his identity might be exposed.

Turning slightly he swung his arm, gestured his hand and projected a fireball at the two witches.

Isadora approached the oncoming attack arrogantly, "Give me light–"

Magically her aura began to glitter as her body quickly absorbed photons. Using her power of Energy Manipulation, energy and air surrounding the fireball warped and it quickly extinguished.

Bermuda walked at her sister's side.

Isadora showed remarkable strength and finesse. Bringing her elbow back past her side she then pushed her arm forwards.

Using her power of Photokinesis, she threw a light dart at the hooded man. Evading, but not enough, it cut his arm as it brushed past him. Swiftly gesturing her arms again she threw another attack, this time using her power of Energy Manipulation to propel the man into her sister's car to the side.

"That was far too easy!"

Slamming against the car, he groaned aloud as the vehicle shook.

The woman mocked, "Idiot man!"

"Hey!" Bermuda protested loudly, "That was my car!"

Swiftly pivoting on the spot, the woman revealed her identity to the two witches.

"You witches are good. But never leave a man to do a woman's job!"

By the widening of their eyes and dropping of their bottom jaws, it became obvious that Isadora and Bermuda knew their foe.

Together they gasped, 'Oh my God!'

Isadora began to name her, "I know you, M—"

The woman roared, "Don't you dare!" as she briskly swung her arm, projecting another replicated power, this time it was a Seismic Pulse.

Engaging in battle, Isadora gestured both her hands in front of her body; making the air ripple and warp she used her power as a shield. Bermuda extended her right hand out in front and utilized her power of Deflection as her hand gave off an impeccable gold shine.

The eight-storey structure shook beneath their feet.

Smashing against Bermuda's power of Deflection, the woman's seismic pulse obliterated it. Shrieking, the force of the impact caused Bermuda to backflip into the air and with a heavy thud, crash onto the ground.

Isadora passed through the wave of energy. Being able to manipulate energy granted her immunity to all forms of energy based attacks and powers.

"Intriguing…" remarked the woman with a sly glare. "You're immune to energy based attacks."

Energy danced around Isadora as it glimmered in the sun's rays. On her cue, the affects of her power disappeared and she confidently, with a brazen look on her face, strode onwards to meet the woman in battle.

Approaching, as she used her power to levitate from the ground, Isadora forced her body into a spin as she struck with a spinning roundhouse kick. Struck in the chest, the woman fell backwards onto the ground.

Landing on her feet Isadora clenched her fists, "I will not let you take him!"

Levitating back up onto her feet, the evil woman remarked overconfidently: "You don't really have a say in the matter!" She grunted, "Urgh!"

Swinging her arm out again, she projected a much more focused seismic pulse.Isadora took a deep breath, puffed her chest and then channeled her power through her vocals to project a sonic scream. The air and energy around her distorted and was projected forwards in the form of a rumbling, streamline funnel of pulsating waves that passed through the seismic wave as it approached.

The woman's beady evil eyes eagerly watched Isadora's power approach.

A hiss in the back of the young witch's mind warned her, "Do not let her touch. She will replicate your power!"

It suddenly became apparent that this evil woman could also replicate a power by touching or absorbing it when it was used to attack her.

Isadora's sonic scream redirected itself but not enough. Blasting against the evil woman, but leaving her unharmed, she was able to replicate that specific trick Isadora could do with her power.

"Hm. An upper-level witch trying to take me on." Morgana made a smile of achievement. The woman kept the extent of her power hidden, the full potency of it was unknown, but to look down upon an upper-level witch implied a powerful nature. "That was hardly a worthy power." Replicating Isadora's sonic scream, the woman now had fourteen powers under her belt.

Slamming against her, Isadora unable to utilize her own power was struck by the woman's Seismic Pulse power. Screaming she was thrown back with dramatic propulsion. Raising his disorientated head, Brady moved his vague eyes. He saw Bermuda lying face down and then turning his head a little more he saw Isadora scream as she disappeared over the edge of the roof top car park.

"Now…" the woman sighed happily as she wiped her hands clean. Behind her an iridescent dome of periwinkle coloured energy moved out from Brady's body. She spoke again, "Where were we…?" Turning around she halted and witnessed with intrigue, "What are you doing?"

Brady looked at her with a look of knowingness. He knew who she was. There was more than a connection between them; a lot more than just an evil witch hunting a siren. It made betrayal even more hurtful.

"I am not scared of you!" he enlarged his dome-shaped barrier. "I know your tricks!"

"Oh?" the woman pretended to be cautious but then manipulatively turned the table on him. "But, you should be! Mummy is not here to protect you nephew!"

Betrayal set firm in his face. His angry eyes strengthened as emotion welled in them and his lips were crumpled with unease.

"Why are you doing this?"

"Because I can…" The evil woman smiled calmly. "and I will! Why have morals when you can have power!"

Brady cried out in retaliation and enlarged his barrier further. The Fly Beings screamed out as his power obliterated their humanoid forms. Their bodies returned to swarms of flies and then individually fell to the ground where they etched black scorch marks into the concrete.

Moving her hand out, the evil woman touched the barrier, allowing it to give off a glow as she both absorbed and replicated his power.

"Fascinating power you have."

In the blink of an eye she was gone and then reappeared behind him as she wrapped her arm around his throat.

A sly gasp slipped from her lips as she held them by his ear, "Wait…" looking ahead the air swayed and the Siren Sorority stepped through a portal of wondrous, shimmering white light. "The boy is mine!"

Leader Clartra Patil warned firmly, "You have no idea who—" but cut herself off as she watched several black blurs rise up behind Morgana. Clartra remarked, "I know you."

Morgana ordered in a booming voice, "What are you waiting for? Do it!"

Clartra looked over the small coven, "You're Ragel Modesto!"

"And you're leaving!" hissed Ragel with her snake tongue.

Clartra's eyes gleamed with power, "Excuse me?"

"We came for the boy!" Sorority member, Lark, intervened with a snarl.

Àtrella Suntory roared, "The boy is ours!"

Clartra turned her head slightly to speak over her shoulder, "Don. Akira. You grab Bermuda Pogue!" All the while she kept eye contact with the evil coven of witches. With a territorial glint in her bewitching eyes, she queried, "You know better than to steal what does not belong to you! Strega!"

In sync the sirens, invisible to the eye, projected their power. Harsh grey clouds quickly swelled as they consumed the clear sky overhead. Thunder rumbled violently.

"You should have stayed on the island," A smug Àtrella remarked with a bigoted look. "Your power is miniscule!" Renowned, the Siren Sorority was a Superior Level faction. It would be unwise on anyone's behalf – good or evil – to underestimate their power. What kind of authority would make their power miniscule?

Raising her hand and gesturing, the evil woman began to use Chain Reaction...another replicated power. In between the two opposing sides, good and evil, the air violently waved like the ocean in a storm. Overhead the clouds grew darker and more ominous. The beautiful sunny day was gone. Thunder rumbled again and a steady downpour immediately followed.

Clartra's eyes shone angrily as she spoke in a deep intimidating voice, "Do not try me, Morgana!" the Modesto Coven did not cower. "We will take the boy by force!" their individual auras burned a seductive cherry as well as giving off a bewitching scent.

Briskly extending her arm out in front, Clartra projected the combined, ultimate power of the Sorority.

The woman remarked modestly, "Stupid girl!" using the power of Chain Reaction she made the group of girls telekinetically move together. Swiftly rotating her gestured hand she remarked with darkened eyes, "You have no idea who you are dealing with!"

In sync they all screamed as a parked car came at them through the air.

Suddenly projected back, the sorority slipped through a veil of invisible energy along with the vehicle.

The woman lowered her hand, "Come." Her smile was sly as her darkened eyes lightened. "We have a boy to ransom!"

Under a clap of thunder and a flash of lightning, the woman, her cohorts and a kidnapped Brady were gone. An ominous sentiment maintained a presence and not even the rain could wash away the black scorch marks.

Standing with her head hung, Bermuda's long, wet, straggly hair clung to her face. Slowly raising her gaze, a disorientated look washed across her face as she vaguely began to look about. She made a murmur, failing to make out words. Brushing her hair away from her cheeks, as she became more lucid, Bermuda stepped about.

She called out, "Indy!" as an unsettling fear began to bubble in her stomach.

She moved her body the wrong way and winced. Lifting her top to make an examination, she saw a harsh looking bruise.

"BASSET!!" she summoned a Custodian, "I NEED YOU!!"

Chapter Twenty-Nine

LADY MORGANA

Bermuda murmured, "Ouch...how?" a sparkle of silver stole her attention.

Raising her head, she let her top fall and she ambled with a stiff posture over to the side of the car park. Grasping the bracelet that littered the ledge, "Indy..." she acknowledged.

Leaning forward she looked over the side.

Lying slumped against the car, the hooded male groaned as he came to. The hood of his thick jacket had fallen to reveal his thick shaggy mop of blonde hair. Hearing him stir, Bermuda straightened her back and glanced over her shoulder. Her emotional eyes strengthened with anger and she turned around fully.

"No way..." she growled beneath her breath,

Her hand slipped away from the ledge with her sister's bracelet in her grasp. Ambling across the large parking lot, intrigue sparked her senses. Thunder rumbled in the harsh charcoal sky.

"You've got to be kidding..." Bermuda announced in an insulted voice. "I know you," halting a short distance away, she watched him get to his feet. By the look in her face she was profoundly shocked that she knew who had helped in both the attack and kidnap of Brady Romani. "You're—"

His eyes glittered as he projected his ability to manipulate perception. Receiving its influence, her eyes glittered. Behind her, some minutes later in the middle of the car park, white smoke swirled up from the ground and a male Custodian with a lean physique appeared.

"Bermuda," Basset announced, naming her as she stood with her back to him. "Bermuda Pogue," He announced again much firmer in tone. Walking up behind her, he questioned, "Why did you call me?" a bewitched, bewildered and slightly emotional Bermuda vaguely gazed at her reflection in the dark tinted windows of her car. "Bermuda…" placing his hand on her shoulder, he turned her body towards him. "Burke. What…?" Her strained eyes met his lurid sapphire ones.

Bermuda murmured his name, "Basset."

Touching the side of her face, he queried again, "What happened?" and upon his touch his hand gave off a subtle white glow that obliterated the enchantment that plagued her. "Why did you call for me?"

Appearing more alert and lucid, she quickly glanced past him to notice the hooded male had vanished, "Where did he…?" Basset replied with confusion, "He who? Bermuda who are you talking about?"

"Erm," She remarked vaguely as a slight headache pained the side of her head. "I know I am not your charge, but they took him."

Basset queried, "Took who?"

In the dank, Woodsons Lane, beside the multi-level car park, white smoke spiralled up from the ground as Bermuda and Basset Ketch reappeared. At their feet, an unconscious Isadora lay face down.

Bermuda shrieked, "Oh God, INDY!" and knelt down beside her sister. Turning her body over, she felt Isadora's neck for a pulse, "She…" looking confused, she remarked in a shocked voice. "How does she have a pulse?" raising her head, she looked up to the roof top level of the car park. "The fall should've killed her!"

Kneeling down, Basset picked the young, unconscious witch up in his arms.

"Seriously I don't care. She's alive; that's the main thing. I'm more concerned withwhat is going to happen to my abducted charge!"

Wrapping her arm around his, they both vanished in a spiral of smoke.

The small street went back to being uninhabited. In the short distance bustling traffic moved along Norvard Boulevard. Suspiciously, Connemara Preston clad in black burlesque attire, stepped out from behind a delivery van as her small crow eyes swelled with intrigue. *Why did she save the young witch from the deadly fall?*

~*~

Hours passed quickly as the ominous black storm clouds consumed the sunny sky. It was now 8:00pm and the news of Brady Romani's abduction spread through the magical community like wildfire, as well as the mortal world. News broadcastings on Treadwell's leading television networks reported:

ABC News, Nina flack, "Brady Romani protégée,"

Luca Gordon, Fox News, "...of Treadwell leading Paediatric Surgeon Pilar Romani,"

"...was abducted earlier today, with officials reporting there was motive and fear the young teenage boy's life maybe at risk!" NBC News, Ross Jaguar.

A female G.S.B. official stood on the steps of the lounge room watching Pilar Romani stare out of the large windows that overlooked the white paved, Grecian-inspired patio and a large swimming pool.

A young man in a suit handed the woman some papers, "Inspector Rowley."

She replied, "Thank you." looking away from Pilar and to the files.

The world was colder than she had imagined; Pilar's strained emotional eyes stared endlessly at her reflection as she struggled to recall a time when it wasn't. Her face was lost as she mentally pondered over and over where her son could be.

"Pilar," A gentle voice summoned her attention and a friendly hand touched her arm. At first the voice was distorted but became clearer as it repeated, "Pilar."

Turning her head, some of Pilar's long brunette hair fell down both sides of her face with the rest of it pulled back in a messy ponytail. Tear lines ruined her makeup, making it look paler while her eyes revealed her silent distress.

"LC," Pilar cleared her throat. She acknowledged the Detective of the G.S.B. who was also a witch. She brushed her long hair to the side as the two greeted each other with a peck on the cheek. "How are you? I have not seen you in a while."

"I wish my visit was not because of such a tragic circumstance." a sympathetic look glimmered in LC's peach coloured eyes. "I am so sorry. But I will reassure you," Pilar pouted as a tear slipped from the corner of her eye. "...The G.S.B. will find him. You have my word."

G.S.B. employees, men and women in suits, littered the ground floor of the plantation mansion making the ambiance uneasy as it took on the form of a mortal inquest.

A woman with dainty glasses and her long brunette hair pulled back into a neat bun, walked the distance of the lounge room to the window where Detective Penn stood with the High Priestess of the Romani Coven.

LC looked to her colleague, "Inspector Florida Rowley.

This is Pilar Romani."

Pilar looked at the woman.

The two exchanged a hand shake as Florida acknowledged, "High Priestess. Mrs. Romani. Your reputation precedes you. Descendant of both gypsies and witches; you're a power all of your own."

"Thank you, Inspector." Pilar replied.

Florida continued sympathetically, "I wish our presence was easier than it has been." Pilar gave a pout as she silently listened. "The entire Bureau's resources are on this case. The

CEO insisted upon it."

Pilar gave a slight warm smile, "Adrian is a good man!"

"You know the King of Magic personally?" Florida queried.

Pilar informed, "Yes. He and Maria are family friends."

Florida gave a respectful smile and then continued, "The G.S.B–"

Pilar spoke the organizations full title, "The Government Supernatural Bureau..."

A gentleman halted at the edge of the lounge room, on the steps of the hallway.

"Inspector, Detective. The conference room is ready."

LC nodded her head, "Thank you, Noël."

~*~

Out in the dark, on the gravel driveway, a wonderment of glimmering green energy manifested. The wondering wisps of green turned into long, multi-shaded, fluttering pieces of green organza. At its centre, a golden wisp shone and long golden blonde hair blew about as a young woman immortalized by an extraordinary green aura, bound in a gown of green, gold and autumn brown lace, organza, satin and silk appeared.

Confidently the six-foot-tall woman strode along the drive. The breeze sung like angels while everything flourished in her presence.

Stepping up onto the front porch, the front doors blew open.

Her piercing green eyes with golden flecks touched every individual agent as they stood, silent and dumbfounded.

"Your name?" squeaked a voice.

She stood tall and regal. Her silence was intimidating as she gazed about.

"Serene Rein," She did not make contact with the person beside her.

Marrying an elf prince put stronger emphasis on the already obvious.

"I am Elf Queen, of the Autumn Forest."

Not much was known about her as an elf but as a witch, Serene's reputation, like her stepmother, proceeded her greatly.

Her power was great, her attitude proficient and upfront. Now placing her full enchanting gaze on the small, male agent she attempted to reply.

"Who are?—"

A relieved and loving voice interrupted, "Serene."

Ripping her gaze away, she immediately formed a smile, "Pilar. I came as quick as I could." The doors swung shut as she left the doorway and approached her stepmother.

Serene's personality was caring; passionate about family she had a strong protective nature.

She halted before Pilar, "I left Denver with the boys." both hugged warmly. "Where's Dad and the others? Are they okay?"

Pilar gave a humble smile as she hid her distraught emotions, "They are fine. Come, the Coven is about to sit a conference."

Serene greeted the two superiors with a warm gaze,

"Florida Rowley, It has been a long time." "Serene…" Spoke an agent.

Looking to the side her smile brightened, "LC. My God," she acknowledged the slight belly on the Detective. "Look at you."

A reluctant LC replied, "Excuse me?"

Serene whispered as they moved on, "How wonderful, you're pregnant!"

The conference room, from the foyer of the Romani mansion was down the hallway to the left. At the left again was a set of timber doors with fogged glass inserts.

A modern ceiling decorated with downlights immediately grabbed your attention when entering. The stone feature wall opposite the entry had three floor-to-ceiling windows decorated in cinnamon coloured drapes. In the middle of the room was an impressive, long stone table with sand coloured chairs. Mounted on the wall at the end of the room was a large plasma television for video link.

Siobhan, Juliann and Zane were seated on the left of whoever sat at the head of the table. The fifth, vacant seat was Serene's. The other members were: Laura Mitnell, a witch who could curse objects; Ryder Romani; Stephani, head witch of the 'Congraga Della Tomba' Coven; Jayme Kristoph, the Cavallo Coven representative; and Karin Dwyer, a Mermaid.

In spirals of white smoke, Custodians Renae and Basset Ketch took their seats. On the plasma, sisters Bermuda and Isadora Pogue attended via video link. As the clock approached midnight, the conference began as Pilar rose from her seat.

She spoke clearly with simplicity, "As you might know a hit was put on our coven." Even though her insides were torn she suppressed it. "Today at roughly midday the hit took place."

Whispering stole the silence as attentive members began to murmur amongst themselves.

"Please," Pilar summoned politely, "Let me finish. It appears," she brushed her hair back behind her ear as her eyes welled with tears. She cleared her throat, "My son was the target."

Stephani interrupted in outrage, "Who would do such a thing?!"

Late upon her arrival, Mavis Gruham, eldest sister to the four Triad members entered the room…unapologetic about the interruption. The room fell silent as all looked to the woman who closed the doors with a loud thud.

Her dark hair with ash grey highlights was placed in a neat bun at the back of her head. Her face was plastered in concrete-thick makeup. Her small eyes were uncaring, like people were supposed to kneel to her rule…but no one ever did. A ruby pendant hung on a chain around her neck.

"You should have waited," She remarked egotistically as she took her seat, giving Pilar a foul glare. "I too am just as important as these people."

Laura Mitnell interrupted with the insult: "Don't make me come over there, Grandma!"

"Please," Pilar raised her hand, drawing the room to silence again. "Mavis, I couldn't care less how important you are." She turned her head and resumed her speech, "As a coven we need to take precautions. I have given The G.S.B. permission to track our movements." Pilar looked at her members for understanding for her agreement. "It is believed that someone intends to use Brady to extort something from us." Looking at her loyal Custodian, Pilar gestured for Renae to take over as she began to sit down in her seat. "Renae if you may…"

"Thank you," Renae's striking amethyst eyes complimented her small face, "Pilar. Brady's abduction occurred moments before all Custodians were issued with a warning." She began to stroll around the table. "A Commander under Rafaela's instruction revealed that sometime within the coming months she is going to launch an attack."

Laura spoke in a cautious voice, "With the Pogue Coven dismantled we are the last line of defence!"

Jayme Kristoph, Cavallo Coven's representative spoke up, "In the absence of the Pogue Coven you are the superior power in the magical community."

Laura, confused, interrupted again, "Where does Brady come into this?"

"Well I believe," Mavis took charge and everyone looked at her with cold stares. "It has something to do with my nephew being deaf!"

"No one cares what you believe!" Zane growled.

Siobhan looked down her nose as she remarked bluntly, "Your nephew?"

"Yes. It is uncommon for a witch to be deaf." Mavis looked at Pilar suspiciously as though she wanted to read her thoughts to seek out an unspoken opinion. "I mean, is it possible he could be something more?"

Pilar gave a sour glare, "Believe what you may. But your politically incorrect insinuations always land you in trouble."

Renae continued as Pilar gave a nod to continue, "We are on the verge of war. Every coven, faction and armada will be questioned. Something Evil is at work here and the Custodian Order–"

LC interrupted accidently, "And the G.S.B."

"In co-operation with the G.S.B. are taking necessary measures to locate Brady and prepare for whatever Rafaela intends to unleash. Every witch, Romani and magical creature will be brought into the fold. Rafaela is unpredictable."

Mavis queried, "You think a coven might be behind this attack on our coven?" Juliann and Zane cleared their throats in response to the comment. Mavis growled viciously, "Oh whatever!"

Bermuda Pogue interjected, "If I may…"

Pilar replied, "Go ahead." as she looked at the Plasma television.

Bermuda continued, "Whoever took Brady…I was able to get a name before they banished the Siren Sorority." Everyone immediately murmured amongst themselves again. "Her name was Morgana."

"We have searched our *Book of Shadows* from cover to cover." Isadora Pogue quickly assumed the speaker role. "It wasn't until we went into books about Camelot and its

Mythology that we found a Lady Morgana."

Mavis burst out in mocking laughter, "Seriously, the fairytale of Arthur and Camelot?" Everyone again gave her cold glares.

Basset Ketch spoke up out of irritation, "We have someone in custody as we speak." And immediately Mavis shut up.

~*~

Some hours later, in the dead of night, in the medieval city of Eris, the red painted doors of Morgana's barn swung open. A figure clad in a baggy cloak entered. The door swung shut and latched. In the middle of the barn Brady sat bound to a chair, gagged and blindfolded with his head hung.

"How is our guest?" a woman's voice enquired.

Atop the look out, a male hooded figure replied, "He has not wakened." In an eruption of black mist he teleported and then reappeared beside Brady as he trailed his hands along the back rest of the rickety wooden chair. "May I beat him some more?"

In the corner, atop several bales of hay, Sharni Suntory sat with her legs crossed and her long black cloak overlapping her lanky figure with her hood removed.

"Be careful. The Romani still might be able to hear you."

The woman who had entered spoke beneath her hood, "Silence you idiots. The Romani is deaf." Ragel Modesto, Àtrella, Dakela and Patricia were positioned around the ground level of the large barn. "Besides, we have bigger problems!"

Àtrella greeted her with respect: "Lady Morgana."

Ragel spoke with repulsion as intrigue danced across her tongue like sour lemon, "What word do you bring from the filthy gypsies?"

The evil lady Morgana noted, "The G.S.B. has someone of interest in custody."

Dakela hissed beneath her cloak, "We do not fear the Bureau. But my suspicions are that it is our brother Illarion that they have in custody!" as she named the only person who would out their coven. "Come Patricia! We have a brother to deal with!" And the two vanished as their cloaks fluttered loudly in an eruption of black mist.

Reappearing beside Brady, Sharni traced his blonde hair with her fingertips.

"What will become of cousin?" she knelt down, raised his head with her hand and admired his charming appeal. "The boy's appeal is overwhelming. He must be Modesto."

Lytton complained, "He is gypsy; nothing more, nothing less."

Above on the second floor, emerging from behind a timber pillar, Brady's Astral Projection cautiously spied on the exhibition below. Their betrayal toward his family, even though they were at odds because of good versus evil, was odious, in his bewitching eyes.

VISIONARY – PART FIVE

"PERRY!!" Noah cried out as he ran up the beach to his brother lying in the sand, "PERRY!!!" he came within meters of reaching out to touch, "I am here–"

Abruptly an invisible presence threw black lightning at the Pogue Witch and catapulted him backwards into the shallow water that lapped the sand. A black ethereal mass began to manifest as it crawled over Perry's body. It began to take a humanoid form; first a head emerged with beaming red eyes complimented by a mouth with shark-like teeth.

Long red hair grew out of her scalp and cascaded down in a single flop.

Arms reached outwards toward Noah as he pulled his wet self out of the water. He coughed and spat sea water out of his mouth. He groaned, turned and gasped as an otherworldly noise rang out and black lightning struck the water causing an explosion...

~*~

A mist lingered for a moment and an odd noise accompanied it.

Clearing, a glimmering protective energy shield reflected the sunlight. In the air, large eagle wings flapped continuously and a large grey cougar levitated in mid-air. It let out a roar and its sapphire eyes glittered with angelic power. To protect himself from certain death by the black lightning attack Noah assumed his Custodian form.

A woman now dressed in a black Grecian gown, not the original white one she wore, stood some meters away from Perry's unconscious body in the sand as she looked down at the water and black electricity sparkled in her gestured hands. Extinguishing her power, she then ran her hands through her hair and sighed with a smile, believing she had brought an end to Noah's life.

"That," she lowered her arms back down to her side and idolized the sun, "was easy. You were miniscule Noah Pogue! Better your dead spirit heard it from me before any other demon got in first!" abruptly she turned around and beamed a sinister and eager grin at Perry. "Perry," her voice changed to authenticate her visage of Lindsay Pogue, his mother. "Perry, my darling boy," she knelt down beside him and elevated his head into her lap. "Mother is here," this announcement seemed awkward, even for her.

Kamenwati, disguised at Lindsay Pogue, revealed her irritation through the narrow glare of her eyes and the pupil in each enlarged to the circumference of the iris. Caressing his forehead like a loving mother, she used her demonic powers to try and access his mind. A glittering purple aura began to appear around her hand.

"Curse those docile Dream-Weaving Witches," she grumbled to herself, fruitless in her attempts. Sensing a telepathic connection to Rafaela, the Avatarian Demigoddess, Kamenwati turned her head slightly and began to talk to the sand, "Yes Rafaela. The barriers they put in his mind to contain the nightmares are very effective. I will try harder. The information we need to resurrect Alera is in those nightmares." Frustrated as she listened to her master, Kamenwati flicked her long red hair out of her face. "My liege, I will die trying."

She suddenly let out a violent scream and then exploded into black mist that quickly disappeared. Revealed to be stabbed in the back, the silver blade of the Athame glimmered in the sunlight as it fell into the sand.

A damp Noah stood some meters away, "Yes! I hope you die trying you bitch!" He appeared to be very outraged that she had taken on the form of their dead mother in order to rouse Perry and goad admission into his thoughts. "How dare you pervert our mother's memory!"

It seemed he had effortlessly defeated his powerful opponent.

He walked the short distance to his brother, knelt down, picked up the knife and made it magically disappear in a gleam of copper energy. He pulled his brother up into his lap and sat him upright against him.

"Perry," he touched his head, "you're safe. I am here!"

He held his brother tight, feeling their souls reconnect. Kindred spirits reunited. Revealed to be so, a white glow resonated in both their chests without Noah's knowledge. Pressing his lips against Perry's head he gave him an unconditional sign of affection.

"Come back to me," he whispered.

A vision of blonde pixie Caydit Packrem, the Vampire Sovereign of Los Angeles Nocturne League and Perry's Maker, manifested beside Noah in an abundance of black mist.

"He is not yours to keep," she snapped at the side of his face as she assumed her full vampire form. "He belongs to the dark! He belongs to me!"

Although apparently invisible, the negativity from her presence made him noticeably comfortable. He sighed. Closed his eyes and then reopened them. In that split second, Perry's body had disappeared from his arms along with the invisible apparition to his side.

Noah quickly got to his feet.

Around him the picturesque beach of Aldinga, Deane County – although in the Dream Realm – had changed to a Gowlland Point beach on South Pender Island, British Columbia, Canada.

He staggered about for a moment, distraught as tears rushed down his face. He was panicking. He had been tricked into believing his brother was safe in his hands. Believing that he was going to be attacked at any moment he wiped the tears from his face, closed his eyes and focused his magic to hone in on any noises around him other than the sound of waves crashing on the beach.

He heard and sensed nothing. Quickly he reopened his eyes and was abruptly greeted by Perry who stared at him. His pupils were dilated and his fangs drawn. Perry was hungry. Caution became obvious as Noah moved uncomfortably on the spot.

~*~

On her own path in the Dream Realm, Kathryn Penthal suddenly found herself separated from everyone she had originally begun her travel here with. She appeared to be inside a house, but not one she had ever visited. It was modern with a tiled floor; the white walls almost seemed to be a sandy colour but only because of the sunlight shining in through the windows.

Halting, she felt a moment of uneasiness; it was ironic though, considering the fact that she was a fearless individual who always had a way of making others around her nervous.

"Noah!" she called out, turning around on the spot, "Noah?"

Taking in her surroundings, she let her guard down, allowing the realm full admission to her subconscious. She brushed her long blonde hair back behind her ear, made another uneasy look with her face and began to turn around.

"Oh," said a woman with delight, "You're home!"

Kathryn's eyes widened with fear as she froze. She witnessed a woman, her eldest sister Connemara come down the staircase to the right of her. Long black hair flowed in the air behind her as she rushed across the hallway and then disappeared into the lounge room to the left.

Kathryn murmured to herself, "Connemara?" appearing to be confused, "Hey," she moved quickly to the doorway, "Connor–" abruptly she halted as she witnessed something out of the ordinary. "Oh...my God!"

Suddenly, in a flash, she was standing on the opposite side of the doorway, looking back at a younger version of herself probably in her late teens.

In the lounge room, Kathryn witnessed something that she knowingly kept a secret most of her life up until now, but which she was somehow reliving.

A second woman, with long auburn hair pulled back into a ponytail and brown eyes laced in seductive eyeshadow appeared at Kathryn's side.

"You knew all this time," the woman acknowledged.

Both of them peered into the room and observed a male from behind with dark hair kissing their older sister passionately.

By the look of intrigue on both their faces it was not Noah Pogue.

Kathryn stiffened her posture, "Carmen?" she whispered. "I don't remember this part, what is this?" Turning her head, she looked at her second older sister. "Oh," she exclaimed inwardly with frustration, "is this me reliving my life because I've died? Goddamn it!"

Carmen raised an eyebrow and smirked, "I'm the dead one little sister! I visit you frequently in your sleep but you don't acknowledge it. You're in the Dream Realm," she seemed concerned for a moment, "you remember that part, right?"

Kathryn appeared vague momentarily and then turned her head to look back into the lounge room. "This however," Carmen acknowledged the revelation before their eyes, "is the past. Huh, I often speculated about this myself to be honest." A displeased look rose in her face like she had missed an opportunity in life, "bitch. She got to bed them both. But you Kat, you little shit, saw the whole thing! Even knew the whole thing like the back of your hand!"

Kathryn queried, "Is this 1988-ish?" with suspicion.

"Yeah," replied Carmen.

Kathryn narrowed her eyes, "that means she lied!"

Carmen queried, "You know, don't you?"

"It means that Connemara was—" Kathryn was cut off midsentence and suddenly found herself standing in a beautiful Canadian forest. "Now, where the hell am I?" she turned around, searching for her sister, "Carmen?" and got no response. "Bloody hell, I hate this bullshit dimension. I like it better when I'm here subconsciously and comfortable in my bed. Not physically walking around!" She grumbled to herself like an incoherent idiot.

Retrieving a turquoise crystal from her pocket, Kathryn closed her eyes and rubbed it between her hands.

"Urania," she whispered and summoned, "Muse of Astronomy," the magical object in her possession gave off a glow and an abundance of glittering starlight moved down from the foliage overhead. "I pray to thee…" Kathryn kissed the crystal, her eyes still closed, "Urania, give me my current location. I am lost!"

The glittering starlight hovered above the ground, gathered into a single glow and then a woman emerged. Long, thick dark blue hair fell over her right shoulder with lighter blue highlights. Her eyes were a bewitching green. She was barefoot and wore a ceremonial Grecian gown.

"I am here Kathryn," her voice so heavenly.

Kathryn opened her eyes, "Where am I, Urania?"

Urania closed her eyes and looked up the sky; she used her divine powers to read the invisible stars in the galaxy to triangulate the witch's current location. Like a computer beaming information up to a satellite in outer space. A brisk wind swept around her as she received her information. Reopening her eyes, they gave off a brief glow.

"You are in the Dream Realm," her response was something Kathryn already knew, "But theoretically you are in Canada, North America in the province of British Columbia. You are on Vancouver Island, in the forest near the Holland Creek Trail. The closest settlement to you is Ladysmith."

Kathryn queried cautiously, "Where are Noah and Shane?"

"Shane is," Urania turned slightly and pointed through the forest, "in that direction, five kilometers away. He has stumbled across the Haus of Romani!"

"Haus of Romani." Kathryn murmured under her breath as though it sounded familiar, "What about Noah?" a spontaneous moment of happiness revealed itself. "Is he safe? Did he find Perry?"

Urania seemed distant now and teleported away in an abundance of starlight leaving the witch confused and concerned. She exhaled, ran her hand through her hair, placed the crystal back in her pocket and spoke to the universe.

"Please God, be safe Noah," she looked about the forest around her, "Carmen, watch over him! Protect him!" Elevating her arm, she pointed in the direction the Muse had pointed. "Shane is that way..." moving off she made her way through the trees.

The ground beneath Noah's shoes crunched as he moved uneasily on the spot in front of his younger brother. His senses were reacting to everything; his nose detected peculiar scents and his ears registered the waves crashing onto the beach, bird noises and the wind in the trees. His eyes moved rapidly, noticing slight golden auras around various objects. Noah creased his left eye slightly, feeling his sight wanting to surge forward like he was being given a premonition even though he did not possess the power.

The Custodian inside of him was becoming increasingly dormant.

"They-they-they," Perry began to ramble incoherently, "found the secrets, Noah," his enlarged pupils fixated on Noah and there was a distinct hunger within them. "They-they-they know."

A cautious Noah replied, "Who Perry?" he kept himself composed, knowing that the slightest movement would trigger a bad reaction from his brother. "What do they know? What did they find out?"

In the the blink of an eye, Perry was gone.

A startled Noah called, "Perry?"

"I told them—" Behind Noah, Perry's voice sounded intimidating, "I told them things!" he pulled his brother around to face him and held him by the collar of his shirt. "If you die,"

Noah struggled, "Perry, stop! Calm down!"

"When you die," Perry corrected himself, "You will name the beast – you will name the beast!" he repeated quickly with delusion. "The nightmares I had as a child. The night terrors that we asked the Sognare Coven in Los Angeles to block...to contain," for a moment there was relief in his eyes, but then the hunger returned, "were a prophecy! But for now, I need to feed!" Reaching his mouth open as he pulled his brother close to him, Perry pierced the skin of Noah's neck as he sunk his fangs in and began to feed.

"Perry," Noah struggled to fight his brother off, "Perry, argh! PERRY STOP!! NO!!"

On the beach, behind Noah, Kamenwati emerged in a mass of black mist. She beamed a smile of delight having achieved what she needed by depriving Perry of food. He looked at her with his hungry dilated pupils and vampire visage.

After a few minutes of almost draining Noah of all his blood, Perry released his brother and dropped his body to the ground. Realizing what he had done as Kamenwati's magic wore off, Perry dropped to his knees and began to cry hysterically.

Kamenwati spoke to him, "I told you, I always get what I want!"

"No!" he yelled in rage, "No! NO! NO!!" he rose from the ground and used his vampire speed to accelerate at her.

Abruptly he halted, "You bitch!"

"You murderer!" she smirked.

With a brisk gesture, she used telekinesis to throw him backwards onto the ground. Laying beside Noah, he watched his brother take his last breath.

Noah murmured, "Alera..."

TO BE CONTINUED……

ABOUT THE AUTHOR

I hail from Adelaide, South Australia, home of the renowned Barossa Valley and McLaren Vale Wines.

My humble city is also the murder capital of Australia.

I love all things fantasy. As a child, I loved writing short stories, but a passion for writing manifested at a turbulent point in my adolescence. My imagination has me away with the fairies most of the time, wishing I had a super power to triumph over all that is bad in this world. Reality has me working a nine-to-five job.

When I'm away from the computer, I love watching anime, drinking coffee to my heart's content, listening and dancing, around the house to music. I'm a child of the 80's nothing gets my imagination flowing like Bon Jovi.

I believe everyone has a book inside them, it just requires something to bring it to the surface.

SOCIAL LINKS

Website - http://www.trkester.com.au/
Instagram - https://www.instagram.com/t.r.kester/
Facebook - https://www.facebook.com/TRKesterBooks/